More Praise for
BIG GIRLS DON'T CRY

By Connie Briscoe
Published by The Ballantine Publishing Group:

SISTERS & LOVERS
BIG GIRLS DON'T CRY

Books published by The Ballantine Publishing Group
are available at quantity discounts on bulk purchases
for premium, educational, fund-raising, and special
sales use. For details, please call 1-800-733-3000.

BIG GIRLS
DON'T CRY

Connie Briscoe

ONE WORLD

THE BALLANTINE PUBLISHING GROUP • NEW YORK

A One World Fawcett Gold Medal Book
Published by The Ballantine Publishing Group
Copyright © 1996 by Connie Briscoe

www.randomhouse.com/BB/

Library of Congress Catalog Card Number: 99-60167

ISBN 0-449-00564-X

This edition published by arrangement with HarperCollins Publishers, Inc.

Manufactured in the United States of America

First Trade Paperback Book Edition: July 1997
First Mass Market Edition: May 1999

OPM 13 12 11 10 9 8 7 6 5 4

For Mama and Daddy, for always being there

BIG GIRLS
DON'T CRY

PART ONE

1963—1968

One

Naomi's heart felt like it was doing the twist when she realized Nancy was about to sneak into the haunted house. The killer was probably in there hiding in some secret passage and could jump out and grab Nancy and finish her off, too. Still, Nancy was dead set on doing it. She had so much nerve. Naomi knew she could never, ever do anything so brave in a million—

"Naomi!"

She looked up from the yellow book in her lap toward the sound of her mama's voice seeping into her bedroom. This had to be the third time in the last half hour that voice had snatched her away from her book. "What?" Naomi asked in the most annoyed tone she dared use with her mama.

"Are you dressed yet? We're leaving in ten minutes sharp."

No, Naomi answered in her head. She wasn't dressed and she had no intention of getting dressed for any dumb piano lesson. That kind of thing was more up Joshua's alley. At thirteen, her older brother was the extroverted one, always ready to show off in front of everybody. She preferred reading and sewing, stuff she could do without a lot of people around. But thinking this and saying it were two different things. She knew Mama wouldn't exactly be thrilled to have her eleven-year-old daughter tell her she wasn't going to do something.

"Naomi, did you hear me just ask you a question?" Mama's voice was louder now, so Naomi knew she was headed that way and was getting madder by the minute. She sat upright on the bed and wrapped her hands firmly around the book, her index finger holding the page.

"I'm not going."

Mama appeared at the doorway, and Naomi knew from the look on her honey-colored face that this time she had definitely gone too far. Mama was wearing pumps and one of her school-teacher dresses even though it was Saturday afternoon, which meant these piano lessons were serious business. It wasn't going to be easy getting out of them.

"Excuse me," Mama said, planting a hand on one hip. "I don't think I heard right. Did you just tell me you weren't going to do something I distinctly told you to do?"

Naomi nodded and set her lips firmly so Mama would know she wasn't kidding.

Mama placed the other hand on the other hip. "And might I ask why?" Mama had a kind of smile on her lips, but Naomi wasn't sure if she was amused or if it was her Girl-have-you-lost-your-mind? smile.

"I'm in the middle of the best part of the best Nancy Drew book I ever read, Mama. I have to find out what happens when she goes in the haunted house. That's why I can't go now."

"Nancy Drew can wait. You have music lessons in one hour, and I want you dressed in ten minutes flat."

OK, so Mama wasn't amused. But surely she felt reading was more enlightening than playing the piano. "Don't you want me to read, Mama?"

"Of course I do. But I also want you to learn to play a musical instrument so you'll be well rounded. I paid more than a thousand dollars for that piano, and you and your brother are going to learn to play it if it's the last thing you do."

A thousand dollars? For some ugly old wood box that practically swallowed up the whole living room? Daddy even had to move the TV from in front of the sofa to a crazy angle on the side to make room for the thing. "Why so much?"

"It's a George Steck, that's why. The best within our budget."

"I still don't see why I have to learn to play a dumb old piano. I read, I sew. Isn't that enough?"

"You need to get out and do more social things instead of staying cooped up in the house so much."

"But I'm not good at stuff like that."

"What do you mean by 'stuff like that'?"

Mama had caught her there. She wasn't exactly sure. All she knew was that going to a stranger's house to learn to play the piano didn't exactly fascinate her, especially since Mama said two or three other kids would be there at the same time. Mama was always saying she was shy and needed to work on it, but Naomi didn't think being shy had anything to do with it. She wasn't scared of people or anything like that. She just didn't like the idea of doing something in front of people unless she could do it better than them. "Stuff like playing the piano," she finally reasoned.

"How can you know until you try?"

"I can feel it in my bones."

"That's enough of this nonsense, young lady. Get dressed and wear something nice. I want you to make a good first impression on your teacher." Mama stood in the doorway, one hand on her hip, the other on the doorknob, so Naomi put the book down and moved to the edge of the bed. But she stuck out her bottom lip as far as she could, just so Mama would know she didn't like this one bit. Mama left the room, but Naomi couldn't pry herself from the bed just yet. She stretched out on her stomach, stuck her thumb in her mouth, and chewed on her nail, or what was left of it. She shouldn't be doing this. Mama was forever getting on her for biting her nails, but she couldn't help it. They were always finding their way to her mouth without her even realizing it.

That didn't go at all like she planned. Instead of spending a cozy Saturday afternoon reading, she had to get dressed and go out to a complete stranger's house to play a dumb old box in front of a bunch of people. Wasn't it enough that she had school every day of the week and homework every night? Now she had to give up her Saturday afternoons too?

Maybe if she had joined the drama club at school last year like Mama wanted, Mama wouldn't have come up with this newfangled idea. At least the drama club only put on a few plays a year. She wouldn't have had the nerve to get up on the stage acting or anything dumb like that, but she could have done something behind the scenes. And she would have been through with it by the end of this year, since she was about to graduate and move on to junior high. Music lessons were year-round and could last forever.

Besides, she wouldn't be as good at it as her brother. Not that she was bad at things, but Joshua was tops at just about everything he did. He got A's in just about every subject at school: math, science, music, you name it. She hadn't gotten an A in math since the days of one plus one equals two.

Joshua was always saying that somebody or something scared her about math, making her think she couldn't do it because she was a girl. Maybe he was right, because she noticed that a lot of girls at school didn't do so hot in math either. And she had to admit that when she really buckled down, she did pretty well in just about anything. But what was the point in slaving over something yucky like math, something she would never use? She didn't know what she wanted to be when she grew up—probably a teacher like Mama and her friends—but one thing was for sure. It wasn't going to involve math in any way, shape, or form.

Naturally, she dreaded report card time. No matter how well she did, Joshua always did better. She had long ago decided never to try to compete with him or anybody else if she could help it, unless she was pretty sure she would come out on top. That meant keeping to herself a lot, but it worked for her. Or at least it had until Mama started making her do these dumb social things.

Martha and the Vandellas, singing "Heatwave," blared down the hallway from Joshua's room. About the only thing she did better than Joshua was dancing. Joshua played his music loud but couldn't dance worth a lick. She took her finger out of her mouth and bobbed her foot to the beat for a few seconds, then took a deep breath and forced herself to get up. She looked down at the Nancy Drew book lying on the bed, tempted to pick it up and read just one more chapter, but she knew better than to delay any longer or Mama would really get ruffled.

She pulled a pleated navy skirt and a sweater from the closet and knee-high socks from a dresser drawer. It only took a minute to shed her Wranglers and slip into them, along with her navy patent leather shoes. She had shoes in just about every color of the rainbow. Joshua called her a clotheshorse, and she couldn't argue with that. It was one of the reasons she took up sewing. Fabric was cheap compared to store-bought clothes, so she could get twice as much with her allowance. Not that Mama and Daddy didn't buy her clothes, 'cause Mama loved to shop too. But Naomi could never get enough no matter how much Mama bought her.

She quickly wrapped a headband around her short pageboy, being careful not to mess up her bangs. She always wore thick, long bangs to cover up her high forehead, not to mention the brown naps around the edges of her face that began to pop out when she was due for a hair pressing. Mama was always trying to get her to push her bangs back 'cause she thought her high forehead looked regal. Naomi thought it made her look like a moron and thanked the high heavens for bangs.

Daddy entered the room puffing on his pipe and wearing his slippers, a sign that he was going to be around the house re-laxing, and she envied him. He sat on the edge of the bed and smiled at her reflection in the mirror as she fiddled with her bangs. They were both the same complexion, about the color of cinnamon. People said she favored him, which always made her feel good, since she thought he was so handsome. And for a father, he dressed kind of hip and listened to pretty decent music. He probably didn't know who Martha and the Van-dellas were, but he liked Little Stevie Wonder.

Joshua was fairer in complexion—about the color of pow-dered ginger—and was also lucky enough to get Mama's wavy hair. Naomi supposed you could call her brother fine; girls were always calling the house for him and fawning over him like he was the last man on earth. Mama didn't like that one bit. She was always saying stuff like "but he's only thirteen" and "what mother allows her thirteen-year-old daughter to call up boys all the time?" Naomi was tempted to tell Mama that some of those girls were only eleven and twelve, but Joshua would kick her butt if she did. Mama would have a heart attack if she thought her daughter was calling boys and flirting with them. Mama didn't have much to worry about, though. Naomi thought her face looked as good as most of the ones she had seen around Joshua, but unlike those girls, her shape was about as round as a string bean.

"I came up to tell your brother to turn that music down," Daddy said. "What's this I hear about you giving your mother a hard time about piano lessons?"

Although she looked more like her daddy, when it came time to discipline her, Mama had more say. Her parents seemed to think that Mama knew best for Naomi, since she was a girl, and Daddy knew best for Joshua. Naomi thought Joshua had the best of that deal, since Mama was the no-nonsense type when it came to behavior. Although Daddy could be pretty strict too, Naomi could sometimes get him to come to her defense when she had a disagreement with Mama.

She took a deep breath and turned to face him. "I don't know anything about playing the piano. I'll probably stink at it."

His smile turned sympathetic. Somehow that smile could always soothe her fears. The problem was that as soon as he walked away and she couldn't see it anymore, the fear returned. Sometimes, she thought if she could just take that smile everywhere she went, life would be so much easier. But of course she couldn't.

"Don't say that," he said. "You're quitting before you even give it a shot."

She flopped down beside him on the bed. "But why try if I know I'll fail? I'll just make a fool of myself."

"Fail? When have you ever failed at something?"

"Swimming lessons."

"That was when you were eight years old and you didn't stick with it long enough. You can do anything if you put your mind to it, you and your brother both. Just the other day, when Joshua was trying out the piano, I was amazed at how much he's taught himself. You could do just as well if you tried."

She couldn't help but smile at Daddy's boundless confidence in their abilities. Joshua had sounded so bad banging on the keys, her ears hurt. She folded her arms across her waist and eyed her father closely. "But isn't that why you decided not to open the liquor store up on Rhode Island Avenue? Because you thought you wouldn't be able to pull it off?"

"That was different. Your mother thought it would be too dangerous, 'fraid I might get robbed. But mainly it was because something like that takes a lot of money when you first start out. It would have meant sacrifices I didn't want to put you all through. We're in a position to give you and your brother the things we couldn't have, and I didn't want to give that up. Like piano lessons, for instance."

She turned up her nose at that tired old argument. "But what if we don't want those things?"

He laughed. So did she.

"Try it out, and if you still despise it I'll talk to your mother. But you have to put forth an honest effort."

She nodded and they shook hands. That seemed fair enough.

"I think I'm lost," Mama said, seemingly to no one in particular. She twisted her head, with its pink pillbox hat perched neatly on top, to glance out the rear window of their new black Buick. If there was one area where Mama wasn't old-fashioned, it was dressing. She was always sneaking bags from Hecht's and Woodie's into the house when Daddy wasn't looking.

"Mama—?" Both Naomi and her brother spoke at the same time.

"Don't interrupt me now," Mama said. "I'm trying to figure out how I got mixed up. I don't know why I'm lost, since this is in the same direction as my building."

By "building" Naomi knew Mama meant the Washington, D.C., school where she taught first grade. Naomi had every confidence Mama would find her way to the music teacher's house sooner than she would like, and she was anxious to get her question in before Joshua got to ask his, since he had a way of hogging the conversation. "Mama, why do you and all your friends wear the same hats?"

Mama shrugged. "It's the style."

"But how do styles get started? I remember when you wore those high heels with the pointed toes."

"And almost ruined my feet."

"Then why did you wear them?"

"Oh, we thought they made our legs look nice, I guess."

"Well, what makes a style come and go?"

"That's a good question. I don't know why we wore those silly pointed-toe shoes, but the hats are because of Jackie Kennedy. She has so much style, everyone wanted to be like her when she was first lady."

Naomi quickly forgot about fashion at the mention of the name Kennedy. She hadn't heard much about the President's assassination recently, but for several days after it happened it was all they talked about at the dinner table. Mama and Daddy said President Kennedy was good for Negroes, since he was the first to speak out and say racial prejudice was wrong. And they were both upset about his death. Naomi was too, but she was more upset to learn that all the presidents before him had practically ignored the problems of colored people. "Did they find out who killed President Kennedy yet?"

"They knew who killed him right after the murder, dizzy," her know-it-all brother said from the backseat. "Lee Harvey Oswald. Where have you been? On the moon?"

Joshua knew perfectly well she knew that; he just wanted to aggravate her. "Some people say he didn't do it."

"They're pretty sure he did it," Mama said. "They're just trying to figure out how. But with Oswald dead, it seems we may never know for sure. And nobody knows what will happen to some laws President Kennedy was trying to get passed to help Negroes. Haven't you talked about this in school?"

"Yes, but—"

"Of course she has," Joshua said, butting in as usual. "Ma, why do you work every day?"

Mama narrowed her eyes. "What kind of question is that?"

Yeah, what kind of question is that? Naomi thought, narrowing her eyes like Mama.

"None of the mothers on TV ever work," Joshua said.

Her brother had a point, she had to admit. Next to *The Bev-*

erly Hillbillies, Dick Van Dyke was her favorite show. He was so funny. But his wife didn't work and neither did Lucy, or Danny Thomas's wife.

"I have to work so we can have nice things, like this car and our house. Your father doesn't earn enough for all the things we want to do."

"Oh," Joshua said.

Her brother suddenly got quiet, but Naomi had plenty of questions. "Why doesn't Daddy earn enough money?"

"Look," Mama said. "Most white men make more money than Negro men because they can get better jobs. Their wives don't have to work."

"But how come white men can get better jobs?" Naomi asked.

"It's 'why,' not 'how come.' And the reason is because when we were young, they would only give certain jobs to Negroes."

"Even if you had a college degree?" Joshua asked.

Mama nodded. "When we graduated it was either teaching or the government."

At least now she understood why all Mama's friends were teachers and Daddy and his friends worked for the government.

"That's not fair," Joshua said.

"No, it's not, honey," Mama said. "But that's the way things are. Negro women have always worked. White women have stayed home."

"Don't you like to work?" Naomi asked.

"I love my job. And since I get off at three-thirty, I can be home almost the same time as you."

"But would you stay home if Daddy made more money?" Joshua asked.

"I can't imagine not working," Mama said. "Your grandmother, your great-grandmother, they all worked outside the home." She paused and chuckled. "But I guess it must be nice to have a choice not to work if you don't want to."

Naomi was shocked Mama even thought that way. She couldn't imagine Mama not working. Mama was one of the smartest people she knew, and since all her girlfriends worked Naomi was sure Mama would get bored to death staying at home with nobody to talk to. Sometimes Naomi thought she wanted to work like Mama. But what Lucy and Dick Van Dyke's wife did looked like fun, too, and sometimes she thought she might want to do that. Now Mama was making it seem like she couldn't. "Does that mean I'll have to work, too?"

"I'm pretty sure you will," Mama said.

Joshua was right, Naomi thought. It didn't seem fair.

"Did you hear about the astronaut who spent a whole day in outer space?" Joshua said, sitting up on the edge of the seat.

Mama nodded. "That's the first time an American's been up there more than a few hours."

"That's what you want to do?" Naomi asked. "Fly around outer space in a machine?"

"It's not just flying," Joshua said. "You're doing research too."

Mama nodded. "What about you, Naomi? What do you want to be when you grow up?"

"Yeah, pipsqueak," Joshua said. "What career are you thinking of this month, circus clown?"

Naomi stuck her tongue out at him. But the truth was she didn't know, and it did seem like she was always changing her mind. One of her choices—being a housewife—had just flown out the window. "A teacher, I guess." That would make Mama happy, she thought.

"Teaching's fine," Mama said. "But you should think about other things. You'd have a hard time getting into some fields, but you have many more choices than we did."

OK, so maybe Mama didn't think teaching was so hot, at least for her daughter. "Like what?" Naomi asked.

"Think about what you like to do, what you're good at."

"Clothes," Joshua said. "That's about the only thing she knows anything about. Period." He reached up and tousled her hair, which seemed to be his favorite way of annoying her now that she wore in it in curls instead of braids.

"It is not," Naomi said, slapping his hand away and smoothing out her hair. "I know—"

"Let's not start fighting," Mama said. "I still don't know

where I am, and we're running late. I need to pay more attention to what I'm doing."

Naomi looked out the window. They were driving across a bridge she'd never laid eyes on before. She looked at Mama. The way Mama's eyes were darting around made Naomi think they really were lost. "Where are we?"

"Crossing over into Virginia," Mama said. Her lips smiled but her eyes didn't. Now Naomi was starting to worry. She had never been to Virginia, and the way Mama and Daddy talked about them not liking Negroes over there, it seemed like a scary, faraway place. She was surprised it was so close to their house.

"I'll turn around right after we get over the bridge," Mama said.

They reached the other side but the road was narrow, so Mama crept along trying to find a place to turn the car around. The road finally widened, and Naomi was just about to point to an alley up ahead when she heard a car swing around from behind and pull up alongside them. She turned to see the faces of four angry-looking white boys just outside her window.

"You stupid niggers!"

The car screeched up the street. Naomi felt as if a snake had sprung out of the bushes and spit poison into her face. She didn't know whether to laugh or cry. She looked at Mama, hoping for her to say something to make it all right, but from the frozen expression on Mama's face she knew crying was in order. Before Naomi could help it, she was all choked up and could hardly breathe. She knew what that word meant, or at least she thought she did. But that was the first time anyone had said it to her face. She wanted to run and hide. She wanted to punch somebody. But she couldn't do either.

Out of the corner of her eye she saw Mama glance at her like she suddenly remembered her daughter was sitting next to her. Mama reached over and smoothed Naomi's hair. "There's no need to cry. It was just some silly teenagers."

"Dumb fools," Joshua said. "Ignoramuses."

"Why'd they have to call us that?"

"Bad upbringing," Mama said. "That's what they've heard

from others, and they're too lazy to bother to learn the truth. They're the ignorant ones, not us."

Naomi sniffed.

"I don't want you to get more upset than you already are," Mama said, "but Negroes sometimes have to put up with things like this. You're going to have to learn to handle them without getting too upset."

"Big girls don't cry," Joshua said. "Remember?"

Naomi had heard that a million times. It sounded good, but things didn't always work out that way. "Then what am I supposed to do when somebody calls me that?" She knew she was whining but she couldn't help it.

"Ignore it and go your own way," Mama said.

"Yeah," Joshua said. "It's just a word."

She remembered another saying that Daddy told her when a girl at school called her a bookworm. "Sticks and stones may break your bones, but words will never hurt you." She swallowed hard and wiped the tears from her cheeks. Mama patted her knee and pulled into the alley to turn the car around.

"Do we still have to go to the music lesson?" Naomi asked. "I don't feel like it now."

"Yes. What happened back there is no excuse for changing our plans."

Naomi sighed and nodded. As much as she didn't want to go, that made sense. Couldn't let a bunch of kooks control them.

As they sped back across the bridge, Mama looked at Naomi and smiled. "I need to ask directions, but I think I'll wait till we get back to the other side."

Joshua chuckled, and she did too. Not so much at Mama's joke, but because it was such a relief to be heading back to Washington.

That night Naomi tossed and turned and punched her pillow for ages, waiting to go to sleep. No matter how hard she tried, she couldn't get those nasty words and scary white faces out of her head. She was tempted to go into her parents' room and climb into bed with them. But she was supposed to be a big girl now. So she did what she usually did these days when she couldn't sleep. She snuck to her bottom dresser drawer, pulled out a flashlight, and crept back under the bedcovers with her Nancy Drew book. Nancy's world was filled with goblins and ghosts, but it was a heck of a lot less terrifying than the real one.

Two

It took almost two years, but Naomi finally convinced her mother she was no more musical than a stone. Still, Mama seemed as determined as ever to implant some culture into her daughter and came up with another idea: ballet lessons. Naomi decided to give ballet a decent chance, though. She had always been good at dancing.

On the first day of class, Mrs. Johnson walked in wearing tights and a leotard with a little sarong wrapped around her waist. Everything about the lady was impeccable, from her graceful posture to the neat little bun at the back of her head to her silky chestnut complexion. Naomi squirmed. She felt dumb in her own ballet getup. What had she gotten herself into? She had a feeling this was going to be a whole lot different from learning to do the mashed potato. From the looks on the other brown faces lining the room, the girls around her felt the same way.

Mrs. Johnson clapped her hands and instructed the girls to line up at the barre. Then she showed them how to stand with their legs straight and their feet just so. Naomi got into position and waited as Mrs. Johnson walked slowly down the line, straightening shoulders and tucking in derrieres. Every time the teacher touched someone, Naomi moved as if her own body was being corrected. When Mrs. Johnson finally reached Naomi, she did some pushing and pulling and then tilted Naomi's chin up.

"You've got good coordination. You should do well at this."

The minute she heard that, Naomi was hooked. She smiled and lifted her shoulders and resolved then and there to become the best ballet dancer in the class.

"How did the lesson go today?" Mama always asked the same old question the minute Naomi got in the car after class, and she always sounded like she half expected Naomi to say she was through with ballet.

"Fine, I guess." Actually she had come to love the class and looked forward to it each week. But she didn't want to seem too delighted or Mama would have her taking lessons in modern dancing, tap dancing, and maybe ballroom dancing too.

"If you're not trying to talk me out of it, that's a start," Mama said. "Do you think you'll stick with it?"

"Probably. I like Mrs. Johnson, and she thinks I'm good at it." Besides, she'd heard that ballet was good for shaping the legs, a part of her body that could use some improvement, along with just about everything else. Every other girl at school seemed to be getting curves these days except her. Mama had her wearing a training bra this year, but Naomi hadn't figured out why. She was still straight as a stalk.

As soon as the morning recess bell rang, everyone in Mr. Parker's Algebra 101 class sat up on the edge of their seats, waiting to be dismissed. Naomi thought Mr. Parker got a kick out of torturing them like this, holding them for a few extra seconds while he piled on the homework. Sometimes it seemed like he was purposely adding extra chapters and equations while he stood there stroking his chocolate-colored chin. The minute he said "class dismissed," thirty-two pairs of feet in various hues of brown made a beeline for the doorway.

During recess all the girls gathered on the playground in their little groups and did different things. There were the fly girls. They were mostly in the eighth and ninth grades, always had the finest boys hanging around them, and wore the latest styles in dresses and shoes. Some of them even wore makeup. Naomi had tried to get Mama to buy her a pair of Nineteens or

Sebastians. They cost twenty dollars a pair and looked so fly. But twenty dollars was far more than she could afford with her allowance, and Mama said there was no way she'd buy them. Not because of the money but because she didn't want her daughter looking like one of those "fast girls," as she called them. Besides, that would mean letting Naomi wear stockings and a garter belt, something else Mama didn't want her daughter to do yet.

Another group was the squares or, if you wanted to be a little nicer about it, the bookworms. They were mostly seventh and eighth graders. They got all A's, dressed corny, didn't seem to know boys existed, and never got in any kind of trouble if they could help it.

Then there were the hard girls. They mostly lived on the other side of Rhode Island Avenue, where the houses and apartments were older and smaller. Some of them were even projects. At school, these girls stood around the edge of the playground wearing black leather jackets, sneaking cigarettes, and joning on each other. It was harmless teasing when they did it among themselves, kind of a game to see who could throw out the worst insults. But sometimes one of the hard girls would crack on somebody in another group—say nasty things about them or their mother.

In Naomi's opinion, if that person was smart she'd smile and go along with it or maybe pretend she didn't even hear it, depending on the circumstances and what she thought would work best to keep from getting her butt whipped. Especially if it was Henrietta Jackson joning on you. Henrietta was the baddest fighter in school, had even creamed a couple of boys who were bigger, and most girls didn't even want to look at her the wrong way. A few of the girls in the hard group were really OK, though. They looked and acted tough but they would speak to you in the hallway and not mess with you as long as you minded your own business.

Naomi was in a group that was somewhere in between the fly girls and the squares. Most of them were in the eighth grade. They tried to dress cool, even if their parents didn't allow them to wear the really fly clothes. They were all pretty smart and studied hard but tried not to seem like bookworms. And they cared about boys enough to sneak and put on makeup at school, even if the boys didn't care much about them.

If one of the hard girls was in the mood to pick a fight, it was usually with one of them. The squares seemed so odd to everybody, Naomi thought the hard girls didn't know what to make of them. And the fly girls always had boyfriends to protect them. That left her group.

Today everything seemed pretty calm. The girls in Naomi's group had changed into their gym shoes and tossed their fall jackets aside and were racing each other. Two girls would run from one marker—a tree, a pole, a crack in the sidewalk—to another. The winner would race the next girl and so on. Naomi had come to love this game, since a week ago she won for the first time ever. Last year, she would have been more likely to curl up under a tree with a good book than participate in the races. But since taking up ballet that summer, her legs were becoming stronger and she felt surer on her feet.

The races finally came down to Naomi and Vicky, a tall skinny girl who was pretty fast, but Naomi beat her last week and was pretty sure she could do it again today. Debbie, her best friend since third grade, had lost way back.

"Shoot. I don't even know why I bother," Debbie had said, putting her eyeglasses back on over her big almond-shaped eyes. "I'm pitiful at this stuff."

They both laughed, because it was so true. Debbie was funny and one of the smartest girls at Monroe Junior High, but athletic she was not. So she picked a spot on the sidelines to root for Naomi as the other girls gathered around her and Vicky. This part got loud as some of the girls who favored Naomi tried to get Vicky's friends to bet on the race. Just as the two of them got into place at the start line, a girl from the hard group named Barbara came over to watch. Barbara was one of the OK ones. She always spoke in the hallways and they'd even talked a few times, so Naomi wasn't bothered. She kind of liked it that Barbara was there watching; if she won, Barbara would go tell the other girls in her group, and that would make her look cool.

She puffed her chest out, knowing the race was hers and the word would get around. Then she crouched a little as one of the girls said "Ready . . . set . . . go!" Naomi flew down the track and beat Vicky easily, barely breathing hard at the finish line. Naomi and Vicky hugged between deep breaths of air and walked back to join the crowd.

Debbie ran up to Naomi and they gave each other five. Debbie's mahogany face was all smiles. "How do you do it, Nay? How'd you get to be so fast all of a sudden?"

Naomi shrugged. "I don't know, you know? If I feel someone closing in on me I just make my legs go faster and—" She stopped as Debbie's big eyes got bigger and moved to something behind her. Naomi turned to see Barbara approaching them. She flicked her cigarette on the pavement and smiled.

"You really fast, girl," Barbara said, shoving her hands in the pockets of her leather jacket. "I seen you race last week, too. You're good."

"Thanks," Naomi said, trying to act as if it was no big deal.

"She's the best. Can't nobody beat her," Debbie said, slipping into her tough-girl dialect.

"Oh, yeah?" Barbara said, smiling. "Think you pretty slick, don't you."

Noami shrugged, trying to maintain her nonchalance. Truth was, she felt ten feet tall.

"I'm always telling her we gotta find somebody who can beat her," Debbie said.

"Yeah," Barbara said. "Hey, I know somebody you can race."

For some reason, hearing that made Naomi feel like she'd shrunk down to two feet. She was fast, but she knew one thing. She had never raced any girls outside their cozy little group.

"You know Henrietta?" Barbara asked.

Now she was down to two inches. She was too nervous to say anything, so she just nodded her head.

"She my number-one ace," Barbara continued. "Sometimes we try, but none of us can beat that girl. Maybe you two should race."

Naomi still couldn't speak. If she said no, Barbara would

run back and tell her friends Naomi was chicken. Barbara was standing there waiting for an answer, so Naomi kind of nodded her head to let Barbara know she heard the question while she tried to think how to get out of this mess.

"All . . . right!" Barbara shouted, leaping into the air.

At first Naomi didn't understand what she'd said or done to get the girl all excited, then she realized she'd goofed big time. Barbara thought her little nod was an agreement to race Henrietta. Naomi thought she would pee in her panties.

Barbara backtracked toward her friends, and Naomi finally found her voice. "Wait. I didn't mean—"

"I'll go tell 'em. Be back in a second." Barbara turned and ran off.

Debbie grabbed Naomi's arm. Now Debbie's eyes looked like they were about to pop out over her glasses. "You're not really going to race Henrietta Jackson, are you?"

"How am I supposed to get out of it?"

"You'll find a way. You're always good at working around things."

Naomi shook her head. "Not this time."

"Then just come out and tell her you can't do it."

"So she can tell everybody I'm chicken?"

"Well, shoot, Nay. Better that than if you beat her and she kicks your butt till it's black and blue."

"I don't think I'll beat her."

"How do you figure that? You're way too fast." Debbie's eyes lit up. "Hey, I have an idea. Let her beat you."

"You mean throw the race?"

"Yes!"

"I guess I could do that."

"You *have* to do that."

There was no more time to discuss it. A herd of leather coats marched their way, with Barbara and Henrietta leading the pack. Not only was Henrietta tough, she was also pretty and light-skinned, with reddish hair down to her shoulders. Henrietta approached Naomi, and the seven or eight girls with her stood behind. By now, some of the others on the playground had sensed something big was happening and were starting to come over too. This included Steve, a boy Naomi had liked since seventh grade but could never get to notice her.

"I hear you want to race me," Henrietta said.

Uh, not exactly. But how could she say that with Steve and half the school looking on?

"Well, do you or don't you?" Henrietta asked, sounding like she was ready to beat Naomi's butt either way. Naomi stole a glance at Steve. He was looking straight at her with that cute baby face of his.

"I'll race you."

The way Debbie looked, you would have thought she was standing over Naomi's casket.

Everybody got into position on the sidelines. Then someone from Henrietta's group got the idea to make the race longer, and they moved the finish line to a tree farther away.

All this was a blur to Naomi. Her mind was whirling, trying to decide what to do. If Henrietta was able to beat her, fine. But what if it looked like she could take Henrietta? Should she deliberately slow herself down? She didn't have a lot of time to think about it, because Barbara was telling them to get ready. As Naomi stood at the start line and looked out at all the excited faces, she made up her mind. She would do her best to beat this girl. She might end up with a black eye or worse, but she could never throw a race in front of all these people, especially Steve. If she won, he'd probably think she was bad. *Everybody* would think she was bad. In a way, she felt relieved now. Instead of worrying which way to go, she could concentrate on winning.

Barbara picked up a stick and held it in the air. She waited for everybody to quiet down some. "Ready . . . set . . . go!" She lowered the stick and they were off.

Henrietta shot out ahead of her. Naomi's first instinct was to let it stay that way. But she couldn't. She willed her legs to go faster, pushing them as hard as she could. She thought of ballet, where she willed her body into all sorts of odd shapes and had become the best dancer in the class. She thought of the pride she felt whenever Mrs. Johnson singled her out to demonstrate a movement to the other girls. She thought of Mama, so tickled with her progress she often came early to pick up Naomi and watch from the sidelines. This was no different, Naomi told herself, as she caught up to Henrietta. All she had to do was push a little harder. The finish line was just ahead, so she didn't have much more time. She forced every ounce of energy in her body down to her legs and sprinted ahead of Henrietta and over the finish line.

She bent over trying to catch her breath. They were both breathing so hard neither could speak. Henrietta had surprised her. She was better than anyone Naomi had ever raced. But Naomi was more surprised with herself. She'd had to dig deeper than ever before to win this one, and it felt good to pull it off. She just hoped—

"Bitch. Think you bad, don't you?"

Naomi heard it, but she didn't want to believe she heard it. She straightened up and tried to keep her knees from trembling. "No. It was just a race."

"You cheated. You started before Barbara said go."

By now the others had gathered around.

"She did not," Debbie said, coming to stand beside Naomi. "You were out ahead of her at the start."

Henrietta glared at Debbie. "Who the hell asked you? This between me and her."

"Yeah, stay out of it," somebody from the crowd said.

Debbie backed down wisely, and Henrietta turned to Barbara. "Didn't she start before you said go?"

"Yeah," Barbara said. "I wouldn't take that shit if I was you."

Some of the other girls chimed in. "Yeah, don't take that shit."

"Bitch don't play fair."

"Whip her mothafuckin' ass."

So much for Barbara being OK. "Wait a minute," Naomi said. "No need to get all worked up. If you want, we can do it over. That would settle it." She was trying to be civil here.

"I don't want to race no cheating hussy," Henrietta said. " 'Sides, I never could stand your stuck-up ass. Think you cute 'cause you got all them fancy rags." She shoved Naomi in the shoulder. "I'ma whip your sorry ass."

"You gonna take that?" somebody asked.

Naomi wouldn't have had any problems taking it if she and Henrietta had been alone somewhere, since she'd never been in a fight and Henrietta was the last person she wanted to learn from. But she couldn't just stand there and let somebody shove her around and call her a snob in front of all these people. Just as she was about to hit Henrietta back, the school bell rang, and a couple of teachers came out and told them all to get moving. Talk about being saved by the bell. She had never been so happy to hear it.

Henrietta wasn't through with her yet, though. She stood inches away and pointed her finger in Naomi's face. "Meet me back here at three-thirty. I'm gonna whip your butt good." Naomi didn't say anything, but she'd just as soon eat a bag full of worms as show up at 3:30. As if reading her thoughts, Henrietta added, "And if you don't come, I'll find you tomorrow or the next day. Either way, your ass is mine."

"What are you going to do?" Debbie asked as everyone headed back.

"Good question," Naomi said, as they walked slowly toward the building. "Guess I'll have to come back. It's now or later."

"Are you crazy? You can't come back here. Even if you could beat her, she'll have some of her friends with her and they'll probably all jump in."

"Don't scare me like that. Maybe she'll come alone."

"Henrietta Jackson? She never goes anywhere without her crowd following her. There'll be at least five of them."

"You got a better idea?" One of the things Naomi liked about Debbie was she always got smack to the point, but that trait was getting on her nerves now.

Debbie sighed. "Guess not."

"That's what I mean. Might as well get it over with."

"You want me to come back with you?"

"I don't see what good it will do if it's just the two of us. It's not like we've got a bunch of friends to invite to stand up to Henrietta and her crowd."

"Two of us is better than one."

"You can come if you want. But maybe if it's just me, I can talk Henrietta into leaving the others out of it. If she sees you, she'll probably just get madder. So just stay home." Naomi couldn't help but notice the look of relief on Debbie's face.

"Why didn't you just let her win?" Debbie asked.

"I don't know. Once we got started, I couldn't hold back. I just don't have good sense, I guess."

"Sure it didn't have anything to do with Steve standing there?"

"No, I'm *not* sure it didn't have anything to do with Steve standing there."

Debbie got this weird smile on her face.

"What?"

"I bet he knows who you are now," Debbie said.

Naomi carefully planted one foot in front of the other on the pavement, being extra careful to avoid the cracks. Maybe if she didn't step on a single crack the whole three blocks to her house, she would wake up and discover that she'd just had a nasty nightmare. That Henrietta Jackson didn't really want to fight her. That she'd live to see another day.

She looked up and saw her house in front and all those missed cracks behind her. Nothing had changed. Henrietta still wanted to meet her on the playground at 3:30. She wasn't going to live to see her thirteenth birthday. It bothered her more to be called stuck-up than to be accused of cheating. It wasn't fair. Just because she wore nice clothes didn't mean she was stuck-up. She worked hard making most of them, and her parents worked hard to get the money to buy her nice things. Was she supposed to be ashamed of that?

She walked into the house and slammed the door behind her. Joshua was stretched across the couch watching TV. "Hey, pip-squeak, what's the matter?"

She ignored him and flew up the stairs to her room and slammed the door. She grabbed her Wranglers and tennis shoes and threw them on the bed. Then she kicked off her good shoes. If she stopped to think about what she was about to do, even for a minute, she would chicken out. She had to keep moving. Suddenly, she stopped everything she was doing, plopped down on the bed, stuck her thumbnail in her mouth, and chewed. She had to catch her breath.

There was a knock on the door and Joshua opened it.

"Get out!" she screamed.

"What's the matter with you?" he asked again.

She flew across the room and pushed him as hard as she could. "Get out of here! Leave me alone!"

"Not until you tell me what's going on," Joshua said, easily resisting her.

She stopped shoving him and tried to catch her breath. At this rate, she was going to wear herself out before she even got to the playground. She lowered her voice. "None of your business."

Joshua folded his arms across his chest. "I'm not leaving this room until you tell me what's wrong."

She could feel her eyes watering and held her breath. She might as well tell him. She'd probably be so black and blue afterward, everybody would know anyway. "A girl at school"—she paused and swallowed hard so her voice wouldn't break— "wants to fight me. I have to go back at three-thirty to meet her. If I don't, she'll—"

"Whoa. Who wants to fight you?"

"A girl named Henrietta Jackson."

Joshua's expression changed from slightly amused to greatly concerned. Dang. She must be in really big trouble if her brother was worried about her.

"You know her?" she asked.

"Who doesn't? She lives over on the other side of the avenue. She should be in my class, but she flunked a couple of grades. She's always been bad news."

It looked like Henrietta's reputation extended far beyond their little junior high school. This was not good.

"What are you doing messing with *her*?" Joshua asked.

"To make a long story short, I beat her in a race."

"And now she wants to fight you? Dumb bitch. She should pick on girls her own age."

"She doesn't care about that. She just wants to look good in front of her friends."

"She's bringing her friends?"

"She never goes anywhere without them."

"I don't think I like the sound of this."

Naomi realized that Joshua was really upset about this too. It made her feel a little better, but not much. She still had to go out there and fight. "Welcome to the club. Now you have to get out of here so I can get dressed."

"I really don't think you should go."

"I have to. If I don't, she'll just get me tomorrow at school. And if we fight at school, we could get kicked out."

Joshua shook his head. "This is crazy."

"Why is it so crazy? I remember Daddy always telling you to stick up for yourself."

"But you're a girl, you're not supposed to fight. You probably don't even know how."

"I guess I'm about to learn."

"Is anybody going over there with you?"

She shook her head. "Debbie offered but I told her not to."

"This is no time to be a hero."

"Joshua, please, just leave so I can get ready. I want to get this over and done with."

"Fine. But I'm going with you."

"What for?"

"You're nuts if you think I'm letting you face a gang of girls by yourself."

"What can you do?"

"Maybe we can talk our way out of it."

She shook her head. "I doubt that. Henrietta talks with her fists."

"Then I can at least keep things fair by stopping the other girls from jumping in. And if it gets too rough, I'll break it up."

Suddenly she was beginning to like the idea of having Joshua tag along. He could at least keep her from getting killed. She smiled for the first time since the race that afternoon.

* * *

On the way to the playground, Joshua tried to give her a few pointers on fighting. At one point, they stopped in the alley and he showed her how to block a punch with one hand and jab with the other. She didn't know how much good it would do, since in the fights she'd seen between girls, they did more slapping and shoving than punching.

"And remember, if you end up on the ground, try to stay on top. You lose control if you're on the bottom."

"OK."

"And try to keep her away from your eyes."

She nodded. She knew Joshua was trying to help, but this was too much to remember in so little time.

"It won't even come to that, if I can help it," he said.

She was definitely rooting for him, but as Joshua liked to say, she wasn't too optimistic. As they got closer to the playground, both of them were quiet. Joshua would be there to help, but this was her fight and right now she was too scared to talk. They looked around but didn't see anyone. "Maybe she changed her mind and won't show up," Joshua said. "A lot of people like to talk tough but don't do anything."

Naomi didn't think Henrietta was one of those people or that she would be that lucky. Just then, she saw someone on the other side of the playground walking toward them, and her stomach turned inside out. Then she realized it was Debbie. Naomi ran up to her. The first thing she noticed was that Debbie wasn't wearing her glasses. "What are you doing here? And where are your glasses?"

"I couldn't let my ace come here by herself. And if I'm going to be fighting, I can't wear glasses. I left them at home."

"You won't be doing any fighting. This is my problem. But can you see OK?"

"Yeah, just don't get more than five feet away from me."

They both giggled, and Naomi hugged Debbie. That was one of the reasons Debbie had been her best friend for so long. Naomi could always depend on her. But more than that, Naomi admired Debbie's smarts. She and her mother lived in a small apartment—Debbie had never even known who her father was—yet she stayed on the honor roll at school and was a genius when it came to math. In fact, she loved the stuff. If there was one thing Naomi admired it was somebody who had a head for numbers. "Thanks for coming. I owe you one."

"You got him to come?" Debbie said, looking at Joshua. "You didn't need me."

"It was his idea," Naomi said proudly.

"They're not here yet?" Debbie asked.

"No." Naomi could tell her voice was quivering, but she couldn't help it. "Maybe they're not coming," she said, daring to hope.

"If they don't show up in a few minutes, we'll leave," Joshua said.

"Why don't we just leave now," she said, suddenly not feeling so brave anymore. "I don't think I can do this. I'm too scared. I want to go home." She was trying desperately to hold back the tears welling up in her throat. But it didn't do much good.

Joshua put his arm around her shoulders. "It's up to you. But if you leave now, the problem will still be there tomorrow."

"I don't care. I want out of here." She freed herself from Joshua's grasp and started walking back toward the house, back toward safety, even if it was only temporary.

"Sooner or later you'll have to face her," Joshua shouted at her back. "It's better to get it over with."

"Yeah," Debbie said. "Do it while Joshua's here."

She stopped and wiped her eyes. They were right, no matter how much she wished it wasn't true. She walked back toward them.

"They'll probably see Joshua and turn around and run home," Debbie said.

Naomi managed a smile, and they gave each other five. But Naomi knew the fun was over the minute she spotted five leather coats rounding the corner of the school building. It felt as if her legs would crumble underneath her, but she took a step forward anyway, trying not to look scared. Joshua reached out and held her back. "Let them come to us."

The three of them waited in silence. When the girls got about five feet away, they all stopped and looked at her brother.

Naomi could tell they didn't like his being there. Joshua stepped up ahead of Naomi and Debbie and looked at Henrietta. "What's this I hear about you wanting to fight my sister?"

"This between me and her," Henrietta said. "I got no problems with you." She looked directly at Naomi. "What's the matter? Didn't think you could stand up to me without bringing your big brother along?"

Seeing these girls look hesitant now that she had her brother there gave Naomi a little courage. "I don't see *you* here by yourself." She looked behind Henrietta. "Had to bring a whole army with you."

Henrietta took a menacing step toward her. "I'ma whip your ass, bitch. I don't care who—"

Joshua stepped between them. "Hold on. This is definitely not the way to handle things. You want to fight Naomi just because she beat you in a race?"

"She didn't beat me," Henrietta said. "She cheated. I don't let nobody get away with that kind of shit."

"I did not cheat. I won fair and square."

"You calling me a liar?" Henrietta said.

"Is the sky blue?" Was that her talking?

Debbie laughed. Even a couple of the girls with Henrietta laughed.

"I'ma fuck your ass up good, nigger," Henrietta said.

The word exploded in Naomi's ear. That was the first time anyone had called her that since those boys in Virginia two years ago. She took a step forward. "You just try it."

"Wait a second," Joshua said, holding Naomi back. He gave Henrietta a hard look. "Call her that again, and it'll be me you have to deal with."

Henrietta rolled her eyes, and Naomi shoved Joshua's arm away. She wanted him out of the way now. She couldn't do much about those boys calling her nigger, but she wasn't taking it from this bitch. As long as Joshua kept the others off her, she was ready to take this girl on.

"Wait a minute," Joshua said. "Seems to me you two should be able to talk this out without fighting. Girls shouldn't fight."

"I'm not letting anybody get away with calling me that," Naomi said.

"Well, I don't let nobody get away with cheating on me, and I damn sure don't let nobody call me a liar."

"You're the one lying," Debbie said. "Naomi didn't cheat and you know it."

"You stay out of this, hussy," Henrietta said, making a move toward Debbie.

"Who you calling a hussy?" Debbie took a step forward, and for a moment Naomi thought it was going to be Debbie and Henrietta. She jumped between them, because she didn't want Debbie doing her dirty work. Henrietta shoved her in the shoulder and she shoved her right back. Henrietta looked surprised that Naomi had hit her, but she was no more surprised than Naomi. Henrietta pushed her again, and before Naomi knew it they were clawing at each other like two angry tigers.

Henrietta slapped and scratched her face something fierce, and Naomi wondered what the devil she had gotten herself into. But after the first few licks, Naomi was able to duck a lot of them and get in a few of her own. She was pretty pleased with herself and felt braver by the minute. Henrietta reached for her face, and Naomi knocked her hand away. Then Henrietta grabbed her by the hair, and Naomi balled up her fists and punched her in the stomach as hard as she could. Henrietta doubled over and backed away. Naomi couldn't believe it. This was it? She won?

Then the girls in her gang started yelling at Henrietta, and Naomi knew it wasn't over yet. "Get that bitch!" one of them shouted. "Don't let her get away with that shit." Henrietta charged full speed, and Naomi hit the dirt, butt first. Henrietta landed on top and slapped Naomi in the face like crazy. Between Henrietta's fat ass sitting on her stomach and all the dirt flying up her nose, Naomi thought she would suffocate. She pushed and shoved but couldn't get the girl off her. It seemed the punches would never stop coming. She raised her arms to protect her eyes, so Henrietta popped her in the mouth. She hit her so hard Naomi thought her teeth had fallen out and she was maimed for life. Then the weight lifted off her body, and she saw her brother picking Henrietta up. Henrietta was still swinging like mad, and Joshua had to shake her to get her to stop.

If Debbie hadn't come over to help her up, Naomi probably would have just stayed there in the dirt until everybody left. She was humiliated and her mouth was killing her. She glanced at the ground, half expecting to see a few teeth lying there. She licked her lips and was surprised to taste blood, but it seemed all her teeth were still where they belonged.

"Fuck with me again, hear?" Henrietta said. "I dare you."

Naomi didn't say anything. She just wanted that dog to go away. She was tired of listening to her funky mouth. Henrietta rolled her eyes at Naomi, and the five girls took off.

"Are you all right?" Debbie asked.

"I'll live," she said, trying to wipe the dirt off her shirt.

"Open your mouth," Joshua said, reaching up to her face.

She brushed his hand away. "I said I'm OK."

"Let me look," Joshua said. He looked in her mouth and said it was nothing to worry about. "Just a little cut in the corner of your lip. You'll be fine, maybe a little sore for a couple of days."

"Unless she comes after me again tomorrow, since you broke it up."

Joshua shook his head. "Not after the way you punched her in the stomach. She won't want more of that. She knows you're no pushover now. You should be proud of yourself."

"Proud?" Naomi asked, touching her mouth. "What do I have to be proud of? She beat me pretty good."

He shook his head. "But you got in some good shots. I was shocked, thought you were gonna lick her for a minute there."

Debbie giggled. "So did I."

Naomi smiled. Maybe she did have a little something to be proud of. At least she had stood up for herself. A year ago, she probably would have hid herself in the house for a week, trying to avoid those girls. "Really? You're not just saying that to make me feel better?"

"Now why would we try to make you feel better?" Joshua said teasingly. Any other time she would have punched him, but not today. If he weren't her brother, she'd have given him a kiss.

Three

Naomi was sitting under the hair dryer going through the routine that she and just about every girl she knew suffered through every two weeks. Mama would wash her hair in the bathroom sink and then sit her under the dryer in her room for half an hour. Then she would take a comb and pull and yank it through Naomi's hair until she got all the tangles out. But the worst part was the straightening iron. Every time Mama brought that steaming hot thing near her scalp, Naomi would suck in her breath and freeze every muscle in her body. She wouldn't breathe out until Mama moved the iron away from her scalp and Naomi could hear the crinkles being smoothed out of her hair. It was pure torture, all right, but worth every minute of it. By the time Mama finished with the curling iron, Naomi had a head full of straight hair with soft curls at the ends.

She crossed her legs and picked up her copy of *Seventeen* magazine. The blond girl on the cover had a short sassy do, and Naomi wondered if she could get her own hair cut to look like that. Not blond, of course, but sleek, with soft little curls at the end and lots of body. Anything would be better than this dumb flip she wore now. Whenever it rained or the wind blew, there went her hairdo.

She thumbed through the pages. All the models were wearing the new miniskirts. Naomi was dying for one too, but it would be an ordeal getting Mama to go along. The woman could be hopelessly old-fashioned when it came to her daughter.

Naomi couldn't wait until she was old enough to make her own decisions about what to wear and do. Lately, she had started to fantasize about someday opening her own boutique. It would have the latest fashions, and women from all over Washington would come to shop there. She'd be rich and famous. It was wild and crazy, she knew—she didn't have the slightest idea how to go about it—but so much fun to dream about. Even crabby old Henrietta Jackson would look up to her.

Joshua had been right about her getting new respect after standing up to Henrietta. The word spread quickly at school that, even though she lost, she was somebody who would stand up for herself. Even Henrietta nodded at her in the hallway these days.

She wasn't exactly what you would call fly, she knew, but she definitely felt hipper. She was even starting to fill out her bra a bit. Nothing to get excited about, but promising; she had started doing little exercises behind her closed bedroom door to help things along.

The only part of her life not looking up was the dude department. Steve had started giving her these looks, but for some reason he never said anything, he just looked. Debbie thought he was shy and wanted her to say something to him. She might be hipper these days, but she was still too scared to do that, and besides, Mama and all the magazines she read always said the boy should speak first.

So she and Debbie came up with an idea to get him moving. Naomi would write him a poem and Debbie would give it to him, since he was in her biology class. She spent days biting her nails while working on the thing in her room, trying to get it to rhyme:

> *Baby love, my baby love,*
> *Instead of staring,*
> *We should be sharing.*

Ugh. That was awful enough to give the Supremes indigestion.

> *Roses are red, violets are blue,*
> *I think you're the cutest dude in the whole darn school.*

If you give me a call on 555-9579,
I'll make sure you have a really fine time.

A poet she was not. But for all her toil and trouble, Debbie ended up slipping it into his biology notebook instead of handing it to him.

"Oh, no," Naomi said, when Debbie told her that. "I thought you were going to hand it to him and tell him who it was from."

"I kind of chickened out," Debbie said. "But he'll find out when he reads it."

"Not exactly. I didn't sign my name."

Debbie threw her arms up into the air. "Shoot. What'd you do something dizzy like that for?"

"Suppose he doesn't like me and goes around showing it to everybody."

"You should have told me you didn't sign the thing. Maybe he'll figure out who it's from."

"I did put my number in it. Maybe he'll call."

A week had gone by with no signs from Steve, except the occasional glance her way, so when Debbie came over this afternoon to help her with her algebra homework, they'd have to come up with plan B.

Mama took the dryer off her head and felt around to see if her hair was dry. Then she combed it out, yanking Naomi's head all over the place, and told her to go sit on the chair in front of the kitchen stove. The straightening iron was already resting in the flames on the gas burner. Mama picked it up and cooled it a bit on a paper towel.

"Mama, can you get pregnant from tongue-kissing a boy on the mouth? . . . Ouch!" Naomi jumped away. They had barely gotten started, and already the woman was frying her scalp.

"I'm sorry," Mama said. "But you startled me, girl." She placed the hot iron back on the stove and planted her hands firmly on her hips. "You haven't been out there kissing some boy on the mouth, have you?"

"No, Mama. But a girl at school said you could get pregnant if you tongue-kiss. That's not what you told me."

Mama was quiet. Even though Naomi was dying to hear her answer, she figured she should wait for Mama to say something since the question seemed to throw her off so bad. Besides, Naomi didn't want to risk another burn. She stuck her pinky finger between her lips while she waited.

"What I told you is right," Mama said slowly, as if she was thinking real hard about every word as it came out her mouth. "You can't get pregnant from any kind of kissing. Only from going all the way. But don't you ever, ever, let a boy touch you like that. Is that clear? And stop biting your nails."

She jerked her finger out of her mouth. How could it not be clear? The way Mama tightened her grip on her hair with each word, Naomi thought she'd yank it all off. This subject always got Mama uptight.

"I would never do that, Mama."

"Good."

"But doesn't a boy expect you to at least kiss him if you go out on a date with him?"

"Certainly not. And if he does, you just tell him to get lost. Anyway, what are you doing even thinking about dating? You're only twelve years old."

"But I'll be thirteen on my birthday." It seemed like a magic number. She'd be an official teenager. A whole new world would open up to her. She had already stopped reading Nancy Drew books. They seemed too childish for an almost teenager. Besides, Nancy Drew's life was so different from her own. Nancy never got into fistfights, no one ever called her names like nigger, and she certainly didn't go through this ordeal with her hair every two weeks.

Mama chuckled. "That's still another month away, Naomi."

"It'll be here before you know it."

"That may be true. But no one said you could start dating when you turn thirteen. That's too young for dating and boyfriends, and certainly for kissing."

"Lots of girls at school have boyfriends."

"They probably just talk to them on the phone and maybe walk home from school with them."

"They go to the movies with them too." Naomi didn't mention that most of those girls were sneaking behind their mothers' backs, saying they were out with a girlfriend.

"You won't be doing that at thirteen. Your father would have a fit."

"But what if I meet a boy I like? How will I get to know him if I can't go out with him?"

Mama put the hot iron down on the stove and tilted Naomi's head up toward her face. She smiled and looked at her daughter in a new way. "Naomi Jefferson, have you met some boy at school?"

Naomi turned her head away. She didn't want Mama to see the big grin that was about to break out across her face as she thought of Steve. "No. But I might later, you know."

"Uh-huh. We'll cross that bridge when we get to it. We might be able to let you invite a boy over once in a while."

Naomi smiled, feeling so grown up.

"But that's it. There won't be any dating at thirteen in this house. I was at least sixteen before my mother even allowed . . ."

Naomi closed her eyes in anticipation of one of her mother's history sermons. At least she had learned something from this conversation. She could invite boys over. Maybe. Now all she had to do was find one to invite. She picked up the copy of *Seventeen* magazine. Since Mama had come around on this, she thought she'd try her on the new miniskirts.

When Debbie came over later that afternoon, they went up to her room to study.

"Steve never did call me," Naomi said, sitting down on the floor and opening her algebra book.

"Write another poem. I promise to give it to him in person this time," Debbie said, sitting across from her.

"Yeah, sure. Do you know how hard it is to come up with poems? Besides, the one I wrote stunk. We'll have to think of something else."

"But what?"

"Maybe I'll just go up to him."

"And say what?"

"I don't know. You're so smart. Help me think of something cool to say."

Debbie pushed her eyeglasses up on her nose. "I'm not smart that way. Gimme some numbers and I'm fine, but I don't know anything when it comes to boys."

"That makes two of us. This is pitiful. Oh, I forgot to tell you." Naomi sucked in her breath, jumped up, and grabbed her copy of *Seventeen* magazine off the bed. "Mama said I can get my hair cut."

"Really?"

She sat back on the floor and placed the magazine down on top of their books. "Help me pick out something," she said, flipping through the pages. "You would look cool in this."

"You're not serious about cutting your hair?" Debbie asked.

"I want a whole new look. If we don't do something, we'll both die old maids."

Debbie giggled.

"Laugh all you want, but it won't seem so funny when you're an old-maid mathematician with nothing but your equations to keep you warm at night."

Debbie giggled again. "At least I'll have lots of money. What kind of old maid are you going to be?"

"Lately I've been thinking about . . . guess."

"Oh, no, not this again. It could be anything. Every time I turn around, it's something different."

"But this is really it this time. I can feel it in my bones. Guess."

"I give up. What is it?"

"You haven't even tried yet."

"Oh," Debbie said, throwing her hand up in the air. "A dancer."

"No, I'm going to open up my own clothing store."

"You're what?"

"Yeah. You know how I love clothes."

"You can say that again."

"So what do you think?"

"It's perfect, Nay. How did you think of it?"

"It just came to me. I'll get to travel all around the world picking out things for my shop. You should go into business with me."

"I don't know anything about clothes."

"But you could handle the money side of it. You know, the accounting and all that icky stuff."

Debbie's eyes lit up the way they always did when anyone talked about numbers. "You're serious about this?"

"I'm dead serious."

"Where will we get the money?"

"Be cool, be cool. I just started thinking about this. But there has to be a way."

"Well, count me in."

"So what am I going to do about Steve?" Naomi asked.

"Forget about Steve. This new idea of yours is much more interesting. Pretty soon, we'll have a whole chain of stores."

"Nothing is more important than boys, unless we want to be old-maid store owners, I guess."

"I wouldn't mind if I could be a rich old-maid store owner."

Naomi giggled and they slapped five.

The Chinese restaurant where Daddy took them for dinner that night was just over the line in Maryland. Most of the time when they ate out they went to a Hot Shoppe a few blocks away from their house. But Daddy said the owners of this restaurant were always real nice whenever he went to the carryout window, so they would give it a try.

The four of them climbed out of the Buick dressed in their Sunday best, and walked through the double glass doors. In the lobby, Daddy and Mama walked up ahead to the host, a Chinese man dressed in a black suit who hurried forward as soon as he saw them. Naomi and Joshua kind of lagged behind, arguing in whispers about which movie they would see after dinner. She wanted *My Fair Lady*, Joshua preferred *Goldfinger*. Not that she didn't like James Bond, but they'd just seen *From Russia with Love* at the drive-in a month ago, and she wanted something different this time. Daddy and Mama came back toward them, and the looks on their faces made Naomi and Joshua stop arguing.

"Let's go," Daddy said, putting his arm around her shoulder.

"What's wrong?" Joshua asked.

"Nothing," Mama said. "Come on."

"We're not eating here?" Naomi asked, looking up at Daddy.

"No," he said in a tone that meant, No more questions, just get moving. He stared straight ahead, pulling Naomi along. She glanced back as they walked toward the door. The Chinese host stood in the doorway to the dining room watching them. He blocked most of the view, but she could see some people seated at tables covered with white cloths. A few of their faces were looking that way.

"OK," Joshua said once they were outside. "What was that all about?"

Daddy was about to say something, but Mama gave him a look and his lips tightened.

"They were too crowded," Mama said.

Naomi and Joshua looked at Mama doubtfully and Mama smiled, kind of embarrassed. Mama could have gotten away with that at one time, but she and Joshua were wiser now and Mama knew it.

"You want to spare their feelings," Daddy said, "but they're old enough now to know what's going on. They're going to have to learn about these things so they'll know how to handle them."

"You're right," Mama said.

"I already know about 'em," Joshua said, shoving his hands in his coat pockets.

"Me too," Naomi said. "They turned us out 'cause we're colored, right?"

Daddy nodded. "I never would have put you all through this, but the help is always so friendly when I come here for takeout, I didn't think they would pull this."

They piled back into the car quietly. It felt spooky to know something like this could happen practically right in their own backyard. Naomi thought this only happened in faraway places like Virginia or way out in the boondocks in Maryland. How was she ever going to open up shops all around the country, if she couldn't even go to eat outside her neighborhood?

"They won't get another dime of my money," Daddy said, slamming his door shut. He started the engine and pulled away from the curb.

"I don't blame you," Joshua said. He folded his arms across his chest and looked out the window.

"The man at the door said *he* had no problems letting us in," Mama said. "But he was afraid he'd lose his white patrons if he did."

"For Pete's sake," Joshua said. "He doesn't need any patrons that won't eat around Negroes. How does he think that makes us feel?"

"You're right, Joshua," Mama said. "But he doesn't care how we feel. It's a business thing for him."

That didn't make Naomi feel a whole lot better. It was crummy being turned away no matter what the reason. When she opened her shops, she was never going to turn anybody away.

"So what?" Naomi said. "We have just as much right as anybody else to eat in there, or anywhere else. We're Americans, too. And they aren't even white, they're Chinese."

"They can be just as bad sometimes," Mama said. "Worse, because they think they have to snub us to be accepted."

"At least now we know where we stand at that place, and we can always eat somewhere else," Naomi said.

"Right," Mama said. "Not all Chinese places are like this."

"But if we let even one place get away with it, others will start thinking they can too," Joshua said.

"Joshua's right," Daddy said.

"Yes," Mama said. "But there's not much we can do about it."

"You can complain," Joshua said.

"I may write a letter to the management," Daddy said. "Or someone downtown."

"Good idea," Naomi said.

"That won't do a bit of good," Joshua said. "Start a riot. That's what people are doing in Harlem and down in the South."

Naomi hated it when Joshua talked that trash. She'd seen awful pictures on TV of black people getting hosed and stomped.

"People are getting killed in those places, too," Mama said.

"Yeah, right," Naomi said.

"It seems to be the only way to get their attention," Joshua said.

"There are other ways, Joshua," Daddy said.

"You mean peaceful demonstrations," Joshua said snidely.

"What's wrong with that?" Naomi asked.

"That's not getting us very far."

"It takes time," Daddy said. "Some of you young people don't have any patience."

"You old people have too much."

It got real quiet for a minute. "It's not that, Joshua," Daddy said calmly. "We can remember a time when violence or even just speaking out could get you into a lot of trouble."

"It still can," Mama said.

Joshua tightened his arms around his chest and stared out the window.

Daddy smiled. "Let's forget about this and go on home and change our clothes. It's warm enough to go to the drive-in tonight. We can eat there."

Mama nodded. "Good idea."

"Fine with me." Naomi looked at Joshua, hoping he would agree so they could forget about rioting and all that stuff and start having some fun. But he just stared out the window with his bottom lip poked out a mile. "Come on, don't be a spoilsport." She reached across to punch him in the ribs, but he knocked her hand away.

"Quit it," he said, giving her the most awful stare, and went back to looking out the window.

Mama and Daddy exchanged looks, and Naomi turned to her window.

"I'm not going," Joshua said. "I don't want to see some silly white flick."

Right then and there, she knew trouble was just ahead. You didn't tell Mama and Daddy you weren't doing something in that tone of voice. You asked politely. Naomi couldn't wait for them to put her high-and-mighty brother in his place.

"And what makes you think you're not going?" Daddy asked.

Joshua squirmed in his seat. "I'd rather go out with Dean, that's all."

"Who's Dean?" Mama asked. "And where are you planning to go?"

"Just a friend," Joshua said. "We're going to see the game over at Roosevelt."

"Well, I'm not sure—"

"For Pete's sake, Ma. It's just a basketball game."

"It'll be OK," Daddy said, patting Mama's knee. She nodded. Naomi couldn't believe it. "You're not letting Joshua get away with this, are you?"

"Get away with what?" Mama asked.

"With . . . with talking to you in that tone of voice." She was shocked but also disappointed. A drive-in movie just wouldn't be the same without Joshua in the backseat to kid around with.

"He's still upset about what happened back there," Daddy said.

"So you're not making him go to the movies with us?"

"Your brother's getting older," Daddy said. "He wants to be with his friends. That's understandable."

Now it was her turn to pout. She folded her arms across her chest. Then an idea came to her. "Can I invite Debbie?" Naomi asked.

"That's fine," Mama said.

That made her feel a little better. Debbie loved going to the drive-in with them since she didn't have a father to take her. "Can we see *My Fair Lady*?"

"Yes," Mama said. "Whatever you want to see."

"Well," Daddy said. "I had kind of hoped—"

Mama gave Daddy a look.

"OK, OK," Daddy said. "I guess it's *My Fair Lady*."

Naomi clapped and Joshua gave her a twisted smile. "Bet you're glad I'm not going to be around now, huh?" he said.

Four

The day Mrs. Johnson announced that her ballet class would be closing was one of the saddest Naomi could remember. The number of girls had dropped from eight to five soon after Naomi started attending, so Mrs. Johnson tried raising the fee. But that made three more quit, and Mrs. Johnson said there just weren't enough girls to keep it going. She had no choice but to close shop.

Naomi pestered her mother until they finally found another ballet class that was just starting up. This one was in upper Northwest, a more exclusive part of town, where Negro families could afford to pay good money to give their daughters ballet lessons.

"Be sure and say hello to Jennifer," Mama said, dropping her off in front of a building in a strange neighborhood. "Her mother's a teacher at the school where I work. She's the one who told me about this class, and she told Jennifer to look for you."

"How will we know when we see each other?"

"If she looks anything like her mother, she's very fair with good hair. If you don't find her, maybe you can ask Mrs. Bailey to introduce you. I'll be back to pick you up in an hour."

Naomi found her way to the dressing room and changed into her slippers. Then she took a quick look in the mirror and fluffed out the bangs to her new short hairdo. She loved her hair like this. It was full and fluffy at the top, short on the sides and in back. She couldn't pin it in a ponytail any longer, but this looked so much more fly.

She walked to the dance studio, where about a dozen girls stood around the room in their tights and leotards, some talking, most just waiting quietly. She knew right off the bat that it wouldn't be easy to spot Jennifer Jones, since the girls ranged in hue from vanilla to manila. One was about Naomi's complexion, but she had black wavy hair down to her waist. Now Naomi's new haircut didn't seem so fly. With her brown skin and brown hair, she'd never felt so colored in all her life.

Mrs. Bailey came in and had them all line up along a mirrored wall and say their names. Since Naomi was on the end, she was first. "Naomi Jefferson," she said, and then watched for Jennifer Jones to introduce herself. When she did, Naomi smiled and tried to catch her eye, but the girl named Jennifer never even looked her way. If anything, Naomi thought she seemed to look away on purpose. She couldn't be sure, but it made her awful suspicious. Some Negroes wouldn't mess with anybody more than a shade darker than themselves. She cut her eyes and looked at the teacher.

Naomi felt better once class started. It was obvious that she was way ahead of these girls, and as soon as Mrs. Bailey realized it, she had Naomi help some of the others. But Naomi did her best not to get too close to Jennifer. Wouldn't want the girl to think she might catch the cooties from her. Afterward, Naomi made a beeline for the dressing room, but stopped dead in her tracks at the doorway. Miss High Yellow was sitting on the bench right next to the hook where Naomi had hung her things. She was bent over putting on her Hush Puppies. Well, so what? Naomi thought. The girl didn't own this place. She marched down the narrow room and put on her skirt and white Dr. Kildare blouse without saying a word. Then she sat down next to Miss It and proceeded to put on her own socks and shoes.

"I like your blouse," said the voice beside her. Naomi looked up to see Jennifer, brown ponytail dangling over her shoulders, smiling down at her. Smile or no smile, Naomi was still suspicious about that behavior back in the studio.

"Oh. Thanks." She bent back down to lace her shoes.

"I have one almost like it," Jennifer said. " 'Cept mine is kind of a beige color."

Beige? Everyone knew a real Dr. Kildare blouse had to be white.

"Your skirt's pretty too," Jennifer said. "It's an unusual color. What is it?"

"Aquamarine. I made it." Naomi couldn't resist bragging a little. It wasn't every day she got compliments from a girl like Jennifer. She might not be as beautiful, but she knew a thing or two about clothes.

"Really?" Jennifer said. "You sew? Wow. By the way, my name's Jennifer."

Naomi looked up from her shoes just in time to see Jennifer flip that fat ponytail off her shoulder. Give her a pair of scissors, Naomi thought, and she'd gladly get it out of the girl's way for good. That, and those beautiful long fingernails. She stood and reached for her coat. It conveniently made her have to turn her back. "I know who you are."

"How do you know who I am?"

Please. Spare me the Gidget act. She turned to face Jennifer. "Didn't your mother tell you about me?"

Jennifer got such a funny look on her face, Naomi was beginning to think she must have goofed.

"My mother? No. Why?"

"She didn't tell you to look for the daughter of someone she works with?"

"No. Was she supposed to?"

The weight on one foot was beginning to feel heavy, so Naomi shifted to the other. "I thought so."

"She must have forgotten, then."

It sounded like Jennifer was telling the truth, which made Naomi feel kind of dumb. Mama was always saying she was too quick to jump to conclusions. This was one of those times.

"Your mother's a teacher too?" Jennifer asked.

Naomi nodded, relieved to have the subject changed. "At the same school where your mother teaches."

"What grade does she teach?"

"First. What about yours?"

"She doesn't teach a grade. She's a special ed teacher."

Naomi frowned. "What's that?"

"She helps the children who have special problems. You have to have a master's degree to do that."

Naomi didn't know what a master's degree was either, but she wasn't about to let on. Even though Jennifer acted nice enough, the girl had a way of making Naomi feel like the biggest idiot living outside the insane asylum. "Oh."

"Well, I have to go now. My mother's probably outside waiting for me. Do you want to walk out together?"

"OK." They both picked up their bags and headed for the front door.

"Where do you live?" Jennifer asked.

"In Northeast, over by Catholic University."

Jennifer nodded. "That's where my grandmother lives."

"Where do you live?"

"On upper Sixteenth Street. Not far from here."

She said this like it was supposed to mean something to her. Naomi didn't tell her it didn't.

"Where do you go to school?" Jennifer asked.

"Monroe. And you?"

"Jefferson."

Naomi knew what *that* meant. This upper Sixteenth Street must be one of those fancy neighborhoods across town.

"Well, there's my mother," Jennifer said. "See you next week."

"See you." Naomi watched as Jennifer walked toward a shiny green Cadillac. She knew what that meant, too.

"How did the lesson go?" Mama asked as Naomi climbed into the front seat of their two-year-old Buick, which didn't seem so hot anymore.

"Fine."

"Did you meet Jennifer?"

Naomi nodded.

"What's she like?"

"She's OK. A little on the uppity side, if you ask me."

Mama smiled. "Her mother's the same way. But she's nice

if you can overlook all the pretentiousness and get to know her."

"What's pretentiousness?" Naomi loved big words. A teacher once told her that if you made a point of repeating a new word, it would be easier to remember it.

"You know. Putting on airs," Mama said.

"Like mother, like daughter then."

They both giggled. "Mama, where's upper Sixteenth Street?"

"It's a very expensive neighborhood north of us with a lot of big old houses."

"How can they afford to live there?"

"Jennifer's father's a dentist. And her mother makes more money than I do, since she teaches special education."

"I thought you said all Negroes with college degrees had to become teachers or government workers when you were growing up."

"Not all of them. A few managed to break out and become doctors and dentists. A very few. And Jennifer's mother has a master's degree. That's a little higher than a bachelor's degree."

"How come you and Daddy didn't become a doctor or dentist or get a master's degree?"

"Because it takes a lot of money. My parents barely scraped enough together to send me to college, much less medical or graduate school. They never even finished high school."

"What about Grandma and Granddaddy on Daddy's side?"

"They finished high school, but they had seven children. The army paid for your father to go to college after he got out of the war."

"Well, where'd Jennifer's parents get so much money?"

Mama let out an exasperated breath of air. "Some Negroes in this city just have more money than we do, honey, that's all."

"Daddy, are we kind of poor? Or, like, struggling to make it?" Naomi asked, sitting across from him on the couch. He was re-filling his pipe with his favorite El Producto Bouquet tobacco and listening to some Nat King Cole. Joshua was in the kitchen, and Mama was out Christmas shopping, so Naomi thought now was a good time to ask this question that had been on her mind without getting Mama uptight and her know-it-all brother interfering.

Before meeting Jennifer Jones, she had always assumed they were rich or close to it. They had everything they needed and a lot they didn't need, like the piano, and she got what she asked for most of the time, like having her own phone. Daddy had once said he could afford to buy anything he wanted. Now she realized that maybe Daddy just didn't want all that much. And she remembered Mama saying that white women didn't work because they had more money. Naomi was starting to notice how white people on TV and in the movies always had bigger houses and fancier cars and clothes. And they were always getting money from a dead relative. That never happened to anybody she knew.

Daddy peered at her over his pipe with a kind of half smile, half frown on his face. "Poor? No, we're not anywhere near poor. Who put that idea into your head?" He took a pinch of tobacco out of the can and dropped it into his pipe.

"Well, you and Mama had to be teachers and work in the government, and there's this girl in my ballet class whose father's a dentist and her mother has a master's degree and teaches special . . . special tea—special something. She's not just a regular teacher."

"Just because her father's a dentist doesn't mean she's rich."

"But it means she can be whatever she wants when she grows up, right?"

"So can you."

"Even if I wanted to be a doctor or something? Would you and Mama have the money to send me to medical school?"

"We'd be more than delighted to do that," he said. "You can be anything you want and you can go to any college you want for as long as you want. We'll pay for it."

A big smile crossed her face. She was happy to hear that. She had been worried for a while there. "What if I want to open a clothing store with Debbie? Would you be able to give me money for that?"

"Whoa. I don't have that kind of dough, but I could probably borrow some. Where did this idea come from?"

Naomi shrugged. "I like the idea of being my own boss."

Daddy chuckled. "You probably got it from me, talking about opening up a liquor store a few years back."

"Where were you going to get the money to do that, Daddy?"

"Save some, try to get some from the bank. But it's hard for colored folks to borrow money for businesses."

He saw the disappointed look on Naomi's face. "It might be easier by the time you get out of school," he added. "Don't let money or anything else keep you from dreaming. We'll think of something. You can be whatever you want."

"Even a trash man?" She was teasing, and her father knew it but pretended to be alarmed by falling back in a faint against the sofa. She laughed and tickled him. He tickled her back, and she jumped away and screamed. Joshua came into the living room with a big bacon, lettuce, and tomato sandwich on a plate.

"Good grief," she said. "Didn't you just finish eating dinner an hour ago?"

He lunged for her hair, but she jumped away and stuck her foot out to stop him. He sat in the stuffed chair and stretched out his long legs and took a big bite from the BLT. "I'm a growing boy," he said between munches.

She rolled her eyes to the ceiling, then looked at Daddy. She had been thinking about the clothing store for a while now, but this was the first time she'd talked to Daddy about it, and she had a ton of questions. "Daddy, what do I need to study in college if I want to have my own clothing store?"

"Now that I don't know. We didn't have all these choices when we were growing up."

"Business," Joshua said.

"Ugh," she said. "Too much math."

"But it's a practical kind of math," Joshua said. "Like economics and statistics."

"I don't care. It's still math."

"That's so typical. Girls always think they can't do math before they even try it."

"Negroes also think that way," Daddy said. "You shouldn't be so hard on yourself when it comes to math, Naomi."

"I never said anything about girls or Negroes not being able to do math. Just *me*. Debbie's good at it, so I'll leave that side of the business up to her."

"You don't want to leave too much up to other people," Daddy said. "If you want to go into business, you'd better start getting comfortable with numbers."

"I'll handle the clothes. I just don't know what to study in school."

"I don't know what to tell you," Daddy said. "Maybe fashion design."

She snapped her fingers. "That's it." Then she frowned. "Exactly what is fashion design?"

"Go to the library to get ideas," Joshua said. "That's what I did."

"What are you going to be when you grow up?" she asked.

"An archaeologist."

That was just like Joshua. He had a different answer every month. "I thought you were going to be an astronaut."

"That was when I was little. Archaeology's more practical 'cause it's easier to find a job. There's only so many astronauts out there."

"Archaeology's just as good," Daddy said, puffing thoughtfully on his pipe. "President Johnson's civil rights bill means no more excuses for them not letting you become anything you want."

Naomi nodded. By now she was smarter about the sorry ways of white folks. Ever since the boys in that car shouted "nigger" at them and the restaurant turned them away, she always paid attention when people talked about whites. What people usually said wasn't good. Seemed they hated us and we hated them, even though we had to try to get along since we lived in the same world. And she was starting to notice things she never did before, like the fact that there were no colored people on TV and the only really famous Negro movie star was

Sidney Poitier. Since he was just about the best actor there was, she couldn't understand for the life of her why they didn't hire more colored actors.

"And it's not just jobs," Joshua said. "The law makes it illegal to discriminate in housing, schools, restaurants, everything."

"It changed all of that," Daddy said.

Thank God they had finally passed it, Naomi thought. It was scary to think she and Debbie might not be able to get the money to open a shop no matter how well they prepared themselves just because they were colored.

"I don't know if it's changed things yet," Joshua said. "Just having a law on the books doesn't mean people will act right. If they don't, we gotta start thinking about doing whatever it takes to make them. We been peaceful long enough. Before he was shot, Malcolm X said we've worked three hundred years in this country without getting a dime in return. And Stokely Carmichael—"

"I don't think it'll come to what they're talking about," Daddy said. "I hope King's way works."

Joshua shrugged. "So do I. But I'm not too optimistic."

"Why aren't you optimistic?" Naomi asked.

"Because they've never been fair before," Joshua said. "Why should they start now?"

"Times have changed," Daddy said. "The President's on our side now."

"Yeah," she said.

"We'll see," Joshua said.

Five

Steve and Naomi spent the rest of eighth grade and part of the ninth sneaking looks at each other. The problem was that every time she saw him at school, she couldn't think of a thing to say. Or if she thought of something, it seemed too dumb. He stopped looking at her around the time he started walking a girl named Delores home from school every day. Naomi felt she'd been let down—mainly by herself.

"He couldn't say anything to you, but obviously he did to her," Debbie said as they walked to gym class the day they found out Steve and Delores were going together.

"How do you know she wasn't the one who said something to him?" Naomi said.

"Come to think of it, maybe she was," Debbie said. "Delores always was kind of forward."

Debbie said it like it was something bad, but it seemed to Naomi that the forward girls always got the boys. She should have kicked herself in the butt for not being brave enough to say something to Steve first. Next year, she would be going to senior high, for goodness' sakes, and couldn't even bring herself to talk to a boy she liked. At the rate she was going, she would never have a boyfriend. And she was practically the only girl in school who didn't have one these days. Debbie had replaced her glasses with contact lenses to show off those beautiful eyes not long after her bra size zoomed up to a 34C. Even though Naomi's legs were shapely from all the ballet, her breasts were still stuck in 32A land, maybe permanently, she sometimes thought. Now Debbie was going with a boy named Gene and even thinking about doing it with him.

"What if you get pregnant?" Naomi asked, the day Debbie dropped this bomb. They were in Debbie's room, supposedly studying for a chemistry quiz, but had spent most of the time on the subject of Gene. Debbie talked; Naomi listened. She didn't have much to contribute because she didn't have much experience with boys. A part of her was jealous that Debbie was getting all this attention from a boyfriend. But she had to act happy. And she was, in a way. It's just that she would have been a lot happier if she had a boyfriend of her own. "My father said if I ever got pregnant, they'd have to ship me off to my aunt in the deep South until I had it because they'd be too embarrassed to let me stay here."

Debbie laughed. "Shoot. They're just saying that to scare you. Your parents would never do that. Besides, Gene says you can't get knocked up the first time."

"Do you think he's right?" Naomi had heard that before but wasn't so sure. And she didn't dare ask Mama, considering how she acted when Naomi asked her about a little thing like kissing.

"At first I didn't," Debbie said. "But Gene sounds so sure of himself."

"Even if he's right, what about the second time or the third time? I heard once you start you can't stop."

"He'll use a rubber."

"Those things don't work. Girls are always getting pregnant with those things."

"Gene says that's 'cause people don't know how to use them."

"And *he* does?"

Debbie giggled. "I hope so."

"Guess that means you've decided to go ahead with this."

"Not right now. But eventually maybe. We've been going together for three months now, and Gene's always bringing it up. Says I've got too many hang-ups. 'Hey, baby,' " Debbie said in a deep voice. She stood up and pimped across the room the way Gene and most of the boys at school did. " 'I'm a man, baby, and I can only go so long without it. If you loved me, baby, you wouldn't put me through this. If you loved me, baby—' blah, blah, blah."

Naomi cracked up at Debbie's imitation of her boyfriend.

Debbie sat back down. "I'm tired of fighting it, Nay. I'm not exactly the prettiest thing on earth. If *I* don't do it, he'll find somebody who will. I don't want to lose him. I'm crazy about him."

Naomi nodded. She didn't know what she'd do. She understood Debbie not wanting to lose her boyfriend, but she also knew if she ever got pregnant her parents would never forgive her. It sounded like a horrible decision to have to make—but Naomi would have given anything to be in Debbie's shoes. "Just don't get pregnant. We're still going to open up that boutique someday."

"You mean clothing store *chain*, don't you?" Debbie held out a hand and they slapped each other five.

As Debbie got more and more involved with her boyfriend, she had less and less time for Naomi. So when they went to senior high, Naomi decided to try and beef up her social life by spending more time with Jennfier from her ballet class. Jennifer had been begging her to come over and help her with a skirt she was sewing for home economics class, but Naomi had always been too busy, or at least that's what she said. The truth was that Jennifer and the girls in her crowd—with their long flowing locks and beautiful light complexions—always made Naomi feel gauche. Naomi felt a little more glamorous with her smart haircut, but she knew she could never look like the girls Jennifer hung out with, unless she bought a wig and bleached her skin.

And naturally Jennifer was going with someone. His name was Aaron and he was a freshman at Bowie State College, not far outside of Washington. He only came home every other weekend, which was why Jennifer had so much free time.

Naomi hadn't met him but she'd seen pictures, and he was as fine as he could be, light-skinned with jet-black wavy hair. Naomi thought she couldn't help but look bad in comparison to a girl who had so much going for her.

Now that Debbie had a boyfriend who took up almost all her time, though, Naomi agreed to help Jennifer with her skirt. Mama was delighted she was making friends with someone like Jennifer Jones and was more than happy to drive her all the way across town to her fancy neighborhood. All the houses were so big, they looked like something in a magazine. Mama said it was called the Gold Coast.

The inside of Jennifer's house made Naomi feel she was visiting the White House or something. Everything was so neat and in its proper place. Jennifer's bedroom looked a little more lived in, with some clutter on the dresser and a sweater hanging on the back of her desk chair, but it was still pretty—all pink and white lace and ruffles. She even had her own sewing machine tucked away in a corner, and it looked like it was hardly ever used. Theirs was in a corner of the rec room, and she had to share it with Mama. Naomi could barely get to it at times, the way it was buried underneath swatches of fabric and pattern envelopes.

Jennifer's skirt was a mess—crooked stitches, pieces sewn together backward. The girl might be rich, but she couldn't sew a lick. Naomi tore it all apart and started from scratch while Jennifer put the Fifth Dimension hit "Stoned Soul Picnic" on her stereo. They talked about *Rosemary's Baby*, which Naomi hadn't seen yet and Jennifer had—with Aaron, of course—and Naomi Sims, the fashion model everybody was talking about since she was the first black woman to hit the cover of *Ladies' Home Journal*. Naomi finished the skirt in about two hours and held it up for Jennifer to see.

"That looks so much better," Jennifer said, hugging Naomi. "I'll probably get an A. But can you make it shorter, up to here?" She indicated a point in the middle of her thigh. "Aaron likes me in short, short skirts. Makes it easier for him to lift them." Jennifer giggled and Naomi gasped. Not so much because Jennifer let Aaron go that far as because she was telling her. They didn't know each other all that well.

"C'mon," Jennifer said. "Don't tell me you never did it with a boy."

"Well, I haven't."

"You're lying."

Naomi gave Jennifer a look that said she wasn't.

"How far have you gone then?"

Now Jennifer was really embarrassing her. This was getting personal, and she didn't have much to brag about. Someone she met at a party at the end of the ninth grade had walked her home from school a few times. She wasn't that crazy about him, but at least she finally had someone walking her home. She let him kiss her the third time, and he slobbered all over her and practically broke her neck. It was the first time she'd kissed anyone, and she prayed it wasn't always going to be like that. Maybe she just had to get used to this kissing thing, but not with that dude. "Uh, just kissing."

"You mean you've never even had your titties sucked?" Jennifer said, flipping her hair off her shoulder.

God, she was vulgar! Naomi thought. Through the little they had talked during ballet class, Naomi had come to realize that even though Jennifer might look and act feminine, she had one foul mouth on her. This was humiliating, not because Jennifer was asking these obscene questions but because Naomi was so inexperienced. Her titties had ripened over the past year but still hadn't been plucked. "That's none of your business." She stuck her thumbnail in her mouth.

Jennifer laughed. "Obviously you haven't. You don't know what you're missing."

"I'll have to take your word for it."

"Do you even have a boyfriend?"

"Not at the moment," Naomi said. Or any moment ever, she thought.

"Damn. We're going to have to do something about that. Even though you're kind of quiet, you have a pretty face. And that new haircut is nice, but you should comb the bangs back off your face. And quit biting your nails."

She took her thumb out of her mouth. "You're beginning to sound like my mother."

Jennifer jumped up, went to her pretty white vanity, and picked up a comb. "Can I try something?"

"I guess," Naomi said.

"Come sit here," Jennifer said, patting the pink cushion to her vanity chair.

Naomi sat and watched in the mirror as Jennifer rearranged her hair. She knew that as soon as she got home she was going to comb her bangs right back the way she always wore them, but it was fun sitting at Jennifer's vanity.

"And another thing," Jennifer said. "You should shorten your skirts and get rid of the tights. You have gorgeous legs. Show 'em off."

Naomi smiled. It felt good getting compliments like that from someone like Jennifer. "Thanks, but my mother won't let me wear stockings yet."

"Haven't you ever heard of sneaking? Take a pair in your bag and put them on in the girls' room when you get to school."

"Is that what you do?"

"I did until this year. My mother just started letting me wear stockings to school."

"You're lucky. Mine is so old-fashioned, I'll probably be wearing socks until I get married and move away."

Jennifer giggled and stepped back to admire her work. "That's much better, don't you think?"

"Yeah," Naomi said. She really hated her hair pulled back like this, but she didn't want to hurt Jennifer's feelings.

"I'm having a party on Saturday. You should come. There'll be plenty of fine dudes there. And if you want to, you can change into stockings when you get here."

"Ooh!" Naomi said, getting excited. She wasn't exactly Miss Popularity and didn't get asked to many parties, but she went whenever she was invited and always had fun. Then she remembered that Jennifer went to Wilson, not McKinley. Wilson was a whole different ball game. The thought of being in a room with a bunch of Jennifers was more scary than exciting. "I don't know. I won't know anybody there."

"You can bring someone, if you want," Jennifer said.

She thought of Debbie, her onetime party buddy, but Debbie would probably be doing something with Gene. Still, she could always ask her. "I'll see if Debbie wants to come."

"Who's Debbie?"

"Debbie Young. She goes to McKinley with me."

"Oh. I think I know who you're talking about. The one with the glasses?"

"She doesn't wear them anymore. She got contacts."

"Don't you think it would be better if you invited a boy? It'll be enough girls there. Must be somebody you like at school."

Obviously not, Naomi thought. Otherwise, they wouldn't be having this whole conversation about her lack of male companionship. When they graduated from junior high, Steve had gone on to a different high school and a different girlfriend, from what she'd heard. Naomi had long since given up on him. There was someone on the basketball team at McKinley who she thought was real cute, but so did every other girl in school, and he didn't seem to know Naomi was alive. She shook her head.

Jennifer let out a deep breath. "That's too bad." She picked up the skirt. "Is this pretty much done?"

OK, so she wasn't imagining it, Naomi thought. For some reason, the second she mentioned Debbie, Jennifer's whole attitude changed. One minute she was her usual bubbly self; now she was acting cool as a cucumber. Naomi was tempted to ask Jennifer if she had something against Debbie but decided against it. She could be totally wrong, and if she upset Jennifer, she might take back her invitation. Maybe she already had. "Almost. Am I still invited to the party? I can come by myself."

"Sure."

Naomi was relieved. It was just as well, she thought, since Debbie was probably going to be with Gene anyway. She took the skirt and showed Jennifer how to do the hand stitches for the hem so you wouldn't see them. She figured Jennifer needed to do something to earn her A.

* * *

"Ma, can I go to a party Saturday?" she asked as soon as she climbed into the car in front of Jennifer's house.

Mama frowned. She was a bit antsy about parties these days, since a gang fight broke out at one not long ago, and there had even been some shooting outside, although nobody got hurt. If Mama knew what went on inside some of these parties, she'd be even more antsy: dimmed lights and lots of slow grinding and making out. Sometimes you even heard so-and-so had gone all the way, in a dark corner or out in back of the house.

"I don't know," she said. "Where is it?"

"Jennifer's having it."

"Oh," she said, relief spreading over her face. "In that case, you can go. But Joshua will have to take you. Your father and I are going out Saturday night."

Uh-oh. Joshua wasn't going to like her interfering with his Saturday-night plans. "He's not going to go for that."

"I'll talk to him. Maybe we'll get you something new to wear."

"That's OK," Naomi said quickly. Mama was always trying to get her to wear silly frilly dresses to parties. "But can I wear stockings? Please, please, please?" This had been a long running battle between them, and she wasn't too hopeful Mama was ready to give in, but she had to try. She was in high school and still had to wear socks or tights with dresses, and it was humiliating. She was dying for a garter belt and some sheer stockings. "I'm fifteen now. There's no way I can go to a party with this hip crowd wearing tights. I would be the only girl wearing them."

"I doubt that."

"It's embarrassing, Ma. I—"

"I think it'll be OK," Mama said.

Naomi's mouth dropped open. "Are you serious?"

Mama smiled. "Yes, but only to parties and church. Not to school yet. I don't want you looking too forward."

Naomi could settle for that for now, at least when it came to the stockings. "Now, Ma, about makeup."

"Uh-uh. No makeup."

"Just a touch of lipstick, Ma?"

* * *

As Naomi had expected, Joshua wasn't exactly delighted about having to chauffeur his little sister on a Saturday night. He had his own thing to do, with Dean Davis and some other dudes, and since she had a midnight curfew it meant he'd have to leave his party early to pick her up and take her home. He protested, he ranted and raved, but it did him no good. Daddy said he had to take her and bring her home or stay in himself.

At first, Joshua was thinking of not going out just to spite everybody, even though Daddy told him Naomi could stay out until 12:30. Neither of them thought that was anything to get excited about, but then Daddy told Joshua he could drive the new Mustang. No way Joshua was passing that up! As soon as Mama and Daddy went upstairs to get dressed, Joshua stuck his finger in her face and told her she would have to ride in the backseat and keep her mouth shut. That was fine with her, she told him, as long as she got where she was going. She stuck her tongue out at him and ran up the stairs to get ready.

Joshua seemed so different these days. He was still basically the same brother—annoying at times, pretty decent at others—but lately he was really into all this black power stuff. Everybody under age twenty was into it to one degree or another, but Joshua was obsessed. You would think he knew Stokely Carmichael personally, the way he was always rapping about Stokely this and Stokely that. Whenever Joshua brought up his name, or the Black Panthers, he would get Daddy all riled up. Daddy couldn't understand how Joshua could support anyone who advocated violence. Neither could Naomi. Joshua even said the riots that had gone on last summer in Newark and Detroit and other cities up north were a good thing. Although at times the arguments got pretty heated, they were really more like spirited debates, and she loved listening to the two of them argue their points.

She was sitting on the bed lacing up her go-go boots when Debbie walked in wearing jeans and a T-shirt and grinning from ear to ear.

"What's happening, Nay?"

Naomi jumped up wearing one boot. "Debbie. What are you doing here?"

Debbie's smile faded as she looked Naomi up and down. "Just stopped by to see what you were up to. You going somewhere?"

Naomi shrugged. "Just to a party."

"Oh."

"I figured you would be with Gene or I would have invited you."

"That's cool."

Naomi slipped into the other boot, then moved to the mirror above her dresser and picked up the tube of pink lipstick Mama let her borrow. It was the lightest shade Mama had, but better than nothing. She leaned close to the mirror to put it on, just the way Mama always did it. "Where is Gene?"

"We had a fight," Debbie said. She walked up behind Naomi. "You're wearing lipstick?" she asked, clearly impressed. "And stockings?"

"Ma said I can wear them to parties now."

"Lucky you."

"What did you and Gene fight about?"

"Sex. What else? He's still bugging me about doing it, but I don't want to talk about that." She kicked off her shoes, sat down on the bed, and crossed her legs, meditation style. "Who's having the party, Nay?"

"Jennifer."

"Jones? From Wilson?"

Naomi nodded.

"Well, 'scuse me. Guess I know why you didn't invite me now."

Naomi turned from the mirror to face Debbie. "Because I figured you'd be with Gene."

"Yeah, sure, Nay. Don't play games with me. Everyone knows they're mostly light-skinned people. The few dark ones have good hair down to their knees."

"Excuse me?" Naomi said, holding her cinnamon-colored arms out for effect. Then she reached up and patted the back of her short hairdo.

"You're just light enough to make it in that crowd," Debbie said.

"You're way off base."

"Oh, am I? Then maybe I'll just come along with you. How do you think they'd like that?"

"Fine, why don't you?" Naomi said. She turned back toward the mirror and bit her lip. She knew her voice didn't sound very convincing.

Debbie waved her hand at Naomi. "I'd probably just scare them all away."

Naomi took a deep breath. "That's so silly. Come if you want. I don't care one way or the other." If what Debbie suspected was true, that crowd deserved some shaking up. Naomi wasn't convinced Debbie was right, but maybe that was because she didn't want to be.

"Forget it, Naomi," Debbie said. "I won't let this chocolate skin and nappy hair embarrass you."

"Debbie—"

"Besides, I'm not dressed right."

That was true. But she could always go home and change. Naomi wanted to suggest that but paused, torn between supporting her oldest and dearest friend and wanting to go to the party without a lot of fuss. Jennifer's attitude had indicated that something was going on, but that didn't necessarily mean it had to do with skin color. Naomi had a hard time believing Jennifer was like that. Maybe she didn't like Debbie for other reasons.

Naomi just nodded, and Debbie sighed and stood up. "Well, I'm gonna get going."

Naomi walked her down the stairs, and when they reached the front door, Naomi turned toward Debbie and smiled. "I'll call you tomorrow."

"Yeah, fine."

As she watched Debbie walk away, Naomi felt bad about how this had turned out. She should have invited Debbie in the first place, no matter how Jennifer acted. Just as she was about to close the door, a dude about Joshua's age stepped onto their walkway. Naomi knew it had to be Dean Davis. All the black power stuff started after Joshua hooked up with this character, so naturally Daddy and Mama had been bugging Joshua about him. They told Joshua he wasn't stepping one foot out the door unless Dean came in and met the family when he arrived at the house that night.

She was kind of surprised when he reached the door and stepped into the house. She expected him to look different, more threatening or something. But he wasn't like that at all. He was tall and slim, with a short neat Afro and a smooth nutmeg-colored complexion. He had nice eyes, but she was a bit worried about the hairdo, 'cause Mama and Daddy weren't too keen on Afros. Joshua wanted to wear one, but Daddy said no son of his was going to run around looking like a wild man.

"You must be Naomi," he said, as he stepped through the door.

She nodded. "And you must be Dean."

He was polite and gracious, telling Mama and Daddy that they had a nice house and all. And he had this smooth voice that made Naomi think of Nat King Cole. When he complimented the quilt Mama had made and hung on the living room wall, Naomi knew he was over. He even worked his charm on her, saying she looked pretty in the new shift she had on. She knew what he was up to, trying to impress them, but it was still nice to get a compliment from a boy for a change. Even though Joshua was acting like she had the plague, Dean smiled whenever their eyes met.

As soon as they got out the door that night, Joshua darted to some bushes at the side of the house and removed a brown paper bag.

"What's that?" she asked, as they piled into Daddy's new white Mustang.

"None of your business," Joshua said, tucking it between the bucket seats.

It was obviously something Joshua had no business with, since he'd gone to so much trouble to hide it from Mama and Daddy. So she waited to make her move until he and Dean were deep in conversation about some girls they were meeting at their party and Joshua had both his hands on the steering wheel, making a left turn. Then she reached between the seats and grabbed the bag.

"What the hell!" Joshua shouted at her, loud enough to be heard across town. But she didn't care. She yanked the bag open and pulled out a cotton pullover top. It was red, black, and green. "A dashiki! You're gonna get it, Joshua."

"Give that to me!" Joshua said. He reached back and snatched it out of her hands. She didn't put up too much of a fight because she didn't want them to get into an accident. She grabbed the back of Joshua's seat and pulled herself up behind him.

"You know you're not supposed to wear that," she said. "Mama and Daddy will kill you if they find out."

"How they gonna find out about it, huh?" Joshua asked in a threatening tone. "If you say one word, I'm gonna bop you good."

"Oh, my knees are shaking."

Dean laughed.

She slid over to the middle of the backseat and stuck her head between Joshua and Dean. "I won't say anything if you get me a dashiki and take me out for a banana split after the party."

"You're dreaming. I'm taking your butt straight home and then I'm going back to *my* party. Dig it?"

She sat back and folded her arms across her waist.

"Besides, Mama and Daddy want you home by twelve thirty," he said.

"They wouldn't mind if I was out with you."

"Forget it. And you can tell them whatever you want. It's only a shirt. I'm not scared of them."

Since her threat to tell Mama and Daddy wasn't working, she decided to try another tactic: being nice. She sat back up on the edge of the seat. "Will you get me one, Joshua? Please? I promise not to say another word before we get to Jennifer's house."

"I can probably get her one from the same place I got yours," Dean said. "The brother makes them in all sizes."

"See, Joshua? Please."

"They cost ten dollars," Joshua said. "You got that kind of money?"

Ten dollars for a shirt? It would take her a lifetime to save that kind of money from her allowance. The dude selling them must be making a ton of money. "Does your friend have his own store?" she asked.

"He works out of his apartment now," Dean said, "but he's saving to open a shop."

"Really? That's what me and my girlfriend want to do." The truth was that Debbie spent so much time with Gene nowadays, they hadn't talked much about it lately. But hearing that someone else was really doing it got her all excited about the idea again.

"I admire that entrepreneurial spirit," Dean said. "We need more people doing things like that."

"She's been talking about that since she was in diapers," Joshua said.

"Yeah," she said. "Only thing is, I'm starting to wonder if we'll be able to pull it off. It takes so much money, and you can't be sure it'll even work out."

"Sometimes you got to take chances to get what you want," Dean said. "After this dude gets set up, I'll take you around to meet him. He might be able to give you some pointers."

"You'd do that?" She was starting to like this Dean Davis. Why couldn't *he* be her brother? "If you'd just get the material, Dean, I could make the dashiki myself."

"I'll see what I can do," he said.

She sat back, pleased to have worked that out.

"You must be dreaming," Joshua said. "No way Ma's going to let you use her machine to sew a dashiki."

"You're right," she said, having to agree with him as much as she didn't want to. Joshua sometimes made extra money cutting the neighbors' lawns and that gave her an idea. "Will you lend me the money, Joshua? I promise to pay you back within a month."

"How are you going to wear it?" Joshua said. "Mama and Daddy won't even let me."

"It didn't stop you, did it? I have my ways, just like you do."

"You? Sneaking around behind Mama and Daddy's back? I don't believe it. Next you'll be talking about black is beautiful."

"Black *is* beautiful," she said.

"And joining the Black Panthers," Dean said.

She tapped Dean playfully on the shoulder. "No way," she said.

"OK," Joshua said. "I'll lend you the money. But you have to pay me back."

"No problem."

"And another thing," Joshua said. "You have to help me practice the bop."

Naomi fell back against her seat and pretended to strangle herself. "Oh, no. Not that. Anything but that."

"I almost have it. I just can't get the turns."

"Joshua, you've been trying to learn that dance since you were in the ninth grade," Naomi said. "If you can't do it by now, it's hopeless. What on earth do you do at parties?"

"I'm fine until a slow song comes on, and some girl tells me she wants to bop instead of grind."

"Just tell her you can't bop," Dean said.

Dean and Joshua both chuckled and slapped five. Naomi rolled her eyes to the ceiling.

"So will you help me?" Joshua asked.

Naomi wasn't looking forward to dancing with her two-left-footed brother, but she'd do anything to get that dashiki.

"OK, OK. Now that we're exchanging favors, let's talk about my curfew. Since Mama and Daddy won't be back until the wee hours of the morning, I figure—"

She nearly landed on the floor as Joshua swung the car into a parking lot in front of a Safeway.

"What are you doing?" she asked.

"I'm going to park so you can show me how to bop."

"You want to do it now? Here? In front of the supermarket?"

"Before the party." He parked the Mustang under a street-lamp, got out, and pulled the back of the seat up for Naomi.

She folded her arms around her waist. "I'm not getting out

of no car to dance in the middle of the street in the middle of the night. Get Dean to show you."

"I'm not dancing with no dude," Joshua said.

"The feeling's mutual," Dean said, climbing out of the front seat.

Joshua leaned inside the car. "Look. If you do this, I'll *give* you the money for the dashiki."

Naomi sat up. "Let me make sure I have this straight. I won't have to pay you back?"

"Right."

"Not ever?"

"That's what I just said, isn't it?"

"Out of my way." She hopped out, and the three of them gathered under the lamp. "This is so silly," she said, as Joshua took one of her hands and placed the other on her waist. "We don't even have music." He swung her out and things went fine until he tried to turn her. She went one way, he the other. Dean cracked up.

"What did I do wrong?" Joshua asked.

"Everything," Naomi said. She took a deep breath. "OK, imagine 'Sitting on the Dock of the Bay.' " She hummed a few notes, and Dean snapped his fingers to the beat as they tried again. But somehow, when Joshua turned her, his elbow ended up smacking her in the jaw.

"No, no. That's all wrong," she said, rubbing her jaw. She placed her hands on her waist, trying to decide the best way to go about this.

"Let me show you," Dean said. He stepped up and took Naomi by the hand. She prayed he was a lot better at this than her brother. They swung out, and after a few steps Dean turned her once, twice, then again. It was smooth, flawless. She smiled. *This* was how you did the bop, she thought.

"OK," Joshua said, following them across the parking lot as Dean swung her around. "Let me try now." But Naomi and Dean were enjoying themselves. To Naomi, there was nothing better than finding a good bop partner on the dance floor—or in the parking lot, in this case. The harmony was perfect, the pace just right. When he swung her around, she felt like she was floating. This Dean could dance!

"Anytime you two are ready," Joshua said sarcastically, as she and Dean danced on.

Six

Naomi was scared something silly when she first got to the party. It was in the rec room, a huge area with wood paneling, mirrored walls, and a big circular bar in the middle of the floor. The air was hot and steamy from bodies pulsating to the beat of soul music. It was full of strangers, and she hadn't spotted Jennifer yet. She had spent so much time trying to come up with something to wear, finally settling on a flowered shift with a miniskirt and white go-go boots, she was relieved to see that her clothes fit right in with what the other girls wore.

Jennifer ran up and hugged her, and she immediately felt better. Jennifer had that effect on her. Actually being around her was always less scary than the thought of being around her. "You finally made it," Jennifer said. "You look so cool, even though you combed your bangs back."

"Thanks," Naomi said. "You look cool too." Jennifer wore a hot-pink miniskirt and pink go-go boots, showing off her shapely legs. Naomi was dying to find out where she'd found pink boots, but it wasn't the right time to ask. Jennifer grabbed her hand and dragged her across the room through a throng of people dancing.

"I want you to meet Aaron," she said, taking hold of a dude's arm and turning him around to face them. Naomi knew who it was before Jennifer said his name. He was even cuter in person than in his pictures, but a little too much on the beefy side for Naomi. She liked them tall and slender. Jennifer cuddled up to him. "Isn't he gorgeous?" she said. Naomi laughed and Aaron smiled, although he looked a bit embarrassed.

They stood around and rapped about school and movies. It felt so hip being with this in-crowd. When "Jimmy Mack" blared from the stereo speakers, Aaron asked Jennifer to dance. "There's sodas and food over at the bar," Jennifer said, as Aaron led her to the dance floor.

Naomi stood around a few minutes, but no one asked her to dance so she figured going to the bar would definitely look cooler than standing alone like a wallflower. "Soul Man" came out over the speakers just as she started to make her way, and a dude grabbed her hand to dance before she reached the bar. Then another, and another. Sometimes she would barely break away from one partner after a record ended before someone else would ask her. Word seemed to have spread that she could dance.

It reached a point where she was out of breath and had to turn down a couple of dudes. She decided to head for the bar again, thinking that if she had a Coke in her hand no one would ask her to dance for a while. She had just started to make her way through the crowd when she noticed a cute boy standing near the wall watching her. He was kind of hard to miss, light-skinned, with a head full of curly reddish hair. She got herself some punch and turned around, trying to pick an angle so she could check him out without his knowing. She liked the way he dressed, hip but kind of low-key in a vest and slacks. That was good, because with hair like that he didn't need much else to call attention to himself. She hoped he'd ask her to dance. When another boy stuck his hand in front of her, she shook her head, wanting to keep herself free.

One record finished, then another, and still Mr. Redhead hadn't asked her to dance. She wanted so badly to go over there and say something to him, but she didn't have that much nerve. She always envied girls who could do that without a drop of sweat. Jennifer would probably do it in a minute. She turned back toward the punch bowl to refill her cup, trying to think how she could get the dude to notice her. Maybe she should move a little closer to him.

She turned back around and looked toward the spot where he had been standing, but he was gone. Vanished. He couldn't have gone far in so little time, she thought, looking all around. Or could he? Of all the rotten luck, she thought, leaning back against the bar. Why did she even bother coming to these things? Dudes always asked her to dance but they never bothered to say much to her, at least not the cute ones.

Just as she turned to set her cup down on the bar, a hand touched her elbow. She was about to say no thank you, since she was too disappointed to dance now, but the fine face that greeted her when she turned back around just wouldn't allow that. It was Mr. Redhead, standing there with a smile that warmed her insides.

"Do you want to dance?" he asked.

She would have danced with this dude even if it meant using up the last breath of air she had left. She hoped none of the dudes she'd just turned down would notice, but the truth was she didn't really care.

They danced through three records, and then a slow song by Smokey Robinson and the Miracles came on. Her mind flipped back to bopping with Dean in the parking lot. That had been so much fun. Before they left, Joshua was even starting to get the hang of it. She was about to ask Mr. Redhead if he wanted to bop when he pulled her in close and wrapped his arms around her. Joshua and Dean and the bop disappeared from her memory.

"Do you go to Wilson?" he asked, turning to look down at her. "I don't remember seeing you around."

"No. McKinley."

"Oh," he said. "Then how do you know Jennifer?"

"She's in my ballet class."

"That explains it," he said.

"What?" she asked.

"You have nice legs and you move gracefully, even when you walk. I noticed you earlier and thought you might be a dancer."

His name was Merlon, and for the next two hours they hung out together—dancing, drinking punch, talking. She discovered he was not only fine but was also a year older and had his driver's license. She was on cloud nine, at least until someone stopped the music and she heard her name being yelled across the room.

"Naomi Jefferson! Your father's here to pick you up."

She almost choked on her punch. The music started up again, but not before she heard a few snickers. She was pretty sure it was not her father upstairs waiting for her, just Joshua trying to be cute. She had planned to be upstairs by 12:15, just so this wouldn't happen, but had been so wrapped up in Merlon, she forgot the time. She could have kicked herself, but she would wait and kick Joshua instead when she saw him.

If Merlon thought it was funny, he didn't let on. "Does that mean you have to go?" he asked.

He sounded so disappointed. Bless his sweet soul. "Unfortunately, yes," she said. "But it's not my father upstairs, it's just my brother trying to be funny."

Merlon laughed. "Can I get your phone number before you go?"

Can Aretha Franklin sing? Can James Brown dance? Can Sidney Poitier act? She nodded and gave it to him. But neither of them had a piece of paper, so he wrote the number in the palm of his hand. She watched in horror as he did that. What if he washed his hands before he wrote it down on a piece of paper? From now on, she thought, she would carry a pad and pencil in her purse whenever she went to parties.

"I'll call you next week," he said, smiling. She backed away to leave, and they were some of the most difficult steps she had ever taken in her life. The thought of leaving him with all these pretty girls was more than she could stand. What if he met someone he thought was more interesting? What if he was the type whose hands perspired and her number faded away? What if—

"Naomi."

She turned at the foot of the stairs to see Jennifer behind her. "I've been just calling you and calling you," Jennifer said.

Naomi giggled, realizing what had happened. She was so

absorbed in thoughts of Merlon, she hadn't even heard her name.

"I saw you talking to Merlon," Jennifer said. "He must have really blown your mind."

Naomi nodded. There was no point denying it. "He's so sweet," she said.

"And fine," Jennifer said. "I hear he's *some* kisser, too."

"Really?" Naomi was dying to hear all the juicy details. She just knew there had to be better kissers out there somewhere than the one she'd done it with. But she was afraid if she didn't get upstairs, Joshua would do something else to humiliate her. "I have to go, but I'll call you tomorrow."

"I'll walk you to the door," Jennifer said, following her up the stairs. "Did he ask for your phone number?"

Naomi nodded. "I just hope he calls me."

"He will. He couldn't take his eyes off you all night. And neither could his ex-girlfriend."

Naomi stopped in the middle of the stairs and turned to face Jennifer. His ex-girlfriend? "You mean she's here?"

Jennifer nodded. "But they aren't talking to each other these days."

"Where is this girl?"

Jennifer took her hand and led her back down the stairs. "See the one standing over there by the wall? In the green dress? Her name's Thomasina."

Naomi's eyes practically popped out of their sockets when she spotted this girl. She was gorgeous—light brown complexion with beautiful hair hanging down over her shoulders. She was proud that Merlon was interested in her after going with a girl like that, she thought, as Jennifer led her back up the stairs.

"You don't have anything to worry about," Jennifer said. "I hear they've really called it quits this time."

This time? "How many times have they broken up?"

"Two, three."

"Who broke up with who?"

"First time it was her, then him. Back and forth like that. Kissing's not the only thing I heard he's good at." She leaned close to Naomi and lowered her voice. "I heard he's hung like a bull. That's why Thomasina can't stay away from him."

Now Naomi was starting to worry. She was going to have to find a way to stay until every last soul went home, or at least Miss Horny in the green dress with the golden complexion and long silken hair down to her knees. She was about to turn around and head back down the steps when Joshua appeared at the top landing. "Where you been, girl? I was just about to go down there and get you. Let's go."

"Joshua, I can't go now."

"What do you mean?"

"There's something I have to do. I need just fifteen more minutes."

"Out of the question. What am I supposed to do in the meantime?"

"You can come down to the party," Jennifer said.

"I'm not partying with a bunch of tenth graders. I got my own party to get back to." He started walking toward the door.

"He thinks he's Mr. Big Shot since he's a senior," Naomi said to Jennifer.

"Why didn't you tell me your brother was so cute?" Jennifer whispered.

"Oh, please."

"Come on, Naomi," Joshua said. "I don't have all night."

"Go on," Jennifer said. "I'll keep an eye on Merlon for you."

"Thanks. I'll call you tomorrow. I want you to tell me everything that happens from this moment forward."

Naomi followed Joshua out the door and down the walkway. "Why do you have to be such a pain in the ass sometimes?"

"Whoa. What's going on for you to get such a nasty mouth? Must have something to do with some dude."

She got in the car and slammed her door as hard as she could. "For once, I meet somebody decent and you have to go spoil it," she said, as Joshua got behind the wheel. "I'll never get a boyfriend."

"So that's what this is about. Don't blame me. I'm just doing what Mama and Daddy told me to."

"It's so stupid. You didn't have to be home by twelve thirty when you were fifteen."

"That's 'cause you're a girl."

"Why should that matter?"

"You're right. It shouldn't."

"Then why don't you let me go back in?"

"Mama and Daddy wouldn't like it."

"They don't have to know. They never get back from their parties before two or three in the morning."

"I can't do that, Naomi. But we can stop for a quick ice cream."

"I don't want ice cream. I want to go back to the party."

"Look. If you go back to the party, it's going to look obvious to this dude that you're checking up on him. That's going to make him uncomfortable. Did you give him your phone number?"

She nodded.

"Then wait for him to call. You got to act cool. You don't need to go chasing dudes around."

"Suppose he doesn't call?"

"How could he resist calling someone as lovely as you?"

"Oh, you!" She couldn't help but smile at her smart-alecky brother. In a way he made sense, though. It *would* look strange for her to go back to the party now. "For once, you might be right. Let's get some ice cream then."

By the time they reached Baskin-Robbins and sat down to share a banana split, she had filled Joshua in on Merlon and his beautiful ex-girlfriend.

"What does this dude look like?"

"He's fine. Light-skinned with curly red hair."

Joshua turned up his nose. "You ought to get out of that light-skinned curly-hair business. That's not where it's happening anymore."

A pang of guilt shot through her stomach, followed by anger the minute she thought of the girls she'd seen around Joshua. "You have some nerve," she said. "None of your girlfriends are ever darker than a loaf of Wonder bread."

Joshua shifted in his seat. "That's not true. I date 'em in all shades."

"Yeah, sure. Anyway, all I was doing was describing him. I can't help it if he happens to be light."

"OK, cool it."

They sat in silence for a few minutes, licking their spoons. "Joshua, do you think I'm OK-looking?"

"What do you mean?"

"You know. Do I look OK?"

"You're more than OK-looking. Even Dean said he thought you were cute."

"Really?"

"Yeah, but don't let it go to your fat head."

She ignored his comment. "Does Dean have a girlfriend?"

"Yes," Joshua said pointedly. "And he's too old for you."

"I was just curious."

"That's why he stayed at the party. She's there with him. With Dean there's always a girl."

"You mean he's a womanizer? He seemed kind of quiet and shy to me."

"He's definitely a one-woman man. And how could anybody get two words in around you?"

She giggled.

"There's nothing shy about Dean. He's one of the most intense dudes I know. I think it's because his father was killed when he was only about ten years old."

"His father was killed? How?"

"Stabbed during a robbery."

"That's awful. What about his mother?"

"She's still around. And he has two younger sisters, about ten and twelve. They were babies when it happened, so Dean has been, like, the man of the house all these years."

"That's awful."

"I know. But don't tell him I told you. He doesn't talk about it much."

"I don't blame him. What if something like that happened to Daddy? He's always going to the store at night."

"It's not going to happen."

"I hope not." She pushed visions of their father going out alone after dark from her head. "I still don't understand something. I mean, if you and Dean think I look OK, why can't I find a boyfriend? Everybody's got one but me."

"You'll get one soon enough. Most of 'em are after just one thing anyway."

She kicked him under the table. "No, they're not."

"Believe me, I know what I'm talking about."

"How do you know so much? 'Cause that's how you are?"

He chuckled. "I didn't say that. But I hear them talking, and getting over is never far from a dude's mind when he's with a babe. So you be careful. Don't do anything you're not ready for."

"But how do you know when you're ready?"

"Don't you talk to Ma about these things?"

"Come on. I mean, we talked about the basics but that's it. She would probably just say wait until I get married."

"She's right. You should."

"Come on, Joshua. Are *you* waiting till *you* get married?"

Joshua faked a cough, and she giggled.

"See what I mean? So how did you know when you were ready the first time?"

"That's different," he said. "Dudes are always ready."

"Thanks. You're a lot of help."

"The best advice I can give is, if you have doubts, then you're probably not ready. Don't let yourself be sweet-talked into anything, especially on the first date, or the second or the third, or they'll think you're easy. Dudes stand around practicing just what they'll say to get you in the sack."

"Really? Debbie said her boyfriend told her he couldn't go but so long without it or he would get sick."

"That's bull. All of them will tell you something like that. But if it's really bothering him, there are ways he can handle it until you're ready."

At first she wasn't following him, then she realized he was talking about masturbation. She couldn't believe Joshua was being so frank with her. That was the nice thing about talking to him rather than Mama or Daddy. She knew he would tell it like it was. "Believe it or not, I'm actually going to miss you when you go to Northwestern."

Joshua smiled at her. "I'm kind of going to miss this place too. But I'm excited. So much is going on now up north. People think all the racism is in the South, but it's just as bad up there, only it's more subtle. In the South they come out and tell you they don't want you around. Up north, they pretend everything's OK, but under the table they're doing everything they can to hold you down."

"Yeah, but there's not much we can do about it."

"Not if we sit back and take it. Things will never change that way. A lot of the students are demonstrating for more black teachers and more classes about our contributions to society. Nothing wrong with that."

"I don't mind stuff like organizing at school to get more black classes. It's all the talk about revolution that scares me. Do you really want to see a revolution?"

"Of course not. But sometimes I get to thinking that's the only way. We can't sit back submissively, afraid to stir up the dust, obediently accepting parcels of liberty as the white man decides to hand them out. It'll be a thousand years before we're equal that way, maybe never."

"It won't take that long. Look how far we've come since slavery."

Joshua shook his head. "If you think we've really made that much progress, you need to go back to the history books. Look at this Madam C. J. Walker. She was a millionaire business-woman way back. How many black millionaire businesswomen do we have now? How many men, for that matter? Maybe a couple, and it's been sixty years since Walker made her fortune. You call that progress?"

Joshua had a point. When you looked at it that way, things didn't seem so promising, at least not on the business front. "Well, we're making more progress politically. Although I guess if you look back at the time right after the war when we had all those black politicians, even that's debatable."

"That's exactly my point. We take one step forward and two steps back."

Joshua was right when you looked at things over time like that. She still got the shivers when she remembered the four little girls who died when a bomb planted by whites exploded while they were in Sunday school. And her heart filled with bitterness when she thought of the three civil rights workers who were killed in Mississippi only a few years ago just for trying to get people to register to vote. But she wasn't convinced that revolution was the answer. "And you think the way to change that is with revolution? I don't buy it. What makes you think we could win?"

"Whether we won or lost, we could definitely wreak some havoc, and whites know that. People talking like Rap Brown, saying stuff like 'This is a dress rehearsal for the revolution,' at least they're scaring white people into paying some attention to us."

"As long as it stays talk it's OK, I guess."

"But no blood, sweat, or tears, huh?"

"I didn't say none, but not too much."

Joshua nodded. "Hopefully it won't come to anything major, but I'm not optimistic."

"You never are. I can't wait until I go away to college. Are you still going to major in political science and then go to law school?"

He nodded. "I may even start my own law firm after I get some experience. I'm beginning to see how important it is for us to start our own businesses. We won't get anywhere, always working for the white man."

"How are you going to pull that off? Where will you get the money?"

"You have to have a plan. All it takes is know-how and connections. White people do it all the time. Why not us?"

"It's harder for us 'cause we don't have the connections."

"We can get them. That's the main reason I'm going to Northwestern. Never underestimate yourself, Naomi. You haven't given up on your dream of opening a store, have you?"

"No, but I'm beginning to realize just how hard it is to do something different like that, especially for black people. What if I try it and lose a lot of money? Sometimes I think I should go after something more normal, like teaching."

Joshua shook his head in protest. "Just make sure you get the best training and credentials you can get. Even if you don't open your own store, you can always put the training to use doing something else. When I was trying to decide if I should spend all that time going to law school, Daddy told me something I'll never forget."

"What?"

"Once you get that degree, no one can ever take it away from you. They can take your car, your house, your money. But not what's up here." He pointed to his forehead.

Naomi knew Mama probably thought it strange that her daughter jumped to answer the phone every time it rang that week, or that if someone else answered and it was for Naomi, she always said she would take it in her room.

"Who are you expecting a call from?" Mama asked as she set a pot roast on the dinner table a couple of days after the party.

"Nobody in particular."

Joshua coughed pointedly from across the table, and Naomi looked up to see this big old grin on his face.

"Are you lying to me, Naomi Patrice Jefferson?" Mama asked, her hands fixed firmly on her hips.

"No," Naomi said, trying to keep her face straight. She didn't fib to Mama often, since the woman had an uncanny knack for later discovering the truth anyway. But she figured this wasn't exactly a lie, since Mama knew she was lying.

"Then why do you jump every time the phone rings and only take calls in your room?"

"Uh . . ."

"It's probably just a phase she's going through," Joshua said. "You know how girls are about their privacy."

Naomi's mouth almost dropped open at Joshua covering for her. Daddy didn't have much to say. He probably figured this was something for Mama to handle.

Merlon finally called the next day and asked if she wanted to go see *Guess Who's Coming to Dinner* that night. She said yes, of course, but felt embarrassed when she told him she had to ask her parents first. She thought for sure he would make fun of her.

"Are you saying this is your first time going out with a dude?" he asked.

"No." That was true if you counted boys walking you home. "But it's my first time going out with somebody in a car."

"I see," he said. "Tell them I've been driving for almost a year now, ever since I first turned sixteen. So you'll be safe with me."

"OK."

"And if they want to talk to my parents or something, no problem."

Bless him, she thought. He really wanted to go out with her. She asked Mama and, after grilling her about Merlon and every relative of his back to the Civil War practically, Mama said she could go if she got Daddy's permission. Naomi thought she was home free, since Daddy usually went along with what Mama said when it came to her. He always said Mama knew best for her, since she was a girl. He would probably ask a lot of questions, just like Mama did, and then would go along. But when she asked him, he had just one word for her.

"No."

No questions, no comments, no conditions. Just "no." He didn't even look up from his newspaper.

"But Daddy, it's just the movies."

"No."

"But why?"

"Because I said so."

"Can you at least give me a reason?"

He removed his pipe from his mouth. "No dating until you're sixteen."

"That's not a reason. Besides that's only, like, nine months away."

"I can count." He stuck the pipe back in his mouth and flipped to the sports page so casually you would have thought they were discussing the weather, not her life. She looked at Mama for help. A fine dude asks her out on a grown-up date, and she has to turn him down because Daddy thinks she's nine months too young? Movie dates weren't exactly handed out on street corners. Didn't he know this could ruin a girl's future?

"Honey," Mama said, "I know we agreed she would wait until she was sixteen, but this boy comes from a nice family, from what she tells me. He goes to Wilson."

"I don't care if he goes to Harvard, Princeton, and Yale all at the same time. If he's such a nice boy, he can wait until she turns sixteen."

Joshua chuckled, but not her. She couldn't believe her ears. Why was Daddy being so strict all of a sudden? He was the one she could usually get through to. "No boy on the face of the earth is going to do that, Daddy."

"There will be other boys."

She didn't want other boys, she wanted this one.

"You'd be better off going along with it," Joshua said. "If you don't, she's just going to start sneaking around on you."

Daddy removed his pipe and looked directly at Naomi. She appreciated Joshua's taking her side, but she wasn't sure telling Daddy she would start dating behind his back was the cleverest way to go about it.

"Naomi would never do that," Daddy said.

"Don't be too sure," Joshua said. "All girls do it. Even nice ones like Naomi."

Naomi hadn't thought that far ahead, but . . .

"I'm sure Naomi would never do anything like that," Mama said. "She's a good girl. But dating's not unusual at fifteen these days."

"Mama should know, Daddy," Naomi said. "Since she teaches school."

"I need some time to think about this," Daddy said. "When does he want you to go out with him?"

"Tonight," Naomi said.

"Tonight? What ever happened to calling up a few days ahead for a date?"

"They do things differently now, John," Mama said.

Daddy took a deep breath. "I don't like this one bit. But I'll let you go if—"

She jumped up and hugged him around his neck.

"Wait a minute," he said. "Before you get too excited, I'm going to take you and pick you up from the movie myself."

Naomi jumped back. "Are you crazy?" She would be the laughingstock of D.C. She would stay home before she went along with that. "Merlon's going to get his parents' car and pick me up."

"I think that will be OK, John," Mama said. "If he comes in and meets us first."

"No problem," Naomi said, then looked at Daddy. "Merlon even said you could call his parents and talk to them if you want."

Daddy took a deep breath. "I want her home right after the movie, Phyllis. Not a minute later."

"Of course," Mama said. She winked at Naomi as Daddy went back to his paper. Naomi jumped up, ran to the phone in her room, and called Merlon back to give him the good news. As she rummaged through her closets trying to find something appropriately hip to wear on her first date, Mama came in and pushed aside all the outfits piled on her bed and sat down. She had this "need to have a talk" look on her face. Naomi appreciated Mama sticking up for her back there, but honestly, she couldn't have picked a worse time to have a chat.

"You remember some of the talks we had earlier?" Mama asked.

"Talks?" Naomi asked, snatching a pair of bell-bottoms and a red halter top from her closet.

"About what to do when you're out with a boy."

Oh, *that*. From what Naomi remembered, those talks had been more like what *not* to do when you're out with a boy. "Yes, but we didn't go into it much."

"I thought I had more time, but you're growing up so fast."

Actually Naomi had been relieved that Mama always sort of danced around the subject. It was embarrassing, rapping about these things with your mother. "Uh-huh."

"I'm sure this Merlon is a nice boy, and I want you to have

fun with him. But you don't want to do anything to get yourself—uh, in trouble. You understand what I'm saying?"

Naomi nodded.

"A baby would disrupt your life. You wouldn't be able to go to college because you'd have to stay home and take care of it. You understand that?"

"Yes, Ma."

"And you wouldn't be able to get a good job to take care of yourself, much less a baby, without a college degree."

"Uh-huh."

"You must never do anything to jeopardize going to college. It's the most important thing you'll ever do. You have to get a good job and be able to take care of yourself when you grow up. Negro women—"

"Black women," Naomi said, correcting her. When would Mama ever learn?

"Black women, then. We can't depend on finding a man to do that."

"I understand," Naomi said emphatically, wanting to reassure Mama so she would get off this humiliating topic. "I would never do anything to jeopardize going to college."

"Good." Mama stood up, looking as relieved as Naomi was that they had gotten this over and done with. "And by the way, I wouldn't wear that halter top if you want to get past your father tonight."

Naomi looked down at the skimpy red top in her hand. She started to protest but then remembered the conversation earlier with Daddy. She was lucky to be going out at all. "Good point. Thanks, Ma. And thanks for helping me out with Daddy earlier."

Merlon came inside to meet her family and passed all the tests. He talked football with Daddy and sat down at the piano and played a couple of tunes for Mama. Daddy and Mama smiled happily as they left.

Everything was going fine until they got in the car and Naomi realized she didn't have a clue what to talk about. She mostly just said yes or no to his questions, since she was so afraid she would say something that would make him stop liking her. She panicked double-time when he stopped asking questions altogether, and things got quiet. She had to muster every ounce of willpower in her body to keep from sticking a fingernail in her mouth and biting as hard as she could. She was sure he was tired of having to do all the talking, with her not holding up her end. This was so different from being at a party where dancing filled up the conversationless moments.

They finally made it to the theater. The good part about going to the movies, she realized, was that she didn't have to say or do anything for a while. The bad part was that she could sit and worry about what he thought of her the whole time. *Guess Who's Coming to Dinner* was a big hit, but she couldn't have told you the first thing about it if her life had depended on it.

By the time the lights came on and they got up from their seats, she was sure this was going to be her last date with him. Maybe her last date with anyone, since she was such a bore. Then he put his arm around her shoulders as they stepped out of the theater, and she was back in heaven.

In the car, Naomi made up her mind she was going to have to do a better job of being interesting. She had a brother she talked to all the time. All she had to do was imagine that Merlon was Joshua—on one of Joshua's good days. So she told Merlon how hard it was to persuade Daddy to let her go tonight. At first, she was nervous that he'd think this was a dumb topic to talk about, but then he laughed when she told him Daddy wanted her to wait until she turned sixteen. He told her he had two younger sisters and a very protective father too, so he understood. He said they'd have to take things slowly with her father, and he'd always be sure to get her home on time. When he said "we" like that, as in "we, a couple," or "we" meaning Merlon and her, it was all she could do to keep from jumping out the window and dancing on the hood.

Then things got quiet, and for a brief moment she thought maybe she was starting to bore him again. But then he reached over and took her hand, and she remembered that she'd read in *Seventeen* or one of those magazines that some of the best moments between couples are silent ones. She hoped he didn't notice her ugly fingernails.

He looked over and smiled at her. "Can I ask you something?"

She nodded and bowed her head. It was going to be something personal. She could feel it in her bones.

"Maybe I should pull over for a minute," he said. "We can still make it to your house before your curfew."

By the time he parked the car, her heart was pounding so hard she thought it would fly out of her chest. Fortunately she didn't need to think to know what was coming. She had lived this moment in her head a thousand and one times. Now she had a real face and a real voice to go with it.

He shut off the engine and turned to face her. He cleared his throat. "Will you go with me? You know, be my one and only?"

She'd heard some girls tried to be cool and all at this moment by saying they needed time to think about it, even though their brains were screaming yes. Well, not her. She wasn't taking any chances that he'd change his mind before she got to say it. "Yes."

Merlon smiled with relief, and it was only then that she realized he was probably feeling just as antsy about all this as she was, that he had actually thought she might say no. How in the world could he possibly have ever thought that?

"Maybe we should seal it with a kiss," he said, and her brain almost blew out of her head. She wondered if he could see her temples pounding as he reached over and gently turned her face toward his. His fingers were warm and his lips were soft and his tongue tasted so sweet. At least she thought so. The truth was she was so numb, she didn't feel much of anything. She had even forgotten to close her eyes. So she shut them, thinking maybe it would help her relax. That was when she realized his hand was traveling slowly up her thigh, and her eyes popped back open. Her first instinct was to slap it away, but then she decided she liked the way it made her feel all tingly inside, so she closed her eyes again.

As he worked his magic with his tongue and hands, she felt herself begin to relax slowly. She thought she could stay in his arms like this forever. Then the tips of his fingers touched her panties, and her eyes flew open again. It was the first time a boy had ever touched her underwear, and she had a feeling it was time to put a stop to things. So she pulled away. "I think it's time for me to go now, Merlon."

He backed off and looked at her with this dreamy expression on his face. "Your lips are so soft," he said, clearing his throat. "I got carried away."

She giggled. This kind of talk was embarrassing.

He looked at his watch. "We've still got a few minutes. Your house is right up the street."

"We can stay a little longer," she said. "But just to talk."

"It's OK," he said, moving closer. "We're going together now." He reached for her but she drew away.

"I never do that on a first date." She said it like she knew from experience, when of course she didn't. It was the first time a boy had tried to go anywhere near that far with her. But every girl knew you just didn't do it on the first date unless you wanted to be called a whore.

Merlon straightened up in his seat, and she breathed a sigh of relief. "So how many dates do you need before you go all the way?" he asked.

Naomi was stunned. She hadn't even thought that far ahead yet, since all this was so new to her. She wondered if he would think she was square if he knew she was a virgin. She was comfortable with Merlon, but not comfortable enough to tell him that. "It depends."

He turned the key in the ignition. "Hope I don't have to wait too long. A man has certain needs."

She remembered the talk with Joshua in the ice cream parlor and realized that Merlon was doing exactly what Joshua said every boy did. She couldn't help but feel a little disappointed.

Seven

All hell broke loose the day Martin Luther King Jr. was assassinated in Memphis, Tennessee, not only across the country, where folks were grieving and talking revolution, but also in the Jefferson home. Daddy and Mama sat glued to the evening news on the TV set after they came home from work. The family even ate dinner in the living room on TV trays. Daddy kept jumping up and pacing the floor, talking about how every time Negroes got someone to look out for them, the white man snatched them away. First President Kennedy, now King.

Joshua was nowhere to be found, so Mama kept jumping up and looking out the window for him. The news said there were some disturbances around town, and Mama kept saying if Joshua didn't come home in ten minutes, she was going to call the police. Naomi wasn't all that worried about Joshua, since she figured he could take care of himself. But she was worried about herself. Merlon wanted her to go to a party the next night, and she had promised to get permission, even though it would feel like asking to go to a party when a friend of the family had just been killed. Naomi wasn't sure how Mama and Daddy would react, but she found out soon enough.

"No, no, and no," Daddy said. "No daughter of mine is going out partying the day after Martin Luther King is killed. Don't you understand what's happened?"

"Yes. But going to the party isn't going to change anything, Daddy."

"No, it's not," Daddy said. "But you can observe a day or two of mourning."

She took a deep breath. "Everyone else is probably still going to go."

"I doubt that seriously," Mama said, getting up to look out the window for the thousandth time. "It's too dangerous out there. The news said gangs of people are on the street looting. . . . Oh, there's Joshua now. Thank goodness!"

Mama reached the door just as it flew open. Naomi was glad Joshua was back too. Now maybe she'd have somebody on her side.

"Where have you been all this time?" Mama asked as Joshua shut the door behind him. Joshua's eyes were as big as golf balls, and he was practically hopping with excitement.

"I went to Fourteenth Street with Dean to see what was happening."

"Didn't you know that would be dangerous after something like this?" Daddy said.

"You should have called," Mama said.

"I would have. But things were moving so fast," he said breathlessly. "People are mad as hell. Fires are starting up and down the streets. This town's gonna blow."

"That's exactly what Dr. King would *not* have wanted," Daddy said. "It goes against everything he stood for."

"Daddy, I'm sorry the man is gone, really. But this just shows why that peaceful stuff doesn't work. They're taking our leaders from us right and left. First Malcolm, now Dr. King. We can't just sit around and let them get away with it."

Oh brother, Naomi thought. If Joshua got them all riled up, she would *never* be able to persuade Daddy to let her go to the party.

"They didn't have anything to do with Malcolm," Daddy said. "His own people did that. And we don't know who shot Dr. King yet. The news said—"

"Later for the news," Joshua said. "We don't need them to tell us the white man is behind it, messing with us all over again."

"We don't know that for sure," Mama said.

"And even if it was a white man," Daddy said. "That doesn't mean—"

"*I* know it," Joshua said, pointing at his chest. "What the hell does it take to get you people to wake up?"

"Don't talk to us like that," Mama said. "I don't know how you talk in the streets, but in this house—"

Joshua threw his hands in the air and stomped toward the kitchen.

"Come back here," Mama said.

"Let him go," Daddy said.

Naomi was shocked that Daddy was going to let Joshua get away with cursing at them. So was Mama, based on the way she looked at Daddy. "Why are you letting him talk to us that way?"

"He's got all the frustrations of generations of black men inside him," Daddy said. "And he hasn't learned to control them yet. That's all."

Naomi was baffled by Daddy's reaction, but now was her chance. "Daddy, about the party," she said, loud enough for Joshua to hear, hoping he would stick up for her. But instead he flew out of the kitchen and glared at her.

" 'Party'?" He spit the word out like she had committed ten mortal sins. "How can you think of partying at a time like this?"

"You don't have to yell at her," Mama said.

"Oh!" Joshua waved his hand and stomped up the stairs.

"But you need to forget about the party, Naomi," Mama said.

"It's out of the question," Daddy said. "I shouldn't even have to tell you that."

Naomi took a deep breath. The way everyone was getting on her case, she felt like a traitor or something. Maybe she was, in a way, for even thinking of going out. By the time she reached her bedroom, she was starting to feel annoyed that Merlon would even put her up to this. She fell across the bed and was reaching for the phone to call him when Joshua came in.

"I didn't mean to jump all over you, but you should realize what this means."

"I know, but Merlon wants me to go to this party with him real bad."

"My opinion of him just dipped about ninety percent," Joshua said.

Naomi smiled sheepishly. "Everyone's not as into this stuff as this family is, you know. Before you came home, Daddy was even saying they killed the dream when they shot Dr. King."

"They can't kill the dream. He was important in the struggle. He had links to the power structure that other leaders don't have. But he's just one person. We have to go on no matter what happens. You've heard of Thurgood Marshall?"

She nodded. "My history teacher talked about him. He's that new black judge."

"Not just any judge. He's the first black man appointed to the Supreme Court. He was the one who argued *Brown* versus *Board of Education* before the Court, and he won, too."

"That's what my teacher said."

"The dude is mind-blowing."

"Is he the reason you decided to be a lawyer?"

"Partly. I mean, all the protests and demonstrations have their place. Sometimes it's the only way to get whites to listen and take us seriously. But I'm no fool. In the long run, we're going to need people working from inside the system. That's why you shouldn't give up your dream. We need people owning businesses, too."

She nodded. Joshua was sounding more like Daddy now than himself, but she didn't tell him that. She also didn't tell him that while a part of her still wanted to open her own clothing store someday, another part was seriously starting to wonder if she could carry it off, especially since she wasn't sure Debbie was still with her. And there were other things a girl had to think about, like getting married and having babies. Going with Merlon had her thinking more about stuff like that, and it was hard to see how she could run a business, raise kids, and take care of a house all at the same time. As to what she would do if she didn't open a store, she had no idea. Nothing else really interested her.

Fortunately, she still had plenty of time to think about all that. For now she wanted to concentrate on her redheaded boyfriend. After Joshua left the room, she picked up the phone and dialed Merlon. "Forget it," she said, when he came on the line. "No way my parents are going to let me go to a party tomorrow night."

"My parents are against it too, but they didn't rule it out."

"So what are we going to do?"

"I may drop by the party for a few minutes with some of my boys."

She was surprised to hear him say that. They'd been practically inseparable the past couple months, going everywhere together except school. She even told him she was a virgin, and he still said he was crazy about her. He said he would wait until she was ready to have sex, but she figured it was only a matter of time before he would lose his patience and start looking elsewhere. Maybe he already was. This was one of those bite-your-fingernail moments, but she had stopped doing that after meeting Merlon. "I don't think you should go without me."

"It'll just be for a few minutes."

She wanted to protest but didn't want to get into an argument with him the night before he ran off to a party alone. All the girls would think he was a free man again and be up in his face. The last thing Naomi wanted was for him to be mad at her tonight.

She had been able to hold him off this long by letting him get a little further each time, and they were already to the point of his routinely stripping her bra and panties and feeling her all over. The last time they were together, she let him rub his dick against her. She knew she wasn't going to let him put it in, but she was curious about how it would feel on her naked skin. She liked it enough to know she wanted to go further, but, unlike Merlon, she had the burden of thinking about pregnancy. Merlon assured her it wouldn't happen if he removed his thing before he came, but if this really worked, why did so many girls get knocked up?

She couldn't take any chances of messing up her future. If there was one thing scarier than losing Merlon it was that she would get pregnant and not be able to go to college. So she read whatever she could find in the library. She found stuff about the pill, condoms, and the rhythm method, but nothing about yanking it out before coming, as she informed Merlon. The pill was beyond her reach, since she wasn't sixteen yet and would need Mama's permission. Mama would chain her to her bed, lock the bedroom door, and saw off the handles before agreeing to that. Merlon had about convinced her that she wouldn't like using a condom, so that left the rhythm method and not many chances to do it, the way she figured it. Since her period was so irregular, the only time she could feel sure of not getting pregnant was a few days after. So she told Merlon they could do it one or two days after her period was over. But she was always putting it off for one reason or another, and he seemed to be losing patience.

"You got your period yet?" Merlon asked over the phone. Before, he always dreaded the arrival of those days, but now that he knew she had decided on the rhythm method, he couldn't wait for the next one.

"Not yet," she said.

"Seems to be taking an awful long time."

"You can't control Mother Nature."

She managed to put Merlon off for a couple more periods, but there was one thing she couldn't put off. In late May, Joshua left for Chicago. Even though his grades were good, for a college like Northwestern he needed an extra math course and the school was allowing him to take it over the summer. It was a bittersweet time for Naomi. She was happy for him, since he was about to embark on the journey to become a lawyer, but it would seem strange not having him around the house from now on.

The whole family went to National Airport to see him off. He and Dean had worked it out so they would be roommates at Northwestern, and Dean and his mother and sisters were at the airport too. They all stood around talking until the ticket agent announced that flight 209 was ready to board. Both families hugged all around. Mama took a long time with Joshua, fussing with his hair and clothes. Naomi hugged Dean, but when Joshua's arms went around her, she lost it and started bawling like a baby. Joshua tucked his hand around her waist and took her aside.

"Hey," he said pinching her lightly on the nose. She put her head on his shoulder and he patted her arm. "You'll be fine. You'll be leaving for college yourself in a couple of years."

She nodded. "I don't know why I'm acting like this."

"In a day or two, you won't even notice I'm gone."

"I doubt that seriously," she said, sniffing.

"You'll be busy with Merlon. You and him still tight?"

Just thinking about Merlon made her feel better, and she smiled and nodded.

"He seems like an OK dude," Joshua said. "But you need to educate him about civil rights."

Naomi smiled. "Everyone can't be as radical as you are. I'm crazy about him and he's crazy about me. That's what counts."

"Uh-huh. Just remember what I told you about keeping your legs together. You haven't gone and done anything with him, have—"

"No," she said before he even finished the question. She was worried Mama and Daddy would overhear. But she was relieved that she could be truthful with Joshua, although she wasn't sure how long it would be the truth.

"Good," he said, and they hugged one more time. Then they all watched until he and Dean waved goodbye and disappeared through the door. Naomi and her parents said goodbye to the Davises, Mama put her arm around Naomi, and they walked back to the parking lot. She could tell Mama was having a hard time, too.

"The first time is always the hardest," Daddy said. "He'll be home for the holidays."

"Will he be home for Labor Day?" Naomi asked.

"He's not coming back until Thanksgiving," Mama said. "He'll be too busy with school."

"He'll be here before you know it," Daddy said.

Mama nodded. "You'll be busy over the summer with your own school applications, and with Merlon and your friends. I've been meaning to ask you, whatever happened to your old friend Debbie? I haven't seen her at the house for a while."

Naomi shrugged. "We talk on the phone every now and then. But we've both been busy doing other things, I guess. She's been going with this dude named Gene for the longest time. And I've been spending more time with Merlon and Jennifer."

"Boyfriends are no reason to forget your old girlfriends," Mama said. "Neither is finding *new* girlfriends. You've known Debbie for so long."

"I haven't forgotten her. We're applying to some of the same colleges. So's Jennifer. Maybe we'll all end up at school together."

"I didn't think Jennifer and Debbie got along," Mama said.

Naomi was surprised Mama had picked up on this, since she'd never discussed it with her. She once tried to get Debbie to come over when Jennifer was at her house, but Debbie didn't want to have anything to do with her. So Naomi let it go and resolved to deal with them separately. "You're right. They don't get along all that well," Naomi said.

"So that's why I haven't seen Debbie much recently?"

"Like I said, Debbie's always with Gene."

"But Jennifer comes over all the time," Mama said. "Doesn't she have a boyfriend?"

"Her boyfriend goes to Bowie, so he's away a lot. I thought you liked Jennifer."

"I do. But I like Debbie too. And I just wondered what happened to her."

"You can't mix oil and water," she said.

"Sounds to me like you dropped the water and held on to the oil," Daddy said. "Or at least what you think is the oil." He said it like he was joking, but Naomi didn't think it was so funny.

The following weekend, Naomi received a letter from Cornell inviting her up to Ithaca in the fall to visit the campus and in-

terview with some of the school officials. She was so excited—
Cornell was one of her top choices. It wasn't that far from
home but far enough so that her parents wouldn't be popping
in to check up on her every other weekend. She called Jennifer
to see if she'd heard from them too. Jennifer had, so they decided to visit the school at the same time.

Then she decided to call Debbie. Cornell had been one of the
schools they discussed most often, back when they used to talk
about opening a clothing store. Debbie was going to major in
business and Naomi in fashion design, and with Debbie's
grades Naomi was sure she must have heard from them too.
Besides, she hadn't talked to Debbie for several weeks, and the
conversation with her folks had her thinking that maybe she
hadn't tried hard enough to stay friends. Naomi hated to admit
it to herself, but it did seem that the last few times Debbie
called to see if she wanted to go out or double-date, she was always busy.

"Hi. May I speak to Debbie, please?"

"Debbie can't come to the phone."

Naomi recognized the voice as that of Debbie's mother. She
sounded annoyed, which threw Naomi off. Naomi thought
maybe she'd done something to offend her.

When Naomi didn't say anything, Debbie's mother asked,
"Who's calling?" Naomi realized then that Debbie's mother
had forgotten her voice, but she was still puzzled by the tone.

"It's Naomi."

"Oh," Mrs. Young said, her voice a little softer. "Hello,
Naomi. I haven't heard from you in a while. I guess Debbie can
talk to you. Hold on."

Obviously it was Debbie that Mrs. Young was annoyed
with. Naomi wondered what the problem was.

"Hi, Naomi," Debbie said. "Long time no hear." Debbie
sounded even worse than her mother did. A year or so ago,
Naomi would have just asked Debbie right out what was going
on. But there was a distance between them now, and she didn't
feel comfortable doing that.

"Hi. Did you get a letter from Cornell asking you to visit the
campus?"

"Yeah," Debbie said. "Last week."

And obviously she didn't rush to tell her. The chasm between them had grown wider than Naomi had thought, at least to Debbie. "Are you going to see them?" Naomi asked. "Jennifer and I are going to try and go at the same time."

Debbie's sigh was so loud it felt like she was sitting right there beside Naomi. "You two have fun," she said. "I won't be joining you."

Naomi couldn't hold it in any longer. "What's wrong? Cornell was your number-one choice. Is it because you don't want to be around Jennifer? You should try—"

"It has nothing to do with Jennifer."

"Then what is it?"

"Nothing."

Naomi couldn't be sure, but it sounded like Debbie was crying. This was so weird. "I'm coming over," she said.

"Don't bother."

"Then tell me what's eating you."

"I can't," she said, then burst into sobs. "It's too horrible."

"I'm on my way."

It had been drizzling all weekend, so Naomi chose a pair of old tennis shoes and put on a green windbreaker with a drawstring hood over her bell-bottoms. While walking the six blocks to Debbie's apartment building, she racked her brain, trying to figure out what kind of trouble Debbie had gotten herself into. Naturally, the first thing that came to mind was that Debbie had gone and gotten herself pregnant. But then she thought, No way. Debbie was too smart, too goal-oriented, to let something like that happen to her. Even if she was going all the way with Gene, she'd have done something to keep from getting knocked up. So Naomi quickly shoved that idea from her head. The next thing that came to mind was that Mrs. Young had caught them doing it—or, if not "it," then something close to it. That would be enough to get a girl grounded for a long, long time, but it wouldn't explain why Debbie didn't want to talk about college.

She began to feel strange as she approached the building's front door. There had been a time when she walked up this path several times a week. She knew each and every crack in the walkway, just as she knew those in her own. As she looked down now, she realized she could hardly remember the last time her shoes had touched the pavement.

As she climbed the stairs to Debbie's second-floor apartment, she noticed something else that felt different. The building seemed smaller and the stairway dingier than ever before. Naomi supposed that was because she'd been spending so much time with Jennifer and Merlon lately. She suddenly felt keenly aware of her own place between the extremes of black society, the haves and have-nots. She was also more aware of Debbie's place on the continuum, and a sense of sadness washed over her. She shook her head just as she reached Debbie's front door. No need to feel sorry for Debbie, she told herself. The girl had a head on her shoulders to rival Einstein.

Debbie's mother opened the door and smiled when she saw Naomi. But it was clear that something was wrong. This wasn't the same bright-eyed, bubbly woman Naomi had come to admire almost as much as she did Debbie for her strength and courage. Mrs. Young's eyes seemed distant, her manner distracted. "I haven't seen you in so long, Naomi. How are you doing?"

"Just fine, Mrs. Young."

"Good. You're here to see Debbie. She didn't tell you she was being punished and can't have company?"

Naomi swallowed nervously. Whatever it was, it was serious. "No. But I wasn't going to stay long."

"I guess it's all right for her to see you for a little while. But you're the only one I'd let her see. Go on back."

"Thanks, Mrs. Young." Naomi walked quickly down the hallway. Debbie's door was partly closed, so Naomi knocked lightly. It swung open, and Debbie's big eyes stared out in shock. "You mean she let you back here?"

Naomi nodded. "Guess so."

Debbie smiled awkwardly and shoved her hands into her front jean pockets.

"OK if I come in for a minute?"

Debbie stepped aside, and Naomi removed her hood and walked in. With all the curtains drawn and the dreary weather outside, the room was dark, but otherwise it looked pretty much as she remembered it. Debbie sat on the edge of the bed, and Naomi sat down beside her.

"What's going on, Debbie?"

"Nothing."

Naomi shook her head. "Don't give me that. You can't have company. You were crying on the phone."

Debbie inhaled deeply and looked down at her hands, lying limply in her lap.

"Did your mother catch you and Gene doing something?" Naomi prayed that was it and not the other.

Debbie looked up at her. A smile crossed her face and she shook her head and giggled. Naomi laughed too. It was such a relief to see Debbie smiling. Maybe it wouldn't turn out to be so bad after all. This was beginning to feel like old times, hanging around in Debbie's room talking and giggling.

Then Debbie stopped laughing and looked back down at her hands. "I wish it were that simple, Nay. God, I wish."

Here she was all ready to relax, and Debbie throws her this. Naomi could only think of one thing worse than your mother catching you doing it with a boy. "Debbie, tell me."

"I'm pregnant."

"Oh, no." Now it was Naomi's turn to stare at her hands.

Debbie stuck the tip of her thumb in her mouth and her eyes got all watery. Naomi knew she should say something, but she was too dumbfounded to speak. She reached over and rubbed Debbie's back.

"Oh, Nay. Don't ever let this happen to you. Don't ever let anybody talk you into doing this."

"I don't understand. How did it happen? Didn't you use something?"

"He used a condom most of the time. But sometimes he wouldn't have one with him, so he said he would stop and take it out before he came. But then he talked me into letting him stay in."

"Even during your unsafe times?"

"I wasn't paying much attention to that. At first I was, but then . . ." Debbie shrugged.

Naomi couldn't believe Debbie had let herself be sucked into throwing all caution out the window. This just wasn't the same sane girl she'd known all these years, not the Debbie who could whip through an algebra equation before Naomi had even deciphered it, who dreamed of someday being a scientist or running a business. "I don't understand, Debbie. You let him do it with no protection? Why?"

"The first time, he said, you know, you can't get pregnant the first time."

"But then you let him do it again with nothing. No condom, no rhythm, no withdrawing. Nothing."

Debbie twisted her hands in her lap.

Naomi exhaled deeply. She needed to calm down herself. She was starting to sound like somebody's mother. "When did you find out you were pregnant?"

"About two weeks ago."

"And you didn't even tell me? I guess if I hadn't come over here, you would never have said anything."

"Didn't think you'd care. You never call or come around here anymore."

That stunned her. Debbie talked like their drifting apart was all Naomi's fault. "But you're always busy with Gene."

"I'm not *always* with him, and the last couple of times I called to see if you wanted to do something you were busy."

"That was just a couple of times. That didn't mean I didn't want to go out with you ever."

"I got tired of being turned down. I bet you don't tell Jennifer you're too busy."

Naomi swallowed hard. "Our timing has just been off. It didn't mean anything."

"Maybe not. But in a way I don't blame you. Jennifer has so much to offer. I heard her parents even got her a new car."

"Uh . . . yeah." She didn't tell Debbie the two of them spent last Saturday night joy-riding in Jennifer's new Plymouth Duster. "But—"

"Never mind, Naomi. You don't have to explain. Just drop it. I've got more important things to deal with now anyway."

Naomi licked her lips. "So what are you going to do?" she asked, relieved to move on to something else, even if it was this.

"Well, an abortion's out of the question. Mama said we just don't have that kind of money. Maybe I'll put it up for adoption."

"What about school?"

"I might miss a semester—you know, when I start showing—until I have the baby. Gene wants me to keep it. But Mama said that will not be happening. She said I have to finish high school before I even think of starting a family. At first, I wanted to keep it." Debbie paused and took a deep breath. "But now I think she's right. It'll be better for me and the baby to give it up for adoption."

Naomi tried to smile. "Maybe then you'll be able to go on to college, and we can still open a store together—a chain of stores."

"Oh, *that,*" Debbie said, shaking her head doubtfully. "We haven't talked about that in ages."

"I know," Naomi said sadly. "Maybe now is not the time, huh?"

Debbie shook her head.

All the way home, Naomi mulled over her visit with Debbie. This pregnancy was a nightmare. Debbie's dreams were slipping between her fingers, and maybe some of Naomi's as well. She couldn't imagine trying to open a store without Debbie.

Something else they talked about bothered her almost as much. Debbie had made her sound so materialistic. She had wanted to be more aggressive in defending herself, but she figured Debbie had enough to deal with. Of course she liked the fact that Jennifer had nice things and friends with nice things. But the way she saw it, that had nothing to do with Debbie and her drifting apart. Naomi could look back and see moments when she might have made more of an effort to find time for Debbie, but she also remembered times when Debbie could have done the same for her and didn't. It wasn't all her fault.

Times changed, and people did too. She had every right to make new friends and to go on to other things.

So why did she feel so guilty?

Eight

As Naomi and her mother folded the laundry in her parents' bedroom, Naomi told her the news about Debbie. Mama reacted just the way Naomi expected her to.

"That's a shame," she said, shaking her head. "Debbie had such promise. She's so smart."

"It's not like her life is over," Naomi said.

"Even so, it will set her back. What's she going to do about college?"

"I don't think she's even thinking about college now. She's trying to get out of high school."

Mama shook her head. "It's such a waste. Is she going to keep the baby?"

"She's thinking about putting it up for adoption."

"That might be the best thing. Otherwise, it'll be so hard to get back on her feet. What about the boy who got her in trouble? Where is he?"

"He's around. He wants her to keep the baby and he said he'll help her raise it."

"And just how is he planning to do that?"

"He finishes school this year, so he'll probably get a job. I doubt he was planning to go to college anyway. He barely made it through high school."

"Then he won't be able to get much of a job, despite good intentions. Even with a college degree, we have trouble getting good jobs. That's why I'm always telling you, you can't think you'll grow up and get married and let a man take care of you. You have to be able to take care of yourself."

"I know. Debbie said some of the strangest things when I was over there. She thinks I've been snubbing her for Jennifer and her crowd."

"What do you think?"

"I would never do anything like that. I can have more than one good friend, can't I?"

"Yes, but do you still consider Debbie a good friend?"

"I . . . well, we haven't seen much of each other lately. It's a problem finding time to spend with her, since Debbie and Jennifer don't mix."

"Why do you think that is?"

"I don't know. Their lifestyles, I guess." Naomi was hesitant to bring up Debbie's belief that Jennifer snubbed her because she was dark-skinned. She didn't want Mama to think one of her best friends was a color snob. But since this thing between Debbie and Jennifer, Naomi had started to notice more and more how black people seemed to prefer hanging around others who were the same complexion, or one or two shades different at most. This seemed to be true in all spheres of life, from friendship to romance to marriage. At school, it was still considered hip to go with someone who was light-skinned. It puzzled her. How did her people get that way? "Ma, why is it that black people mostly associate with others who are about the same complexion?"

Mama frowned. "What do you mean?"

"You know. They hang around people who are about the same as they are; they marry them. You rarely see a dark-skinned man or woman married to someone who's much lighter."

Mama nodded understandingly. "It's probably because of how we were separated during slavery: the dark-skinned ones in the field, the light ones in the house."

"And we still do it after all this time? Why?"

Mama shrugged. "Light-skinned people still get the advantages. They're treated better because whites feel more comfortable around them. They get better jobs and things like that, so they live better lives."

Naomi immediately thought about how many of the people who lived in Jennifer's well-to-do neighborhood were doctors and lawyers. They were also mostly light- or medium-skinned. She shook her head. "We shouldn't let them pit us against each other like that."

"You're right, we shouldn't. Is this what you think is the problem with Jennifer and Debbie?"

"No," Naomi said quickly. That was exactly what she didn't want her mama thinking, because it simply wasn't true. Or at least Naomi didn't think it was. "I was just asking."

"Uh-huh. Well, it's good you're able to get along with different kinds of people. We never encouraged you not to associate with anyone because of their complexion."

"Yeah. Sometimes I feel like I'm caught in the middle of a tug-of-war, but Debbie will always be my friend."

"Then you need to make sure she knows that, especially after what just happened to her."

Mama had a point. But in some ways, Naomi thought, it would be even harder for them to remain close now. Their lives would be so different. As sad as it was to think it, Debbie's future seemed limited. She had called Debbie once after getting the news, but Debbie sounded so down about her future, it made Naomi depressed and she hadn't called back since. It scared Naomi to think that life can be rolling along smoothly and then *bam*!—everything starts tumbling downhill all because of one mistake. "Ma, can I ask you something else?"

"Go ahead," Mama said, standing to put some things away in a dresser drawer.

"I don't want you to get the wrong idea, but it's something I've heard a lot of people say, and—uh, I was just curious."

"What is it?"

"Can you get pregnant the first time?" Naomi really didn't want to ask Mama anything about sex. But Mama was the only person she could count on to give her a true answer, now that Joshua was at college.

Mama turned to face her. "The first time? Oh, you mean . . ."

Her eyes and voice wandered off, like she was having this intense internal debate with herself. "Yes. You certainly can."

"Then why do so many people say you can't?"

"Who said that? Is that what happened with Debbie?"

"Sort of. People always say that."

"Naomi, it takes just one time. Remember that."

"Got it."

"You're not thinking of doing something you shouldn't with Merlon, are you?"

She looked at her mother, making sure a good dose of horror was on her face. "You don't have to worry about me. Especially after what happened to Debbie."

"Good. I'm sorry about Debbie, but I hope this serves as a warning to you."

No question about that. In fact, for a while, she wouldn't even let Merlon do some of the things she'd allowed before, like fingering her or reaching up under her bra. Debbie's experience rammed all Mama's warnings right smack into the middle of her brain. Merlon said their sex life seemed to be going backward instead of forward, but that was fine with her.

After a couple of weeks, though, things started heating up again, and they were pretty much back where they'd been before. Naomi was more tempted than ever to give in. One thing she'd learned about sex was that it was pretty hard to retreat once you'd gone a certain distance. She couldn't turn off her feelings or forget how good it felt to have Merlon touch her bare skin just because she was scared. On top of all that, Merlon was a good catch: he was cute, cool, and from a good family. They weren't as well off as Jennifer's parents, but they were close enough, and Naomi definitely didn't want to lose him. She didn't have a lot of competition over the summer, but once school started again that could change. Merlon would be a big man this year—a senior at Wilson High—and she'd be all the way across town at McKinley.

She'd done a lot of reading on the subject and felt pretty confident she could do it without getting pregnant. To be doubly careful, she would insist on a condom and doing it only during her safest times. And she would never, ever, let Merlon talk her out of sticking to those two rules.

On the very weekend she was planning to tell Merlon the news, Ralph Jones walked into her life—or, more precisely, into his sister Jennifer's bedroom. He was tall with a honey-colored complexion and wavy jet-black hair. And he had a smile that was sexy enough to charm a snake. He looked so smooth in his turtleneck sweater and cuffed slacks, he could have been a fashion model. She knew Jennifer had a brother, but not much else except that he was three years older than Jennifer, was away at college, and wanted to be a doctor or dentist like his father. She had seen some pictures in an album that had been taken many years before and hadn't paid much attention. But no way could this fine fox be ignored in the flesh.

Jennifer introduced him, and Naomi tried hard to be cool, calm, and collected, even though she could barely look at the dude without hyperventilating. He held his hand out to her, so she stood up and extended hers, reminding herself to put both feet flat on the floor, keep her lips together, and breathe. Thank God she had stopped biting her nails.

He shook her hand and smiled a sexy smile. "You're a friend of my sister's?" he said, still holding her hand. "You look so much more mature." She smiled back but was too dazed to say or do anything more, not while his hand was wrapped so intimately around her own. She was kind of relieved when Jennifer took her off the spot by bopping him in the head with a pillow.

It turned out that Ralph was in Washington for the summer break before the start of his sophomore year at Morehouse College, so Naomi found every excuse she could to spend time at Jennifer's. When Mama couldn't drive her over, she took the bus. Jennifer was puzzled by her behavior at first. When Naomi finally came out and admitted she was mad about Ralph, one day as they lounged on Jennifer's bed talking, her friend was seized with a fit of the giggles.

"Oh, no," she said between chuckles. "You can't be serious."

Naomi sat up and planted her hands firmly on her hips. "I'm dead serious."

Jennifer rolled off the bed laughing.

"Why is that so funny?" Naomi asked. "Your brother is fine."

"But he's too old for you. He'll be in his second year of college."

"That's one of the things that's so exciting about him. He's a Morehouse man with his own car. And he's studying to be a doctor. The dude is blowing my mind. Besides, your boyfriend will be a sophomore at Bowie this year."

Jennifer got off the floor. "Ralph seems so much older than Aaron though. He's more mature and he's had a million girlfriends."

Naomi batted her eyelashes coquettishly. "Like your brother said, I'm more mature than most girls my age."

"Ah, excuse me. I think he said you *looked* more mature. A big difference. And that was just typical Ralph, always flirting."

"At least he found me worth flirting with."

"I hate to disappoint you, but Ralph flirts with everything in a skirt. He sometimes has half a dozen girls calling him up. If you ask me, he treats most of them like shit."

"Maybe that's 'cause he just hasn't found the right one."

"Don't say I didn't warn you. But if you want to know the truth, he did ask about you a couple of times. He—"

"Damn. Why didn't you tell me?"

"Because I thought you were so wrapped up in Merlon."

"Oh, him."

"Yes, remember dear old Merlon, the love of your life?"

"What did Ralph ask you about me?"

"My, how quickly we forget and move on to other things! He just asked how old you were and if you're seeing anyone."

"You're kidding! What did you tell him?"

"The truth. That you're almost sixteen and have a steady boyfriend who—"

"Oh, no. Quick. Go tell him we broke up."

"But that's a lie."

"It won't be if Ralph is really interested."

"God. You're so capricious. You and my brother are perfect for each other. But don't say I didn't warn you."

A week later, Naomi was still faced with the dilemma of whether to have sex—but not with Merlon. After Jennifer told her brother she was interested, Ralph called the very next day and asked her out to a movie. Things started moving really fast between them, since he only had a couple of months before he was due back at school, and he said he wanted to spend as much of it as he could with her. She couldn't believe her luck, that this fine Morehouse man wanted to spend his summer break with little old Naomi. And contrary to what Jennifer said about him, she didn't see any signs of other women around him. He seemed completely devoted to her.

So after a few dates with him in as many days, she broke up with Merlon. She felt bad about that, but next to Ralph, Merlon felt like a fake leather coat from Lerner's. Why settle for plastic when you can have the real thing? He was so much more mature than Merlon. That was to be expected, of course, since Ralph was two years older than Merlon, but it wasn't just maturity; Ralph was sexy as hell and had a way of making her feel alluring too, the way he looked at her like he could see straight through everything she was wearing. He couldn't keep his hands off her, and she didn't want him to. No one had ever made her feel this way. She was hooked, and the feeling seemed to be mutual. By their third date, Ralph had already gotten as far with her as Merlon did in three months.

Her folks weren't exactly thrilled that she was spending all this time with a man three years her senior. She thought they only went along with it because he was Jennifer's brother, and they knew he'd be splitting for college in a matter of weeks. She guessed they also saw how happy she was. For the first time ever, she was completely satisfied with her life. She no longer felt jealous of the Jennifers or scared of the Henriettas or inferior to the Debbies and Joshuas. It had taken her long enough to reach this point—longer than most, she thought— but she was finally there. And while she knew Ralph wasn't the only reason—she'd been weaving her way up this bumpy, twisted road of confidence for years before she met him—he was the extra bit she needed to steer around the last corner.

She felt as if the whole world were spinning around and she didn't know which way was up. They went as far as two bodies can go without going all the way—twisting and grinding stark naked in his red Sting Ray—but she always stopped short of letting him put it in. She didn't tell him she was still a virgin, and he didn't ask. She thought that a man with Ralph's experience would be turned off by a virgin, so she read a bunch of dirty novels and magazines, hoping she could fool him if and when the time came. Still, she kept putting it off. A little voice in her head kept reminding her of her mother's warnings.

Ralph helped quiet that voice during the next-to-last week of his vacation by surprising her with a pearl ring and inviting her to visit him during Morehouse's homecoming that fall. She decided she had to do everything within her power to hold on to this dreamboat, this future doctor. If she played her cards right, she might someday be the doctor's wife. If she wasn't going to get rich herself by someday starting a business, maybe she could do it through marriage. She could just see herself, living in one of those big houses on the Gold Coast with a pool out back and two luxury cars in the driveway.

So she decided to give in a few days before he left for Atlanta. She didn't want him to have any excuses for pursuing those Spelman College women. She told him she was ready, and to celebrate he took her to a nice seafood restaurant out in Rockville, Maryland. It was her first date somewhere besides a movie or McDonald's, but she was so nervous about what they had planned for afterward she could barely taste her lobster. She kept trying to visualize the photos in some of the dirty magazines stuffed underneath her mattress, so she'd know what to do.

He drove out to a wooded area and parked in an isolated spot. Funny how dudes always knew about these spots. Must be a million of them around town, she thought. He borrowed Jennifer's Plymouth Duster instead of driving his 'Vette, for obvious reasons. Before she knew it, they were rolling around in the backseat naked from the neck on down, and he had spread her bare legs wide open. Then, just as she was getting into it, he stopped and fumbled around in the darkness through his rumpled clothing until he found a small square package. Even though Naomi had never seen one before, she knew it had to be a condom. She couldn't imagine what else would make him stop at a time like this. She was surprised when he opened the package and removed the contents. She didn't know why, but she expected that something powerful enough to prevent pregnancy would be more substantial. Instead it was this flimsy piece of translucent plastic. She was even more amazed as she watched him squirm into it.

"That's all?" she asked, thinking surely there must be a part he'd forgotten. As soon as she said it, she regretted it. All her efforts to seem experienced had just flown out the window.

He laughed. "That's it."

She shut her mouth and breathed a sigh of relief, thankful that he hadn't notice her goof, but her relief was short-lived. After he got it fitted over his thing, he looked down at her with suspicious eyes. "If you've never seen one of these, what did you use for protection with Merlon?"

All she could manage was this dumb look. Ralph fell back against the seat and rubbed his temples. "Don't tell me you're a virgin."

She lowered her eyes.

"Why didn't you say so before?"

She shrugged. "You didn't ask."

"Still . . . Well, no problem. I've got enough experience for both of us. Come here, baby."

He kissed her, and she closed her eyes and tried to concentrate on the good feelings she always had when they were intimate, rather than what she knew lay just ahead. She was curious but also scared. What would it feel like? Worse yet, what if it didn't go in? Those were the thoughts running through her head as he climbed on top of her and spread her legs until she thought they would split apart.

They immediately ran into trouble. He got it in about an inch or so, and then it stopped. He rocked and pushed gently at first, then a little harder, but still couldn't get it in.

"It would help if you'd move," he whispered between grunts.

Move? Oh. She imitated his movements and finally felt him slide inside. Then she closed her eyes and waited for the fireworks to begin. About a minute later, she opened her eyes again. Not much was happening, at least not with her. She enjoyed being this close to him and hearing his deep rapid breathing, but was this all there was to it? She started thrusting harder and faster; then, just as she was getting warmed up, his body went rigid. He wiggled a little and went rigid again. Then he collapsed.

She was trying to figure out just what had happened when he lifted himself up. She slid over so he could squeeze onto the seat beside her and then reached for her bra and panties.

"How was it?" he asked, slipping into his boxer shorts.

She hesitated, not sure how to answer. It was nice, but she had expected more.

He patted her head. "That's 'cause it's the first time for you," he said, as if reading her mind. He smiled. "You made me wait so long, I was excited and couldn't think much about you. I promise to make it better next time."

That was nice to hear. She just wished he didn't have to go back to school so soon. They wouldn't have much time to experiment. "How was it for you?"

"Me?" He chuckled. "I'm on cloud nine."

"You don't mind that I'm a virgin—or was, anyway?"

"Nah. I'm kind of honored that you chose me. I'm glad we did this before I leave to go back to school."

She smiled and snuggled up close to him, and he put his arm around her. "What's Morehouse like?" she asked.

"Like I told you. It's a lot of work, especially the premed program. Sometimes I can't believe how much they expect from us."

"Oh, I'm sure you can handle it, but I meant since King's assassination, and Robert Kennedy's. I got a letter from Joshua yesterday. He said the black students in Chicago are demanding courses in black studies."

"I don't get involved in that stuff. Some of my friends are

into that whole black-white thing, but I don't need anything distracting me from my studies." He slapped her thigh. "Let's get dressed so I can get you back home."

As she slipped into her skirt, she couldn't help but think how different Ralph was from Joshua. She was sure Joshua loved being right in the thick of everything. Knowing him, he probably considered it part of the college experience. "Do you believe in Dr. King's philosophy or the more radical ones?"

"I'm against violence because it won't get us anywhere. I mean, think about it. There's so many more whites than blacks, and they have all the power. If they wanted to, they could just ship us all back to Africa like that." He snapped his fingers.

"I know. But is that any reason not to demand our rights?"

"That's not what I'm saying. I support everything people like your brother are standing up for. I would just go about it in a different way. I can do more by getting my medical degree and fighting from within the system than fighting outside it."

"It seems to me we need to do both. Fight both from inside and outside the system." She was about to explain her reasoning when he slipped up to the front of the car.

"Let's get going," he said. "It's almost your curfew time."

She looked at her watch. She loved being with him, but he was right. On this of all nights, she didn't want to be late getting home.

Ralph was right when he said sex would get better for her. Since he was leaving soon, they did it every night for three nights in a row, and each time she managed to relax and like it more. It still wasn't exactly the Fourth of July, but it was getting closer. Ralph said the more you did it, the better it got, so she should plan to visit him at Morehouse often.

Since she was spending every minute with Ralph, she didn't see much of Jennifer. Most of the time they talked, it was over the phone, when she called for Ralph and Jennifer answered.

"I can't believe you're seeing my brother," she said, one day when she called and Ralph was out.

"Neither can I."

"Are you screwing him?"

It was just like Jennifer to come right out with it. The girl had no sense of decorum, despite her bourgeois upbringing. Since talking about sex still kind of embarrassed Naomi, all she could do was giggle.

"You must be," Jennifer said. "I haven't seen any other girls hanging around him all summer, and Ralph isn't one to go too long without it."

"He invited me down to Atlanta," Naomi said, trying to change the subject.

"And I'm sure you're taking him up on it."

"He makes it sound nice."

"I'm surprised Ralph has anything nice to say about Atlanta. He always used to bad-mouth it, talk about how country it was, since Morehouse wasn't his first choice."

"Oh? What was his first choice?"

"He applied to Harvard and some other Ivy League schools. But they rejected him. He didn't tell you?"

"No."

"He was very bitter about it at first, but maybe he's starting to like Morehouse better."

"It's a good school from what I hear, especially the medical program."

"I doubt that Ralph plans to stay there for medical school. He really wants to get into Harvard or Johns Hopkins or someplace like that."

"I'm surprised he didn't get in for premed, since he's doing so well at Morehouse and your father's a dentist."

"Ralph didn't take his studies seriously until around his junior year in high school. He was too much the lover boy, and now he's paying for it. It's a wonder he never told you. For a while, he was really bitter."

"Maybe it's like you said. Maybe he likes Morehouse better now." Naomi didn't like to think Ralph wouldn't have mentioned this if he was still bothered about Morehouse. That was the kind of thing couples were supposed to share.

About a week later, on the night of their last date, Ralph and Naomi lingered in the parked car and talked until well past her 1 A.M. curfew. But she knew that no matter what happened, even if she was punished for months, it was worth it to have the extra time with Ralph. When they drove up to her house at three in the morning, lights were streaming from every window.

She kissed Ralph goodbye, and he promised to call in the morning before he left for the airport. Frankly, at this point she was more worried about what her parents were going to do when she walked through the door than about Ralph leaving. She ran up the walkway, not bothering to get her key out since she figured one or both of them were probably looking out the window. She remembered the time she was only a little over an hour late and Daddy yanked the door open the minute she put her foot on the porch. This time, though, she got all the way to the door without anybody coming out to greet her. She turned the knob; it was locked. Strange, she thought, as she fished through her shoulder bag for her keys.

Just as she found them, the door swung open and Daddy stood there with this grave look on his face. Her first instinct was to defend herself, but then she noticed something peculiar: Daddy's face was more sad than angry—his cheeks puffy, his eyes red. He pulled her inside the doorway and hugged her tightly. "Thank God you're home," he mumbled into her hair.

"What's wrong? I'm not *that* late." Without answering, he put his arms around her shoulders and guided her to the living room. Did they think something bad had happened to her? Something bad enough to make Daddy cry?

In the living room, she saw something so odd the nerve endings along her arms began to tingle. Mama was sitting in the corner of the sofa, her head buried in her hands, rocking back and forth. Mama looked up, and Naomi could tell she'd been crying quite a while. A relative must have died, Naomi thought, or maybe a family friend. Or . . .

"Did you tell her yet?" Mama asked, practically whispering.

Daddy shook his head. "I thought we should do it together." He placed one hand on Mama's shoulder. The other hung at his side, as he clenched and unclenched his fist.

Mama touched the sofa next to herself. "Sit here, Naomi."

Naomi sank down next to her mother.

"We have bad news. Your brother . . ."

Joshua? A feeling of fear unlike any she'd ever known before washed over her. She could feel her heart pounding in her chest.

"He . . . he . . ." Mama seemed unable to go on.

"Something terrible happened at school," Daddy said. Naomi looked up at him and remembered the last time she'd seen her father clench and unclench his fist like that was when his own father died, more than ten years before. "There was some kind of demonstration." Daddy paused and swallowed.

"Will somebody please tell me what's going on?"

"A car accident. He . . ."

"Is he all right? *Please.* Say he's OK."

Daddy let out a long deep breath. "He's dead, Naomi."

She fell to her knees; then she screamed.

PART TWO

1971—1975

Nine

Atlanta pulsated from the bodies of thousands of students streaming through the gates of the city's colleges, as they returned from their summer vacations refreshed, happy to see their school friends again, and eager to take on new challenges. For many of them, this was one of the best times of their lives. They had finally escaped from their parents' apron strings, with all the freedom and responsibility that meant, and yet were still young enough to believe that a lifetime of choices and adventures lay ahead of them.

Naomi Patrice Jefferson couldn't have been further removed from all of that. She got up at first light one Sunday morning in November, bathed and dressed, and walked across the campus of the Atlanta Institute of Technology. She hadn't seen a soul until she reached the bus stop, and now she was alone again as she stood in front of the Martin Luther King gravesite.

She sat on the ground in front of the crypt, crossed her legs, and pinched the hem of her bell-bottom blue jeans. Everyone, including her parents, tried to tell her it was a car crash, nothing more, nothing less. And at first she had agreed. But as the family learned more about the events surrounding the accident, she'd found it harder to accept their simple explanation. Joshua had been in the car with Dean Davis and two other people, rushing from Evanston to a civil rights demonstration in Chicago, where they had heard the police were using tear gas to break up the crowd. Dean ended up in the hospital for weeks with several broken bones. The other two, a man and a woman whose names Naomi had forgotten over the past three years since the accident, suffered minor injuries. Joshua was the only one killed.

She swiped the pant leg and gritted her teeth. Racism had put Joshua in that car, and it killed him. No one would ever convince her otherwise.

"If people weren't so racist," she pointed out to her parents not long after the accident, "my brother would still be alive."

"You don't know that, Naomi," Daddy said.

"*You* may not, but I do. If it weren't for racism, Joshua wouldn't have been in that car going to a civil rights demonstration and—"

"But what's to say he wouldn't have faced some other tragedy?" Mama said.

"I don't buy that for a minute. We're always forced into these dangerous situations. Why is that? Can you please tell me why? It's not fair."

Daddy swallowed hard and shook his head. Mama choked back tears and ran from the room. For months after Joshua's death, Naomi woke up sobbing herself nearly every morning. And she clenched her teeth in her sleep so hard, headaches became a part of her daily life. Sometimes she caught herself clenching them in the middle of the day. At first, she told her parents whenever it happened, but when they began talking about taking her to the dentist, she started keeping her jaw-clenching to herself: that and her dark, angry thoughts about Joshua's death. Her parents would never understand. They wanted to let it go, pretend racism had nothing to do with anything. But she couldn't do that.

She felt rudderless in a sea of confusion, couldn't concentrate on anything, and her grades began to slip. But what did that matter? Her dream of opening a clothing store seemed as far away as the moon. What was she, a little black girl from nowhere, doing even thinking such lofty thoughts, dreaming the American dream?

In the middle of her junior year in high school, she told her parents she was going to take a year off after she graduated to think about whether she even wanted to go to college. Mama and Daddy didn't argue with her. They seemed to be sleep-walking too. Mama said it was a chore just to get up and go to work in the morning. Daddy seemed not to be able to wait to get out of the house. In the evening, when he came home, he'd sit in his chair in the living room after dinner and stare at his hands for hours. And Mama would go up to her room and cry.

But then Daddy snapped out of it. He told Naomi she was going to have to do better in her senior year and that she was still expected to go on to college. Forget this talk about taking off from school. They'd honor Joshua's memory best by getting on with their lives.

At first, Naomi protested. But Daddy was adamant. So after weeks of thinking, she decided to go away to college. She needed to get out of this town, out of this house, where the memories were so vivid. But the idea of living in an area as remote as upstate New York, where Jennifer was still planning to go and where the complexions of the people were generally about as white as the snow-covered hills, seemed out of the question. She would go to Atlanta, a city that, like her hometown, had plenty of brown, black, and yellow faces—faces that would give her comfort and security and peace of mind. And she would major in communications, something practical, reasonable, and attainable, even for a little black girl from nowhere.

Besides, Ralph was in Atlanta. Even though she had decided to major in communications, it could just as well have been macramé. What she really cared about was being near him. He'd been a big help to her, at least in the beginning. When the accident first happened, he would call at least once a week from school and listen patiently as she talked endlessly about her brother and his death. He even came to D.C. to try to cheer her up. Thank God for those moments! Ralph's visits were about the only time she felt alive. She didn't know how he stood it, since at times she even got sick of listening to herself.

But as the months went by and it continued to affect her moods, he began to complain that she was no longer fun to be with. His visits and phone calls became less frequent. Then it hit her that she was going to lose her man if she didn't lighten up. So she tried to stop talking about Joshua so much, at least when she was with Ralph.

When she'd told him that she'd been accepted at Atlanta Tech, he didn't seem all that enthusiastic. At first she thought it was because of her moods. She could hardly blame him, but she'd promised she wouldn't bring her sullen disposition to Atlanta with her, and she'd made a real effort, not only for his sake but hers as well.

She stood up in front of the King crypt and brushed off her hands. That had been a year ago. Now she was a college sophomore. She had lost nearly twenty pounds in the three years since the accident, shrinking from a size seven to a three. And she still clenched her teeth from time to time. But the tears had long since stopped. What was the point? Her brother had been given a rotten deal, his life snuffed out before it had a chance to blossom, but no amount of tears would ever change that. The only thing to do was put it aside, no matter how bitter it made her. And the best way to do that was to focus on Ralph. He was such a prize—smart, handsome, and sure of himself. And he was studying to be a doctor. About the only thing that still excited her these days was the possibility of someday being his wife.

She lowered her head, shoved her hands into the pockets of her pea jacket, and made her way to the bus stop. She got off at Edgewood Avenue and walked up the block toward Ralph's house. The cemetery freshened so many memories, it seemed as if it all happened only yesterday. That was just the point of her visits to King's grave. She didn't want the memories to fade.

As she climbed the hill to Ralph's house with her head bent against the wind, her throat felt scratchy. She wasn't sure whether it was the brisk fall weather or her emotions. Probably some of both.

"Naomi?"

She stopped and looked up to see a brown face that transported her to another time and place. "Dean? Dean Davis?"

"I can't believe it's you," Dean said, smiling.

She looked into his eyes and felt like snow melting on a

warm hillside. She hadn't seen Dean since the night they danced in the parking lot. He had spent weeks recuperating in a hospital in Chicago after the accident, so he didn't even get to Joshua's funeral. Then he dropped out of sight. "Neither can I."

"Here," he said, holding his arms out. "Can I get a hug?"

He wrapped his arms around her, and the wool of his jacket brushed softly against her cheek. Then he held her at arm's length. "Let me look at you."

She'd changed, she knew. Gone were the pretty little dresses and shiny shoes. Jeans and T-shirts were her usual attire now and had been for some time, not only because they were a college staple but because she no longer had the energy or desire to look turned out.

"I like your hair," he said. "The short Afro looks cute on you."

Her bangs were gone too, and no longer did she think of straight hair as good hair. Right after Joshua died, she hacked off all her perm, leaving barely a half inch of natural growth. She thought her parents would get upset when they saw it, but to her surprise Daddy just shook his head, and Mama mumbled something about being glad when it grew back.

"Thanks, Dean. Yours looks nice too. It's much bigger than it was before." It was one of the biggest she'd ever seen, almost a foot long at the top of his head. He looked good from head to toe, especially considering that he'd been badly injured in the accident.

"It's like this mainly because I'm too lazy to bother getting it trimmed half the time," he said. "What are you doing in Atlanta?"

"I was about to ask you the same thing. I'm going to Atlanta Tech. Been here since last year."

"Really? What's your major?"

"Communications."

He wrinkled his brow. "I always thought you would go into fashion design or something."

"Pipe dreams. This is more rational."

He nodded. "I see. Planning to go into television or print?"

She shrugged. "Haven't made up my mind yet. What about

you?" She gestured toward the books under his arm. "You're in school around here?"

"Morehouse, econ. Transferred this year." He squinted as if trying to remember something. "Weren't you planning to go to school up north?"

She shrugged. "Changed my mind about that too, after . . . you know. Changed my mind about a lot of things."

He nodded with understanding. "I finished up my freshman year at Northwestern, but then I had to get away. I ended up drifting for a couple of years—Philadelphia, New York. I only went home every now and then to check on my mother and the girls." He shook his head. "Rough times."

She blinked. It had been nearly two years since she'd felt even a hint of tears. But this was her first time talking to Dean since the accident. He had been Joshua's best friend, and as he talked Naomi felt time drift backward.

"After I got out of the hospital," Dean continued, "I found I couldn't concentrate on my studies, so I just . . ."

She barely heard him as her mind slipped back to the night she and Dean danced in the parking lot, while Joshua begged them to let him try. She shut her eyes to hold back the tears and bit her bottom lip. Dean paused and shifted his books from one arm to the other. "I'm sorry," he said. "I'm being insensitive."

She shook her head. "I don't know what got into me," she said, searching through her shoulder bag for a tissue. "I don't do this anymore. I guess it's seeing you for the first time since it happened. You meant a lot to him, and it brought back so many memories."

Now *his* eyes were starting to moisten. She reached in her bag for another tissue. "I'm getting you started too." She held the tissue out to him as a couple of students walked by and looked at them strangely.

"No, thanks," he said, blinking. "I'm OK." He sniffed. "We're a pathetic couple, aren't we?"

She smiled. "Want to start walking? I was going to see a friend right up the block."

"I wish I could, but I need to head the other way."

She nodded. "It was good seeing you again, Dean."

"Nice seeing you too. Are you coming to the pep rally here next Saturday?"

"I didn't know anything about it."

"It's something to motivate the students to be more politically active. We've even invited some local bands and speakers. I'm one of the organizers. You should come if you're not too busy."

So he was still very much involved in the struggle. She would have to ask Ralph if he was interested in going, although she knew without asking that he wouldn't. "I'll think about it."

They hugged again, then walked in opposite directions. After taking a few steps, she turned and watched as he walked down the hill and disappeared around a corner. She smiled. Seeing Dean again brought back so many happy memories of Joshua. She walked up the hill, passing Ralph's red Sting Ray as she approached the old house he shared with three other Morehouse students, and the smile fell from her lips. Since coming to Atlanta, she wasn't so sure her dour disposition had been the only reason Ralph hadn't seemed so keen on the idea. In her freshman year, she tried to get used to the women of every size, shape, and complexion who were always on the scene at this house. Now she was a sophomore and still wasn't used to it. Instead of keeping her away, though, it made her that much more determined to hold on to him.

As she climbed the stairs to his house, Diana Ross's hit, "Ain't No Mountain High Enough," floated down to greet her, and a petite woman with a huge Afro that dwarfed her tiny chocolate face opened the door. Pamela Thompson had just started dating one of the other men living there and was also in Naomi's statistics class. They smiled at each other the way acquaintances often do. Naomi always felt awkward around Pamela because she'd seen Keith, Pamela's so-called boyfriend, take other women up to his bedroom when Pamela wasn't around. Naomi was tempted to tell Pamela but reasoned it was none of her business since she didn't know the girl that well. Sooner or later, Pamela would find out for herself what a rotten skunk her boyfriend was. Men could only get away with that stuff for so long.

"Ralph's in his room." Naomi loved the way Pamela dragged out the "a" in Ralph's name. She was from a rural town in Georgia and had this cute southern accent.

"Thanks," Naomi said, heading upstairs.

She knocked and Ralph opened his door and smiled at her. "What took you so long?"

"I ran into one of Joshua's best friends," she said, then kissed him briefly on the lips. Seeing Dean and his big Afro made her aware of Ralph's hairdo. He was one of the few men around who had never grown an Afro. He claimed his hair wasn't frizzy enough to stand up. He was kind of an oddball among black students in Atlanta with his straight hair, but that was all right. He was cute enough to get away with wearing his hair any way he wanted. She removed her pea jacket and flopped down on his unmade bed.

"He just transferred from Northwestern to Morehouse," she said.

"What's his name?"

"Dean Davis. You know him?"

"Sounds familiar."

"He's very active politically. He invited me to a rally on Saturday."

"I think I know who you're talking about. I've seen him around here handing out flyers."

"Want to go?"

Ralph shook his head. "You know that's not my kind of thing. Besides, I have to finish this anatomy report by Monday." He sat at the desk at the head of his bed. "I'll be ready to go pick up something to eat as soon as I finish this page."

"Why don't we eat out for a change instead of bringing it back here?"

"Because that takes up too much time, Naomi. You know I have a ton of work to do."

She folded her arms under her breasts. Yes, yes, she thought. He was a medical student now and really had to buckle down. That was understandable. But somehow he always had time for sex and was always ready, willing, and able when she wanted to come to his place.

She was tempted to point this out, but she didn't want to get into another argument. The tone of his voice told her he was already short on patience. The last time they argued, she was so pissed off she stormed out of his room and ended up spending the entire evening alone in her dorm, worrying about how he was filling up his time without her. She prayed he would come to her room to make up, but he never did. Just like every other time they'd argued, he seemed to have no trouble waiting for her to come to him. She supposed if she ever didn't give in first, he would come to her eventually. But it was hard for her to go more than a couple of days knowing he was upset with her. It was always at the back of her mind that there were plenty of other women who would love to snatch him away. She didn't want to make it easy for them by having him mad at her for long.

"What am I supposed to do while I wait for you?" she asked, trying to keep the bitterness in her heart out of her voice.

"Why don't you make up the bed if you want to keep busy?" he said, without taking his eyes from his work.

She stood up and put her hands on her hips. "You think I'm your maid or something?" Oops! She covered her lips with her hand. That popped out before she could help it. Instead of getting upset, Ralph just chuckled.

"No," he said, smiling up at her. "But it would be nice of you."

"Never mind," she said, and sat back on the bed. "I'll sit here and wait." The sitting was boring, so after a few minutes of rocking her foot and tapping her knee with her fingers, she picked up her shoulder bag from the bed and set it on the floor. Anything to keep her mind occupied and her mouth from arguing while she waited, she thought, as she straightened the sheets.

He glanced at her out of the corner of his eye.

"Don't say a word or I won't finish," she said, yanking the sheets around a little harder than necessary.

He smiled. "Wasn't planning to." He reached over and squeezed her thigh.

The things she did for this man, Naomi thought. "Did I tell you about my statistics professor?"

"Uh-uh," he said, already back into his books.

She knew he wanted peace and quiet, but she was bored and this was something she'd been meaning to tell him. "I think he's a racist. He hardly ever calls on the black students, and he's always talking this crap about the right and left sides of the brain to explain why some people have trouble with statistics."

"That's a common theory, that the left side is for analytical things and the right is for more artistic things."

"Yeah, but he implies that some of us are idiots because our left sides are undeveloped."

"You probably just misunderstood him."

"You weren't there. He said in *certain* people the left side is less developed. You distinctly get the feeling he means blacks and women. He always calls on white men first and gives their responses more weight, like what they say is more important."

"They probably just speak up."

"Honestly, Ralph, you can be so infuriating at times! If they speak up more, it's because Mr. Hill doesn't give the rest of us a chance. I admit I have a problem with math, but not all of us do. Look at you. And some whites aren't so hot at it, either. My friend Debbie is brilliant at math. She's black *and* a woman. So there. And you know—"

He stopped writing and held his pen in midair. "OK. You've made your point. Can I get some quiet? I need to concentrate."

But she was pumped up now and couldn't stop. "Can you listen for just a few more minutes? This is bothering me."

He sighed. "Go ahead," he said, without looking up.

She wished he'd give her all his attention, but half was better than none. "You know what he said the other day? That women are better off staying at home taking care of the house and kids. That their minds are more suited to that kind of thing."

He looked up from his desk at her fluffing the pillows on his bed. "And you don't believe that?"

She threw the pillow at him.

He threw his hand up to block it and chuckled. "I'm only

kidding," he said, tossing the pillow back onto the bed. "I don't think women should necessarily stay at home. But there's probably something to his theory."

She couldn't believe her ears. But she shouldn't be surprised. Ralph had a way of reasoning unlike any other person she knew. Sometimes she was actually embarrassed when he expressed his views around others. "How the hell can you say that?"

"Think about it. A lot of women do stay at home. And even when they work, it's at less demanding jobs. How many women do you see running corporations?"

She planted her hands on her hips. "How many blacks do you see running them? Are you saying that means we shouldn't?"

"We don't have the know-how to run them."

She stared at him, speechless.

"Things are changing, but that's the way it is now," he said. "Think about it. We often don't have the education and experience that whites do. I mean, if you were running a company and wanted to hire someone to run the financial department, who would you choose? Someone with an accounting degree from Harvard whose daddy was vice-president of a bank? Or someone with a degree from Howard whose daddy was a janitor?"

"The one from Howard," she said, between clenched teeth.

"You can't really mean that."

"Yes, I do. Part of the reason we don't have the experience is people with attitudes like yours and my professor's."

"Well, yeah."

"He has no right talking that trash in class. It's bad enough having to put up with racism out in the streets, but in the class room too? I came here hoping I could concentrate on my studies." She flopped down on the bed.

Ralph put his pen down and turned in his chair to face her. "Then why don't you do just that? Put it aside and focus on your studies. It's not like it's the first time this kind of thing ever came up. And it won't be the last."

"But it's hard to ignore."

"You're so touchy about everything now. You weren't like that when I first met you."

"Guess not. Didn't have a dead brother then."

He inhaled and turned back toward his desk. "Here we go again."

"Well, sorry," she said sarcastically. "Every time that professor says something stupid, I hear Joshua screaming in my head not to take that from him. But I just sit there 'cause I don't have a clue what to do, and to tell you the truth I'm scared to say anything."

"You're better off ignoring it. That's what got Joshua—" He stopped.

She jumped up and stood behind him. "Go ahead, say it: 'That's what got him killed.' See? Nobody wants to come out and admit that. But deep down inside, you know it's true."

"I agree it had something to do with it. But only indirectly."

"Directly, indirectly. What difference does it make? He's still dead."

Ralph clenched his jaw and picked up his pen. Even though she was tempted, Naomi knew better than to continue with this subject unless she wanted to ruin their afternoon together.

She sat back on the bed and brushed some imaginary lint from her jeans. "Pamela's in my statistics class."

"You mean Keith's woman?"

"Ha! One of his *many* women is more like it."

"That's none of your business, Naomi."

"I just feel so deceitful around her, knowing and not saying anything."

"There's no point getting her all upset. You women never understand these things."

" 'These things'? Are you involved in any of 'these things'?"

"I'm not now, but—" He shrugged.

"But what?"

"We've talked about this a million times, and I don't want to discuss it now. But you know, if you don't work on that problem of yours, I could be tempted. Any man would be."

He kind of smiled as he said it, but Naomi didn't like it one bit. She knew he was alluding to more than just her moody disposition. "So you're going to look for someone less frigid," she said bitterly.

"I never said you were frigid. I said you have some hangups."

"What's the difference?"

"You need to be less inhibited, loosen up some. You'd get more out of it. And so would I."

Naomi didn't know what to say to that. She never did know what to say when Ralph started talking about her lovemaking skills—or lack thereof, as he seemed to think. At first he thought it might be the restrictions imposed by using a condom and suggested she get the pill. So she did. He loved it, since he didn't have to stop at the crucial moment. But it hadn't made much of a difference for her.

"Do you even enjoy it?" he asked.

She laughed nervously. "I always like being close to you." It was true. She loved the feel of his smooth skin and the sound of his heavy breathing when he got excited. But Ralph wanted more. Maybe she should too.

"You need to let go, you know? Stop holding back."

She didn't think she was holding anything back. But if Ralph thought something was wrong with their lovemaking, then something must be wrong with their lovemaking. Although damn if she knew what. She didn't exactly have a lot to compare it with. She was going to have to do something about "her problem," and fast, if she didn't want to lose her man, though. A dude like Ralph could have any girl he wanted. She had to make sure he never wanted anyone but her.

"OK," Professor Hill said, peering at the class over his reading glasses. As usual, his thin, wispy blond hair needed combing, his scruffy shoes needed polishing, and his pale cheeks could do with a good dose of sunlight. "Who wants to come up to the board and work out the first homework exercise?"

Naomi's hand shot up in the air. From her view at the edge of the classroom, it was obvious that hers was the first one up. She'd spent hours working on the assignment the night before.

But instead of calling on her, Professor Hill waited a brief moment until other hands went up and then called on one of the white dudes in the front of the classroom. Then he called on another, and another. Finally, just before class ended for the day, he called on Pamela. By the time the period ended and he dismissed the class, Naomi was fuming. She grabbed her books, jumped up from her seat, and stomped down the hallway. She was just as upset with herself for not speaking up as she was with Professor Hill.

Pamela, wearing a brightly colored dashiki under her denim jacket, ran up to Naomi. "I saw what happened in there when you raised your hand," she said, removing a Salem from her jacket pocket as they stepped outside Jackson Hall. "That man is sickening, isn't he? The racist bastard."

"I'm damn sick and tired of it," Naomi said. She felt a headache coming on and realized she was clenching her teeth. She released her jaw and rubbed her temples. "It's hard enough getting through statistics without all this bull. I should report him to the head of the department."

"Don't waste your time. I already talked to Dr. Smith." Pamela held the pack out to Naomi.

"No, thanks," Naomi said, shaking her head. "What did he say?"

"That Professor Hill had a superior record here, was brilliant, blah, blah, blah, so I must be imagining things. Bullshit. He did say he would speak to Mr. Hill, which I think is why he called on me today."

"Whatever they said to him didn't have much of an effect. He just ignored me."

"You'd better get used to it, kiddo."

"Maybe it was a mistake, coming to school in the South," Naomi said.

"That doesn't have anything to do with it. A friend of mine at school in Boston was beat up by three white guys."

Naomi stopped in her tracks and turned to face Pamela. "You're lying. A woman?"

Pamela nodded. "I swear. She was just walking down the street and they were coming toward her and she bumped one of them. He turned around and said, 'You better watch where you're going, bitch,' or something like that. Well, my friend *has* got a mouth on her. She turned right around and told him he better watch where *he* was going. So they jumped her right there in broad daylight."

"Damn. Is your friend OK?"

"She landed in the hospital with a broken nose. That's why I say being in the South has nothing to do with it. I look over my shoulder all the time when I'm out by myself."

Naomi rubbed her forehead. They couldn't escape. It was everywhere—in the classroom, on the streets.

"Headache?" Pamela asked.

Naomi nodded.

"Migraines?"

"No. Comes from clenching my teeth."

"Why do you do that?"

"Tension, I guess. It's a long story. Stuff like what you just said makes me more determined not to let Professor Hill think he can get away with spewing that racist venom," Naomi said. "If enough of us complain, they'll have to do something about him."

"You can try. Maybe we can get a few other blacks and women in the class to complain too."

"What if we could get a whole bunch of students to march in front of the building during his class? Bet those suckers would listen to us then."

"That's a dynamite idea. I'm with you all the way. What do we do first?"

"That's the problem. I don't have the slightest idea. But I know somebody who does. He's going to be at a demonstration at Morehouse on Saturday. Want to go with me?"

"You bet."

"Don't get your hopes up too high," Naomi said. "I'm not sure anything will come out of it. But we can try. I'm tired of this crap."

"You and me both."

"Dress warm. I heard it's supposed to snow this weekend."

"I know. I hate snow."

"Where is your friend now?" Naomi asked. "Did she go back to school?"

"Are you kidding? She met a Muslim guy. Now she's thinking of converting. Doesn't want to have anything to do with whites."

Naomi let out a deep breath of air. "Can't say I blame her."

Ten

Saturday was suddenly cold enough to bite through a bearskin. Naomi and Pamela walked around trying to find Dean without much luck until they spotted a man at the edge of the crowd telling people where to go. Naomi approached him. "Do you know where Dean Davis is?" she asked, stomping her feet to warm them.

"Probably up front somewhere."

They made their way to the front, and she finally spotted him. He had a bullhorn in his hand and was climbing onto the hood of a car.

"All right!" Dean shouted into the bullhorn. His deep voice carried across the crowd easily. "Let's get started." He lowered the bullhorn and waited for people to quiet down. "I appreciate you all coming out here in the cold. You won't regret it. We have an interesting program for you. The focus of this gathering is serious because we need to get the word out about where we are in the struggle today, where we need to take the movement next, and how you all can help. But that don't mean we can't have some fun here, all right? So after the speakers ignite your minds and spirits, we'll have some local groups here to get your bodies warmed up." With that he did a little dance step, and a roar went up through the crowd.

He climbed down from the hood and several people rushed up to ask him questions. He was obviously very busy, so Naomi walked to the edge of the small crowd gathered around him to wait her turn. When he looked up and saw her, he smiled and excused himself. "Naomi," he said, obviously pleased. "I'm glad you came."

He kissed her lightly on the cheek and she smiled. "So am I. Looks like a good crowd."

"We were hoping for more, but we'll take what we can get."

"Let me introduce you to Pamela. She goes to Atlanta Tech with me."

Dean touched Pamela's arm. "Welcome," he said. "Any friend of this sister's a friend of mine."

"My reasons for coming are probably not what you think," Naomi said.

"Oh?"

"I wanted to talk to you about one of my classes."

"Oh," he said, feigning disappointment. "I was hoping it was more personal."

Pamela laughed loudly, and Naomi felt her cheeks go hot. Suddenly it felt like Haiti out here. She couldn't believe Dean was flirting with her. "Sorry to disappoint you," she said.

"What class is it?" he asked.

"Statistics. We're thinking of organizing a protest, but we don't know the first thing about doing it."

"Then you've come to the right place. What's the problem with this class—other than the fact that it's statistics?"

She laughed, but before she could answer his question, a man rushed up to Dean and tugged on his sleeve. "Dean, they need you up front. Pronto."

"Be right there."

"You're busy," Naomi said. "I guess now isn't a good time to go into it."

"Yeah, I do have a lot to do around here, but the rally should be over about noon. If you can stand the cold and stick around, we could get something to eat and talk about it then."

Naomi hesitated for a second. Ralph was expecting her at his place at noon. But this was important. She'd have to call Ralph and tell him she would be late. "Good idea."

He nodded. "Don't go far, so I can find you afterward."

"Lordy," Pamela said, as he walked off. "Why didn't you

tell me the man was so fine? That voice of his sends shivers down my spine."

"Dean?" Naomi had never thought about him that way. She was so inexperienced when they met, she hadn't even yet laid eyes on Merlon. And as one of her brother's friends, Dean had seemed so much older than the boys at school. But now that Pamela mentioned it, Naomi had to agree. He was tall and much more muscular now. He had a beautiful brown complexion, and his eyes . . .

"He's got the sincerest eyes," Pamela said, as if reading her thoughts. "And he can't keep them off you. Ralph's cute, but Dean's divine. I've never seen a man look so good in a pair of ragged old blue jeans."

"Pamela, please. He was my brother's best friend. He probably thinks of me as a little sister or something."

"Uh-huh." She took a deep drag off her cigarette and twisted her lips to let the air out in a circle.

"Seriously."

"Uh-huh. Anyway, you'll have him all to yourself after the rally. I promised Keith I'd meet him."

"Damn, Pam. Can't you put it off till later? I'm supposed to go see Ralph, but he can wait a couple of hours."

"Yeah, I could, but I don't want to. Besides, it's so blasted cold out here," she said, hugging herself. They both had wool coats on, but they didn't do much good.

"It's not that bad," Naomi said, trying to convince herself.

"Maybe not to you, but I'm from the deep South and I don't like this kind of weather. Thank God we don't get much of it."

"I thought we were in this together."

"I'm still with you. You can tell me what Dean says."

Naomi couldn't believe Pamela wouldn't put her boyfriend off just a couple of hours for something so important, especially a boyfriend like Keith. He was probably screwing someone else this very minute.

"You know," Naomi said, "I wasn't going to tell you this, since it's none of my business. But Keith brings other women to his room when you aren't around." As soon as she saw the look of horror on Pamela's face, Naomi regretted her words.

Damn, she thought. She'd said it partly out of a feeling of loy-
alty, but she also realized with shame that she was trying to
stop Pamela from deserting her.

"What the fuck are you talking about?" Pamela asked, her
face tight with tension.

Naomi looked away. "Nothing. I shouldn't have said
anything."

"Don't give me that shit now!" Pamela screamed so loud
that Naomi jumped back. The girl's southern accent seemed to
get deeper when she shouted. Others around them turned to see
what the fuss was about.

"Finish what you started, damn it," Pamela said, throwing
her cigarette on the ground. She stomped on it and scowled.

Naomi took a step back. For a moment there, it looked like
Pamela was going to punch her in the stomach. Memories of
that day on the playground with Henrietta Jackson came
rushing back. She didn't know Pamela all that well, so there
was no telling what the girl would do. She had to get out of this
carefully. "I've been wanting to tell you for a long time, because I hate what he's doing to you. I hate it when any man
does that. But it's the truth. I wouldn't lie about it."

Pamela's jaw got tighter by the second, and all Naomi could
think was that she was just glad Pamela was so tiny.

"Who is this bitch?"

Now Naomi was really in a fix. The truth was that there had
been several "bitches." But she didn't say that. She decided to
mention only the one she'd seen most often. "Her name is
Judy. I don't know her last name." That was a lie, but Naomi
didn't want them to find Judy lying in a ditch somewhere tomorrow morning.

"How long has this been going on?" Pamela asked.

"Since the beginning of the semester. A couple of months."

"Why the hell didn't you say something before now?"

"I didn't think it was any of my business. I didn't know you
all that well, and Ralph told me to stay out of it."

"Ha. I'll just bet he did, since they're two of a kind. The
bastards."

Something in Naomi's gut jumped. "Why do you say that?"

"Think about it."

Naomi didn't want to think about it, or talk about it either. How had they gone from planning a demonstration to this crap? She turned and walked away from Pamela. "Forget this shit. Go on back. I'll see you later."

"You can walk away if you want, Naomi, but that doesn't change a damn thing, does it?"

"It doesn't have to change anything, 'cause you're lying," Naomi said. This was the thanks she got for trying to help out a friend. She comes back with this garbage.

"You wish," Pamela said. "Her name is Marlena Robertson and she's a senior in premed at Spelman. So there."

Naomi stopped but didn't turn around. She didn't want Pamela to see the tears forming in her eyes. She scrunched up her face, determined to keep them from falling.

"Lord, Naomi, why would I lie about something like that? I never said anything to you for the same reason you never told me. Keith said, 'Leave it alone, it's none of your goddamn business.' Don't you see what they're doing? They're cheating on us, and they've got us blaming each other."

Naomi still wasn't convinced. She believed Pamela had seen something but must be mistaken about what it meant. She had been with Ralph more than three years. She'd sense it if he cheated on her. But there was no point arguing about it with Pamela, a woman she hardly knew. She turned around and walked back.

"Do you believe me?" Pamela asked.

Naomi shrugged her shoulders. "I don't know what the hell to think. I believe you when you say this woman was there, but they're probably just studying together."

Pamela grunted. "Yeah, like anatomy and physiology."

Naomi twisted her mouth. She didn't think that was even a little funny.

"Well, I know what I'm gonna do," Pamela said. "I'm marching straight over there."

"What about the rally and the meeting with Dean?"

"You're crazy if you think I'm putting this off for some rally."

"But this is important," Naomi said. "Your shaky boyfriend can wait."

"Maybe so. But my temper can't."

Naomi let out a deep breath. She was tempted to forget about the rally too, and head straight over to Ralph's room. But she didn't know how to get in touch with Dean, since they'd never exchanged phone numbers or addresses. Besides, Ralph had a lab that morning and wouldn't be free until noon. It was just as well, she thought. She needed time to think this over. "You go on and find Keith. I'm going to hang around here."

"You are? Well, see you later then, kiddo."

Naomi found a spot in the middle of the crowd and watched the parade of speakers and musicians, but her mind kept wandering back to Ralph and this Marlena Robertson, whoever she was. Naomi had to admit that she'd always been a little jealous when it came to Ralph. He was so good-looking and had so much going for him, she couldn't help it. But it was more than that. He never wanted to be with her in public, only between the sheets. He might think she was frigid or whatever, but he couldn't seem to get enough of her when they were alone.

She was pretty sure it was all some horrible mistake. Maybe some woman named Marlena was spending time in Ralph's room, but it wasn't what Pamela thought. Ralph took his studies seriously, so it wasn't hard to believe that he and this other woman were studying together. If she was a premed student, Ralph could be helping her out. Naomi was sure there was a simple explanation and that Ralph would clear it all up when she saw him.

At a little after noon, Dean got on the stage and gave a wrap-up speech, telling the crowd about upcoming rallies and demonstrations and urging them to stay motivated. After the crowd dispersed, Dean had to stay to tidy up some business. It was one by the time they hopped in his Firebird and drove to a small cafeteria.

As she listened carefully while he explained how to distribute flyers, make posters, and manage crowds, she realized why he was so good at this kind of thing. He had a way of looking at you while he talked that was comforting, even encouraging. Every time she expressed doubts about her ability to carry it off, he would gently boost her confidence. And yes, she thought, sitting across from him, he was quite pleasant to look at. She found her mind drifting more than once to his eyes and the soothing tone of his voice. But she quickly pushed those thoughts aside and focused again on what he was saying.

"You have to start somewhere, Naomi," he said. "When I first got into this, I made some mistakes, believe me. But if it's something people can come to believe in, it'll build its own momentum."

"You make it sound easy."

"I don't want to give you the wrong impression. A lot of it is just legwork—organizing things. The hard part is motivating people to get out there, especially in the beginning."

"That's just it. How do you do that?"

"Let me ask this first," he said. "You want to demonstrate against a professor who's making racist comments in the classroom?"

"Right."

"And comments about women being inferior, too?"

Naomi nodded.

"He sounds like a real character."

"Tell me about it. But I think I want to concentrate on the racist part. The sexist part is bad, and I could probably get more people involved if I included that, since not a whole lot of blacks go to Atlanta Tech. But the racism definitely bothers me a lot more. It's hard to try to deal with what he says about women when we've got racism to contend with, too."

"Oh, I agree with that approach. Things would get muddied if you try to do both. Concentrate on one or the other."

"That's what I thought. I just hope I can pull it off."

"There's something I should warn you about," Dean said.

She looked up at him.

"Be prepared to face hostility from the administration. They're going to side with this professor, at least initially, and things could get ugly."

"Why would they necessarily side with him? He's the one

who's wrong. Any fool should be able to see that if we point it out."

"That's just the way it is, Naomi. He's one of them."

"Well, you said it could get ugly. You mean I could get expelled?"

He nodded. "I don't want to discourage you. But I've seen it happen, and it's only fair to warn you. If the administration takes a position against you and you refuse to budge, at some point they'll just get rid of the organizers."

Naomi moaned. "My parents would have a fit if I got expelled. So would I."

"Then be very clear with yourself exactly what your goals are and how far you're willing to stick your neck out to reach them. What exactly do you hope to accomplish?"

"I want Professor Hill kicked out. Somebody like that has no business teaching."

"Fine. But what if they refuse and offer some middle ground, like maybe disciplining him? Would you accept that or would you press on, knowing it could lead to expulsion?"

She wasn't sure. She hadn't considered the risks to her own well-being, which was probably naive. All she knew was that in no way, shape, or form could she allow herself to get kicked out of school. Maybe she was making a mistake here, getting herself into dangerous territory she knew nothing about. It would be so much safer just to forget about it, suffer through her statistics course, grab that piece of paper, and get out of here.

"This is starting to sound too complicated," she said.

"You can do it. You just have to plan and organize."

"This is the kind of thing you and Joshua were involved with in Chicago, isn't it?"

"We were just getting our feet wet before the accident. Joshua was getting really good at motivating people. He had a natural touch."

"So do you."

"I'm better at the organization side of things. What I've learned about moving people came from watching how Joshua worked. He was so passionate, it was like he was born for this kind of thing. He would have made one hell of a lawyer or a politician."

"He was good at everything. I don't know what makes me think I can do what he did and not make a fool of myself. I wish he were here so he could tell me what to do. I miss him so much."

He reached across the table and covered her hand with his. "So do I. But I know he would have been real proud to see you doing this."

She nodded and smiled. "*If* I can do this. He would have been shocked. Even I can't believe I'm doing it."

He smiled. "I don't think he would have been surprised."

"You know, I was walking around in a daze for so long after the accident happened that I never even thought to contact you," she said.

"I always thought it kind of a shame that we all went our separate ways: you, me, Maurice, and Tisha—the other two in the car. Joshua was the glue connecting us, I guess."

"What happened to Maurice and Tisha?"

"Maurice is still in the Evanston area as far as I know, but I don't think he ever went back to school. He wasn't injured much physically, but he was pretty messed up emotionally. He felt responsible, since he was driving. Tisha got away with barely a scratch too. I haven't heard anything about her since. You knew she was involved with your brother?"

Naomi shook her head. "I had no idea."

"He met her right after we got out there."

"Was she a student?"

"No. She was from Chicago. I only talked to her once or twice afterward. She took his death pretty hard."

Naomi took a deep breath. "All these lives turned upside down. It's depressing."

Dean nodded. "But we've got to get ourselves back on track and keep going. It doesn't do any good to sit around moping and blaming, no matter how much we might want to. It took me a while to figure that out."

"Then you think racism had something to do with his death too? Everybody else seems to think I'm crazy for feeling that way. But I can't help thinking—knowing—that Joshua would be alive if it weren't for racism."

"I don't think you're crazy. I mean, we wouldn't have been in that car if we didn't have to deal with this kind of shit all the time. Sorry to use that kind of language around you, but I feel strongly about it. We're always faced with these impossible situations where we take personal risks because of racism in society. A lot of times we can't even see the connection or we turn a blind eye to it. Like Vietnam. Nobody's talking much about it, but the brothers are getting killed right and left over there. And they signed up because they don't have much to look forward to in this racist society. I don't know if Joshua ever told you what happened to my father."

"He told me."

"Well, how many white dudes are likely to get stabbed just going out to buy a pack of cigarettes? It was a rough neighborhood, but lots of black people live in neighborhoods like that because it's all we can afford. In this situation with your professor, you've been forced into a position where you feel a need to risk your welfare, or your education at least. You can't just go to class and deal with the usual problems students have."

Naomi nodded enthusiastically. It felt so refreshing to talk to someone who saw things the way she did. "I resent even having to think about disrupting my life and going to all this trouble because of some racist professor. I'd give anything to go back to the carefree days when I didn't have to deal with this. I mean it was there, but I had my parents to shelter me and I didn't always see it. Joshua's death woke me to the realities. I can never go back to being so innocent."

"A lot of us have something happen at some point in our lives that wakes us up. Sometimes it's one big thing; other times it's a collection of things. But once our eyes are opened, we can never shut them again."

"Pamela told me about a girlfriend of hers who was jumped by three white guys in Boston in broad daylight just for bumping into them on the sidewalk."

"That Boston is a mess. Something like that almost happened to me when I was visiting a friend at Boston University last year. A gang of white boys started circling me, calling me nigger and everything else in the book."

"You're kidding? Why?"

Dean shrugged. "I was just in the wrong place at the wrong time. I had left the campus. I don't know where the hell I was, but they obviously didn't think I belonged there."

"What did you do?"

Dean chuckled. "Hightailed it out of there. They chased me all the way back to my friend's dorm. Luckily he was with a group of brothers, and we scared 'em off."

"That's crazy."

"That's life, at least as we know it. When I was in Birmingham staying with a friend last summer, I got stopped by the police and ended up in jail."

Naomi's eyes grew wide. "How did that happen?"

"One of my taillights was broken. I had backed into something just the day before and hadn't gotten it fixed yet. And I didn't have my driver's license with me since I was just dashing out to the store. Big mistake. I admit I was wrong for not bringing it. Black men should never ever drive a car without making sure they have their license, registration, and everything else in perfect order. Well, when the cops found out I didn't have my license—it was two of them—they handcuffed me and put me in the backseat of their cruiser. I kept asking why the handcuffs until one of them reached back and popped me in the mouth."

Naomi gasped. "You mean they hit you?"

Dean nodded.

"What did they say they were arresting you for?"

"Some other dude was wanted, and one of his aliases was Luther Dean. They said I was him."

By now, Naomi was on the edge of her seat. Talk about bizarre. "But why did they think you were him?"

"They knew I wasn't him. They just decided since they got hold of this nigger, they were going to make his day as miserable as possible. You think they would have treated a white dude like that for not having his license with him? I was only a few blocks from my friend's house; my license was there. Kept telling them that, but . . ." He paused and shook his head.

Naomi sat back and took a deep breath. As horrible as the stories were, she loved listening to Dean talk. She admired his way of thinking, his passion. He was also warm and caring. Even though they'd only talked a few times, she felt she could come to him with anything on her mind and he would take the time to listen. He reminded Naomi of her brother in so many ways. Every girl should have a Joshua or a Dean to look after them. Sometimes she wished Ralph would be more like that, more understanding of her needs, passionate about the issues of the day, but he cared very much about his studies and his future career. She swelled with pride whenever she remembered that he was a Morehouse medical student and he belonged to her.

Or so she hoped. She glanced at her watch and then shoved her pen and notebook into her shoulder bag. They had been talking for two hours. She was so late getting to Ralph's, he probably thought she wasn't coming. "I could talk to you forever, Dean, but I need to get going." She removed her wallet.

"Don't bother," he said, touching her hand. "I'll get it."

"I don't mind paying for myself."

He shook his head. "I insist." He put a few bills on the table, and they both stood up.

"Have you decided what you're going to do?" he asked as they walked out the door.

"I don't know. I have to think about it. But thanks for all the advice."

"Glad to help. If you need anything else, anything at all, call me." He wrote his number on a slip of paper and gave it to her. "I'll give you a lift back to your dorm."

"You don't have to do that. I'm used to taking the bus. Anyway, I'm not going back to Woodruff. I have to stop by a friend's."

"Then I'll drop you by your friend's. Why should you take the bus when I've got a set of wheels right outside?"

"If you insist."

It was sweet of him to offer to go out of his way to see her home. He reminded her how nice it felt to have an older brother to do things for you. Actually, Dean treated her even better than Joshua had. Maybe because he had to look after his sisters when his father died. "How are your sisters doing, Dean?" she asked, once they were in the car.

He smiled. "Fine. The oldest one is going to college next year. I've been taking her around to visit different campuses."

"That's nice of you."

"I wanted to ask you something," he said, turning down the radio.

"Yes?"

He turned and looked directly at her. "Are you seeing anyone now? Romantically?"

Her heart nearly jumped out of her mouth, but she tried to keep a straight face. Here she was thinking of him as a brother, when he obviously had other ideas.

"Yes," she said. It might be wishful thinking, based on what Pamela just told her, but it was the best way to avoid getting more deeply into something she found awkward to talk about. And she wanted to be careful not to offend him. She liked Dean and hoped they could be friends.

"Too bad," he said. "For me, anyway. If the situation ever changes, I hope you'll let me know."

She smiled and turned toward the window. She wished he'd stop flirting with her. It made her feel funny. She was both re-lieved and apprehensive when they pulled up in front of Ralph's house at 3:30 that afternoon—relieved to be getting away from Dean but uneasy about what might lie ahead with Ralph.

His Sting Ray parked in front of the house told her he was back from his lab. So many questions raced through her mind as she walked to the door. Should she talk about other things first, then bring it up casually, like "By the way, who's Marlena Robertson?" Should she go on a fishing expedition by asking him roundabout questions, like "Do you ever have other people up here to study?" Or should she come right out with it the minute she saw him: "Hey, are you fucking some other chick?"

Keith opened the door, and a funny look crossed his face

when he saw her. Naomi figured Pamela must have told him she'd squealed on him about Judy. Served his two-timing butt right. She waited for Keith to step aside so she could enter, but he didn't.

"Excuse me," she said.

"Ralph's not here," he said. Just then, Pamela came up and stood quietly behind Keith.

"But I just saw his car parked downstairs," Naomi said.

"I know, but . . ."

Naomi's eyes traveled away from Keith. Pamela was making faces trying to get her attention. At first Naomi didn't understand what was going on, then Pamela rolled her eyes toward the stairs and Naomi got the hint. She shoved Keith away, and he fell back easily, since it was probably the last thing he expected.

She darted past him and ran up to Ralph's room. She didn't bother to knock, just pushed the door open. What greeted her eyes was a nightmare come true. Ralph was on top of some woman, screwing and panting like mad. Both of them were naked, and the woman's legs were wrapped around him like a vise, bouncing rapidly with his thrusting. The bedcovers and pillows lay in a heap on the floor, so Naomi could see everything plain as day, down to the look of pure ecstasy on Ralph's face. It felt like her heart had been ripped out of her chest.

They were so absorbed, they didn't even hear her. Until she screamed. Then Ralph's eyes shot open, and the woman jerked her head back to look. Ralph leaped up and scrambled off the bed, as the woman sat up and looked at Naomi defiantly. She had the biggest pair of titties Naomi had ever seen. Ralph fumbled around on the floor for some clothes and threw the sheets over the woman at the same time.

"Jesus, Naomi!" he said, hopping into his slacks.

She realized she'd been standing there staring at those boobs with her mouth hanging open as if in a trance. At the sound of his voice, she snapped out of it, whirled around, and fled down the hall. Then she stopped, turned, and ran back to his room. He was zipping his pants, and the woman was sitting on the bed fastening her bra. The scene made Naomi sick all over again.

"You stinking, no-good, two-timing son of a bitch," she screamed, as loud as she could. "How could you do this? I hope you rot in hell!"

"Nao—"

"Shut up." She turned to the woman. "And you. You think you're the only one he's been fucking? Well, I've got news for you. It was me, just last night."

The woman's expression told Naomi it *was* news to her. She fixed Ralph with a stare as cold as Siberia. That made Naomi feel better, but she was still as mad as hell. She glared at Ralph. "You make me sick to my stomach."

He started to say something, but she turned on her heel and fled down the stairs. Out of the corner of her eye, she glimpsed Pamela and Keith in the living room. The looks on their faces told Naomi they had a pretty good idea of what had happened upstairs. She ran out the door and down the street. At the bus stop, she was so out of breath she had to bend over and open her mouth to keep from hyperventilating.

Bastard, bastard, bastard. How could she have been so blind, so trusting of someone so utterly deceitful? She'd been naive—downright stupid. She tried to catch her breath and get hold of herself as the bus came down the street. Then she climbed on board and walked to the rear, where she sat frozen to the seat with her eyes focused on the aisle, all the way to campus.

Eleven

Naomi stayed buried beneath the covers the rest of Saturday, not even bothering to go to the cafeteria for dinner. When Kathy, her roommate, asked what was wrong, Naomi said she had an upset stomach, which wasn't far from the truth. Every time she remembered the scene at Ralph's, she wanted to throw up. She barely slept all night, tossing and turning. The thought of Ralph making love to another woman was more than she could handle.

Sunday afternoon she put on her robe and Dr. Scholl's sandals, dragged herself downstairs to the vending machines for a candy bar and a soda, and then returned to her room, dropped her robe on the floor, and climbed back into bed. Kathy had gone on to church without her. It was one of the few things they ever did together, since they were nothing alike. Kathy was a hippie, spaced out and into Peter, Paul, and Mary. She rarely left the room without first lighting some incense and smoking a joint. Naomi tried one with her once but never really got into it, since Ralph refused to touch the stuff. Kathy was easy enough to deal with if you could overlook the occasional strangeness, and they both realized they had to try to get along since they lived in a room that couldn't be more than ten by fifteen feet. Attending church together had become a Sunday ritual to help keep the peace.

But how could she go to church when her mind was haunted by obscene thoughts? Over and over, she visualized Ralph humping that woman and the look of pure pleasure on his face, put there by someone else. Did she make him feel like that? Probably not. He thought she was frigid.

How could he do this to her? How could she *let him* do this to her? Here she was thinking about someday being this man's wife. She'd given everything to him—her body, her mind, her soul, her hopes and dreams. Obviously it was a one-way street. She was giving, and all he did was take.

She jumped up, put on a Jackson Five album, and switched on the TV, turning the volume up on both as loud as she thought possible without provoking complaints from anyone. She had to get her mind off that man before she went mad. She was never going to have anything to do with him ever again, even if he came begging on all fours, although of course Ralph would never do that.

She was nibbling on the candy bar when someone knocked on the door. For a second, she thought it was Ralph. She glanced down, horrified about the way she looked: old ragged T-shirt for a nightgown, hair uncombed. Then sanity prevailed. He almost never came to her room on campus, she reminded herself. So she dragged herself out of bed, cracked the door open, and breathed a sigh of relief when she saw Pamela standing there.

"Lordy," Pamela said, walking in and shutting the door behind her. "You look plain awful."

"Thanks," Naomi said sarcastically. She plopped down on the bed. Pamela turned down the stereo, flicked off the TV, and sat down beside her.

"What happened up there?" Pamela asked, slipping her arms out of her coat. "Marlena came out right after you left, and she looked mad enough to spit."

"That's about the best news I've heard in twenty-four hours. Now he can look for *two* new women to cheat on."

"Will you please tell me what the hell happened? You're driving me insane."

"I caught them fucking the daylights out of each other."

"Holy shit. You mean the whole nine yards?"

Naomi couldn't help but grin at Pamela's reaction. It was

even funnier as she thought about the look on Ralph's face when he saw her standing over them in their moment of passion. She found herself giggling with Pamela.

"At least you know what the bum's been up to. I'm still in the dark about Keith."

"Yeah. What happened with him? I was shocked to see you there yesterday."

"I asked him about this Judy, but he said they were just friends."

"He's lying his ass off, Pam."

"You might be right. But I need him, and unless he admits it or I catch him, I'm not giving him up. Has Ralph called?"

"No. And I hope he never does. I don't care if I never see him again."

Pamela laughed. "Sure you don't."

"I'm dead serious. He thinks I'm frigid anyway."

"He thinks you're what?"

"That I'm too uptight. You know, when we have sex."

"He said that?"

Naomi nodded.

"Lordy. Are you?"

"I guess I must be, if he's running to other women."

"Maybe the problem is him."

"I don't think so. Ralph's had so many women, I don't see how it can be him."

"Honey, that don't mean a damn thing."

"But why can't I be looser or whatever he wants? Wilder, freer?"

"He's probably not doing the right things for you."

"How do I get him to do the right things?"

"Now that's tricky. You can never tell a man he's no good in bed, even if it's true. Especially if it's true."

"So what do you do?"

"You have to coax him. Or fake it."

"Fake what?"

"Orgasm. You know, coming."

"Oh, *that.*"

"Now why do I get the feeling you don't know what the hell I'm talking about?"

"I know what it is. And I like being with Ralph, it's just that . . ." Naomi paused.

"You've never reached the mountaintop?"

"I'm not sure."

"Lordy me. Honey, if you had, you'd know it. What about the other men you've been with?"

"What other men? Ralph's the first."

"Well, there you go. That's part of the problem right there."

"And how many have you been with?"

"More than one, for crying out loud."

"Are you saying I need to go out and get laid by some more dudes?"

Pamela laughed. "Not a bad idea, but no. I bet Ralph likes the fact that you haven't slept around. Our men don't want us to have a lot of experience."

"And yet they want us to be these hot mamas when we're in bed with *them*."

"Ain't it just rotten? But it's not so much how many you've been with that counts. You just need to find the right one."

"Or get it going with the one I have."

"Amen. Well, I must say this has been interesting, but it's not what I came to talk to you about. What are you going to do about the demonstration?"

"I don't think I'm up to it now."

"C'mon. You can't let this get in the way. Isn't that what you told me at the rally?"

"You didn't just catch your man screwing another woman. And anyway, it's not just this. Dean made it sound so complicated. I don't know if I can handle it."

"Then we're going to let Professor Hill get away with spreading his bullshit brain theories?"

"Let someone else start a protest against him. Why does it have to be me?"

" 'Cause no one else knows how."

"Neither do I, for that matter."

"But you've got Dean to help you. What did he say was involved?"

"It's not that difficult to organize. You have to print up flyers, hand them out."

"See there."

"But it's too risky. We could end up getting expelled or something. I hadn't thought about that."

"That ain't going to happen. People are doing this kind of thing all over and not getting expelled. I think you're just using that as an excuse because you're depressed about Ralph."

"There really is some risk involved. We need to think carefully before we get into it."

"I don't need to think another minute. The man is a racist."

"I know."

"And this is just the kind of thing you need to get your mind off your man troubles." Pamela picked Naomi's robe up off the floor and shoved it at her. "So get dressed. We'll go get the stuff to do the flyers."

"Maybe tomorrow. I'm—"

"Now, Naomi."

Forty minutes later, she had showered and dressed and felt better. In fact, she was starting to get worked up about organizing the demonstration. This was just what the doctor would have ordered—a healthy dose of meaning, something to distract her from thinking about Ralph.

They were headed out the door excitedly making plans for the flyers when her intercom buzzed. "Yes?" she asked, pressing the button.

"Naomi Jefferson?"

"That's me."

"You have a visitor in the lobby."

Naomi's heart skipped a beat. The odds that it was Ralph were slim but not nonexistent. After all, he'd lost both his women in one weekend. Maybe he wanted one of them back. If he was downstairs, that meant she was the one. "Did you get the name?"

"Just a minute. I'll see."

She tried to stay calm while she waited. She wasn't ready to forgive him yet, but it would be nice to know he'd made the effort to come by.

The intercom crackled. "It's Dean Davis."

"Oh," she said, unable to keep the disappointment out of her voice. "Tell him I'm on my way down."

"*You* may not be excited about seeing this baby, but I am," Pamela said as they left the room.

Naomi laughed. And when she saw Dean in the lobby, she realized she *was* glad to see him. If he was here, that meant she hadn't turned him off yesterday when she told him she was involved with someone else.

They explained what they were up to, and Dean offered them a lift. The three of them spent the afternoon shopping for supplies, and then they went to Naomi's room and spent an hour talking about when to hold the demonstrations and what to put on the flyers. They decided to hand them out for a week and begin the demonstrations the following Monday. When they finally came up with wording that all three liked, Dean called a friend who owned a printshop and persuaded him to open up even though it was Sunday. He went to have two hundred copies made while Naomi and Pamela made the posters. By the time Dean returned, brightly colored posters with slogans like RIGHT-BRAINERS AGAINST RACISM lined Naomi's room. Then they went out for dinner at the Underground.

"So, have you decided how far you're willing to go to get this cat fired?" Dean asked.

"I think we have to wait and see how it develops," Naomi said. "If we get a lot of students involved, we'll have a lot more power."

"Don't count on that happening too soon and without a lot of conflict," Dean said.

"Under no circumstances are we willing to be expelled," Pamela said. "This is important, but it's not worth sacrificing our educations."

"Right," Naomi said.

"Then you need to start giving some thought to how much you're willing to compromise. This thing could go down to the wire, and even then it's doubtful. You might not get what you want."

"I don't agree," Pamela said. "How can they keep a racist professor around if the students refuse to go to his classes?"

"And they can't kick all of us out," Naomi said. "We're going to win this one."

"OK," Dean said. "I admire that spirit. I just wanted to warn you."

Naomi and Pamela spent every free minute between and after classes handing out the flyers. The response was just what they'd hoped for. Several students told them they thought it was about time someone did something about this professor. A few even offered to help hand out the flyers during their free time. Others volunteered to make posters and then brought them to Naomi's room. By Thursday they had distributed all two hundred flyers and had to have more printed. Pamela and Naomi were so busy working on the demonstration they had trouble keeping up with their classes.

Naomi was glad she'd decided to go through with this, mainly because it kept her too busy to think about Ralph or wonder why he didn't call. The only time she thought about him was during the wee hours of the night. But by then she was so tired, she soon drifted off to sleep.

Twelve

The first thing Naomi did on Monday morning when she woke up was to look out the window of her dorm room. The weatherman had been predicting snow for the longest time but nothing had fallen, and as she crawled over the covers on her hands and knees to the window at the foot of her bed, Naomi prayed his predictions would stay wrong for at least one more day. But they didn't—the campus was blanketed with at least half a foot of snow. She moaned and sat back on the bed. It hadn't snowed since she'd been in Atlanta, but if it was anything like her hometown of D.C., six inches of snow could cripple the city. She only hoped that on campus, where just about everybody walked everywhere, the snow wouldn't be as disruptive.

At 8:00 A.M., Naomi and Pamela lugged the posters, extra flyers, and a bullhorn they had borrowed from Dean across campus to Jackson Hall, where Professor Hill taught his classes. The going was rough, because many of the roads and walkways on campus hadn't been cleared yet. And with their hands and arms full, it was hard to keep their balance.

By 9:00 A.M., only three students had joined them, and two said they could only stay an hour. Naomi gave them posters, and the five of them formed a circle and marched, but it was a weak showing. Black students were coming and going all around them, but they all had excuses for not joining the protest. Naomi spotted two black women she knew were in Professor Hill's class entering the building and asked them to join the march. They said they would come back later. That was pretty much how it went all day. By 1:00 P.M., Pamela was ready to give up.

"Looks like we're wasting our time," Pamela said. "Nobody seems to care about this but us. Can't say I blame them. It's so damn messy out here."

But Naomi refused to quit. She was tired, wet, and hungry and had missed a morning's worth of classes, but she was damned if she'd give up so quickly after taking so much trouble. Besides, stopping the protest scared her. She knew it was the only thing that kept her from crawling back to Ralph. "At least it's melting, and tomorrow it's supposed to be warmer."

"I hope like hell you're right, 'cause otherwise this has been a monumental waste of time."

Naomi handed Pamela a stack of flyers. "Here. We'll hand the rest of these out to people going by and come back in the morning. It should be better tomorrow. It *has* to be better tomorrow."

On Tuesday they carried everything back across campus to Jackson Hall. The snow had turned to mush and Pamela fell, ruining a bunch of posters.

"Shit, fuck, shit," Pamela said between clenched teeth as she brushed the snow off the posters and her jeans.

It was warmer, and much of the snow had melted. Still, things were not much better that morning. Only a half dozen students showed up. Naomi started having second thoughts too. She should have listened to her feelings before, instead of letting herself be talked into doing this. And yet she was so sure of the rightness of what she was trying to do that it was difficult for her to believe she couldn't make others see it too.

At noon she spotted Walter Johnson, a short stocky black man, coming out of the building from that morning's statistics class, and waved him over to their little group. The high-waters

Walter always wore didn't seem so out of place in the slush covering the campus.

"Why aren't you out here demonstrating?" she said. "We need you."

"I was going to come," Walter said, pulling his navy skull cap down snugly around his head, "but the weather's been so bad."

"Chicken," Naomi said. "Letting a little snow stop you."

"Shame on you," Pamela said.

Walter grinned sheepishly and looked around. "Maybe if you had more people out here."

"Everybody's got excuses, just like you," Naomi said. "They seem to forget what this professor's like in class."

"We're just trying to get in and out of this place," Walter said. "The sooner the better."

"I understand that," Naomi said. "But you think once you leave things are going to be different? You're going to face it out there too, unless you speak up."

"It's hard missing classes a month before finals," Walter said. "Especially when this might not even work."

"I know," Naomi said. "But racism's not going to wait until it's convenient for you to do something about it."

"What do you expect them to do to Professor Hill?" he asked.

"Nothing, if we don't get together on this," Pamela said. "He'll just go on with his racist attitude and comments forever."

"Even if the administration ignores us," Naomi said, "if we put on a convincing protest, Professor Hill might stop talking that nonsense. But if we don't do anything, he'll never change."

"You're right," Walter said.

"It's your lunch break now," Naomi said. "Can't you at least stay during that?"

"I would," Walter said, "but what good can just a few of us do?"

"I'll get more people out here," Naomi said. "I promise."

Pamela and Walter gave Naomi doubtful looks. "And just how the hell you going to do that?" Pamela asked.

Naomi gave Walter her poster. "Give me ten minutes."

With Pamela and Walter staring at her like she'd gone bonkers, Naomi headed across campus. She didn't know what the hell she was going to do, but she had to try. If she failed, it wouldn't be for lack of effort.

She opened the big metal door leading into the cafeteria. It was filled with the noisy clatter of students talking and eating. Naomi spotted a table of black students at one end of the room and walked over. She only knew one of them, a woman named Louise who was also a communications major. Pretty and always smiling, Louise was the only black woman on the cheerleading squad.

"Hi, Naomi," Louise said, as she approached the table. "I heard you're organizing a protest against Professor Hill. It's about time. I'm in one of his classes, and some of the things he says are unbelievable."

All the students at the table stopped talking and looked at Naomi. She stood at one end with her hands on her hips. "Then why aren't you out there with us? All of you."

"I have classes all day," Louise said.

"You're not in class now."

"No, but I have cheerleading practice at two, so I have to eat lunch."

"I walked by yesterday," one man said. "Only saw a couple of students so I thought it had been called off because of the weather."

"It hasn't been called off. It's going on right this minute."

"Then why aren't more people there?"

"You tell me," Naomi said. "They probably think, Let somebody else do it. Just like you. Nobody wants to take responsibility. If we just brush this kind of thing off every time we come across it, things will never change. You expect whites to suddenly one day say, 'Oh, we've been wrong all along, we'll be nicer to them from now on'? It doesn't work that way."

It was quiet for a moment as people turned and looked at one another.

Louise spoke up first. "What do you want us to do?"

"None of you are in class now. Come on over to Jackson Hall with me."

"You mean right now?" a woman said.

"This is important," Naomi said.

Louise stood up. "I'll go."

Another woman stood up. "Me too. Even though I don't have class with Hill, one of *my* professors also seems to have trouble calling on black students."

A man stood up. "Count me in."

"Me too," said another, and another.

As they made their way across campus, the initial group of half a dozen students attracted attention until it had more than doubled in size. Pamela's mouth dropped open and she tossed her cigarette on the ground. "Lordy me. How did you do that?"

Naomi laughed at their startled expressions. "Don't just stand there. Hand out posters. We're ready to get going."

By 3:30 that afternoon, as classes wound down and the students in front of the building attracted curiosity, the group had grown to more than forty. They marched in a big circle and chanted for Hill's dismissal. Naomi was so proud of what they had set in motion. This must be how Joshua felt when he got involved in stuff like this, she thought. It was a pretty heady feeling.

Dean dropped by at four to see how things were shaping up, and Naomi and Pamela dropped from the line to greet him.

"This looks pretty good for two days' work and a week of leaflets," he said.

"It was her doing," Pamela said, jerking her thumb toward Naomi. "She went to the cafeteria and dragged a bunch of folks over. Then more started coming."

Dean gave Naomi a big smile. "That's what you have to do sometimes."

"But what do we do now?" Pamela asked.

"We wait," Naomi said. "If we disrupt things enough, they'll come to us."

"Right," Dean said. "You'll probably have to keep this up a few days."

"This is much better than yesterday," Pamela said, "but I doubt it's enough to get more than a glance from the administration."

"It'll grow," Dean said. "They'll go back to their rooms tonight and talk about it."

"Tonight I'm going around to all the dorms and—" Naomi paused. She heard the Sting Ray before she saw it, and she turned and followed it with her eyes as it cruised by the crowd.

"Well, I'll be," Pamela said, looking in the same direction. "If that don't beat all."

Naomi turned back toward Dean and Pamela and tried to act like nothing unusual had happened. "Anyway, I'm going to leave flyers in all the dorms." She knew she was talking too fast, but couldn't help it.

"He's parking," Pamela said.

"So what?" Naomi said.

"Now he's getting out of the car."

"Who is that?" Dean asked.

"Nobody important," Naomi said.

Dean looked at her. "Uh-huh."

"He's coming over now," Pamela said.

"Will you stop it?" Naomi said.

Pamela didn't say another word, just smiled. Naomi thought she would go out of her mind trying not to look in the other direction. Her temples were throbbing, her heart pounding, her stomach flipping. But she was determined to act like it was no big deal, especially with Dean standing right next to her. He was watching her closely, and she didn't want him to see her acting foolish about some dude. But when Ralph came up right beside them, she could ignore him no longer.

"Hey," he said to everybody.

"Hi," they all said at once.

"How are you doing?" he said, wrapping his fingers around the back of Naomi's neck.

She pulled away from him. It was only a slight movement, but he got the hint and dropped his hand.

"Uh, this is Dean," Naomi said. "Dean, Ralph."

They gave the black power handshake. Naomi couldn't help but notice that Ralph seemed to struggle with it.

"I heard what was going on over here," Ralph said. "Thought I'd come take a look."

"You heard about this all the way over at Morehouse?" Pamela asked, a big smile on her face.

Naomi smiled too. She couldn't believe the word had spread that far. Dean must have had a lot to do with that.

"These ladies have done a hell of a job," Dean said.

"Looks that way," Ralph said. "It was just the two of you putting it together?"

"And Dean," Naomi said. "He was in on it."

"I didn't do anything," Dean said. "I haven't even been over here until today."

"But your advice helped a lot," Naomi said.

"It was only advice," Dean said. "Give yourselves the credit."

Naomi smiled at him, and an awkward moment of silence passed as the four of them stood around in a circle.

"Naomi," Ralph said. "Can I see you for a minute?"

"You're looking at me now," she said, not budging from her spot.

Pamela and Dean laughed uncomfortably, and Ralph smiled awkwardly. "I meant over by my car, if you don't mind."

"I'll be right back," she said to Pamela and Dean.

"Take your time," Pamela said, moving closer to Dean. Naomi couldn't help but smile at her flirtatious little friend.

"I'm surprised," Ralph said, leaning against his car.

"About what?"

"To see you into this kind of thing."

She shrugged. It figured, she thought wryly, given he took so little time trying to understand her.

"I'm sorry about what happened," he said. "I'm not even going to try to make excuses."

That was probably wise, she thought, given that she'd caught him bare-assed.

"I don't know what came over me. But she's been after me for weeks."

"Excuse me?"

"Marlena. That's her name. She's been after me since school started and—"

"Oh, you poor baby."

"Naomi, I'm trying to explain."

"Then why don't you start with the truth? Are you about to tell me that was your first time with her?"

"You heard different?"

"Yes."

"From who?"

Naomi cut her eyes to the side. "Never mind who."

"Whoever it was, they're wrong. Saturday was the first time anything ever happened."

"You expect me to believe that?"

"It's the truth. She caught me in . . . well, a moment of weakness, I guess you could say."

"Don't expect me to feel sorry for you."

"I'm not expecting anything. I'm trying to apologize."

"Did you apologize to her too?"

"What?"

"Did you tell *her* you were sorry too? That all the times you were with me were moments of weakness?"

"Naomi, stop being difficult."

"Me? I'm not the one who was fucking somebody else."

"Look, I said I was sorry. Besides, you know the problems we've been having in bed. And, well, I . . ."

He paused when he saw the look on her face. She didn't like his attitude one bit. Not only was he lying about it, he was acting like it was her fault. She turned to walk away, but he grabbed her elbow.

"Wait a minute."

She snatched her arm from his grasp and stomped so hard snow splashed all over her legs. Ralph jumped back. "If that's the way you feel about us, you can go back to your little premed student."

"I shouldn't have said that. The real problem is school. I've been having a rough time in some of my classes lately. The pressure is unbelievable."

"You think that's an excuse?"

"No, but will you just listen to me? I'm not saying it's an excuse, but maybe it helps explain my temporary lack of judgment." He came up close and leaned over and whispered into her ear. "Look, with her it was just sex. You're the one I'm in love with."

Those were the words she'd wanted so much to hear. He said them so rarely that her heart soared whenever he did. She'd wanted him to come to her and apologize, and he'd done that too. Still, the vision of him in his bed with another woman was etched on her brain. She had to swallow hard just thinking about it. "You still seeing her?"

"I never was seeing her."

"I wish this had never happened," she said, her voice cracking with the memory. "I'm so crazy about you. Maybe too crazy. What do I have to do to make you happy? I've tried everything."

"You're already making me happy." He reached out for her, and this time she didn't resist. He held her, and she snuggled her head in the crook of his neck. She was still torn between anger and love, but the anger was slowly receding. This was where she belonged.

"Come to my place," he said. She started to pull away but he pulled her back. "Please?" She appreciated the way he sounded a bit unsure of himself, unlike in the past, when he knew all he had to do was ask.

"I can't tonight. I have to stay until this is over. Then we have to organize things for tomorrow."

"How much longer will you be here?"

"An hour at least."

"I'll wait for you."

"But I have so much to do afterward. Why don't you help out? It would go faster that way."

He shook his head. "I don't have time for that. I have an

exam tomorrow. Look, we'll only stay at my place a couple of hours. Then I'll bring you back and you can do your work and I'll study. C'mon. We haven't seen each other for more than a week."

He didn't have to remind her. All the busywork hadn't filled the void in her heart. She missed the sound of his voice, the seductiveness of his smile, the feel of his flesh pressed against hers. All the causes in the world couldn't make up for the warm body of this man. She realized that more than ever now, with him standing here so close. And the idea of Ralph waiting for her and taking her back and forth was too much to pass up. Maybe he would be different from now on.

"That your old man?" Dean asked, a smile playing around his lips, when Naomi rejoined them.

"Uh-huh."

"Nice car," Dean said, shoving his hands in his pockets.

Naomi turned to Pamela. "I'm going to meet him in an hour." Ralph had gone to visit a friend on campus and would return for her.

"You're going to leave me just like that?" Pamela asked.

"I won't be long."

"But there's so much to do tonight, especially since we're expecting more people tomorrow. We have to get more flyers made and fix the posters I dropped. And Dean said it would be good if we set up a stand with hot chocolate in the lobby of the building next door."

"It was just an idea," Dean said.

"A good idea," Pamela said.

"But I already told Ralph I would go."

"Well, tell him to get lost," Pamela said. "Especially after what he did to you."

Naomi stole a glance at Dean, who was trying to look nonchalant about the whole thing. Naomi didn't want her dirty laundry aired out in front of him. She took Pamela by the arm. "Excuse us for a minute, Dean."

"No problem," he said and walked off toward the crowd.

Naomi led Pamela away. "That was uncalled for."

"Well, shit, I haven't seen Keith much since this started," Pamela said, digging in her shoulder bag for a cigarette. "I don't think you're being fair."

"You and Keith didn't break up either, did you? If you want to spend time with him later, I'll cover for you. But I need some time with Ralph."

Pamela lit her Salem and blew out a big puff of smoke. "Fine. I'll do it by myself."

"Pamela, anything you can't get done just leave and I'll finish up when I get back."

"But the printshop, the stores, everything will be closed by then."

Naomi sighed. "You're right. Damn. I guess I'll just have to—"

"Oh, never mind. Go on. But tomorrow night you're going to have to take care of things while I spend some time with *my* baby."

"It's a deal."

Pamela shook her head and chuckled at the same time.

"What's so funny?" Naomi asked.

"I was just thinking. Why do we go through so much trouble for these no-good men?"

"Good question."

"I mean, it's not like there's no other fish in the sea," Pamela said. She grinned. "Maybe I'll get that cute friend of yours to help me out tonight. I just love that voice of his. Do you know if he has a girlfriend?"

"You mean Dean? No, I don't." Then she remembered what Joshua told her years ago—that there was almost always a woman around Dean. "Probably so," she added.

"Let's hope not," Pamela said. "That voice alone is enough to give a woman an orgasm."

"Pamela!"

"Sorry, but I can't help myself. You don't mind if I ask him to help, do you?"

"I thought you were so in love with Keith."

"Ha! Two can play at this two-timing game, you know."

"If you're planning to cheat on Keith, he deserves it. But don't use Dean."

"Then you do mind."

"That's not what I said. Do whatever you want." Actually, Naomi didn't think Pamela and Dean were such a hot match. Pamela was kind of flighty, and it seemed Dean would prefer a more serious type. But then what did she know—or care?

As soon as Ralph drove up for her, all thoughts of Dean and Pamela vanished from her head. They spent the evening making up and making love. Naomi still didn't reach the mountaintop, as Pamela would say, but Ralph seemed pleased, and as far as she was concerned that was what counted. A few hours later, they parked in front of her dorm. Their time together hadn't been nearly long enough for Naomi, and she didn't want to let him go.

"Will you have time to stop by the demonstration tomorrow," she asked, "and help me carry some things back to the dorm?"

"I'll come by after my last class, about four."

They kissed goodbye and she walked to her room smiling. Everything was going good now. He still showed little interest in the things that were important to her, like the protest, but he had his own battles to fight trying to get through medical school. She would have to learn to live with that and try to be more supportive.

"Pamela said to tell you she'd meet you in the lobby an hour earlier tomorrow morning," Kathy said as soon as she opened the door to their room. "So you'd have time to set up the doughnut and hot chocolate stand."

So Pamela had made arrangements for hot chocolate and doughnuts, as well. Her partner had been busy. Naomi felt a little bad about not being around to pitch in. "Did Dean help her out, do you know?"

"She didn't say. Just said for you to be ready."

Naomi went to bed that night relieved that she'd made up

with Ralph but wondering just what might have developed between Pamela and Dean. Not that it was any of her concern. They were two adults, free to do as they pleased. "Voice enough to give a woman an orgasm." Naomi chuckled into her pillow. That Pamela was a mess.

Thirteen

"You look so happy," Pamela said on Wednesday morning when they met in the dorm lobby. "I guess last night paid off."

Naomi nodded. "Mmm. Ralph was so sweet."

"For a change, huh?"

Naomi laughed as they struggled with the front door, their arms filled with posters and stacks of flyers. "So, I heard you arranged for hot chocolate and doughnuts."

"The doughnuts fell through. Too expensive. But we'll have hot chocolate." She held up a paper bag.

"How'd you pay for it?"

"Out of my pocket. How else? But we're charging five cents a cup."

"Is that enough to cover what you paid?"

Pamela shrugged.

"I'll give you some money," Naomi said. "And maybe we can get Walter and some of the others who helped out yesterday to pitch in."

"I can use every penny you dig up."

"Uh, was Dean around after I left?"

"Shit, no. I asked him, but when I said you were occupied for the evening, he told me he had something else to do. So much for supporting the cause. I think it's you he wants to support."

Naomi couldn't help but smile. "Maybe he really was busy. Ever think of that?"

"I bet he would have gotten out of anything if *you'd* asked him."

Naomi rolled her eyes skyward. "Where are we getting the hot water for the chocolate?"

"A coffeepot I borrowed from the cafeteria. But I'll have to go back to my room to get it. It was too much to carry."

"I'll go back for it. You've done more than your share."

By 9:30 that morning, more people were marching than had participated in the previous two days put together. At lunchtime, the crowd grew so big they couldn't march in a circle with any kind of orderliness. So the crowd just stood in front of the building shouting "Black is beautiful!" and tried to discourage other students from attending classes.

At 5:00 that evening, as things were winding down, Pamela rushed up to Naomi as she picked up discarded paper cups at the table holding the coffeepot.

"Isn't this exciting?" Pamela said. "I counted at one point and there were, like, almost a hundred people."

"I know, around lunchtime," Naomi said, dumping a bunch of cups into a plastic trash bag.

"I can't believe we pulled this off. Do you think this many will show up again tomorrow?"

Naomi shrugged. "Hopefully."

Pamela looked at Naomi more closely. "What's the matter? You seem distracted."

"Nothing. Just tired, I guess." The truth was she'd expected to see Ralph pull up by this time, but he was nowhere to be seen. Already he seemed to be slipping back into his old ways, running late. Maybe he wouldn't show up at all.

"Want me to help you with that?" Pamela asked.

"Nope. I'm almost done. You can stack up the posters."

"Somebody else already did that. And Walter said he would carry the coffeepot back. That's another thing. We're getting all these volunteers. It's unbelievable."

Naomi nodded.

"It's Ralph, isn't it?" Pamela asked.

"What do you mean?"

"Something's got you upset. I'm excited, but your mind is, like, out there." Pamela waved her arm in the air.

Naomi smiled. "He said he would stop by to help out, and I'm just wondering what happened to him."

"Maybe he'll still show up."

"I'm not going to hold my breath," Naomi said, knotting the stuffed trash bag. "Are you going to see Keith?"

Pamela nodded. "I told him I'd be over after this."

"I'll handle things tonight. You go have some fun." Naomi heaved the trash bag over her shoulder. "I'm going to dump this."

"OK, I'll see you in the morning."

Probably no need to brood, Naomi thought, as she struggled alone across campus with her arms full of demonstration para-phernalia. He'd probably just been held up in one of his classes. The previous night he was so sweet and attentive, she couldn't imagine he wouldn't have come if he could have. Maybe there was a message from him back at the dorm.

Someone *had* left her a note on dorm letterhead, but she knew the minute she took it from the dorm manager and saw her name scrawled hastily on the front that it wasn't from Ralph. She didn't recognize the handwriting, and it was un-usual to get an envelope this way. She tore at the flap and skipped over the body of the short note to the signature. She al-most dropped the stack of posters in her arms when she saw it: *Marlena Robertson.*

I didn't have time to wait around for you, since I'm meeting Ralph at 5. I'm the woman who was with him when you barged in on Saturday. I have been his woman off and on for almost five years and I intend to stay that way forever. I have been to his house in D.C. and had dinner with his family, and he's been to mine in New Orleans. But since Ralph has a way of not telling the whole truth sometimes, I wanted to come and set things straight to your face and tell you to stay away from him.

By the way, you're not the first woman he's cheated on

me with, but I will do everything in my God-given power to
see that you're the last.

Yours hatefully,
Marlena Robertson (Jones-to-be)

Naomi's knees felt so wobbly she had to sit. She found a
chair in a corner of the lobby and sank into it, letting the posters
scatter at her feet. Her hands trembled as she clutched the note
in her fist. It felt as if her brain would burst with the thoughts
racing through it. *Ralph . . . cheated on me . . . his woman for
five years . . . not the first.* Could this have been going on all
this time without her realizing it? No. Impossible. She refused
to believe it. Ralph had insisted this woman was a one-night
stand. And while Naomi wasn't necessarily sure it had been
that brief, she wasn't ready to believe it had been an ongoing
five-year affair. This woman was just plain lying—an obses-
sive, crazed bimbo trying to scare her off.

Naomi spread the note out and looked at it again, searching
for a clue that would expose the woman for what she was. It
said she was with Ralph right now. Well, that would be easy
enough to check. She was supposed to go out and get more hot
chocolate for tomorrow and had planned to call Dean for a
ride, but all that would have to wait.

She stood, gathered her things, and took the stairs two at a
time all the way to the third floor. She dumped everything on
her bed and ran down the hallway to the phone booth. She
turned the corner and nearly collided with a woman already in
the doorless booth.

"Sorry," she said, backing away. Normally, she would have
asked the woman to knock on her door when she finished with
the phone. But this couldn't wait. She ran down the stairwell to
the floor below. Just as she reached the phone on that floor, it
started to ring. Naomi sat down on the bench, lifted the receiver a few inches out of the cradle, and softly put it back
down. God, she thought, clutching the receiver. It was embarrassing how desperate she was acting. But she quickly brushed
the thought aside and dialed Ralph's number. Keith answered.

"Can I speak to Ralph, please?"

"Hold on."

The phone clattered in her ear as he dropped the receiver on the hallway table. Rude bum, she thought. Why wasn't he over here picking up Pamela instead of making her get the bus? After she got this mess straightened out with Ralph, she was going to tell him that from now on he would pick her up or do without her. She was sick and tired—

"Hello?"

"Ralph. What happened?"

"Oh, hi. I was going to call you when I thought you'd had time to get back to the dorm. I just had too much work to do."

"Can you take a break now and take me to get some things for tomorrow?"

"Well, I still have a lot to do."

She knew he would say that. Always a million excuses. She paused a moment to get up the nerve for her next question. "Marlena's not over there, is she?"

Silence. Naomi panicked, waiting for him to respond.

"Is she?"

"I told you that was a onetime thing, didn't I? I don't want to have to keep going over this."

"Then tell her to stop leaving me these crazy notes."

More silence.

"Did you hear what I just said?" She didn't meant to shout, but these silences were driving her nuts.

"What notes?"

"I had a note from her when I got back to the dorm. She said she's been going with you for five years and I wasn't the first woman you cheated on her with."

Heavy breathing.

"Is it true, damn it?"

"No, it's not."

"Then why is she leaving me these goddamn notes?"

"Good question."

"Tell her to stop this shit."

"I will. Believe me, I will."

"Oh? When do you expect to see her?"

"Uh, I'll have to call her."

"What are you doing calling her if it was a onetime thing?"

He exhaled impatiently through the phone. "Damn it. Didn't you just ask me to tell her to leave you alone? How am I going to do that unless I talk to her?"

"Fine, just fine." This conversation was going nowhere. She was as much in the dark as she had been when she called. "Is Pamela there yet?"

"She just walked in."

"Put her on."

"What for?"

"I need to talk to her about getting supplies for tomorrow."

"Just a minute."

"Hi, Naomi," Pamela said. "What's up?"

"Is that bitch there?"

" 'Scuse me?"

"That woman Marlena."

"Uh, I don't think so."

"Is Ralph still standing around?" Naomi asked, sensing Pamela's evasiveness.

"Yes."

"Is anyone with him?"

"Keith's here."

"And you haven't seen that Marlena?"

"Nope. Why?"

"When I got back to the dorm, I had this crazy note from her saying to stay away from Ralph and she was with him this very minute."

"You're jiving."

"I wish. Have you been upstairs?"

"Not yet."

"When you do, see if she's in his room."

"Can't." Pamela's voice dropped to a whisper. "All the doors are always shut up there. You know that."

"Then open it." Naomi had to giggle at the outrageousness of her own request, but she was dead serious.

"You're out of your mind," Pamela said.

"Pretend you need to ask him something."

"Forget it, Naomi."

"Some kind of friend you are."

"Listen, even friendship has its limits. I'll keep my eyes open, but I'm not about to open any doors in a house full of horny men."

As soon as Naomi hung up, she dialed Ralph's sister, Jennifer. In the middle of her dialing, a woman with waist-length strawberry-blond hair approached and stuck her head in the phone booth. "How long are you going to be?"

"As long as it takes to get my business straightened out."

"Why can't you go use your own phone? This is for our floor."

"Well, excuse me. But I'm paying just as much as you are to live in this dorm, and I'll use any damn phone I please."

The woman backed away, looking at Naomi like she was a mental case. Naomi knew she had gone overboard, but it felt good to let off some steam and she wasn't about to apologize.

Someone on the other end picked up, and she turned her attention back to the phone. "Jennifer, is that you?" she asked. Jennifer had a private room at Cornell with her own phone.

"Naomi! It's good to hear from you. How's it going?"

"Terrible. Your brother is driving me bananas."

"I think that's his hobby, driving women up the wall. What's he done now?"

"That's what I'm trying to find out. Do you know anything about a woman named Marlena Robertson?"

"Oh, no. That's his old girlfriend. Why?"

Naomi took a deep breath as the frustration in her gut boiled to anger. "Why the hell didn't you tell me about her? You're supposed to be my friend."

"I thought she was long gone. He told me they broke up just before he started seeing you."

"Then why is she sending me these threatening notes saying they're still together and to stay away from him?"

"That sounds just like Marlena. I never could stand that chick. She's too possessive. She hated it when he came home during school breaks instead of going to New Orleans with her. And when he was home, she would call all hours of the day and night. They were always breaking up and getting back together because she's so jealous. But Ralph told me years ago they broke up for good. So she's probably lying. Did you ask him about her?"

"I didn't have to. I caught them together."

"You mean fucking?"

"That's exactly what I mean."

"Oh, hell, don't tell me that bitch is back in the picture."

"He tried to tell me some bull about it being a onetime thing with her. You warned me about him. I should have listened to you."

"I don't know what to say. Maybe I've already said too damn much."

"No, I'm glad you told me."

"I'm going to kill that brother of mine when he comes home."

"If he's still alive when I get through with him, be my guest."

As soon as she reached her floor, a woman standing at the phone booth told her she had a call. Naomi walked up and started to take the receiver, then hesitated. She didn't want to talk to Ralph again until after she had some time to think about all this. She hated herself for thinking it, but it was possible that Ralph had been telling her the truth in a way when he said that Saturday afternoon had been a onetime thing. At least it was possible for the recent past. Jennifer said they'd broken up. Maybe Ralph was just having a hard time getting rid of the woman. God knew she seemed persistent enough. Maybe his slipup Saturday afternoon had given Marlena a reason to think they were back together. Breaking up with Ralph could be just what that woman was trying to get Naomi to do.

"Is it a man or a woman?" Naomi asked.

"A woman."

She took the receiver. "Hello?"

"It's me. Pamela."

"Why are you whispering?"

"I did what you asked me to," Pamela said, still speaking softly. "I went in his room. Didn't even knock first. Lord, the things I do for you." –

Naomi closed her eyes and held her breath. "And?"

"Oh, God. I saw the same thing you did that Saturday afternoon."

That night was one of the worst of Naomi's entire life. After chewing Ralph out on the phone, screaming loud enough for everyone on the dorm floor to hear, she was too distressed to go out and get hot chocolate. Instead, she spent the night buried under the bedcovers, pummeling her pillow with her fists. She barely slept a wink, thinking about Ralph all night. Why did he insist on treating her so rotten? People around campus were beginning to look up to her as a leader in the demonstration. Strangers gave her the black power salute. And her boyfriend treated her like shit.

In the time she had to think about him before falling off to sleep in the wee hours of the morning, it was with shame. Shame for all the times she'd taken the bus to meet him at some so-called midpoint so he wouldn't have to drive a few extra miles to pick her up. Shame for all the times she'd let him talk her out of going to a movie or a concert or out to eat because he claimed he had to study. Shame for all the times she'd begged to see him but he was busy. Shame for running over to his place at all hours of the day and night, no matter what she was doing, because he was feeling horny. Shame for wanting him so desperately, she had had no shame for herself.

Those days were over.

Fourteen

When Pamela came to the room the following morning, Naomi had showered, dressed, and arranged all the flyers and posters in a neat pile near the door. But she could barely look her friend in the eye, she felt so humiliated.

"You OK?" Pamela asked, picking up a bunch of the posters.

"I'm fine."

"Whenever you're ready to talk, I'm here."

"Thanks," Naomi said, gathering the flyers. "But I'm going to focus on this for now. It's much more important."

Just as they were about to leave, someone knocked at the door. Naomi opened it to see Walter Johnson standing there with a huge grin on his face. "The chairman of the math department wants to see you."

"Dr. Smith?" Naomi asked.

Walter nodded. "He just sent someone over. He wants both of you to meet him in his office at ten."

"Oh, God," Pamela said, covering her mouth with her hand. "I wasn't expecting this so soon. What will we say to him?"

Naomi shrugged. "Just what we planned. That we want Professor Hill out of here."

Naomi hoped she sounded more convincing than she felt. Now that they had a meeting set with the department head, she was reminded of an old saying: "Be careful what you ask for, you just might get it."

The first thing she did when they reached the lobby was call Dean. But he wasn't in. She walked slowly back toward Pamela. The girl was yakking as usual as they made their way toward Jackson Hall, saying something about what to say to Dr. Smith, but Naomi was having a hard time concentrating. She could hear Pamela's voice, but not the words. Her mind kept drifting back to Dean. Some brother he was turning out to be. Where was he when she needed him so desperately? Why were all the men in her life falling away at this crucial moment? Then she stopped herself. That was selfish. Dean had his own life to live: classes to go to, causes to fight for. Maybe he was even with his girlfriend, assuming he had one.

"Are you listening to me, Naomi?" Pamela said.

"Sorry," Naomi said. "But the crowd is making so much noise, I'm having trouble hearing."

"Let's move over here," Pamela said, indicating a tree some distance from the crowd.

"Are you OK?" Pamela asked.

Naomi sighed. "I'll be fine."

"It's a bad time for you, I know. Are you nervous?"

"A little, maybe."

"I'm scared to death. Probably why I can't stop running my mouth."

"We just have to be firm when we go in there."

"Did you reach Dean?"

"No, unfortunately."

"Where is he?"

"I don't have the faintest idea. We'll be fine without him, though. This is what we wanted, isn't it?"

Pamela nodded forcefully as Naomi looked at her watch. "Guess we'd better go."

They walked toward the administration building in silence. Pamela must have smoked three cigarettes on the way, lighting one from the butt of the last. Naomi imagined Pamela was also wondering what Dr. Smith would have to say to them. What should *she* say to him? She had Ralph to thank for being so out of focus.

Before she had worked anything out in her mind, they were

standing before the dean's secretary, a middle-aged white woman with a head full of silvery hair piled high on her head. "Oh, yes," she said when they introduced themselves. She didn't make any effort to hide her disapproval. Naomi half expected her to shout "Communists!" or something along those lines. Instead, she came around from her desk and walked ahead of them to a room with a dark wooden conference table. Dr. Smith would be there shortly, the woman said, and retreated from the room, shutting the door behind her.

Naomi glanced at Pamela as they stood on opposite sides of the table. Pamela patted her hand rapidly across her chest, indicating the pace of her heartbeat, and Naomi nodded with understanding. As she took in a big gulp of air to calm her frayed nerves, the door swung open and Dr. Smith walked in.

He was small for a man, with a stern face and a pallid complexion. It seemed to Naomi that every time she saw him walking around the math department, he was wearing the same navy suit and blue-and-white necktie. And he was always carrying papers, like the manila folder under his arm now.

"Sit down, ladies," he said, dropping the folder in front of the chair at the head of the table. Naomi and Pamela sat across from each other. Dr. Smith sat and flipped through the folder, pinching his bottom lip with his fingers as he studied one page in particular. Naomi and Pamela exchanged glances. Naomi thought that if she looked as scared as Pamela did at that moment, they would never get through this. Dean had said to try and get the upper hand in the conversation if she ever met with the college officials. Well, here was her chance. Naomi licked her lips and cleared her throat.

"Dr. Smith, it might be a good idea if I start by explaining what the demonstration is all about."

He glanced up at her sharply. "I know what it's about."

"I . . . I thought I could explain our—"

"I don't need you to do that. I've known Dr. Hill for many years. He is one of the math department's finest professors."

"Yes, but—"

"He's extremely dedicated and hardworking. He has helped many students and has been commended by myself and by the previous chairman of this department. Now, in looking over your records, I see that you, Miss Jefferson, are from Washington, D.C., which may go a long way toward explaining your behavior in this." He turned and looked directly at Pamela. "I must say that I'm surprised about you. Being from Georgia, I would think you'd know this is not the way we do things down here."

Yeah, Naomi thought. Down south, you get unhappy about the way things are going, you just shoot our leaders—King, JFK, and God knows how many others. As soon as he looked toward Naomi, Pamela rolled her eyes to the ceiling.

"Nevertheless, I see from your transcripts, Miss Jefferson, that you are obviously a bright young lady; you both are. So I'm hoping you'll listen to reason. You have disrupted the productivity of this department. Students are missing not only the class you attend but others as well. I insist that you call off this nonsense immediately."

Naomi blinked. "I . . . we can't do that."

"What do you mean, you can't do that? You started the whole thing, didn't you? You and Miss . . . Miss . . ."

He gestured with one hand toward Pamela and scratched through his papers with the other. Pamela winced and seemed to shrink in her seat.

"Miss Thompson here," Dr. Smith continued. "Aren't you the ones responsible?"

"What I meant," Naomi said, "is that we don't think we *should* stop it, until . . ."

"Until what?"

"Until you let Professor Hill go," Pamela said forcefully.

Thank goodness! Naomi thought. Pamela seemed to have found her voice.

"That's preposterous. I will not allow a professor of his caliber to be dismissed simply—"

"But you haven't even listened to our reasons yet," Naomi said. "You—"

"Just a minute, young lady. I will not tolerate this. I will not be interrupted when speaking. That's the problem with you young people today. You have absolutely no respect for your elders, for authority figures. All this rioting going on at college campuses across the country, about anything and everything you disagree with."

"Most of it is peaceful," Naomi said. "We're not—"

"You call what happened at Kent State peaceful? They don't call in the National Guard for peaceful demonstrations. In my day, we wouldn't have dreamed of doing anything like that, under any circumstances. And we will not allow it to happen here. Do you understand?"

"We're not—"

"Do not interrupt me, Miss Jefferson. I will not tolerate it!"

Naomi slumped back in her seat. This was going nowhere fast, and she didn't have a clue as to what to do about it.

"I insist you call this demonstration off immediately or face dire consequences. I'm warning you."

"We have to think about—"

"What the devil is there to think about? Are you willing to face expulsion over this? I have the full backing of the administration. If you're thinking of superseding my authority by going over my head, you may as well forget it."

Naomi looked at Pamela, but that was no help. Pamela had the same scared look on her face that was there at the beginning of the meeting. If anything, she looked even more nervous now. "I still say we need time to talk things over among ourselves." Naomi hoped her voice didn't sound as timid as it felt.

He puffed out his chest and set his jaw while thinking for a moment. "You have until tomorrow morning at ten."

"That's not enough time," Naomi blurted out without thinking. As soon as she heard her voice she regretted it. The tone was almost a whine, when she wanted to sound forceful.

"That's all the time I will allow. You have completely disrupted this department, and I will not permit it to go on any longer." With that, he closed his folder firmly, stood up, and stalked off, leaving the two of them seated at the table.

"I can't get kicked out of school," Pamela said. "I could never face my folks. Do you have any idea what they would do to me?"

"We're not going to get kicked out," Naomi said.

The four of them—Naomi, Pamela, Dean, and Walter—were sitting in Naomi's room planning what to do next.

"They'd probably throw me out of the house," Pamela said, smashing her cigarette out in an ashtray. "I was pitiful in there. And Dr. Smith was so damn stubborn."

Naomi leaned up and rested her elbows on her knees. "We'll do better tomorrow."

"You were much better than me. I mean, I freaked out."

Dean sighed and sat next to Naomi. "At least you didn't give in to him. Sorry I wasn't around."

Naomi noticed he didn't volunteer information on his whereabouts. But it was none of her business.

"I wish I could take you in there with us tomorrow," Pamela said.

"I'm not a student here," Dean said.

"I could go with you," Walter said.

"Yeah." Pamela grabbed his arm. "Maybe he won't talk down to a man."

"If anything, he may be harder on us if I go. Black men aren't exactly popular in situations like this."

"He couldn't possibly be any tougher than he was today," Naomi said. "You should come."

"I'm in, then," Walter said. He pushed his glasses up his nose. "Now just what are we going to tell him?"

Naomi jumped up and paced the floor. "We're not backing down on our demand that they get rid of him."

"But what if he follows through on his threat to expel us?" Pamela asked.

"I'm worried about that," Dean said. "Maybe you can work out a deal. What if they reprimand Professor Hill and promise to keep an eye on him? In exchange for you negotiating down on your demands, they would have to guarantee no repercussions for you or any of the demonstrators."

Naomi shook her head forcefully. "No, no, no. He was so bullheaded, he just made me more determined."

"Damn it, Naomi," Pamela said. "What's wrong with a compromise? At least it's something. We need to resolve this soon. We're already behind in our classes, and if we don't get back soon, we'll never catch up."

"That would be fine if they'd follow through and make sure he stops making racist comments. But I don't see him stopping *or* them following through. After meeting with Dr. Smith this morning, I don't trust him one bit. They'll say anything just to get us to stop."

"Naomi's right," Walter said. "He'd still be a racist through and through. He'd probably stop making racist cracks for a while and then go right back to it."

"Well, I don't see Dr. Smith firing Professor Hill," Pamela said. "I see him kicking our butts out and saying to hell with us."

Naomi stopped pacing and faced Pamela. "Why are you getting cold feet all of a sudden? We said we'd go down to the wire."

Pamela stood and glared at Naomi. "Excuse me? I don't remember saying any such thing."

"We're not settling for anything short of getting that man out of here," Naomi said.

"Maybe we could agree to letting Professor Hill resign," Walter said.

Naomi sat down. "That's an idea."

Dean nodded. "That will be harder, but the very fact that Dr. Smith called you into his office means they're worried."

"Please explain something to me," Pamela said, placing her hand on her hip with exasperation. "What difference are they going to see between letting him resign and sacking him?"

"They might be more willing to go along with letting him quit because it wouldn't tarnish his record," Dean said. "You'll probably have to agree to nothing being put in his record about why he resigned."

"I don't like the idea of nothing going in his record," Naomi said. "But I could live with it."

"Then it's settled," Walter said. He removed a notepad from among his books and placed it on his lap.

"Not quite," Dean said. "You have to decide at what point to lower your demands. Do you go right in with the idea of his resignation or do you try to get them to fire him first?"

"I think we should go in with the original demand for them to fire him," Naomi said.

"Oh, brother," Pamela said.

"Then if he doesn't agree . . ."

"You mean *when* he doesn't," Pamela said.

". . . we bring up the idea of letting him resign."

"Provided he doesn't expel us first," Pamela said.

Naomi continued to ignore her. "What do you think, Walter?"

"Sounds good to me. I doubt he'll expel us right off the bat without trying to do a little convincing first."

The intercom buzzed and all eyes turned toward Naomi. The first thing that came to her mind was that it could be Ralph, and her stomach turned to jelly. She'd been busy enough with the demonstration to put all thoughts of him out of her mind. The buzzer was bringing back all the painful, disgusting memories of him with that woman.

The intercom sounded again, and she snapped out of her reverie to see everyone staring at her strangely, especially Pamela. She stood and turned away from them. It might not even be for her. Could be for Kathy. For the first time in all the arguments she'd had with Ralph, Naomi really didn't want it to be him. She pressed the button on the intercom. "Yes?"

"Naomi?" asked the voice on the other end.

She blinked. "Yes?"

"You have a visitor in the lobby."

She frowned, trying to think what to do. Under no circumstances did she want to see Ralph now. "Is it a man or a woman?"

"A man."

"Can you find out who it is?"

"Just a minute."

A second later. "Said his name's Ralph."

Naomi could feel her blood begin to boil. If he was planning to try to sweet-talk his way of out a jam again, it was an insult to her intelligence, not to mention her feelings.

"Tell him to get lost," she said, practically spitting the words out of her mouth.

"Are you serious?" asked the voice on the intercom.

"Is the sky blue? No, wait," she said, after giving it some thought. "I'll come down and tell him myself."

"I don't believe that man's gall," Pamela said as Naomi jammed her feet into her shoes.

"What's going on?" Dean asked. "Sounds like Ralph's in the doghouse."

Naomi didn't say anything. She was too angry to speak without shouting.

"Do you want us to come back later?" Dean asked.

"No," Naomi said. "I'll only be a minute."

She ran down the stairs and into the lobby and looked around until she spotted him standing near the doorway. She clenched her fists and marched in his direction. He started toward her, but stopped when he saw the look in her eyes. His glance dropped quickly to his feet. Probably trying to hide the embarrassed expression that had crossed his face, Naomi thought. It was a look she would never forget: guilty, guilty, guilty.

She marched up to him and pointed toward the door. "You can just get the hell out of here and out of my life. Forever." She was attracting the attention of everyone else in the lobby, but she didn't care.

"Look," he said. "Can we go up to your room to talk?"

"I have company."

"Then we should go outside."

"I don't have time for this—here, upstairs, outside, anywhere."

"It will only take a minute, and the way you're shouting is—"

"Who the hell cares? I could give you a lifetime to explain this and it wouldn't do you a bit of good, 'cause it's not just about you and that woman. You don't care about me or anything that interests me. You never did. All you ever do is take, take, take. Well, I'm fucking tired of giving."

He shoved his hands in the pockets of his leather coat.

"And I have more important things to do with my life right now than listen to your lame excuses."

"So I hear."

"You may think it's a waste of time, but I happen to be proud of what I'm doing about these racist professors around here."

"Have you thought about the risks involved? Word is going around that you could be expelled."

"Don't you think I know that?"

"You're willing to risk your education for this? That's crazy."

Who the hell was he to talk about taking risks? He was willing to risk their relationship for that woman and God knew how many others. Naomi had never before felt the urge to slap anyone, but at that moment it was taking every ounce of will-power she could muster to keep her hand from flying through the air and landing flat on his cheek. The face that once seemed so irresistible now made her feel nothing but shame. "What about you fooling around? You were willing to take a chance with our relationship for that. Do I mean so little to you?"

He frowned with bewilderment and shook his head slowly. "I . . . you can't compare . . . That's not the same."

"Then you admit you screwed up royally. Well, that's progress."

"Naomi, I . . ." He threw his hands up in the air.

"Unfortunately for you, it's too late."

"You want me out of your life? Fine, I'm gone, for fucking good." With that he walked out the door. Naomi was at first startled that he left so abruptly, then angry because she felt cheated once again. She should have been the one to stalk off, not him. Then she realized why he'd done it and felt better, re-lieved even. He knew she could no longer be jerked about like some puppet on a string. She had feelings and thoughts just like he did. And they needed to be acknowledged just like his. But she couldn't blame him entirely for being slow to realize that. He had had a lot of help from her. Well, no longer.

She walked up to the glass door and watched as he strolled across the courtyard, his hands shoved inside his pockets, his head bent down. Goodbye, Ralph.

It was almost midnight by the time Pamela and the others left the room and Naomi pulled the bedcovers up over her shoulders. Walter was proving to be a big help, coming up with all sorts of ideas. But Pamela was another story. Naomi didn't think she would hold up if things got rough tomorrow. For all her tough talk, the girl was running scared.

Well, not her. Just about every time Dr. Smith opened his mouth, Naomi felt her blood get hotter. It was as if she was back in their old Buick being called a stupid nigger or being turned away from the Chinese restaurant. The disguise had gotten cleverer over the years but it was the same old ogre underneath, and it pissed her off just as much today as it did then. The difference was that now she was fighting back.

It felt as though running into that racist professor was fate, that she was being tested: the new Naomi versus the old. The old one would have complained but taken no action. The new one welcomed the challenge. This kind of thing was tailor-made for Joshua, but he wasn't around, so it was up to her to see it through. Her brother would approve, and knowing that made her feel stronger. It was as if he was the wind beneath her wings, guiding her, encouraging her, cheering her on. She hadn't clenched her teeth since this began.

She was risking a lot, she knew. If she was kicked out of school, it would be a big disappointment, not only to her but to her parents, especially now that Joshua was gone. They expected her to make good on an education, and she wouldn't disappoint them; there were other schools. It might be hard to find one that would admit her if she were expelled, but not impossible. She wasn't so sure she wanted to come back to Atlanta Tech next semester anyway, even if she wasn't kicked out. Now that she and Ralph were through and she'd seen the ugly side of these ivy-covered halls, she couldn't think of a single redeeming quality about the place.

Amazing how life changed so quickly. Here she was confronting expulsion from college and life with no boyfriend or prospects for a replacement. And she was facing it all alone. Joshua was dead, and her parents were hundreds of miles away. She might have memories of their words and deeds but she no longer had them around in person to tell her what to do every step along the way. She could very well fall flat on her face.

It was hard to believe that a few years ago, her biggest worries were facing up to a bully and having sex with her boyfriend. It was even harder to think that as little as a few weeks back, all she cared about was holding on to Ralph and getting through college by the shortest route possible. And that she longed for the carefree, painless days of ballet class, high school parties, and sweet boys like Merlon. Well, not anymore. She was a woman now. She didn't have time for that other crap.

Fifteen

Judging from Dr. Smith's demeanor when he entered the conference room, Naomi figured he was ready to do battle too. He walked in and went straight to the head of the table without so much as acknowledging the three of them, and his stack of papers had grown taller. She and Pamela exchanged looks from across the table, but Naomi quickly looked away. Naomi didn't want any of Pamela's obvious uneasiness to rub off on her. Walter, sitting next to Naomi, opened his pad to the notes he had taken the night before.

Just as Dr. Smith reached for his chair, he noticed the newcomer. He paused, hand in midair, and fixed Walter with a vicious stare. "Who is this?" he barked.

Walter pushed his glasses up on his nose and stood up. "Walter Johnson. I'm also in Professor Hill's class."

Dr. Smith grunted and shook his head. "You were not involved in our meeting yesterday."

"No," Walter said, "but I've been involved with this problem almost from the beginning."

"I asked him to come today," Naomi said calmly. She was not going to let this man rattle her.

"Well, I'm sorry, but he'll have to go. I met with only two of you yesterday, and we're not changing the framework at this point."

"I don't see why," Naomi said.

"I'm not changing my mind on this," Dr. Smith said, sitting

195

firmly in his seat. "I will meet with only two of you. You decide which two that will be."

The three of them looked at one another. It was going to be a long morning. Walter picked up his notepad and pen, but Pamela quickly stood up. "I'll go," she said. Everyone looked at her with surprise, including Dr. Smith.

"Are you sure?" Naomi asked.

Pamela nodded, already halfway to the door. "You stay, Walter, since you have all the notes and everything. I'll wait outside." She left, and Walter leaned back in his chair.

"What was your name again, young man?" Dr. Smith asked, fixing him with a grave stare as he picked up a pen.

Walter cleared his throat. "Johnson, Walter Johnson."

"Now," Dr. Smith said, placing his pen back down on the table after writing down Walter's name. He looked at Naomi. "Have you given much thought to what we discussed yesterday?"

Naomi nodded.

"And?"

"And we don't feel we can call off the demonstrations yet."

Dr. Smith was speechless. Naomi suddenly realized he had expected them to back down.

"We—uh, we still feel Professor Hill should be let go." She paused. She had to get hold of herself, she thought. She had to sound more forceful. "In fact, we're sure," she added. "We don't think we should have to take classes from someone who constantly makes racist and sexist comments. It's demeaning and counterproductive."

Dr. Smith sat silently for a moment, rubbing his chin with his hand. "Do you know the meaning of free speech, young lady?"

"Of course I do," Naomi said. "But—"

"Let me finish," Dr. Smith said. "I'm not saying that Professor Hill ever made these comments, but supposing he had. This is an academic institution. Nowhere is the right to free speech more important than it is here. We must be free to express our thoughts and ideas without the threat of censorship."

"But with that right also comes responsibility," Walter said.

"And how can students be expected to learn in an environment that is hostile to them?" Naomi asked. "Professor Hill is not criticizing our ideas or thoughts. He's criticizing *us*. There's a difference."

"He's expressing an opinion," Dr. Smith said. "And he has every right to do that, just as you have the right to challenge those opinions."

"This is a statistics class," Walter said, "not a social studies class."

"I understand that, so I've spoken to Dr. Hill and told him to stick to statistics in the future."

"Did he admit to making the comments?" Naomi asked.

"He admits to discussing the concept of the right and left sides of the brain, but he insists there was no racial or sexist connotation and any belief that there was is a misunderstanding."

"Are you saying all the students out demonstrating are mistaken?" Walter asked.

"I'm saying a few students misunderstood him and the rest are probably just going along. Why, half the students out there are not even in any of his classes."

"That's not the point," Naomi said, losing her cool. She was tired of holding back and trying to be respectful when he wasn't. "We shouldn't have to put up with him any longer. We want him out of here."

"Listen, young lady," Dr. Smith said, shaking his finger at her. "What you're asking for is out of the question. I've gone over this matter in depth with President Delaney, and he and I have come to an agreement. Either you call this off and get back to your classes, or we will expel you and everyone else out there. Is that understood?"

Naomi was stunned. She gasped out loud. She had expected him to threaten to expel the three of them. But all the others too? Why, there must be two hundred students out there! The idea that a bunch of white men in positions of power could so casually and ruthlessly decide their fates burned her up. The administration hadn't heard a thing they'd been saying, even though they'd been shouting at the top of their lungs. Maybe they needed to shout louder, if such a thing was possible. She still found it hard to believe she couldn't make them understand how frustrating a professor like Dr. Hill was to them. She was tempted to ask Dr. Smith what he would do if one of the few black professors at Atlanta Tech insinuated that the whites in his class were too ignorant to learn. But that would probably just make him more defensive. Instead, she'd try compromise.

"We're willing to consider other options in dealing with Professor Hill."

He closed his folder so fast the papers in it blew out and scattered across the table. Naomi jumped in her seat.

"I don't care to hear about 'other options.' Who are you to give me options?" He pointed a finger at her. "I warned you about this yesterday."

There was that finger again. She wanted to slap it back into his white face. "You could at least listen—"

"I have no intention of wasting any more of my time. Either call it off or get off this campus, every one of you."

Naomi sat back in her seat and set her lips firmly. It was no use, she thought.

"What about disciplining Dr. Hill?" Walter asked. "Suspending him for a semester or something of that nature?"

Naomi noticed that Walter had already skipped over the idea of getting the professor to resign instead of firing him and had moved to the least severe option they had agreed to the night before. Naomi now thought even that was a waste of time. Dr. Smith wasn't going to agree to any of their ideas, because he didn't care whether they stayed and got an education or not. To Dr. Smith and the others, they were a bunch of expendable nuisances. They were so far apart in the way they saw this, she would never be able to make him understand.

"Out of the question," Dr. Smith said. "This meeting is over. Finished." He stood and gathered his papers.

Walter was about to say something, but Naomi tugged at his sleeve. When Walter looked at her, she closed her eyes and shook her head.

"If those students haven't dispersed by the end of the day, you will both be expelled. And I'll send someone out there tomorrow morning to tell the students they face similar consequences if they don't get back to their classes immediately." He walked from the room, and Naomi and Walter exhaled at the same time.

"That was a major disappointment," Walter said. "I've never felt so damn powerless in my life."

Naomi nodded, and they sat in silence for a moment.

"What do you want to do?" Walter finally asked. "I'm with you, whatever you decide. If you want to go on with it, I'm there. To hell with this stinking place."

"No, Walter. His threat to expel everybody puts a different spin on things. We'll have to tell them what happened and let them decide."

"What do you think they'll do?"

"If they're smart, they'll go back to their classes. We're a bunch of nobodies."

It was one of the hardest things she'd ever had to do, standing before that crowd with a bullhorn and raising her voice to tell them something that wasn't in her heart. But it would be even harder to be responsible for their being expelled. Jeopardizing her own education was one thing; encouraging others to put theirs on the line was another.

When she told them they would be expelled if they didn't return to their classes by the next day, many of them booed and shouted that they wanted to continue anyway. But Naomi told them the chances of getting what they wanted didn't look good and urged them to break up. She agreed to back them up if at least fifty students showed up the next morning but encouraged them to think of other less risky ways to make their voices heard.

"We may not have gotten what we wanted today," she said through the bullhorn. She was so disappointed, it took every ounce of energy she could muster to raise her voice so they could hear her. "But I think we made a dent in their resistance. And we must continue to make our voices heard in small ways to keep wearing them down. Speak up when you don't like what's being said in classes. Write letters. Call the administration and bug them. Think of other ways to fight, but don't jeopardize your education."

Naomi, Pamela, Dean, and Walter stood together and watched in silence as the crowd broke up.

"Do you think any of them will come back tomorrow?" Walter asked.

Naomi shook her head. "Maybe a few, but not enough to go on."

"Feels like we're fighting a forest fire with a backyard hose, doesn't it?" Dean asked.

Naomi nodded. "I've certainly learned my lesson."

Walter exhaled deeply. "Well, I'm off. Got to hit the books."

"Don't we all," Pamela said. "Thanks for your help, Walter."

"Yeah," Naomi said. "Thanks for everything."

Walter shrugged. "Don't have to thank me. It became my cause as much as yours." He kissed them both, slapped Dean with a high five, and took off.

"I need to get moving too," Dean said.

"I don't know about you two," Naomi said, "but it's going to be hard for me to get back into the old routine."

"Not when you return to your classes and realize how far behind you are," Pamela said. "That should get you going."

"Now that this is over," Dean said, "it should make Sonya happy."

Naomi and Pamela exchanged looks. "Your girlfriend?" Pamela asked.

Dean nodded. "She hasn't liked all the time I've been spending over here."

So he *was* seeing someone, Naomi thought. It figured. Everyone had somebody to go back to except her. She had only her books. But when Naomi sat alone at her desk later that afternoon, all she could do was stare at them. Even if she hadn't broken up with Ralph, he would be absolutely no comfort to her now. He didn't really understand her, and she had to admit that wasn't entirely his fault. She'd changed so much since they first met. So had the world around her.

Her hand went to her forehead and she realized she was clenching her teeth. This was not the way it was supposed to play out. She was going to finish college and marry the doctor and live in the big house on the Gold Coast and run the little boutique. Then, when all that fell apart, she was going to make a difference by making Atlanta Tech a better place for black students. Every time she seemed to get a handle on life, it was wrenched from her grasp. If she was being tested, she was failing miserably. She folded her arms on the desk and buried her head.

The last week of the term, Dean walked Naomi to her dorm.

"There's still some things you can do when you get back next semester if you want to keep this alive," he said. "Like organizing a letter-writing campaign."

Naomi shook her head vigorously. "Forget it. I won't be coming back next semester."

"What are you talking about?"

"Things haven't turned out the way I expected them to. Not by a long shot."

"So what? That's true for all of us. You can't just throw your hands up and give in when things get rough."

"Why can't I? I know when I'm licked. I hate this feeling of going up against them and losing totally. We got nothing. Nothing. We went through all this trouble, and for what? They just do whatever the hell they want anyway. This kind of thing might work for you and for Joshua, but not for me. I need to get out of here."

Dean stopped walking and stared at her. "You mean leave Atlanta altogether?"

"Yes," she said, walking on ahead.

"Fuck, Naomi. I can't believe you want to just give up and take off."

The sharp tone in his voice made her stop. She tried to calm herself. But she felt so rotten about this place, it wasn't easy. She looked down at her feet.

He walked up to her. "Have you thought of trying one of the black schools, like Spelman?"

She shook her head. "It's not just racist professors. I need to get away from all of it—school, this city." The ex-boyfriend. The lost dreams.

"Where are you going to go, a convent?"

Naomi smiled wryly. "Very funny, but I'm not in the mood for jokes, OK? I'm just going back to D.C., until I figure out what the hell to do next."

He exhaled deeply, and they walked again.

"I think you're going about this all wrong," he said. "But I'm the last one to knock needing a break from the rat race. I took a year and a half off."

"I can't take that much time. Maybe a semester. My parents would never go for more than that."

When they reached Woodruff Hall and Naomi turned to face him, it suddenly occurred to her that he would be finishing up next year. "Are you going to hang around Atlanta after you graduate?"

"Maybe. If I get a full-time job at the organization where I'm doing part-time work now."

Naomi blinked. She didn't even know Dean had a job. "Where do you work?"

"With a group that does research on Africa. Right now, I'm just a research assistant. But I hope to get something better after I graduate."

Naomi realized that she knew very little about Dean. She'd only found out about his girlfriend at the end of the demonstration, and now his job. It was her own fault. Their brief friendship had been one-sided. She let him take care of her but gave little in return. She didn't know a thing about his likes and dislikes, dreams and ambitions. She was so consumed with her own problems, she hadn't thought to ask about his, or consider whether he even had any. That was silly; of course Dean had problems. Everybody did.

"Do you want to come up for a while?" It would give them a chance to talk, she thought. And give her a chance to learn more about him.

"I'll pass."

She couldn't blame him for turning her down. She wasn't

much fun to be around right now. "Dean, I didn't mean to snap at you back there. This place has got me on edge."

"Don't even think about it."

"I mean it," she said. "I'm sorry. You've been a big help to me here. I'm going to miss you. We were just starting to get to know each other."

"To my way of thinking, we hadn't even begun." He took her hands into his and kissed her—on the nose. For a moment Naomi thought the kiss was going to land on her lips, and her stomach flipped. She was slightly disappointed when it didn't, which surprised her.

"Thanks for the invite," he said, letting her go. "Maybe another time before you leave."

"Are you planning to spend any time in D.C. during Christmas?"

"A few days; then I'm off to Birmingham to visit Sonya and her family. She's going through a rough period. Her grandfather died a few days ago, and she was real close to him."

Naomi shoved her hands into the front pockets of her pea jacket. "I see. Sorry to hear that."

What she was really sorry about was that he was only planning to spend a short time in Washington. As she watched him skip back down the stairs, she found herself wondering what it would be like to have Dean hold you in his arms and comfort you when you were feeling the blues. Or any time. Lucky girl, that Sonya.

Sixteen

Naomi felt like a stranger in her old bedroom. At first, she had always thought it was because her mother kept the room so neat. All the clothes she'd left behind were put away in the closet and drawers, her stuffed dolls were perched prettily on the bed, and her old Jackson Five and Supremes records were stacked on a shelf. The white dresser and desk were clean of the clutter of jewelry and toiletries and papers and books that she once kept there. Now she realized it felt so foreign because the woman using this room was a stranger to the girl who had lived here all those years before. The girl had dreams, hopes, and ambitions. The woman had none of those things.

She removed a framed photo of her brother from her trunk and placed it on top of the dresser. His absence from the house felt different now, too, and she realized with sadness that was because it felt normal. Before she left for college, there were often moments when, beyond reason, she expected Joshua to walk through her bedroom door and call out her name. She no longer had those moments and often had to struggle just to remember the sound of his voice or the way his eyes had sparkled when he teased her. She wished so badly that she could talk to him now. Where did he find the strength to fight even when he knew there was almost no chance of winning?

She stared at the photo. What do I do now, Joshua? What am I supposed to do with my life? Studying communications wasn't the answer. If she thought she had a good chance of becoming a television broadcaster or an editor at a major news-paper, it might excite her. But as a black woman, she would face too many barriers along the way. Who would put her face on television? Even if she could land a job, she would have to prove herself again and again to whites who would doubt her ability simply because of the color of her skin, not to mention her sex. She would have to spend as much time and effort fighting everybody as she would learning the field.

She closed the lid on her trunk and pushed it into a corner. Then she took a deep breath and headed downstairs to help her parents decorate the Christmas tree, an annual family ritual. Their first Christmas without Joshua had been rough. He'd only been gone a few months, and they didn't even buy a tree. They just stuck a small artificial one on top of a table. Now they were back to real trees, and each year it seemed they picked a bigger one. This year's tree almost touched the ceiling, and the scent of pine filled her nose as she made her way down the stairs.

Daddy smiled when he saw her. He was sitting on the living room sofa with a big box of tree lights at his feet.

"Come help me with this, will you?" he said. "Phyllis is giving me a hard time for taking so long getting them untangled."

"He does the same thing every year," Mama said, sorting through the Christmas balls. "Throws them back in the box, instead of packing them neatly. Then the next year he wonders why it takes so long to straighten them out."

Naomi smiled. She felt better already, just being around her folks. They were the only constant in her life, the only thing she could always count on. They weren't thrilled that she had decided to take some time off from school, but they had been surprisingly calm when she phoned home and told them the previous week. Naomi had expected a protest, and at first she got exactly that until they realized her mind was made up. Nothing had been said about it on the drive from the airport that morning, although she knew they had a million questions.

She sat on the floor in front of her father, grabbed a bunch of lights from the box, and held them up. They were so snarled she couldn't see where they began or ended. "Daddy, we'll never get these untangled."

"We will if you stop complaining and get to work," he said.

He stood and held up a line he'd just straightened out. "There, you see?" he said triumphantly, as he handed it to Mama. She began to wrap it around the tree while Daddy sat down again and picked up another bunch.

"Well, let's have it," he said, as he sat back down.

"Have what?" Naomi asked innocently, although she was pretty sure what he was getting at.

"What are you planning to do with yourself?"

She cleared her throat. "I think I'm going to try to find a job. Just until I figure out what I want to study in school."

Her folks gave each other the look that Naomi had long since learned meant proceed with caution.

"A job doing what?" Mama asked.

"Good question," Naomi said. "Maybe something in publishing. I took some journalism classes, and I was always good at writing."

"It's going to be hard to find something without any experience," Daddy said.

"Or much of an education," Mama said.

"I know that. But I'm not sure what I want to do yet, and it would be foolish to waste time studying something for four years only to find out it's not what I want."

Mama sighed. "When do you think you'll figure it out?"

Naomi shrugged. "Sooner or later."

"Sooner," Daddy said, setting his lips firmly.

Naomi smiled. "Probably."

"Probably, nothing," Mama said. "I don't even like to hear you talking like that. If you want to live in this house, you have to go to college. And soon."

Daddy frowned at Mama and then looked at Naomi, as if to say her mother wasn't really serious about kicking her out if she didn't go back to college. But Naomi wasn't so sure.

"You don't realize how lucky you are to have parents who can afford to send you to college without you having to work," Daddy said. "Your mother and I both had to work our way through; even now, most black children going to school have to work or get a scholarship. It's silly for you to let this opportunity slip by."

"I'm not so gung-ho on the college thing anymore." She waited for the bomb she'd just dropped to land.

"What are you talking about?" Mama said.

"I don't see the big deal about college. I mean, why waste all that time and money when whites aren't going to give you a decent job anyway?"

"That's the silliest thing I ever heard," Mama said.

"It's not so silly. You said yourself that you had to become a teacher and Daddy had to work for the government because those were the only jobs you could get."

"So? We still did it. And things are different now. You have many more choices."

"We still go to college and come out and make half the money whites do. They'll never treat us as equals, so why bother?"

"That just means you have to work harder," Mama said.

"But why should I have to work twice as hard for half the reward?"

"Because that's how it is," Mama said.

Some reason, Naomi thought.

"What exactly happened down there at school?" Daddy asked.

"We protested against this white professor. Some of the things he said in class were unbelievable. Like blacks are stupid at math because their brains develop differently."

Daddy shook his head. "He had no business saying something like that."

"Well, he said it. And most of them think like that."

Mama sighed. "That's not true, Naomi. And even if it was, that's no reason not to try to get ahead."

"That's just a reason to try harder," Daddy said.

"Why? So they can just keep kicking you in the face?"

"You're going to come up against this kind of thing all your life, Naomi," Daddy said. "You'd better learn to handle it."

*   *   *

None of the local newspapers were looking for writers with no experience or degree, so Naomi turned to magazines. The first two she called told her they weren't interested, and she realized she was going to have to lower her sights. She hung up the phone and put on Carole King's *Tapestry* album. The newspaper listed dozens of jobs for typists and clerk-typists. That was not the kind of work she wanted, but hey, she wasn't exactly a Harvard graduate. The key, she supposed, was finding a typing job in a field that interested her. She scanned the ads for jobs as clerk-typist or receptionist, and by the end of the day she had set up four interviews. Three were in publishing and one was with the general counsel of the D.C. city council.

She was surprised when she got two offers, one from a small newsletter on politics and the other from the city council. She reasoned that the chance to work in politics and experience the day-to-day happenings in the flesh might never come up again. And she'd been surprised and happy to discover when she went on the interview that the lawyer for the council was a black woman. She accepted the offer, and they asked her to report to the District Building the following week.

She hadn't been this excited about anything for as long as she could remember. As soon as she hung up the phone, she picked it up again, dialed information, and asked for Dean's home number. She wanted to share the good news with him.

"Hello?" she said when someone picked up at his house. "May I speak to Dean, please?"

"He's not here. May I ask who's calling? This is his mother."

"Oh, hi, Mrs. Davis. This is Naomi Jefferson."

"Hi, how are you?"

"Fine. Is Dean still in Atlanta?"

"No. He was home for a couple of days, then left to go to Birmingham."

Birmingham. Sonya. Of course. "Would you tell him I called, please?"

"He said he was going straight back to Atlanta from Birmingham."

"Oh. Maybe I'll call him down there then. Thanks."

It was disappointing not to be able to reach Dean, and even

more so to realize he'd come home and didn't bother to call her. But she wasn't going to let anything spoil her good mood. She put on a Sly album and danced around the room until her eyes caught her reflection in the mirror hanging over the dresser. What she saw was a wild Afro, faded blue jeans, and a tattered sweatshirt. When she interviewed at the D.C. council office wearing one of the few skirts she still had, she noticed that most of the women were dressed in smart knit suits. She wondered how she ever got the job offer looking so corny.

She ran to her closet and threw the door open. Other than what she'd worn on the interview and a couple of dresses, she really had nothing appropriate for an office job. She had to update her look, and she had to do it fast. Jeans and dashikis were fine for college, but for the office she needed something more businesslike. And although she didn't want to give up her Afro, it could use a good trim. All that would take money. Time to go to the bank.

"What's wrong with the clothes you already have?" Mama asked when Naomi bombarded her as soon as she walked in the door from work.

"Ma, please. You want me to wear those rags to the District Building? I mean, I'll be working with the chairman of the D.C. city council. Do you know what that means? I'll be at the pinnacle of power."

Mama rolled her eyes to the ceiling but couldn't resist smiling. "Naomi, why do you have to exaggerate so?" She went to her purse and took out a twenty.

"This is enough for shoes," Naomi said. "Now I need something for a dress or two."

"Can't you make something? That's cheaper."

"I *will* make some things. But I start work on Monday. Can't make much by then. I need a whole new wardrobe."

Mama sighed and gave her another twenty. "If you need more than that, ask your father when he gets home. That's all I can spare for now. We have a contractor coming in to look at the roof tomorrow."

"Can I borrow your car tonight?"

Mama frowned. "What for?"

"To go shopping."

"Fine. But don't go alone in the dark."

"That doesn't bother me."

"Why don't you call Debbie? Or Jennifer. Is she still home from school?"

"Maybe. I'll see." She ran upstairs to put the money with what she'd saved from her allowance.

A couple of hours later, as he slowly took out his money clip, Daddy asked, "What about all those dresses you left behind in the closet when you went away to college?"

"You mean the ones I wore in high school? Daddy, please. Let's not be funny."

"What about your allowance?"

"I used that for Christmas presents. And I'm going to get my hair trimmed."

"In that case"—he quickly peeled off two twenties and held them out—"that enough?" he asked.

"For now," she said, grabbing them from his hand before he could change his mind. "Thanks, Pops."

She went to her bedroom and put on a clean sweatshirt to go shopping. It would be nice to have some company, but calling Jennifer was out of the question. Ralph might be home and could even answer the phone. She wasn't in the mood to hear either his voice or Jennifer's "I told you so." So she dialed Debbie's number. They had drifted even further apart over the past year and a half, although they usually talked on the phone whenever Naomi came home from Atlanta. It would be good to see her.

Debbie answered on the first ring.

"Hey, girl. It's Naomi."

"Nay! Are you home?"

"Yep. I have so much to tell you about school and all. Want to go out to Wheaton Plaza with me?"

"Oh, I wish I could. But I don't have a dime to my name."

"You don't need any money. And I'll treat you to a movie afterward. Have you seen *The French Connection*?"

"No, and I'm dying to. I guess Ma can watch Serena for a

couple of hours. Hell, yeah, why not? It's so rare I get out to have some fun these days."

"Solid. I'll pick you up in an hour."

Naomi spent a few minutes talking to Debbie's mother and visiting with Serena, then she and Debbie climbed into the new family Buick.

"Serena's gotten so big," Naomi said. "How old is she now?"

Debbie beamed. "Three. And she's a handful. I don't know how I'd make it without Ma's help."

"She seems to be tickled to death with Serena."

"Ma adores her."

Naomi smiled. "So things worked out OK for you."

Debbie twisted her mouth. "We're managing, although just barely. It was really awful when I first got pregnant. I thought my life was over. So did Ma. And the first months after she was born were almost impossible, with Ma having to go to work and me still in school. That was the hardest time of my life."

Naomi felt a pang of guilt cross her stomach as memories of that time came flooding back. Naomi knew even then, of course, that Debbie was having a hard time, but she'd been so absorbed with Ralph she hadn't felt she had anything left to give to Debbie. And Debbie's life after she got pregnant was so alien to anything going on in her own that Naomi hadn't been sure she would fit in with Debbie anymore. All that seemed so silly and selfish now. Everyone's life had tough spots, and she should have been there for Debbie.

"Sounds rough," Naomi said.

"We're finally getting the hang of it, though, and it's fun watching Serena grow and learn. Only thing is, I'm always tired these days, since I work three nights a week at Sears." Debbie removed her eyeglasses and rubbed her eyes.

"What happened to your contacts?"

"Oh, please. I lost one and didn't have the money to replace it. The baby takes all my money. I've been back to wearing glasses for over a year now. Only good thing is that this job has made me even more determined to go back to school. No way I'm doing this the rest of my life."

"I always thought it would be such a waste if you didn't, 'cause you're so damn smart. Have you applied anywhere yet?"

"Yeah, everywhere around here. Howard, George Washington, Georgetown, American U."

"You'll be accepted at all of them. If you're good enough for Cornell and Columbia, you're good enough for them."

"Yeah, but that was before. My grades slipped after I got pregnant, and I've been out of school going on two years now. When I have interviews, all of them want to know why, and I have to tell them I had a baby. None of these schools are exactly dying to get some poor black girl who's got a kid of her own. And I have to get a scholarship because we can't afford tuition."

"You're just looking at the last couple of years, Debbie. What about all those other years when you were practically a straight-A student? I know you'll be accepted somewhere."

Debbie smiled. "Keep your fingers crossed for me."

"I will."

Debbie let out a big yawn and leaned her head back. She looked so tired that Naomi was unsure whether to talk or just let her rest. It seemed petty to bring up her disenchantment with the whole college scene when Debbie was struggling just to get enrolled. A long moment of silence passed between them as Naomi tried to think of a safe subject to bring up.

"So," Naomi finally said. "Any new men in your life?"

Debbie laughed bitterly. "Are you joking? It's almost impossible to meet dudes when you have a baby and never get to go anywhere."

Naomi nodded. So much for safe subjects. "Does Gene ever spend time with Serena?"

"He comes around once in a while. But it's hard since we don't get along anymore. Every time we see each other, we end up arguing 'cause he wants to take her somewhere, and I don't trust that sucker for nothing. Most of the time he's not working, doesn't go to school. What did I ever see in that bum?"

Naomi shrugged. "What did either of us see in those high school dudes? Remember Merlon and that red hair?"

"Did you hear about him? He got in with this bad crowd and was into drugs and drinking."

"You're kidding! How did that happen?"

"I don't think it was anything serious, because he got drafted, and they wouldn't have taken him if he was an addict or anything like that."

"Merlon got drafted? I can't believe it. Is he in Vietnam?"

"I think so."

"God, I hope he's OK."

"I just wish they'd end this stupid war," Debbie said. "All our men are getting killed."

"That Nixon gets on my nerves. He keeps saying he's going to pull out, but I don't see it happening."

"Are they demonstrating against it at your school?"

Naomi shook her head. "Not against the war but against other things." Since Debbie asked for more details, Naomi told her about the protest she'd organized at Atlanta Tech.

"That sounds so exciting," Debbie said.

"Not to me. I was upset about the whole thing."

"When is Christmas break over?"

"It was over last week. But I'm not going back."

Debbie sat up and turned to look at Naomi. For the first time that evening, her big eyes didn't look sleepy. "What?"

"I'm taking a break."

"For how long?"

"Who knows. I'll have to see."

"Damn. Not going back to school? That doesn't sound like you, Naomi."

Naomi shrugged. "People change. College isn't everything."

"It is when it looks like you might not get to go. What are you going to do?"

"I start Monday as a clerk-typist at the D.C. council."

Debbie shook her head. "I can't believe you're not going back to school. Here I am dying to get to go, wondering where I'll get the money if I ever get accepted. And you have all that and don't even want it." She chuckled.

"What's so funny?" Naomi asked as she pulled into the parking lot in front of Hecht's.

"It's just that a couple of years ago we both thought we'd be sitting in Ivy League schools by now and then running our own boutique. Remember that? Funny how things change."

"We were so naive."

Debbie nodded and smiled. Then, for some reason, the smile changed to tears.

"What's wrong?" Naomi asked.

Debbie took off her glasses and wiped her cheeks, but it didn't do much good. The tears kept coming. Naomi quickly found a parking space and shut off the engine. Then she reached over to hold Debbie. "Why are you crying?"

"Because it's so sad. We had such big dreams. What went wrong?"

So many things flashed through Naomi's mind: Joshua's death, Ralph's philandering, school, Gene, Debbie's pregnancy. "We got hit by life, I guess. It's not as simple as we thought, back then."

Debbie sat up and sniffed. "But I don't think our dreams were all that far-fetched. Other people do these things all the time. And I, for one, have no intention of giving up, no matter what."

"Neither do I. It's just that we're going to have to sprinkle our dreams with a heavy dose of reality from now on."

"Yeah," Debbie said. "Reality's tough, isn't it?"

Naomi nodded. "But so are we." She hoped she sounded more convinced than she felt.

Seventeen

Naomi's hopes of finding adventure and opportunity in the world of work were dashed the first week on the job. The most thrilling thing to happen to her that week took place the very first hour she was there, when Lisa James, the general counsel, said she was taking Naomi to meet the councilman she'd be working for. Naomi felt excitement building up in her stomach as her new boss led her down a stately corridor to the council offices. Lisa was tall, with a silky dark complexion. And she looked so elegant, just as she had when Naomi came for the interview. Heads turned when she walked—the men in appreciation of her model-like figure, the women trying to sneak a glimpse of the latest wool or double-knit suit she carried so well.

After the introductions, the councilman, Jeffrey Harrison, smiled and asked Naomi a few polite questions, but he was obviously in the middle of something important. So Lisa cut the meeting short, and Naomi's day went downhill from there. Lisa led her to a tiny room and sat her in front of the only piece of furniture that would fit inside, a square table pushed up against the wall. On top sat a tape recorder and headphones, a typewriter, and a stack of audiotapes about a foot high that she was expected to transcribe. Naomi took one look at them and knew that with her meager 45-words-a-minute typing skills, she'd be in that room for a long, long time. Worse yet, she discovered an hour into the work that they were boring as hell. By Friday she had to struggle to keep from nodding off.

The tapes were from council hearings that dealt with Thomas Turner, a local businessman who wanted to build a small strip mall near the waterfront but was looking for some pretty hefty tax breaks and other incentives from the D.C. government. About half the council members were in favor of his project, but the other half balked. Turner was threatening to take his money and plans elsewhere unless he got the concessions he wanted.

A few minutes before noon on Friday, she removed the headphones and stretched until she thought her body would splinter. Even after she shut the stupid machine off, the voices hummed in her head like a broken record. She sat and stared at the typewriter while thinking where to head for lunch.

This had become the biggest challenge in Naomi's day. The District Building was downtown, and while the city was not exactly thriving, it had lots of little places to eat. Unfortunately, she always went alone. Lisa James came into Naomi's little cubbyhole at least once a day to chat briefly and find out how the work was progressing, but no one else had tried to befriend her. All the staff members were older, and a nod or a smile seemed to be all that was forthcoming. At first, Naomi was a bit hurt by their unfriendliness. Nobody seemed to have time to waste with a lowly tape transcriber. But as the week wore on, she began to realize that the attitude toward her was closer to indifference than to hostility. These people were professionals, and probably too busy to be bothered. The council members often had lunch with business associates, and the staff usually ate at their desks or skipped lunch altogether. Naomi tried bringing a sandwich to eat at her desk one day, but that just made her realize how much she needed to get out of that room during her lunch hour.

She stood and stretched again. She still hadn't decided where to go. Maybe she would just walk until she saw something that tempted her. She was reaching for her coat when Lisa opened the door and stepped in. As usual she was dressed in a smart-looking suit. Naomi reached down and tried to smooth the wrinkles from the lap of her skirt.

"You're doing a good job with the tapes," Lisa said.

"Thanks. I might be able to finish next week."

Lisa shook her head. "More will be coming, since the hearings are still going on."

"Oh," was all Naomi could manage, although she tried to keep the disappointment out of her voice.

Lisa smiled. "A little boring for you, I imagine."

Naomi didn't know what to say to that. It was an understatement, but she was uncomfortable admitting that to her new boss. "Well, I . . . I mean, it's got to be done."

"You're exactly right. But I might be able to get permission from Jeffrey to let you sit in on some of the hearings one day next week. They aren't nearly as dull live, and it'll break up your day. Interested?"

Naomi's eyes lit up. "Yes. How much longer will they go on?"

"Another week. Maybe longer." Lisa looked at her watch. "I need to get going; I have a meeting. I'll take you to lunch one day next week, OK?"

Naomi smiled. "OK." After Lisa left, Naomi stuck her tongue out at the junk on her desk, put on her coat, and picked up her shoulder bag. Now she hoped the hearings would last long enough for her to sit in on a few, but not so long that she'd be transcribing the tapes until doomsday. She nodded to a couple of secretaries she passed on the way to the main entrance. Then she opened the big double doors, stepped out—and bumped right smack into the mail cart.

"Are you OK?" Jimmy, the mail clerk, stood on the other side of the cart, looking at her anxiously.

Hell, no. Her thigh was killing her, she had the dullest job on earth, and she needed a man. "I'll live."

"Are you sure?"

Naomi nodded, although the prospect wasn't so thrilling.

"How's it going?" he asked.

Jimmy brought the mail to the council suite twice each day, morning and afternoon, and since Naomi wasn't exactly immersed in her work they'd sometimes chat. They didn't talk long, since he had runs to make, but Naomi had begun to look forward to his visits. It was about the only time during the day that she got to hear the sound of her own voice. Jimmy was twenty-six, older than the men she was used to, and it was refreshing to talk to him. He was also easy to look at— light-skinned with curly dark hair.

Naomi didn't like catching herself thinking in the old ways. It sounded disgusting, and she was embarrassed that people ever talked that way. She certainly never described men in those terms out loud. And she found herself noticing the dark ones more these days. Some of them were downright lovely. Like Dean. But old habits died hard, she supposed, since she still found herself getting excited around men who looked like Jimmy.

"Some days, I think I'll go out of my mind with boredom," she said. "How about you?"

"I'm hanging in there. You know, I've been meaning to ask you if you'd like to go out sometime. Maybe take in a movie?"

Naomi had been half hoping he'd ask her out. Jimmy was not exactly the type she usually went for. Although no dummy, he wasn't the most intellectual dude in the world. But he was cute and easy to talk to. Besides, she didn't exactly have guys lined up at her doorstep.

"Fine," she said.

He looked surprised. "Really? I would have thought a good-looking babe like yourself already had a dozen brothers hanging around."

"Goes to show you," she said, smiling.

"No man in the picture?"

"We broke up in November."

He nodded. "I knew there had to be one not too far back. Well, his loss is my gain. I have to go up to New York this weekend, but are you busy next Friday night?"

That was a joke, Naomi thought. "Not really."

"Good. Give me your phone number and I'll call you when I get back. Got me a new set of wheels the other day, so maybe we can ride down to Hains Point."

"What kind of car did you get?" she asked, as she scribbled her number on a sheet of paper he dug out of the mail cart.

"Cadillac Eldorado. It's a used one but only two years old and that baby sings on the road."

Naomi almost dropped the pen. What was a good-looking man like Jimmy doing with such a tacky car? Every time she heard the name Cadillac, she had visions of a pimp cruising around in a white one with a red top, leaning hard to the side. Jimmy must be spending every dime he made on the car, which didn't say a hell of a lot for him.

It was enough to make her want to try to wiggle out of the date. And for a moment she considered it seriously. But she reasoned she hadn't been out with anyone since she and Ralph broke up last fall. During the Christmas break, she'd been so lonely on Friday and Saturday nights she was tempted to call Ralph just to suggest they meet briefly. But she knew if he so much as hinted at their getting back together, she'd be like putty in his hands. Anyway, what the hell did she have to lose by going out once with Jimmy? It was only a date, not a wedding ceremony.

She handed him the piece of paper with her phone number on it and chuckled after he entered the council suite and the door closed behind him. Whatever happened, at least she would have something to do next Friday night besides sitting around in her room watching TV. She'd just have to be sure to take cab fare, in case things got to the point where she had to get away from him.

Jimmy's black Eldorado was so big and shiny it was triply embarrassing. As she walked with him toward the car, she was reminded of a blubbery whale. She thought she'd be swallowed whole when she got in. She glanced over her shoulder to see if any of the neighbors were watching, but all she saw was her parents looking out of the window, probably in horror. She'd get an earful when she returned home. She could hear her mother now. "Where on earth did you find that character?" Good question.

As flashy and downright ugly as the monstrosity was, Naomi had to admit the ride was a smooth one, despite the fake leopard upholstery and imitation-fur floor mats. It was all Naomi could do to keep from giggling out loud at the thought that she was sitting there. At least it wasn't white with a red top.

They rode down Fifteenth Street toward Hains Point and the Tidal Basin along the Potomac River. The area was a popular spot when the cherry blossoms were in bloom, but it was practically deserted now. Naomi thought it strange that he'd want to ride around down here, since it was always windier than elsewhere in the city and too cold to get out of the car. But as they talked and Jimmy slowly circled the peninsula along Ohio Drive, she realized that cruising in his car and talking was probably his idea of the perfect date.

"Did you know that three thousand cherry trees were planted during the Wilson administration?" Jimmy asked.

Naomi turned and stared at him. It was exactly the kind of stuff Jimmy was always coming up with. "That many, huh?"

"I don't know how many there are now. They dug up a lot of them when they built the Jefferson Memorial and they've planted others since."

"Interesting," she said.

"So, how long do you think you'll stick it out at the council?"

Naomi shrugged. "Depends on what else they give me to do. If it doesn't get more interesting soon I'll have to find something else or maybe go back to school."

"Go on back to school. You don't know how lucky you are that your parents can afford to send you. I'm planning on doing the same thing myself someday, as soon as I get the moola together."

"Really?" Naomi was tempted to ask if he thought buying a Cadillac when he was supposed to be saving for college was a smart move. But she didn't. At least he wanted to go.

"I don't plan to be handling somebody else's mail the rest of my days."

"What will you study if you go back?"

"Probably business, since that's where the money is. What about you?"

"I was majoring in communications before. Now I'm thinking about political science. But the truth is I don't know yet. I can't seem to make up my mind."

Jimmy waved his hand. "Forget politics. You'll never make

any money in that, unless you plan on cheating somebody. Those cats work their butts off for nothing."

"It's not for nothing. They're working to change the laws and the way things are run."

"You can get things changed faster if you have money to spread around. Why do you think the big corporations spend all that dough on lobbyists and campaign contributions? Not to mention the kickbacks."

"Are you suggesting we should do things illegally to get our way? That just gets you into more trouble when you get caught."

"Nine times out of ten, you don't get caught. That kind of stuff goes on all the time. The ones that get caught are just stupid."

"It doesn't happen much."

"More than you think. And the main reason politicians take the money and run is 'cause they don't make any doing what they do."

"Not everybody is thinking only of the money, Jimmy."

"Then they're wasting their time, the way I see it. If you want the power to change things, go into business, not some little do-good government gig."

"I think we need people to do both. You can't say everybody who goes into something besides business is wasting their time."

"No, but it would be a waste of *my* time."

"You sound awfully greedy, Jimmy," she said, only half joking.

Jimmy snickered. "Damn right I am. I want my share of the pie and I'm gonna get it. And if you don't watch out for yours, I might just take that too."

Naomi laughed. At least he was honest about it. She had never suspected he held such high ambitions. He also seemed smarter than she'd figured. Just went to show that you never knew what was going on inside someone's head. "What do you see yourself doing ten to fifteen years from now?"

"Running General Motors. Something like that."

Now that was a bit much, she thought. "No, really, Jimmy."

"I'm serious. Those white cats do it, why not me?"

"Those white cats have been through business school at your age, too, and they've started working for some big-time corporation by now. And their daddies before them did the same thing."

"So I'm at a disadvantage. There's more than one way to get there. As soon as I get the money together for school, I'm out of here. Another year, two at the most."

They drove downtown and got a bite to eat. Then Naomi suggested they go dancing. She couldn't remember the last time she'd been on a dance floor, since Ralph didn't like it. Jimmy had a friend who was a member of the Foxtrappe, D.C.'s hottest and most exclusive night spot, so he called and got him to put their names on the list. Naomi had heard that if you didn't have the right credentials and make at least fifteen thousand a year or know someone who belonged, you couldn't get past the front desk, so Jimmy's friend must have something going for him.

Jimmy gave his name at the desk, and they were waved ahead of a group of people trying to get in. Since Jimmy liked to dance as much as she did, they stayed on the floor until nearly three in the morning.

When he pulled up in front of her house, she noticed that all the lights were out. She smiled. Not like in the old days, when the house would have been ablaze and her parents sitting up in their nightclothes waiting anxiously. She invited him in and put on a Jackson Five album, turning the volume down low. They slow-dragged a bit, then sat on the living room couch and talked. He asked her if she'd like to go see *Shaft* the following Friday night, and she readily agreed. Jimmy was nothing to get too excited about, but he was better company than her TV.

She walked him to the door and was surprised to find herself feeling a little down that the night was ending. He reached out and gave her a gentle, lingering kiss. She was just starting to relax when she felt a hand dip beneath her hemline. She pushed it away gently, but not his lips. She was enjoying them, and it had been much too long since the last time. But when she felt his hand groping for her breast, she backed off. That was enough. It was only the first date, not to mention that her parents were right upstairs sleeping.

He smiled and kissed her forehead. "I'll call you tomorrow."

Just as she began to close the door after him, he turned back toward her. "I meant to ask," he whispered. "Do you ever get high?"

"You mean on grass?" she asked.

He nodded.

Ralph never touched the stuff, but she had smoked it a few times with Kathy in the dorm. It never made her high until she and Pamela smoked a joint together at a party their last night on campus. The demonstrations were over, exams were completed, she and Ralph had broken up, and Keith was otherwise occupied. Nothing like a party, a little grass, and plenty of screwdrivers to cure a couple of girls' blues. The two of them partied hard until dawn.

They woke up the following afternoon, their heads at the opposite ends of Naomi's tiny twin bed, their feet in each other's faces, their temples pounding fiercely. Naomi felt like she'd slept with her head in a crocodile's mouth. Pamela was so wasted, Naomi had to drag her out of bed and shove her out the door. She hated doing that to the girl. But by the time they woke up, she had only two hours to get ready for her flight home. She ran around the room throwing things into suitcases and barely had time to shower. That was her goodbye to Atlanta Tech.

"I have a few times," Naomi said.

Jimmy frowned. "What, you didn't like it?"

"It's not that. I wasn't around it much, since my exboyfriend didn't like it."

"I'll get us some, and I guarantee it'll be the best you ever had."

Lisa finally found time to take Naomi to lunch early the following week. As they took the elevator down to the first floor of the District Building, Naomi had visions of herself poring leisurely over a heavy menu at one of the classier downtown restaurants. Moments later, she found herself standing in front of a hot dog stand, trying to decide whether to ask for relish.

"Sorry it's not something more interesting," Lisa said as they made their way to a bench in a small nearby park. It was a bright, sunny day and very warm for February. "But I have to be back in less than thirty minutes."

Naomi nodded and smiled. At least she finally had some company for lunch. She didn't think she'd ever get over the sight of Lisa biting hungrily into a hot dog, taking care not to drip mustard on her suit.

"What do you think of the hearings?" Lisa asked as they sat down on a bench.

"Much more interesting," she said. Her only regret was that she couldn't spend more than an hour or so a day in them, since she now had typing assignments from several of the council members. At least there was more variety now in what she typed. "I wish I could spend more time attending them, but the work is starting to pile up."

"That's because word has gotten around that you're a thorough typist. You're doing a fantastic job."

Naomi smiled. She tried to make up for her lack of speed by making sure there were no mistakes. And she was typing so much now, her speed had probably picked up a notch or two. "Thanks."

"You know, you should be doing much more than typing."

Naomi was glad to hear that somebody realized that. "There's not much people will offer you if you don't have a college degree or any work experience."

Lisa nodded understandingly. "Are you planning to go back to school?"

Naomi was so tired of that question. "Probably. But I wanted to spend some time working first. I don't know what I want to do."

"That's probably not a bad idea. I've always thought we're much too young to decide what we want to do for the rest of our lives right after we get out of high school. After college, I worked for several years as a teacher before I decided it wasn't right for me. Then I went to law school in my early thirties.

Now I think, if I had it to do all over again, it would be business. So take your time, but make sure you go back."

Naomi was surprised. Lisa didn't look that old. Naomi had assumed she was somewhere in her early thirties now. "That's what everyone tells me, especially my parents."

Lisa smiled. "What was your major?"

"Communications. Now I'm thinking about political science."

Lisa turned up her nose. "I wish more young black people would go into business. Politics is not the only answer to our problems. If we really want to have influence, we're going to have to start opening businesses. And I don't mean Mom and Pop stores. I'm talking about real estate, industries, that kind of thing. You know, Tom Turner sometimes hires young people for six months to a year to give them a chance to learn about his business. Think you'd be interested?"

Naomi sat up on the edge of the bench. She was more than interested. Right then and there, she made up her mind it was exactly what she wanted. She'd seen Thomas Turner in the hearings the past couple of days, and today she had passed him in the hallway talking to two councilmen. The man exuded power and confidence. Even the council members seemed in awe of him. "Yes, a thousand times yes!" A million times yes!

"It would mean leaving us, and you'll be hard to replace. But you're too smart for this kind of work. If you're interested I'll talk to him."

"Would you? I'd love to work for Thomas Turner."

"I don't think you'd see much of him. And it's only for six months to a year. After that, you'd be back out there looking."

"Doesn't matter," Naomi said. "I'll take it."

Lisa laughed. "I'll talk to him. But it's going to have to wait until the end of next week, since I leave for a conference tomorrow."

Naomi was crestfallen as she remembered Lisa's business trip to Detroit. It would be a whole week and a half before she got back. Naomi hated waiting around once her mind was set on a particular course of action, but she tried not to show her disappointment. That would be childish.

"Thanks. I can't wait to hear what he says."

"Now don't get your hopes up too high. I don't know exactly how the program works and I've never asked him before." She paused as she looked at Naomi. "But I can see it's already too late to tell you not to get excited about it. Do you have a résumé?"

Naomi's eyes grew wide with alarm. "Oh, no. I filled out a One-seven-one for this job. I never—"

"Don't panic. You can make one while I'm gone. Use the typewriter in the office."

"But I don't know the first thing about doing a résumé."

"I'll give you a copy of mine. Don't worry, it's easy. Just follow the same style. Of course, you'll have to emphasize your schooling and extracurricular activities."

"And the fact that I didn't finish college," she said wryly.

"That may not matter. Tom Turner never finished college."

Naomi's admiration of the man shot up tenfold. "Really?" That just proved her point that college wasn't the only route to success.

Naomi spent so much time writing and polishing her résumé, she fell drastically behind on her other work. But if the résumé paid off, she reasoned, she wouldn't have to do that other drab stuff. As she worked on it, she was thankful to her mother now for all the music and dancing lessons she'd insisted on.

"See," Mama said one evening as Naomi tried the résumé out on them, "your old folks know a little something, don't they?"

Naomi smiled. "I never thought otherwise."

"You think your parents are a couple of old fuddy-duddies," Daddy said.

"I do not."

"Who is this Thomas Turner again?" Mama asked.

"He's only one of the most powerful men in D.C.," Naomi said.

"You know, that businessman," Daddy said. "He probably owns half the real estate in town."

"Not that much," Naomi said. "But he owns more than any other single person."

"And he's going to give you a job?" Mama asked, fixing Naomi with an incredulous stare. "You don't even have a college degree."

God, she thought. If she heard that one more time, she would scream. "Neither does Thomas Turner," Naomi said, not bothering to hide her annoyance at her mother's skepticism. "Apparently it doesn't matter for this job."

Naomi hoped that was true. When they had returned to the office after their lunch, Lisa did some asking around and learned that the young people Thomas Turner hired were usually college students, if not recent graduates. He'd always regretted not finishing himself and wanted to encourage young people today. Naomi had been brokenhearted to hear that, but Lisa insisted she still try. After all, Naomi did have a year and a half of college, and Lisa promised to rave about her when she spoke to Turner. Naomi was still hopeful. The last thing she needed was her mother reminding her of her deficiencies.

"What will you be doing?" Mama asked.

"How do I know? I haven't gotten the job yet. We'll have to see."

By Friday morning, the résumé was as perfect as she could make it. She removed it carefully from the typewriter and read it over for what must have been the fiftieth time. It was much skimpier than Lisa's, naturally, but not half bad. The only problem now would be waiting until Lisa got back, an almost impossible task.

When Jimmy went out with her to lunch that afternoon, he said he had to go to New York that weekend and would have to postpone their date. Any other time, the thought of being dateless another weekend would have disappointed Naomi, but she was so consumed with the possibility of working for Thomas Turner that his news didn't faze her.

"That's fine," she told him. "We'll go when you get back." Then she changed the subject to Turner. She knew Jimmy was probably sick of hearing about the man, but he was the only thing she wanted to talk about. She would probably spend most of the weekend at the library reading everything she could find out about him. By the time Lisa returned, she'd be an expert on both the man and his business.

As soon as she got back from lunch and saw the résumé sitting on her desk, Naomi decided not to wait until Lisa got back. Why wait for Lisa, when she could do it herself? He was right there in the building every day. She had noticed that when the sessions broke at noon, he would stand in the hallway and talk to the council members and the others attending the hearings. The very first day Naomi attended, she had used a water fountain in the hall after the meeting stopped for lunch, and when she stood up he was right there behind her, waiting his turn. She smiled and backed away. He returned her smile and bent over for a drink. Naomi couldn't help but turn back a couple of times as she walked away from the fountain. He was a tall man in his fifties, not bad-looking, with light brown hair that was thinning at the top. He had on a dark expensive-looking suit and a brightly patterned tie. Naomi thought he'd probably been very handsome when he was young.

In the days that followed, she noticed that he often stopped at that water fountain before heading for the elevators. Most of the time he was with one of the councilmen, but sometimes he was alone, if you didn't count the assistants who always seemed to tag along behind him. All of them were white, but that just strengthened Naomi's resolve. His staff obviously needed a little integration. Naomi vowed that if she caught him alone before Lisa returned, she'd get up the nerve to approach him herself.

Her chance came on Tuesday afternoon. As soon as the chairman pounded the gavel signaling the end of the morning session, Naomi headed outside and watched the fountain from across the hallway, just as she had the day before. She had her résumé and had spent the weekend at the library reading newspaper and magazine articles about Thomas Turner. She was ready for anything he might toss her way. He approached the fountain alone, and by the time he stood up, Naomi was beside him.

"Mr. Turner?"

He seemed startled to see a face right there in front of him, and Naomi realized immediately that her timing was bad. But she couldn't back off now. She cleared her throat. "My name is Naomi Jefferson. I work in the council office."

"Uh-huh." He'd quickly regained his composure and stared at her intently. Naomi had never before been so aware of being sized up.

"I wanted to give you this," she said, holding out the résumé. He looked down but didn't seem eager to take it.

"It's my résumé. Lisa James, my boss, said you sometimes hire people to work on a temporary basis. I'd love a chance to do that."

He nodded and smiled for the first time. "So you work for Lisa, huh?"

"Yes," she said, returning his smile. From his tone, that was obviously a plus.

"And you've got guts, coming right up to me that way. I like that."

Naomi's smile spread from ear to ear as he took the résumé from her hand. "Where do you go to school?"

There it was again. Up until now, Naomi had been surprised at how calm she felt. She was ready for questions about his business or the hearings, but that was one question she did not want to hear. "I'm—uh, not in school right now. I was at Atlanta Tech until last semester."

He frowned, and Naomi sensed that the tide was turning. "Did you finish?" he asked. "You don't look old enough."

"No, I didn't. I went for a year and a half. I wanted to try working for a while."

He thrust the résumé back toward her. "Come see me after you're back in school. All our interns are college juniors and seniors or grad students."

"I'm only one semester short of being a junior, and I have work experience. I—"

He held up his hand to silence her. "Not good enough."

Naomi's mouth dropped open. She wanted to ask him how he could be so hypocritical, since he'd never finished college himself. But she didn't have the nerve. He signaled one of his assistants and they took off.

She looked down at the résumé. It was wrinkled now from when he'd shoved it back at her. He never even bothered to look at it.

Eighteen

The episode with Thomas Turner left Naomi so frustrated she took off sick that afternoon. The thought of transcribing even one more tape, knowing she'd blown her chances of working for Turner, was more than she could stand. She should have waited until Lisa got back. Lisa would have known better how to talk to him. Lisa could have said nice things about her. Lisa . . .

"Damn," she said aloud, flopping down on her bed. It didn't make a damn bit of difference. Mr. Turner wouldn't have hired her even if she had a Ph.D. He could get away without having a college degree. Hell, maybe he didn't even finish high school. But did it matter? No, because he was the right color. She was sick of this system, sick of fighting it, sick of living in it.

She kicked off her shoes. It felt like she was falling into a ditch. And whenever she seemed to be climbing out, just reaching over the top, something dragged her back. Why did she even bother trying to get anywhere?

She couldn't talk to her parents about a lot of the things happening in her life. They were from another generation and faced a whole different set of hassles when they were growing up. It seemed that whenever she did take a problem to them, they looked at it through this ancient prism, from a time when things were so much simpler. Not many blacks back then attended white schools, so they didn't run into racist professors.

And they never even entertained the thought of working for a prominent white businessman.

She stretched out on the bed, still dressed in her work clothes. The next thing she knew, the sound of the front door shutting was waking her up. Mama usually got home from work a little after four, but it couldn't be that late. She lifted her head and looked at the clock on the dresser: 4:10. She couldn't believe she'd dozed off like that, with so much on her mind. A part of her wanted to get up before her mother saw her, knowing she'd have a million questions. But she didn't feel like moving. She turned onto her back and listened to the sounds of her mother moving around downstairs, then her footsteps as she came up.

"Naomi, what are you doing home so early?"

She didn't say anything, just stared at the ceiling.

"Are you sick?" Mama asked. The tone of her voice grew anxious as she approached the bed.

Only in the head, Naomi thought, covering her eyes with her arm. "Just tired."

Mama put her hand on Naomi's cheek, feeling for her temperature. "How long have you been home?"

"Since after lunch."

"You took off from work?"

Naomi nodded.

"Why, if you're not sick?"

She wanted to tell her mother what happened but knew she'd just get a lecture for being so rash. But then maybe that was what she needed. Sooner or later some of it might sink in.

"Maybe Lisa can still talk to him," Mama said when she finished. By then, she'd moved to sit on the edge of Naomi's bed.

"It won't do much good," Naomi said, punching the pillow she was holding. "I already ruined it."

"There you go, jumping to conclusions."

Damn, she thought. This habit *was* pretty bad. "I know."

Mama got up. "All you can do is wait until Lisa gets back. But don't take any more time off from work. You just started the job and that doesn't look good."

"I know." Here it comes, she thought. The grand lecture.

"I'm going down to start dinner. Are you going to be OK?"

Naomi bolted up. She couldn't believe Mama was about to take off without scolding her. "You're not going to get on my case about being rash and impatient?"

Mama smiled. "I think you've done enough of that yourself. You don't need me to tell you your behavior was rash."

"I'm so confused about everything. Nothing seems to go right for me."

"Some confusion at your age is natural."

"You mean because Joshua died?" Sometimes, that was what Naomi felt was causing all her confusion. "Ever since that happened, my life has gone downhill."

"I think that's because you blame society for his death, and you're still bitter about it."

"I do blame society. For that, and for a lot of other things. I know you don't see it that way, but I do."

"Even if you do feel racism is responsible, that's no reason to give up trying to get somewhere."

"But it's hard when white people do everything they can to stop you. No matter what I do to try to get ahead, they win and I lose."

"No, Naomi. They only win when you give up."

Naomi exhaled deeply and shook her head. Mama just didn't understand how much harder it was to make it these days. "Things have changed so much since you were my age. They were much simpler back then."

"Where did you get that idea?"

"It's true. Your world was smaller and simpler because things hadn't opened up for black people yet."

"You think opening them up for your generation was simple?"

"That's not what I meant. But it was a different set of problems. The things that worked for you don't work now."

"That may be true to a certain point. But the basics never change, Naomi. Like needing to be twice as prepared as anyone else. If anything, that's more important if you're competing with white people for the same jobs."

"That's just the trouble," Naomi said. "Why should we have to work twice as hard for half the reward? It's not fair."

"No, but it's the reality. What's that expression you young people use? Deal with it."

"If you were white, that dude would have hired you in a minute," Jimmy said. They had been rehashing her conversation with Turner for weeks. He took a deep drag from the joint and handed it to Naomi. "But since you're not, he expects a college degree."

They were sitting on the balcony of Jimmy's apartment, gazing up at the stars, shooting the breeze. Naomi took a drag and handed the joint back to him. She felt relaxed and content at this moment, despite all the things going wrong in her life. Getting high with Jimmy had that effect on her. It was about the only thing that did these days.

"I definitely think he would have taken me more seriously if I'd been white. I'm only one semester away from being a junior."

"Damn right," Jimmy said. "We've always been expected to have more and know more to get the same kind of job as a white person. A great-uncle of mine had a law degree, and all he ever did was teach high school. Back in the early part of the century, half the Pullman porters had college degrees. That was the only job they could get. And now . . ." He paused and added a clip to the roach. Naomi watched as he took several quick drags. When they'd first started getting high together, he would hold it out for her, but she decided she didn't like all that smoke going up her nose. So he'd stopped offering her the roach. Besides, by the time they got down to the end of the joint, Naomi was already floating.

"And now . . ." Jimmy paused again and looked at Naomi. "What the hell was I just saying?"

"Huh?" Naomi looked at him and realized she didn't have a clue. "Damned if I know," she said, giggling. "Whatever it was, I agree a hundred percent. I'm tired of these white people, every last one of them."

Jimmy snickered. "That's got to be the third time I did that shit. Oh, I know. I was talking—" He stopped and got this dumb look on his face, like he'd forgotten again. Naomi burst out laughing. Jimmy did too.

"Oh, me," Naomi said, trying to catch her breath. "What you're saying about blacks needing more to get the same things as whites is so true. I don't see how we can be expected to compete under those terms."

"Yeah. Now we need an advanced degree to compete with whites who have high school diplomas."

"It's not that bad," Naomi said.

"Sho' it is." Jimmy's doorbell rang and he dropped the roach into an ashtray and disappeared into the house. Naomi leaned back in her chair and looked up at the stars. Although it was only early April, it was already warm enough that they only needed jackets at night. This was Naomi's favorite time of year: cool clear days and nights with low humidity.

Jimmy was different from any man she'd dated before. He seemed to prefer getting high to having sex. Once or twice a week was plenty for him. Naomi didn't complain, since sex with Jimmy didn't exactly set off any fireworks for her. But then, did it ever? Did *anything*? Life was such a drag.

What was wrong with her? She'd never experienced the wild abandonment she always read about in *Cosmo*. Only one thing she'd read gave her hope—that women matured sexually as they got older. She just hoped she wouldn't have to wait until she was thirty to have an orgasm. Or to start enjoying life.

She heard deep laughter coming from inside the apartment and got up to take a peek through the sliding glass doors. Two black dudes were standing near the front door talking to Jimmy. One was about Jimmy's height, the other shorter. She went back to her seat. Men were always stopping by, but they never stayed more than a few minutes. Jimmy only bothered to introduce them if she was in the living room when they came. Something was fishy about the whole deal, but she couldn't put her finger on it. She asked Jimmy about it, but he always said they were friends or dudes who lived in the neighborhood.

When she mentioned it to Debbie, the first word out of her mouth was drugs. Debbie was sure he was selling. "Either that or he's bisexual," she said. Naomi didn't think he was bisexual. Why would he parade the men in front of her if he was sleeping with them? That didn't make sense. But then, as Debbie had said, a lot of people out there didn't make sense. And Naomi had always felt that even though she'd been seeing Jimmy for three months now, she didn't really know him.

Jimmy came back out to the balcony and sat in his chair. "Now where were we before we got interrupted?" He was smiling broadly. That was another thing. He was always so chipper after some of his friends stopped by.

"Jimmy, who were they?"

"Just a couple of friends of mine."

"You certainly know a lot of people."

"Can't help it if I'm a sociable kind of guy, can I?"

That was just it, Naomi thought with exasperation. Jimmy was the least gregarious person she knew. A lot of dudes stopped by, but they never sat down, never even stayed more than a few minutes, and none of them seemed like more than casual acquaintances. He didn't seem to have any real friends.

"Are you selling drugs, Jimmy?" She said it quietly, not accusatorially. She wanted him to tell her the truth. If Jimmy was selling drugs, it would explain a lot of things: the Cadillac, the men, the sudden trips to New York, and why he always had so much cash on him. When she discovered several thousand dollars in a drawer, she asked him why he didn't put it in the bank. He said he didn't trust them with his money.

Jimmy exhaled deeply. "I guess it's time you knew," he said. "Yeah. I'm selling."

Her mouth went dry. Now that he'd told her, she didn't know what to make of it. She was dating a drug dealer! "You should have told me."

"I didn't know how you'd handle it."

"Why do you do it?"

"For the money. What else?"

"Don't you worry about getting caught?"

"Nah. I did when I was out there on the streets pushing like the brothers you see coming around here. But now I only deal with them."

"You could still get caught."

"I won't be doing it much longer. I just need to clear a few more thousand for college and to pay my living expenses while I'm there."

"I must have seen enough for a couple of years of college in that drawer."

He smiled. "That's not all mine. I have to use some of it to pay my suppliers."

"In New York?"

"New York and here."

"Do you just sell grass?"

"I'm just starting to get into other things. Mainly 'cause the money's better."

"Like what?"

He shrugged. "Just other things. Pills, angel dust now and then."

"Doesn't that make it more dangerous?"

"Not if you're careful."

"What about coke or heroin?"

"Look, that's enough questions. The less you know, the better."

That was when it hit her just what Jimmy was really doing. She was surprised to feel a tinge of excitement. This was beginning to seem like the movies.

"How do you feel about it, now that you know?" he asked.

She shrugged her shoulders. It might be a little exciting but it was still against the law. "Mixed. I don't like the idea of being around something that's illegal."

"Nothing's going to happen to you. I would never get you involved in any way."

"Don't worry, I don't intend to let you."

"You're not going to stop seeing me, are you?"

She shook her head slowly. But she now knew what she had sensed from the first date. Their affair was doomed to be short-lived.

* * *

"It's drugs," Naomi said, as she stood in the bathroom doorway and watched Debbie help Serena with the potty.

"I knew it. What did I tell you?"

"I never tried to deny it," Naomi said.

"What are you going to do?"

"What do you mean?"

"You going to keep seeing him?"

"I guess."

"What if he gets busted while you're with him? Have you thought of that?"

Of course she had, but she didn't think it would happen. "Jimmy's careful."

"So are the police."

"Very funny. I'm not ready to give him up just yet. It's not like I've got guys lined up outside my door."

"So you'll hold on until somebody better comes along?"

"You make it sound so cold."

Debbie giggled, picked up Serena, and handed her to Naomi. "You just be careful," she said, leading Naomi back into her bedroom. She went to her dresser drawer as Naomi sat on the bed and tickled Serena. The child giggled with delight and scrambled away, only to come back a few seconds later for more.

"I have something to show you," Debbie said, holding out a slip of paper. Naomi let Serena go and took it. As soon as she saw the Georgetown logo, her mouth dropped open. She smiled the whole time she was reading the acceptance letter; then she jumped up and hugged Debbie. "I've been here almost an hour and you're just getting around to telling me this?"

"Well." Debbie handed Naomi another letter. This one had George Washington University's logo at the top.

"Another one?" Naomi asked. "How can you be so calm? You're so lucky. No, I take that back. You're smart; they're the lucky ones. Did you get a scholarship?"

"From both of them." Debbie sat beside her and held Serena in her lap.

"You're kidding! Have you decided which one you'll go to?"

"Probably GW. It's easier to get there on the bus."

"I still don't see how you can be so calm about it."

"The only thing I worry about is that something will go wrong like it did last time. Not that having Serena was wrong, but you know what I mean."

"Nothing's going to go wrong," Naomi said, patting Debbie's knee. "This is in the bag. What are you going to major in?"

"Accounting. I want to be a CPA."

Naomi whistled.

"Why not?"

"I think it's great you've gotten so ambitious."

"I was always ambitious. I just got sidetracked. But seeing Serena growing up makes me determined to get back on track. I think of all the things I want to do for her. And I want to be a good role model."

"I admire that."

"What about you?" Debbie asked. "Aren't you going back?"

"Guess I'll have to, to keep up with you."

"No, seriously. You really should."

"I probably will. Maybe sooner than I thought, 'cause this job of mine is the pits."

"What would you study? Communications again?"

"Hell, no. I don't know. Remember when we used to talk about someday opening our own clothing boutique?"

"How could I forget? We still could do something like that, you know."

Naomi shook her head. "Do you realize how hard that would be for two black women? Almost impossible. I would have to study business or something like that, and I don't have the head for that kind of stuff."

"Since when?"

"Don't tell me you've forgotten how you always had to help me with my math homework."

"In business you wouldn't have to take the hard-core stuff. Maybe just some accounting and economics."

"Ugh!"

"Oh, go on. You could do it."

"Maybe," Naomi said. "Right now my head is so screwed up I don't have the faintest idea what I'm going to do." That was no joke about her head. Before coming to Debbie's, she had sneaked into the backyard at home to smoke a joint, although most of it had worn off by now. She shoved Debbie on the shoulder playfully. "But you, girl, I won't even be able to talk to you, Miss CPA."

"Yes, you will," Debbie said. She batted her eyelashes and crossed her legs with mock vanity. "Maybe I'll hire you as my personal assistant."

"Thanks a lot." She said it with mock envy, but then it hit her. She really was jealous of Debbie.

"You getting so you like this stuff," Jimmy said as he lit a second joint.

Naomi smiled thinly. She didn't like the way that sounded, but it was true. Sobriety was brutal. Marijuana made her feel that all was OK with the world, even if only for the moment.

"I'm ready to hit the clubs whenever you are," he said, handing the joint to her.

She put it to her lips and inhaled deeply. "Mmm-hmm," she said, holding the smoke in her lungs. She leaned back against the couch and released it slowly. She'd felt miserable ever since Debbie told her about her grand ambitions. It was wonderful for Debbie, and no one was more deserving of happiness. But her own life, if you could call it that, seemed more futile each day. Her job was dreadful, and going back to college was about as exciting to her as . . . as the thought of having sex with Jimmy was, some days. She tightened her lips to keep the giggles spouting inside from reaching them. And forget living happily ever after on the Gold Coast with the man of her dreams. Here she was getting high with a damn drug dealer. It had gotten so she didn't even want to wait until she saw him to get high. If he was planning to take off on one of his weekend buying trips, she would get him to give her enough to hold her until he got back. She was pitiful.

Jimmy was always shooting off his mouth about how he was going to stop when he got enough money to go back to school. Ha! Naomi had come to realize that was just talk. He seemed to get a thrill out of what he was doing, some perverted sense of power. He had given up on getting anywhere a long time ago. Only he didn't know it yet.

She tried to get him to stop selling. It was safer to get it from other people, she told him. But it was pointless. The last time she brought it up, after opening the glove compartment and finding a package of cocaine, they got to screaming and shoving each other as they drove down Georgia Avenue, one of the busiest streets in the city.

"I thought you only sold grass," she said, jerking the bag in his direction.

"I never said that."

"You did. You lied."

Jimmy snickered. "You just heard what you wanted to hear. Now put that back."

He lunged for the bag, but she yanked it out of his reach and slapped his arm. "You're putting me at risk carrying this stuff around in the car. Suppose you get stopped? Don't you think about anybody but yourself? I ought to throw this shit out the window."

He grabbed at the bag and nearly sideswiped a truck. Naomi waited until he had the car back under control, then slapped his shoulder.

"If you don't put that back this minute," he said, grabbing her T-shirt at the neck, "I'm gonna throw *you* out the window."

She struggled to free herself. "Let me go!"

He swung the car to the curb and jerked it into park. Then he grabbed Naomi's wrist and forced the bag out of her hand. "Don't mess with my stuff like that anymore, bitch."

"Fuck. Take me home."

"With pleasure."

They didn't talk for a week after that one. Then he called. Naomi was sure that if he hadn't, it would have been over between them. She certainly wasn't calling him. But she agreed to go out with him. At first, she couldn't understand why and cursed herself when she hung up the phone. "Stupid dummy. What the fuck's the matter with you?" But she thought about it and soon had her answer. Jimmy was safe. She liked his company, but there was no love between them and they didn't pretend there was. With Jimmy, she didn't have to worry about the dangers of getting attached. If he disappeared from her life, so be it. And he always had good grass.

She made up her mind never to bring up his selling again. She had no right to. She was dating a drug dealer who would never be anything else and she had to either accept that or get out.

She handed the joint back to him and sat up. "I'm ready to party now."

"Sure, baby. But first I got something else you might want to try." He walked to his bed on the other side of the room and lifted the mattress. He came back to the couch and dangled a small package with something powdery in it in front of Naomi. "You game?" he asked.

A month earlier Naomi knew he wouldn't have dared offer it, the way she had ranted and raved about his selling. But now they got high on grass every time they were together, and lately she'd been complaining it didn't always do as much for her as it used to. She didn't know if it was the quality of the stuff Jimmy was getting or because they smoked it so much.

"Why not?" she said. Once couldn't hurt, could it? Besides, she was curious about coke. She stuck the joint in her mouth while he got it ready.

They snorted some, then went to a club and danced and drank tequila until the lights went out. Then they went back to Jimmy's apartment, snorted some more, and made love, or at least went through the motions. Then, while Jimmy dozed, Naomi got up and lit another joint. She was beginning to think Jimmy was right. Getting high was more fun than having sex, at least with him.

By the time Jimmy dropped her off in front of her house, it was 5:00 A.M. and the lights were on all over the place. She'd hoped her folks wouldn't have missed her, since it was Saturday—or Sunday now, rather. No such luck. The marijuana and coke had mostly worn off, but not the liquor. She cupped her hand over her mouth and blew out. Jesus. She smelled like a brewery.

She was jiggling the key in the lock when the door swung open. She stumbled inside, catching herself before she bumped into her father. She straightened up, saluted, and walked on by him, hoping he'd let it go at that. But her progress to the safety of her room was halted by her mother coming down the stairs, her long robe blowing behind with her brisk steps.

"Where are you coming from at this hour?" Mama asked, tying the belt around her waist. Her hair was rolled on sponge curlers with a silken scarf tied neatly at the back.

"Clubs," Naomi said softly.

"At this hour?" Daddy said, approaching from the rear. God, she was trapped. She tried to slip around them.

"We were worried sick about you," Mama said, grabbing her arm.

"Sorry," Naomi said. "But I . . ." She closed her mouth. Even she could smell the stench coming from it.

Mama backed away. "You've been drinking," she said, affixing her hands on her hips.

Naomi shrugged and headed for the stairs.

"We're not finished with you," Mama said, a tone of rage in her voice that Naomi had never heard.

She stopped and exhaled but only from her nose. She didn't want to fuss with her mother when it was taking all her energy and concentration just to stand upright.

"What do you think you're doing?" Daddy asked. "Going out and getting drunk and coming in at this hour. You may be going through some rough times, but that's no reason to act like a damn fool."

"I haven't had that much to drink." She hiccuped. Oh, hell, she thought. That *would* have to come out now.

"You're lying," Mama said.

Naomi rolled her eyes to the ceiling. If these people knew the truth, they wouldn't be bitching about a few drinks.

"We're wasting our time talking to her while she's in this state," Daddy said. "Let her go to bed and we'll talk to her later."

Yes, Naomi thought. They weren't making it any easier on her with all this yakking. Better to let her out of here before she fell flat on her face.

Mama threw her arm toward the stairs. "Go on. I don't want to see you like this anymore. You're acting like *you're* the one whose life ended instead of Joshua's."

Naomi lowered her eyes. She could feel her parents' scalding stares on her back as she walked up the stairs. A lump swelled up in her throat and she swallowed it away. They were probably more disappointed in her now than they had ever been, and she didn't blame them one bit. But she couldn't think about that with her head going around in circles. She kicked off her shoes and dropped across the bed. . . .

The next thing she knew, the sun was shining brightly through the curtains and a blanket was covering her. She squinted against the light and lifted the blanket to see a badly wrinkled dress, and the previous night slapped her in the face. This was the pits, she thought. The absolute worst. She wanted to sit up, but she couldn't. The thought of going downstairs and facing her parents was more than she could bear. She shifted to her side to look at the clock on the dresser, and the first thing to reach her eyes was Joshua's portrait. She turned on her back and threw the blanket over her head. She didn't need to be reminded of him. Not now. Every time she thought of him, it seemed harder to go on. That was the antithesis of what Joshua had stood for, she knew. Joshua was always so full of ideas, so full of hope. But look where it got him. Look where it got *her* whenever she tried to do anything. It was a cruel world out there.

Yes, it is, Naomi. But stop blaming everybody and everything and get up off your butt and deal with it.

She yanked the covers from her face, stood up beside the bed, and looked quickly around the room. Joshua? She was always trying to think what he would say, trying to remember the sound of his voice. But rarely did she come close anymore. Then she realized that the voice in her head wasn't Joshua's. It was her own.

Nineteen

"Where are my old college catalogs?" Naomi asked.

Mama gave Daddy a look from the sink, where she was washing dishes. Daddy had given up pipes and sat at the table nibbling on a toothpick. Naomi knew the minute she walked into the kitchen that they had been talking about her. "In a box in the basement with all your old school things," Mama said.

"Thanks," Naomi said.

"Do you want some lunch?" Daddy asked.

"Maybe later." She didn't think her stomach could take much of anything at the moment. She turned toward the stairs.

"Naomi, we have to talk," Daddy said.

"I know I messed up last night, but can it wait until after I dig up the college catalogs?" Her mind was on a run now, and she didn't want to stop for any lectures.

"Come right back here when you finish," Mama said.

No question about that, Naomi thought, judging from the tone in their voices. As she walked down the stairs, the air grew chillier. This area wasn't used for much more than storage space. In a corner, her mother had piled all the things she didn't have the heart to throw out—old baby clothes, toys, even Naomi's collection of Nancy Drew mysteries—on top of a sleeper sofa that she remembered from her elementary school days. Joshua's things were sitting on an old dining room table.

She picked up one of the Nancy Drew books and blew the dust from its faded cover. Then she flipped through, being careful not to let any of the loose pages fall from the tattered spine. It was hard to believe that these mystery stories, with their blond-haired, wide-eyed heroine, had at one time been all she needed to keep herself happy on a Saturday afternoon.

She carefully placed the book back on its pile and looked around until she found the college catalogs. At least a dozen of them were stacked in a box, from schools she applied to and those she didn't. She picked out the local ones—George Washington, American, Howard, and Maryland—and flipped through them. They all had programs in business administration, and all those programs required loads of courses in economics and statistics.

She stopped flipping through the pages and took a deep breath. They would also have professors who would doubt her ability to succeed, except maybe at Howard. She would have to work her butt off, especially in the beginning. She'd probably have to take extra courses along the way and spend all her time studying. If a B average was expected, she'd need an A average. In other words, she'd probably have to work twice as hard for half the reward. But so what? Her folks were right. She was acting like she was the one who died. She had no business letting a few setbacks get her down or thinking she was a victim, not as long as she was breathing. What was it Mama had said? "You don't lose until you give up." Something like that.

This was perfect for her. With a degree in business she might even be able to start her own company someday, just like she'd always dreamed of doing. Why had it taken her so long to reach this point? This was something she would feel passionate about, something she'd be hungry for, something that all the doubtful looks and words in the world wouldn't be able to keep her from accomplishing.

She was so excited about this new way of thinking that she sat down on the cold, hard floor and flipped through the pages to find the schools that had the toughest, most demanding programs. Why settle for half the reward? If she was going to do it, she was going to go for all of it, and if that meant working

ten times as hard, that's what she would do. She was still flipping through the catalogs when she heard her mother call her
name from the top of the stairs.

"Yes?"

"Dean is here."

She stood up and went to the bottom of the stairs. "Did you
say Dean?"

Mama smiled. "Yes, he's right in the living room."

Naomi was petrified. She had on an old robe and slippers,
and she'd hastily braided her hair that morning before coming
down. They weren't pretty braids, either, but stuck out all over
her head. Then she relaxed. It was only Dean. One of the nice
things about him was that she never felt he was judging her
looks. Still, the hair was a bit much. She would have to try to
slip by the living room and get to her bedroom for a scarf.

All her plotting flew out the window as she reached the top
of the stairs and Dean slipped up behind her mother. He was all
smiles, and she smiled too. It was fantastic to see him after all
these months. He was looking as good as ever in a new pair of
jeans that fit just right.

Mama backed away toward the kitchen, pointing toward her
head as she fell out of Dean's sight. Naomi's hand flew to her
hair. In her excitement at seeing Dean, she had completely forgotten about the braids. "Sorry I look such a mess."

He reached out for her. "Come here and give me a hug."
They embraced warmly. "It's good to see you," he said.

"I'm glad to see you too. You look different somehow,
though."

"Good different? Or bad?"

"No, good, definitely good. Happier or something."

"Maybe it has to do with what I came to tell you."

"Good news?"

He nodded.

"I sure could use some of that. Go sit in the living room
while I get something for my hair." She ran up the stairs.

"Do you want something to drink?" she asked when she returned, a brightly patterned scarf tied at the back of her neck.

He shook his head. "I can't stay long. Come sit next to me."

He patted the sofa next to where he sat, and she sat down. "I'm moving to Niger."

"Niger? That's in Africa, isn't it?"

He nodded. "My job is sending me. I only have a two-hour layover before my flight to New York. Then I get an Air Afrique flight this evening."

She was disappointed to hear he would be leaving the States, but it would be selfish of her to let on when he sounded so excited. "Wow. Africa, huh?" That was all she could manage.

"Pretty amazing, isn't it? I still can't believe it."

"Me either. How long will you be there?"

"No telling. Until my assignment is up."

"Are we talking months, years?"

"One year, maybe two."

A whole year? "I'm in shock. But you sound so happy."

He chuckled. "It's a big change, I know. But I can't wait to get away from here."

"Really? Why?"

"I'm looking forward to living in a country where dark-skinned people are the majority, and the color of my skin won't matter. That's not to say they don't have problems over there. They do. But different problems. I won't be hampered just because of my race when I'm trying to accomplish something."

"Lord knows, I can understand your feelings. But remember what you said to me about running? Don't you think in a way you're just running from the problems instead of staying and trying to fix them?"

He smiled. "I'm not running away. I'm just taking a break, like you are. At least, when I do come back, I'll have a fresh perspective."

Naomi nodded. Running, not running. Didn't make a whole lot of difference. "I'm upset that you're leaving me here all alone, but you deserve whatever will make you happy."

"If I learned anything in Atlanta, it's that you're more than capable of taking care of yourself. Heaven help anyone who crosses you. They were talking about the demonstration for weeks after you left."

That was the furthest thing from her mind now. She looked down at her hands. "I'm really going to miss you."

"Then come with me."

She looked up at him. "You're joking."

"Well, I was when I said it, but you could, you know."

"That's impossible."

"Why? What's stopping you?"

"I . . ."

"Are you back in school?"

"No, not yet."

"Is it your job?"

"Heck, no. I'd leave that in a minute."

"Then what is it? Your boyfriend?"

"Not really."

"You mean you're not seeing anyone?"

"That's not what's stopping me. Are you still with Sonya?"

"No, we broke up. So you see? No excuses either way."

He slid over to close the distance between them. "Come with me, Naomi. It would be fun."

He ran his finger along her jawline, and she laughed nervously. His face was so close she could feel his warm breath on her neck. "I can't just jump up and leave. I don't have a job over there. I—"

He touched her lips with the tip of his finger to silence her. "I'll have enough for both of us for a while. The cost of living is much cheaper there. And you could find a job in no time. They'd be glad to get someone with your education and skills. And if you didn't like it, you could always come back."

"Dean, I'm flattered you would ask, but it's so far away from—"

"Wait. Let me finish." He exhaled. "You remember the day in Atlanta when I drove you back to campus and asked if you were seeing anyone?"

"Yes."

"Well, my feelings haven't really changed. I know you probably think of me more as a brother, and that's fine if that's the way you want it. I can live with that. But the point is, I'd never let anything bad happen to you, over there or anywhere."

Yes, she knew that. She closed her eyes and for a fleeting moment let her imagination run with the thought of living with Dean in Africa. A second ago, as he ran down his list of what might be stopping her, she realized how little she had to keep her here. Africa sounded so exotic. If she could feel safe with anyone in a strange land it was the man sitting here beside her. Adventure, security, maybe even a little romance. It felt funny thinking of Dean that way, but who knew what might happen thousands of miles away? It was so tempting. But she couldn't. She had to get her life in order here at home before she tried to make it someplace else.

She opened her eyes. "It sounds exciting, and I'm flattered you asked me. But I think I'll take my chances here."

He slid back to his side of the sofa. "Fine. I understand."

Did he? Because she wasn't sure she did. She was already starting to miss him.

A few minutes later, she walked him to the door and then watched from the living room window until he hailed a cab. The good ones always go away, she thought, as he pulled off.

"Naomi?"

She turned to face her mother, not bothering to hide the grief on her face.

"What's wrong?" Mama said, alarm crossing her face. "Did something happen to Dean?"

Naomi shook her head. "No, he's fine. But he's leaving for Africa."

"How long will he be there?"

"He doesn't know, but a long time. His job is sending him."

"I'm sorry, honey. But it sounds like a good opportunity for him, living in Africa."

Naomi nodded and sniffed as Daddy walked into the room. "What's wrong?"

"Dean is moving to Africa for a while," Mama said.

"Where in Africa?"

"Niger," Naomi said. "It's not just that. It's everything. My life has been pure chaos."

Mama sighed and sat beside her. "It's not that bad. You just have to make up your mind what you want to do with it."

"You're still young," Daddy said. "You have time."

Naomi stood up. She might have time but not patience. Her life was pathetic, but she had nobody to blame for it but herself. She couldn't think about the what-if's and maybe's with Dean. Right now, she was a mess. Dean deserved better, and so did she. She pushed up the sleeves to her robe and headed for the basement stairs.

Twenty

Naomi stepped onto the curb and cut across the grassy lawn in front of the Colefield House. She took the same shortcut across the University of Maryland campus every Tuesday and Thursday on her way from macroeconomics class to the library, and something different seemed to be happening on the lawn every time. This was known as protest central, since somebody or other was always out here demonstrating against something, from women's rights to animal rights, sometimes more than one group at a time. Last Tuesday, black students were out demanding more black professors at the university. One of the organizers had asked Naomi to join them. She declined, although she did agree to sign their petition.

The biggest and loudest group by far was the one protesting the war. It had grown even larger recently, as U.S. involvement in Vietnam heated up. A few students had even set up tents and sleeping bags and seemed to live on the lawn. It was a huge campus, and this one little corner didn't disrupt much, but Naomi was at first surprised and then resentful that the administration hadn't put a stop to the overnight camping. She wondered how long they would put up with it if it were a group of *black* students hanging around the Colefield House twenty-four hours a day drinking beer and smoking grass and doing goodness knows what else.

As she walked past the edge of the crowd, a long-haired fellow wearing beads handed her a flyer. "Peace," he said, holding up two fingers as she took it. Then he strolled off to hand one to somebody else. Naomi glanced at the flyer. It announced a major rally this coming Saturday against the war. She dropped the flyer into the first garbage can she passed by. She sympathized with all the causes, but she had her own war going on inside her head right now, with her brain cells battling each other over statistics, economics, accounting, and the principles of business administration.

Since starting school that summer, she had neither the time nor the temperament to come out from under her books. Protesting might work for others, but not for her. She was convinced that the best way to fight power was to become powerful herself. Whenever she ran into a racist professor—and she'd come to realize that Maryland had as many as Georgia—she made a personal pledge that nothing short of an A would do in the course. She'd spent many a night with nothing but a package of No Doz and her textbooks for company, but so far she'd kept every one of her promises.

As soon as she left the field, the commotion quieted down and the late fall breeze picked up a notch. She shifted her books under her arms and wrapped her trench coat around her, tying the belt snugly. She needed a hat, but her Afro was so big now it would be hard finding one that fit.

She had just stepped off the curb when a red Midget came flying up the street. She dashed across, and it swung around her. "Stupid fool," she muttered, as she hopped up onto the curb. Then she realized the driver was pulling over, and she paused to look. It was Jennifer Jones.

"Hey, what's up?" Jennifer said as she hopped out of the car.

Naomi stared, speechless for a moment. She hadn't heard from her old high school friend since breaking up with Ralph almost a year ago. "I don't believe it. How on earth did you find me?"

"Luck more than anything else," Jennifer said. "I called your house, and your mother said you usually go to the library around this time. I asked somebody for directions after I got on campus but got all mixed up. I've been riding all around. This place is huge. Lucky I saw you."

Jennifer stepped up on the curb, and they hugged warmly. Naomi stepped back and looked at her and smiled. Jennifer had cut her hair into a short curly Afro and was wearing a beautiful rabbit fur jacket. As always, she looked adorable. "It's good to see you," Naomi said. "Your hair is so cute."

"Thanks. You look good too. You've put on some weight since I last saw you, in all the right places. Were you on your way to the library?"

Naomi nodded.

"Is it far?"

"Everything's far on this campus."

"Get in. I'll give you a lift."

They climbed into her little sports number, and Jennifer shifted gears and took off. "Nice car," Naomi said. "What are you doing in these parts?"

"I'm home for Thanksgiving."

"That's not until next week."

"So I cut a few classes to come home early. Shoot me."

Naomi laughed. "How are things up at Cornell?"

"Fine. It's always freezing cold this time of year, and I've changed my major again. But otherwise, fine."

"What are you majoring in now?"

"Accounting. Before it was economics."

"Didn't you start out in art history or something?"

Jennifer laughed. "I don't want to talk about it. What's your major? And why did you leave Atlanta?"

"Business administration. And Atlanta is a long story. I'll tell you some other time."

"Did Ralph have anything to do with it?"

"In a way, yes."

Jennifer shook her head. "I feel like I should apologize for my brother."

"Don't. You warned me about him, but I wouldn't listen. I'm over it now."

"Good. I hate to say this about my own brother, but you deserve better."

Naomi nodded. "I finally came to that conclusion myself."

"So, want to get together tomorrow night? Go roller-skating or something?"

"Skating? When did you get into roller-skating?"

"When I discovered it was a good place to meet guys. I haven't been seeing anyone since the end of last semester. That's almost five months, and I'm horny as hell. Besides, it's fun."

Naomi laughed and shook her head. "Count me out. I have too much work to do."

"You can't study twenty-four hours a day."

"No, only sixteen. I do try to get eight hours of sleep."

"You're not serious?"

"Oh, but I am."

"Are you seeing anyone?"

"Not since last spring," Naomi said. "Same as you."

"Aren't you dying to meet a man and get screwed?"

"Jennifer, please." These days she didn't have time to think about sex or much of anything besides school. She filled the lonely spots with homework. She didn't want to get involved with some man purely for the sake of it—she wasn't doing another Jimmy—and real relationships took time.

"Come with me to the rink tomorrow night."

Naomi shook her head. "I usually study with Debbie on Friday nights. We're both taking accounting courses, and Debbie's a natural at that kind of thing."

"Where is she going to school?"

"GW."

"Didn't she have a baby?"

"Uh-huh. A girl."

"Get her to come too, if she can find a sitter."

Debbie's mother could probably watch Serena, but Naomi didn't think Debbie would be too keen on the idea of going skating or anywhere else with Jennifer. Naomi never did figure out exactly what was going on the night of Jennifer's party, whether Jennifer didn't want Debbie around because she was dark-skinned and didn't fit in with Jennifer's crowd or if it was something else. And much as she hated to admit it to herself, she'd been too intimidated by Jennifer back then to ask, too afraid of losing her friendship. "I don't think Debbie would be interested."

"You're like two peas in a pod. You're missing out on all the fun."

"It's not that. It's . . ." Naomi paused. She would still hate to lose Jennifer as a friend. But if what Debbie suspected was true, the break would be Naomi's own doing, not Jennifer's. She had no time or patience for people like that anymore. "Can I ask you something?"

"Sure."

"Do you remember the party you had in tenth grade?"

Jennifer nodded. "The one where you met Merlon."

"Uh-huh. And I said I wanted to bring Debbie with me?"

"I don't remember that."

Naomi paused. How could she forget that part? "You told me I could invite someone, and I mentioned Debbie."

Jennifer shrugged. "OK, if you say so."

"Anyway, when I said that, you suddenly got all uptight, like you weren't so hot about the idea."

Jennifer frowned. "I hardly remember."

Naomi exhaled. Jennifer wasn't going to make this easy. "I distinctly remember feeling you didn't want me to bring her."

"Why would I care one way or the other?"

"Maybe you didn't think she'd fit in because she's dark-skinned."

Jennifer was silent.

"I may be wrong," Naomi said. "Tell me if I am."

"It wasn't me, but some of my friends might have felt that way."

"Uh-huh."

"You know how it was back then."

"That's no excuse. Debbie's one of the nicest people I know. And if you associate with people who think that way, you're not much better than they are."

"You're right, and I don't do that anymore. At Cornell, I hang out with all kinds of black people. But D.C. was different back then."

"Yeah, right," Naomi said.

"All of us were guilty in a way, Naomi."

"Excuse me?"

"You always went with light-skinned guys. Merlon, my brother."

Naomi bit her bottom lip. Jimmy.

"So don't go jumping on me when you're just as guilty."

Naomi smiled thinly, and they rode the rest of the way to the library in silence. OK, so she wasn't Miss Perfect either, back in those days. When Jennifer pulled up to the curb, Naomi put her hand on the door handle and turned toward Jennifer. "Thanks for the lift."

"No problem."

"About skating?"

"Yes?"

"I'll ask Debbie and give you a call tonight."

Jennifer smiled. "Good. I think you'd both have fun."

Persuading Debbie took a bit of work. At first, she flat out refused to have anything to do with Jennifer Jones.

"Forget it, Nay." Debbie said, flipping through the pages of her statistics book. "I don't hang around rich little vanilla-colored princesses who can't see past my complexion."

"She's changed, Debbie. Everybody deserves a second chance."

Debbie looked up from the book. "So you finally admit she didn't want me around before?"

"Jennifer even admits it. But she doesn't think like that anymore."

"I'm happy she finally got some sense, but no thanks."

"You know, you're doing the same thing in a way, Debbie."

"Come again?"

"You're snubbing Jennifer 'cause she's light-skinned and has money."

Debbie seemed about to protest; then she paused. "So what if I am. Can you blame me?"

"Maybe not before. But now, yes. Come on, Debbie. You're the two oldest friends I have. I'd love to see you get along. At least try. Jennifer can be a lot of fun."

Debbie exhaled. "OK. But if that girl even looks at me funny, I'm outa there."

It was tense at first, with the three of them piled tightly into Jennifer's two-seater. But by the time they pulled up in front of the skating rink on Sixteenth Street, Debbie and Jennifer were chattering about accounting and the upcoming skating adventure like two old friends. It turned out that Debbie had learned to skate when she started taking Serena to the rink. Naomi was so happy to see them getting on easily that she didn't even mind when they skated off together and left her wobbling on her feet.

After falling twice, she decided her bruised butt had seen enough action for one night. She was trying to make her way through the skaters whizzing by to the edge of the rink when a young boy bumped into her. He skated on by just as her legs buckled beneath her, and she saw the cold hard floor of the rink rising up to greet her once again. She'd put her arms out to catch herself when a pair of big brown hands caught her in midfall. It took a little jiggling but soon she was standing straight again and staring up into the face of a black Adonis.

"Are you all right?" he asked.

"Huh?" She was so mesmerized by this good-looking chocolate baby that all her senses seemed to have turned into mush. "What did you say?"

"I said, are you OK?"

"I'm fine, fine." Just then her legs gave out from under her again, but he reached out and caught her just in time. This was humiliating, she thought, trying to steady her feet. She couldn't even keep her balance while standing still on the darn skates.

"This your first time?" he asked, holding on to her arm. He seemed afraid to let her go, and that was just fine with her. She was falling in love with those big steady hands of his.

"How did you guess?"

He smiled, showing a set of pearly white teeth. "I'll help you around a couple of times."

"Actually, I was about to take a break." A permanent one, she thought, glancing wistfully at the benches scattered just outside the rink.

"You'll never learn that way. Come on." Before she could protest further he was leading her around the rink. He was so poised and graceful, and so good at holding her up, she could almost forget her own clumsiness.

"Now balance yourself," he said, holding on to her arm.

What did he think she was trying to do, audition for a job as a circus clown? "How long have you been skating?"

"Since I was a little brat."

Naomi laughed. "How long did it take you to get good at it?"

"Not much time. It's easier when you're little. But if you keep coming, you'll get the hang of it soon enough."

He let go of her slowly, turned, and skated backward, watching her as she watched her feet.

"Look up at me," he said. "It's easier that way."

Looking up *was* easier. But she suspected it had to do with what was in front of her. He was about six two, with a muscular build and a complexion that brought velvet to mind. All the commotion around her faded into the background.

"What's your name?" he asked.

She actually had to think for a second before it came to her. "Naomi."

"I'm Chuck." He extended his hand, and she grabbed it and refused to let go.

He smiled, skated around beside her, and tucked an arm about her waist.

"Don't let go this time," she said.

He squeezed. "I won't."

They made it around the rink twice without Naomi falling once. That was enough time for her to find out that Chuck was a third-year law student at Howard, so he spent a lot of time hitting the books too. Skating was his way of relaxing.

"Who was that?" Jennifer asked later as the three girls sat on a bench and removed their skates.

"His name is Chuck."

"He sure is fine," Debbie said. "You gave him your number, I hope?"

Naomi nodded. "I'm going skating with him again next weekend. I just hope I don't break my neck."

"You're waiting a whole week to see him?" Jennifer asked.

"He's in law school," Naomi said. "So he's busy with work all week too."

"I thought you weren't dating these days," Jennifer said teasingly.

"Someone like that would make a nun think twice about giving up men," Debbie said.

The three of them laughed and slapped high fives.

Within a few weeks of meeting Chuck, Naomi was drawing little hearts around his name in her econ books and fantasizing about his beautiful hands. All they did was go skating a couple of Friday nights and out to dinner and the movie *Lady Sings the Blues* one weekend. But she was hooked. He treated her like a lady, and a special one at that. He opened doors for her, helped her lace up her skates, ordered for her at dinner, mailed her intimate little notes telling her how he couldn't wait to see her again, and always paid her way.

All that old-fashioned genteel stuff was a potent aphrodisiac for a girl who wasn't used to it. Not to mention those sexy hands. Still, she was a bundle of nerves as he shut the door to his studio apartment after the movie and gave her that lusty look that made her feel like he was undressing her with his bare eyes. It was at times like this that she wished her underwear was from Frederick's of Hollywood rather than the lingerie department at Sears. He made her feel so sexy, and that lean chocolate body looked so tempting, she thought she would pass out right there on the spot.

But he wasn't going to allow that. He grabbed her and kissed her hungrily with those warm, soft lips she had come to love. She'd known this was coming all evening—from the way he cuddled her hand in his lap throughout the whole movie, the way he licked the tips of her fingers in the car. She also knew she was ready for it. It was only the third date, way sooner than usual for her, but never mind that. Her body had been ready for this man since she first laid eyes on him.

Her mind was another matter, though. It kept intruding with memories of Ralph ridiculing her lovemaking and of Jimmy's incompetence. Then there was the matter of her breasts, she thought, as his hand glided up her back and found the bow to her halter top. She was embarrassed by their lack of volume. She wanted to be perfect for him. She wanted to look more like Lola Falana or Diahann Carroll than Twiggy.

She shuddered as the top dropped down to her waist, and he seemed to sense her anxiety. He sat on the bed, put his hands on her hips, and pulled her toward him. "What's wrong?" he whispered, between deep breaths of air.

"Nothing," she said, a bit too quickly. What was the matter with her? This wasn't Ralph, and it certainly wasn't Jimmy. This was the man of her dreams. This was Shakespeare's Romeo, Michelangelo's David and Hollywood's Billy Dee Williams all rolled into one. And right now, he was all hers. She closed her eyes and guided his head to her breasts, determined to clear her mind.

That became easier as his lips brushed her nipples ever so tenderly, and he planted a trail of feathery kisses down to her belly button. It became easier still as he slowly undressed her with those big, strong hands, his tongue trailing along as he un-buttoned, unhooked, unzipped, and slowly peeled away all her resistance. He was so eager, yet so gentle. So this was how it was supposed to feel, she thought, running her fingers down his back.

Then he lifted his shirt over his head, exposing firm muscles, and every nerve ending in her body stood at attention. Her eyes never missed a beat as he opened his jeans and let everything fall in a heap on the floor. When he pulled her on top of him, she was too delirious to think. By the time he slid inside her, her brain cells had turned to mush. She wanted to tell him not to stop, to go on doing this to her forever. She'd finally reached the mountaintop.

He lifted his body up and pulled her over so her head was resting on his shoulders. Then he reached down, brushed her hair away from her face, and kissed her forehead. She looked up and kissed him, then snuggled up close. They were both too breathless to speak. She thought about how she'd gone from waiting three months to just three dates to have sex. She had the women's movement to thank for that. No longer was it considered necessary for a woman to wait even when she was feeling horny enough to explode. If she'd known it was going to be like this, she'd have been ready after three minutes.

She rubbed her hand across his firm flat tummy. She loved his dark complexion. It made him exciting, sexy. It was like a whole new category of men had opened up to her. Not that she wouldn't have dated a dark man before simply because of his color. But what Jennifer said was true, as much as she hated admitting it to herself. She hadn't been as open to them. Now, though, she'd be as willing to seek out good-looking dark-skinned babes as she would the light ones. Maybe more willing. She looked up. He had dozed off. She wrapped her arm around his waist and smiled. If things went well with this one, she wouldn't have to think about other men in the future.

Lying there at that moment, she felt her life was perfect. She was back in school studying business and lying next to a super-fine dude who treated her like a princess. He would someday be a lawyer, and visions of the big Tudor house on the Gold Coast danced in her head—again. Despite what Mama always told her, she simply couldn't seem to shake the Cinderella fantasy.

But it wasn't long—a few weeks, maybe—before the clock struck midnight. It started in small ways, like Chuck complaining whenever she didn't look her best: nails perfectly manicured, hair just so, lots of makeup, and the latest fashions, preferably dresses. Naomi knew she was no slouch when it came to dressing, but this man was never satisfied. For a while, she was flattered that he took such an interest in her. But it soon got to be a nuisance, especially the day he asked her to wear makeup to the beach.

They were spending a week in the Bahamas celebrating a whole bunch of things—his graduation from law school, passing the bar, and landing a job as an attorney for the Legal Services Corporation. It wasn't exactly his dream job; all the big Washington law firms he applied to had turned him down. But it was a good place to park until he found a better spot.

"You don't go in the water much anyway," he said, when

she came out of the hotel bathroom in her swimsuit wearing only a touch of lipstick. "So why not fix yourself up?"

"I'd feel like a fool in full makeup on the beach, Chuck."

"Then just put on some rouge and a little something around your eyes. I like my woman to look good all the time."

Naomi was tempted to ask him if he thought she was so bad-looking without it why he bothered with her in the first place. It was at times like this that she thought of Dean and his carefree laid-back ways. If she were in Africa with him, she'd probably still be wearing her hair in a big Afro with no makeup, dressed in jeans and a dashiki, and shooting the breeze. But she wasn't. She was here with Chuck. So she smiled and marched back into the bathroom. She had learned within a few short weeks of dating Chuck not to argue with him, especially when he was around his friends.

"That was uncalled for," he'd said as they flew down the Beltway after a party at his best friend's house. Naomi had to hold on to her seat to keep from being jerked around.

"What are you talking about? And would you please slow down before you kill us both?"

"When I said I didn't think Nixon should be impeached 'cause it's not all that big a deal, you said you thought he should be."

"Well, I do. Watergate is—"

"That's not the point. Don't go around contradicting me like that, especially in public."

"I wasn't contradicting you, I was just saying what I think."

"Then keep your thoughts to yourself when we're in public. You made me look like a damn idiot."

"If that's all it takes to make you look like an idiot, it doesn't take much. And would you please slow down."

He pressed his foot to the floor, and they fumed in silence all the way back to her house. He didn't run around the car to open the door for her this time, didn't even bother to get out. By the time Naomi slammed the front door shut, she was convinced it was over between them. Two nights later, her hands gripped the bars on his brass bed while he rocked inside her, and she knew she couldn't live without him.

OK, so her Prince Charming was really a raging chauvinistic pig. Sometimes he made her feel so bad, the way he took every little thing that went wrong in his life out on her, she wanted to cry. He hated his new job, and that didn't help things between them. But she told herself there had to be hope for a man who could be so sweet when he wanted and could make the earth move under her feet. She would just have to be patient. Sooner or later, he would see that she wasn't the enemy.

Graduation day was one of the most satisfying in Naomi's life. As she stood in front of her bedroom mirror tucking the front of her newly permed hair under the graduation cap, she thought back to the days when she would stand in this very same spot trying to hide behind her bangs. That was not much more than five years ago, and yet with all she'd been through it seemed like ages. But here she was, standing in her cap and gown, about to get her degree in business, and no one besides herself knew just how torturous a road she'd traveled. No one except maybe Joshua. She glanced at his photo and smiled. She had a feeling he knew, and that he was just as happy.

And her parents—no matter what was in store for her from here on, she would never forget the looks of pure pride on their faces on this day. Mama kept fussing with the cap and gown and batting moist eyes, and Daddy must have used up a dozen rolls of film, taking pictures of his daughter and everything that moved around her.

That night, Chuck took her out to dine at Benihana in Rosslyn to celebrate. She had a good life now, she thought. The only thing missing was marriage. She and Chuck had circled around the subject, naturally, since they'd been together for almost two years now. She could definitely see herself being married to him but was old-fashioned enough not to push it. She'd settle for dropping the occasional hint—like admiring diamond rings in jewelry store windows when they shopped together—and wait for him to pop the question. She was hopeful, since they were getting along better than ever, mostly because she'd learned how to stay on his good side. She always tried to look her best around him; he was the main reason she'd given up her cherished Afro. She wanted to cut her hair short, but he said he liked long hair, so she let it grow out. And she never contradicted him in public. So what if he wasn't the hotshot corporate lawyer they'd both envisioned back during his law school days. That bothered him more than it did her. He was going through a rough period, with his career not going the way he wanted, and she tried to be encouraging and supportive.

When she landed her dream job as a research assistant at System Solutions, Inc., one of the biggest consulting firms in the Washington, D.C., area, and learned she would be making almost as much money as he did, she downplayed the whole thing. At times she felt like she was cheating herself, but in return she got a man who was attentive, treated her well most of the time, and was explosive in bed.

Life wasn't perfect but it was close. And she knew from experience it could be a hell of a lot worse.

Twenty-one

OK, so her job wasn't the dream she had anticipated. Instead of heading up teams working on exciting research projects, she spent most of her day sitting on her butt in the computer room entering numbers onto punched cards and feeding them into machines with a zillion buttons and lights. Then she would carry the printout back to her desk in the office she shared with two other research assistants and spend hours proofing it before handing it over to one of the analysts.

It didn't take her long at all to realize that although most of the analysts had advanced degrees, a few of them had been hired right out of college. And all the other assistants on her level had only associate degrees, except Rob. She didn't like to think about how a white dude with a degree in psychology ended up at SSI doing the same thing she did.

She hadn't the faintest doubt that she should have been hired as an analyst. Of course, that would have been breaking a long-standing tradition, since none of the analysts at SSI were black. But Naomi knew she could perform much of the work they did, despite what everyone else might think. A couple of times she offered to do just that but was simply turned down and handed another stack of cards.

After putting up with this crap for a year, she became convinced she was going to have to prove herself to these cats. Otherwise she'd be stuck in this two-bit job forever. On her next project, she came in on Saturdays and stayed late during the week so she could finish entering the data onto the cards and still have some spare time to analyze it. But despite all the extra hours, she still hadn't finished the analysis by the time she was supposed to hand the data over.

"Naomi, have you finished entering the data yet?"

Naomi jumped and glanced up from her desk to see Patrick Anderson standing above her head. Patrick was a pencil-in-the-breast-pocket, wallet-bulging-in-the-hip-pocket kind of guy. She quickly covered the papers she was working on.

"Not quite." Actually, she'd finished entering the data days ago and was now analyzing it. But if she told him that, he'd probably demand that she hand the data over, which she was determined not to do.

"Can you speed it up?" Patrick said. "I have to finish the analysis by the end of the week, and I need the raw data. All the other assistants have handed theirs over."

Well, good for them, she thought, sneaking a glance at Rob, sitting at his desk at the other end of the office. His head was buried nonchalantly in a printout, but that didn't fool Naomi. She was sure he was fixed on this exchange between her and Patrick. "I just need a couple more days."

He let out a frustrated sigh and walked from the room.

Two days later, she met Patrick in the hallway on the way to his office and handed him the analysis.

"What's this?" he demanded to know, flipping through the printout.

"I went ahead and did some of the preliminary analysis myself. Standard deviations and errors, regressions."

He huffed and puffed and looked at her as if she'd gone off the deep end. "You weren't supposed to do that. Where's the raw data?"

"Some of it's in there. On page seventeen of the printout."

"I need all of it, so I can analyze it."

"You have the analysis in your hands."

"Naomi, I need the raw data, all of it."

"I'll have to dig it up."

"And just how much longer will that take?"

"A couple of days."

"That's too much time. I'm going to have to talk to Robert about this!" With that, he stomped off down the hall.

Naomi panicked big time when he said that. She had expected some resistance, at least until he looked at the printout and saw she'd done a decent job. But she never expected this talk about going to the division head. Now she was having second thoughts about her work. What if it wasn't as good as she thought it was? This was her first time using real data, not some made-up figures in a statistics class. Suddenly her mind flipped back to Thomas Turner and the awful scene with him in the hall outside the D.C. council office. Was she getting ahead of herself again?

All that day and the next, she felt as if she had a time bomb strapped to her back. She had no one to talk to about this, since none of the other assistants were black. So she sat at her desk alone and tried to concentrate on punched cards and printouts while praying that the bomb wouldn't explode.

When the president's secretary called and said the boss wanted to see her, she thought she would gag. This thing had gone all the way from Patrick to Robert to Edwin Gallows? She was in real trouble. They were all probably laughing at this very moment over the printout she'd given Patrick. Who the hell did she think she was, a lowly assistant trying to analyze data? Mr. Gallows would point out all her mistakes. Maybe he'd even fire her for insubordination.

Sitting outside his office, she tried to think how she would explain her behavior, how she would get out from under this tangled mess, but nothing seemed to do. Not even the secretary's smile soothed her. "You can go in now," she said.

Mr. Gallows was smiling too, as he stood and signaled for her to sit in the chair across from his desk. Maybe this wasn't even about the analysis, she thought. Maybe he wanted to talk about something else. Maybe Patrick hadn't gone to Robert and Robert to Edwin. But before she sat down, she caught a glimpse of the printout in the middle of his desk, and her heart sank. She was tempted to snatch it and run down the hall.

"I thought maybe I could save Patrick some time by doing

some preliminary analysis of the data," she said. "But I probably didn't consider—"

"You did a very good job."

"Huh?"

"What's here is very good. Robert says they need more multivariate analyses and some other stuff, but they're going to let you know exactly the format to use so you can get to work on it. I'm impressed."

Naomi swallowed hard. So the time bomb didn't go off. It was only when she felt the muscles in her body relax that she realized how tightly wound up she had been. "Well, I . . . I was a bit rushed because I knew Patrick faced a deadline."

"Fine, fine." He tapped his fingers on the desk. "The reason I called you in here is because—well, they don't have any need for more analysts in Robert's unit. But the health systems division is competing for a contract with the Department of Defense, and Gary's looking to hire a couple of analysts over there. Are you familiar with that project?"

"Yes, DOD is redesigning the information systems for their hospitals, all over the country, and they're contracting the work out. I helped the division do some calculations for the proposal a couple of weeks ago."

"So Gary tells me. Have you had any experience designing survey research projects?"

Naomi cleared her throat. "I took several courses in survey methods and sampling at Maryland University and had to do a project from design to the final verbal and written report in my senior year."

"How did you do?"

"An A. I can show you the report if you like."

He smiled. "I'll take your word for it. That settles it. I'm going to move you up to a position as research analyst in the health systems division. What you've done here is equal to what many of our analysts are capable of when they join us. Provided you're interested. Are you?"

Hell, yeah. It was high time. "Of course."

"Fine. Keep up the good work. I'm pleasantly surprised. We

don't get many blacks who are capable of this kind of work. You're obviously an exception."

Naomi winced but tried not to show it. She didn't know what to make of that comment. It was true that not many blacks went into research, but only because of their circumstances, not their capabilities. Lord knew, if she had reached this point, others could too. She thought of Debbie, who could run circles around these white cats and all their fancy analyses any day of the week. She wanted to tell Mr. Gallows that, but she was no fool. She didn't want to jeopardize the promotion. She had come to believe she could do more by proving herself than by ranting and raving about all the injustice she faced along the way.

She loved the new position. It gave her the chance to finally put her analytical skills to work. And for the first time ever, she had a private office. It wasn't much bigger than a walk-in closet, but it was her very own. The downside was that she was the only black analyst. She felt proud of being a trailblazer, but climbing the corporate ladder alone was—well, lonely, especially when things got rough.

It wasn't long before she again sensed something fishy in the air. When it was almost time to write the proposal, she was told to hand her research over to another analyst when it was done. At first she assumed it was because she was new at this. Then she learned that most of the other analysts working on the project were helping to write sections of the proposal. If Naomi was confident about anything, it was her writing skills. She'd seen some of the reports written by other analysts and knew she could outwrite them any day of the week. So she decided she would have to show them again.

She did the same thing she'd done before. She worked extra hours to finish the analysis early, then she took a bunch of old proposals home, studied them, wrote up her own section, and handed it in.

A week later, Gary's secretary came into her office and dumped a stack of papers on her desk.

"What's this?"

"Gary said to give them to you," Anita said.

Naomi flipped through the pages and saw they were sections of the DOD proposal written by other analysts. "What on earth for?"

"He wants you to fix them up."

"You're kidding." Before the week was over, Naomi found herself wishing Anita *had* been kidding. Not only was she to rewrite major parts of the DOD proposal, Gary gave her the job of organizing and writing many of the other proposals for the division. Then, after they won the DOD contract a few weeks later, the work really began to pile up. Other divisions came to her office, proposals in hand, and asked her to rewrite theirs too. It soon got to the point she couldn't do anything else at the office and still had to take work home.

Chuck didn't like any of this one bit. He was furious about all the time she spent working. Naomi complained and pretended not to like it either, but she really loved it: all these white people depending on her to get the job done. Although she wasn't getting paid any more money for the work she took home, she didn't mind. It was valuable experience. Her mind began toying around with the idea of doing this on the side as a consultant. But first things first. For now, she would aim for a bigger promotion at SSI. And for that she needed to go for her MBA. She sent in applications but didn't breathe a word to Chuck. She had a feeling he wouldn't be thrilled to know she would have even less time for him once she went back to school. When the time came, she would have to tell him, but she didn't see any point in getting him upset until then.

In the weeks that followed, it was almost as if he sensed she was slipping away from him. One evening shortly after she got her acceptance letter for the MBA program at GW, they went out to dinner near her office. As she tried to come around to telling him the news over coffee, he popped the question. *The* question. Or sort of.

"Let's get married," he said.

She blinked. "What did you say?"

He smiled. "I don't want to have to shout it. But you've

hinted around. Or at least you used to." He leaned forward. "Let's get married."

She picked up her cup, took a sip, and set it back down. "Oh, Chuck." What she really needed was a stiff drink. This was a total, complete, utter surprise. She was almost twenty-four years old, and at times she had thought she would never hear those words. It seemed all her friends were getting hitched and having babies. Jennifer had gotten married right out of college to some guy she met at Cornell and moved to San Diego. Naomi hadn't seen her since the wedding. They talked on the phone when Jennifer came home to visit, and that was often enough for Naomi to know Jennifer was living a good life. She had had a daughter a year ago and was director of personnel for a large computer firm. Her husband was an engineer. They had a big new house and two luxury cars, a Mercedes and Jaguar. All of it was so Jennifer. Even wild and crazy Pamela had settled down and gotten married. The last time Naomi talked to her, Pamela was pregnant.

"I don't know what to say." She picked up her coffee cup again, but when it reached her lips she realized it was empty. She set it back down, and folded her hands in her lap.

"Say yes. You want to get married and have a family, don't you?"

"Some day."

He frowned. "What are you saying, not now?"

She shook her head, more out of confusion than in response to his question. A year ago, she would have jumped in his lap and been tempted to shout out her answer: yes! She practically lived at his apartment and had grown to know and love him the way only two people who spend a lot of time together can. But one thing she had come to realize only recently was that she could never be married to this man unless he changed his ways. She didn't even feel comfortable telling him when she got a raise or a promotion, or that she was going back to school. She could put up with that foolishness now, because when she got tired of it she could walk away for a while. But that wouldn't be true if she accepted his proposal. She couldn't see herself permanently tied to someone who wasn't strong enough to handle her success. She had big dreams, and they were getting bigger all the time.

"With me being so involved with my work, I don't—"

"Why do you let them work you like that?"

"I don't mind. I like it."

"Obviously more than you like spending time with me. Especially lately."

"Don't say that. You know how it is when you're starting out. You have to prove yourself."

"No, I don't know. I just work for the government. Are you sure it's the timing that's stopping you, or is it me?"

"The timing, of course."

"You sure that's it?"

She nodded. "It won't always be like this," she said. It's going to get worse, she thought.

"Then I should ask you later?"

"Later is better."

"Fine. But don't keep me waiting forever."

She didn't tell him that night about going for her MBA after all.

PART THREE

1983—1985

Twenty-two

Naomi kicked off her heels and paced back and forth across the carpet as she waited for her résumé to print out. Damn slow printers, she thought, eyeing the page as it moved up, line by line. She hated going up against powerful white men. It made her tense and edgy. She did it so often, though, it seemed to be her destiny. The last time was three years ago, to get promoted to her current position as manager of the proposal writing department. Now she was back at it. But it seemed to be the only way to get anywhere in this company. At least for her.

She stood in front of the picture window of her nineteenth-floor office and looked down at the traffic below. The streets of Crystal City, Virginia, right outside Washington, D.C., were always noisy, but the only sound reaching her ears all the way up here was the hum of the printer behind her. Reaching this perch above the masses had been a long hard fight. The powers-that-be at SSI were all middle-aged white men, used to doing things a certain way. When Naomi suggested they set up a proposal writing unit and make her the head, they balked. They weren't used to giving chocolate babes real power. She had to use every tactic she could think of to persuade them—assertiveness, flattery, reasoning, charm, cold hard facts. She started dressing in smart business suits and had her hair cut short and sophisticated.

It had paid off. After a year of meetings and memos, they finally agreed to set up the unit in the contracts and grants division and make her the manager. She was the first woman and the first black in the entire firm to be made a manager, and she was immensely proud of that fact. To this day, she was still the only black manager.

So she'd won that one. But Naomi knew that at best she seemed a peculiar breed to most of the brass, and at worst a nuisance that wouldn't go away. Now she was clamoring for another move up the corporate ladder, or so the word was going around, this time for a position as director of the division. Her boss was retiring, and Naomi felt she was the most logical successor. That didn't mean *they* would see the logic. Managing a unit was one thing; running a division was something else entirely, especially this division. Its director met with government and corporate heads—the ones who decided who would get their dough—and then dished out the funds. They were often department heads of federal agencies and *Fortune* 500 companies. And the person representing SSI had always been polished, articulate, and, to this point, white and male. As a black woman, single and thirty-one years old, Naomi knew she'd be butting up against a brick wall trying to land this baby, not a glass ceiling.

But she had plenty going for her besides her MBA. The number of contract awards had increased by more than 20 percent since she'd taken over. She had just learned that Patrick Anderson, the other manager in the division, was also going out for the position. Patrick had a master's degree in operations research, but he was notorious for hating to work after hours and was one of the worst writers in the firm. With the boom in the consulting business, especially technology consulting, SSI had to better position itself to compete for awards. That meant spending long hours putting together well-written proposals.

Patrick, also the resident nerd at SSI, always said they had a Bill Gates out on the West Coast to thank for the boom. In the nine years Naomi had been at SSI, they had gone from a big clunky mainframe and shared work stations to having personal computers on every desk. Punched cards were a relic of the past. The downside for the company was that with the size and cost of computers coming down so rapidly, anyone who'd had a course or two in statistics could buy one and some software, hang out a shingle, and compete with the biggies like SSI.

Naomi was giving that idea more and more thought. The dream of owning her own business was never far in the background these days. She had started taking freelance consulting work from other firms right after she got her MBA and couldn't believe how much people were willing to pay her. But first she wanted this promotion at SSI. A black woman striking out on her own would need all the credentials she could get.

She stopped pacing long enough to glance at the résumé as it came out of the printer. This was what her life had come to: contracts and grants, data analysis and research reports, and cutthroat competition. A lot of people would think it boring, but she thrived on it—especially when she thought how far the little black girl from nowhere who hated math had come.

She smiled, until she thought about her drab love life. If only she could light a fire under that. She'd dated many men over the years, but she didn't think she'd been in love with anyone after Chuck. They broke up shortly after he proposed marriage. The ending wasn't dramatic, more like a whimper than a bang. Gradually, she started spending less time at his apartment until one day she realized she hadn't seen or heard from him in almost two weeks. Her first instinct was to pick up the phone on her desk and call him, but she didn't, because she realized with sadness that it was over. No point dragging it out, she reasoned.

That was six years ago. Since then, it had been a long dry spell. She would go out with a man on a few dates and then quickly lose interest. Or he did. It was hard finding a man who was strong enough to handle her success yet gentle enough to take care of her when she needed it. And the more successful she became, the harder it seemed to be. The men with less education and money shied away, and those who had taken command of their careers seemed to want to take control of her too. The minute she sensed that a relationship was headed in that direction, she packed her bags and hit the road. She'd put in a lot of miles, but she knew exactly what she was looking for in a relationship. Someone strong enough not to be intimidated by her achievements yet confident enough not to need to dominate her. Someone who would take her work as seriously as she did. As for love—well, she'd tried that route and always seemed to crash and burn. She hoped that if she found a man with all the right traits, that love—the real thing, based on shared goals and a shared outlook on life—would come eventually. No more blind passion, no more giving and not getting, no more one-way streets.

The minute the printer stopped, she tore the résumé off at the perforated line, and sat back at her desk to read it for what must have been the hundredth time. Tomorrow was the big day. She was going to submit it and was working late tonight to update it. She had mentioned her plans to only a couple of people, but SSI had a rampant grapevine and her office buddy, Carla Reed, had told her at lunch that day that Patrick was also going to ask for the job.

"But my money's on you," Carla had said at lunch. "Patrick's too much the nine-to-five guy."

Naomi poked at her seafood salad with her fork. She was surprised to hear that Patrick was going after the position, for the very reason Carla mentioned. Patrick rarely worked more than forty hours a week and complained bitterly whenever he had to stay past five. He prided himself on being a family man and often boasted about how much time he spent helping his wife with their two boys.

"Hmm," Naomi muttered, while sizing up the competition. "He's got some things going for him."

"Yeah, like his writing skills," Carla said sarcastically.

Naomi smiled. "Seriously. He's been here a year longer than I have." Naomi didn't add that he was also a white male. Carla had become her closest friend at the office since coming on board two years earlier. She was about the same age as Naomi, also single, and had a tough no-nonsense attitude about her that Naomi liked. Yet she was open-minded and easy to talk to. She was a brilliant systems analyst, and Naomi had no doubt she was going places with the company. But Carla was also white. And although Naomi felt she could say almost anything to her—they'd had frank and spirited discussions about race and just about every other issue of the day—that didn't mean Carla would really understand her viewpoint.

"That doesn't matter," Carla said, her brown hair bouncing as she shook her head. "The company's policy is to promote on merit, not seniority. And I heard they've been looking to hire or promote a woman as director for a couple of years now."

Naomi nodded. She'd heard that too, although she often wondered what was taking them so long, since during that time two new directors had been installed, both white men. Even if they were talking about hiring a woman director, a black woman was probably the furthest thing from their minds. It would be up to her to change that.

"That's what I'm counting on," Naomi said. "But I can't help but wonder if they're really ready to do that, especially a black woman."

"They *have* been excruciatingly slow about it, no question. But if they're ready to appoint a woman, they should be ready for a black person too."

"I'll have to bop them over the heads about it, but I've had experience doing that. Still, I had hoped I wouldn't have to do that this time. I proved myself to them long ago."

"Maybe you won't."

"On a cold day in hell."

"Why do you have to assume the worst?"

"Sorry, it's the way I was raised. But maybe it's for the best. Makes me work that much harder."

"But things are changing around here."

"Depends on your viewpoint. Have you looked around you recently? The company's hiring a lot more women analysts these days, but—"

"That's just my point. You said when you started there were only a handful. And when I started there weren't many more. But now almost half of us are women."

"You came during a wave of hiring women. I've been waiting for the black wave, but I'm not holding my breath. How many black analysts do you see around here?"

Carla smiled sheepishly and flipped her brown shoulder-length hair back. "Only one now."

"And from what he tells me, he won't be around much longer."

"He told you that?"

"Yes."

"Why?"

"I keep telling you, being the only one is rough."

"But why is that so difficult? We're all professionals in the same field."

"It's fine most of the time. But when you run into problems or particularly difficult challenges and need someone to unload stuff on, someone who will understand without needing a lot of explaining, that's when it gets difficult." Like now, Naomi thought.

"I thought you felt you could talk to me."

Naomi sighed. "I can, and you're a big help. I like talking to you because I can say pretty much what's on my mind. But it's not the same. Try to imagine what it would be like if you thought you were being held back or having some other problem on the job because you're a woman and you were the only one around. You could maybe find a sympathetic man in the bunch, but it wouldn't be the same as talking to another woman. Can you imagine how that would feel?"

Carla smiled. "I'd rather not try."

Naomi laughed. "See what I mean? I know white women have problems too, but at least you usually have other women around these days, and certainly others of your race."

"It takes time to change things, Naomi. At least they're trying. They made you a manager, didn't they?"

Naomi twisted her mouth. "I had to practically beat them over the head to get it and I'll probably have to do it again. But like I said, I've got experience. And the challenge just makes me more determined. Which reminds me. I need to get back to finish up some things so I can work on my résumé."

"Good luck," Carla said, as they both stood up. "By the way, how's it going with the house you're planning to build?"

The house. She had an appointment with an architect in the morning. It had completely slipped her mind. "It's not definite. I may end up just buying one. But I like the idea of building a house just the way I want and I'm looking into it. I'm interviewing architects."

"If you'd like, I can get a number for you. He's a friend of the guy I'm seeing."

And white no doubt, Naomi thought. She had resolved to try to find a black architect. "Thanks, but I'm looking for a black one."

"Oh."

"They sometimes have a harder time finding clients, and I figure if I'm going to spend my money that way, I want to help someone of my race."

"I understand. I think it's a good idea."

Naomi was surprised but relieved. At least she wouldn't have to go to the trouble of explaining herself this time. She never knew when Carla would understand something like this and when she wouldn't.

Naomi moved from the printer, as it chugged out yet another version of her résumé, back to the picture window overlooking Jefferson Davis Highway. The Crystal City skyline was all black sky and silvery lights. But traffic was still heavy, with workers leaving their offices and people looking for parking spaces in front of the restaurants and shops sprouting rapidly along the highway.

Sometimes it was hard to believe this was the same street in Virginia where those ignorant boys had yelled at her family all those years ago. She wasn't sure exactly where it happened, because the street had changed so much in the meantime. But she remembered the words and their angry voices as if it had happened yesterday: "You stupid niggers!"

With the benefit of time and experience, she was able to look back on it now without getting all riled up. Just as her mother and Joshua had said, they were a bunch of ignoramuses. When she told the story to friends they always got a good chuckle out of it, a kind of shake-your-head-at-the-stupidity-of-some-whitefolks chuckle.

Something like that would probably not happen here today, but that didn't mean racism had disappeared—it hadn't. It was still very much alive and kicking, even in this very building. Racism was usually more subtle now, though no less damaging. But after years of struggling, she'd finally learned to cope with it. She was no longer the scared little girl who cried when racism reared its ugly head or the young woman who lashed out one minute and then buried her head in defeat the next. She had learned to play their game with skill—to take advantage of their rules when they suited her and bend them tactfully when they didn't.

She was also able to smile when she thought of Joshua these days. Sometimes the smile came with moisture around the edges of her eyes, but the bitterness that once consumed her had dulled over the years, and she felt lucky to have had a brother like him, even for just a little while. She couldn't count the times when being able to imagine what he would have said had helped her solve a problem or get out of a jam. But now she realized that even though the words came in Joshua's voice, the wisdom was her own.

The telephone rang, jolting her back to the present. It seemed extra loud now, with the building practically deserted. The only other sound in her office was the printer spitting out her résumé. Ed Gallows had asked for a copy of it when she met with him that morning about the director's position. Naomi wanted to finish it and leave it on Ed's secretary's desk before she left, since her morning meeting with the architect would make her a little late for work. She didn't want to give them any excuses for turning her down.

She picked up the phone on the second ring. "Naomi Jefferson speaking."

"Hi," Mama said. "Are you still coming by after you get off work?"

Naomi slapped her forehead. With so much going on, she'd forgotten she was supposed to stop by her parents' for dinner that evening. "I'm sorry, Mama. I forgot."

"Oh."

"I had to work late. Maybe tomorrow."

Mama smacked her lips, and it dawned on Naomi that Mama's voice was off. "What is it, Ma?"

She heard Mama breathe deeply through the phone. "It's something about Joshua. I wanted to tell you face-to-face, but I don't want to wait until tomorrow."

"The phone's fine." Naomi couldn't imagine what her mother would have to say about Joshua.

"Some woman called here from Chicago this morning saying . . . well, she has a son and you'll never believe this. She claims it's Joshua's boy."

Naomi's mouth dropped open. "That's ridiculous."

"I know."

"After all this time?"

"I know, I know."

"How old is he?"

"Fourteen. Which would make it possible. But I don't know what to think. Your father doesn't believe it."

"Neither do I. Why did she wait all this time to get in touch with you? Did she ask for money?"

"Of course."

"Don't give her a dime."

"But what if it's true? She said she's been having a hard time financially. And she also seems to be having a hard time with Joseph."

A chill ran up Naomi's spine when she heard the name. It was so close to Joshua. "What do you mean she's having a hard time with him?"

"He cuts school, stays in the streets, won't listen to her."

Naomi sighed. "That's her problem. I don't like the sound of this, Ma. Check it out real carefully before you do anything."

"Your father is going to call someone to look into it. But we wanted to let you know first."

"She lives in Chicago?"

"That's what she said. And there's something else. She said she was the woman in the car with Joshua when they had the accident."

"Even if that's true, it doesn't mean it's Joshua's son."

"She also said he's the spitting image of Joshua."

"Oh, God."

"We told her to send us a photo. I'll know if I can just get hold of a picture of this boy."

"Mama, you can't be sure with just a picture. Get a blood test."

"If it comes to that. I have to get off the phone now, so your father can call the detective."

"Jesus, Ma. What if it's true?"

"Then we'll have to do what we can to help them out."

As Naomi put the phone in the cradle, her thoughts were spinning a mile a minute. The résumé sat in the printer ready for her to proof it, but she had to consider this news first. It was bad any way you looked at it. If this woman was lying, Naomi hated the thought of her parents being jerked around, of someone trying to take advantage of them. But she could take comfort in knowing that her parents wouldn't be easy to fool. They were no dummies, especially her father. He'd probably insist on all kinds of tests if there was the slightest doubt.

If this woman was telling the truth and the boy really was Joshua's son, that would be even more painful in its own way. Naomi's stomach felt queasy just thinking that Joshua may have had a son growing up somewhere for the past fourteen years and the family knew nothing about him. Her parents didn't need this kind of complication at this point. They were both looking forward to retirement in a few years and to a life of relaxation and travel. They shouldn't be saddled with the burden of a grandson whose mother couldn't take care of him. Naomi knew if it turned out to be true and the boy was having problems, her parents would feel obligated to help out. She hoped for their sakes it would turn out not to be true and the whole thing would go away.

She looked at her watch. She had to put this aside for the moment. It was already past eight. She rolled the résumé out of the printer and tried to focus on it. But her mind kept slipping back to thoughts of this woman. If it was true, she was one of the last people besides Dean to be with Joshua before he died. Naomi then realized that she had forgotten to ask for the woman's name. It had been fifteen years since the accident, and the name had slipped her mind. What was she like? Had they been in love? Did Joshua know she was pregnant? Stop it, she thought, looking at the résumé. She would never be able to figure out the answers to these questions sitting here, so why torture herself?

It was after ten before she left work that night.

Twenty-three

The architect's office was in a brick row house off Connecticut Avenue, near Adams Morgan. It was one of Washington's more desirable neighborhoods, with a mixture of homes and small businesses. Naomi was impressed. If he could afford digs here, he must be good at what he did.

She parked a few blocks away and walked up the short flight of stairs to the office. She rang the buzzer and gave her name when a voice came over the intercom. The door buzzed and she entered a small foyer with a high ceiling. To the right was a small room, where a black secretary sat behind a desk facing the lobby. Naomi smiled and stepped into the room.

"Mr. Underwood will be out in a second," the secretary said, taking Naomi's coat. "You can have a seat if you want."

"Thanks." Naomi sat in one of two chairs and picked up a copy of *Architectural Digest* lying on a small round table. The homes in the magazine were so beautiful and expensive-looking that Naomi began to think she was out of her league. But the idea of designing something just as she wanted was so appealing she had to at least investigate it. And all the houses she'd looked at were built with a family in mind.

Naomi still hoped to get married someday and have children. Although she was already over thirty with no prospects on the horizon and sometimes sensed that time was running out, she was determined to wait until the right man came along. Still, she felt like the odd woman out. The only one of her friends not married was Debbie. But Debbie had bought a house several years back and lived there with Serena, now fourteen. Debbie and Serena were close, more like friends than mother and daughter. Naomi had to hand it to Debbie. Serena got all A's in school, just like her mother had, and Debbie hadn't done badly for herself either. She was a senior accountant at one of the big eight accounting firms.

So everyone had done what you were supposed to do—get married, or at least have children, and buy a house—except her. Although she had moved to a town house in Silver Spring, Maryland, once she was promoted to manager, she was only renting. But she was determined not to put her personal life on hold waiting for the right man any longer. She would buy her own house. Not on the Gold Coast—she couldn't afford that alone. But she would work hard and someday buy that dream house. And as soon as she got the promotion at SSI, she was going to start working more reasonable hours and do some traveling. Debbie was always trying to get her to go somewhere. She and Serena took a trip together every Christmas—Mexico, the Bahamas. This year they were going to Africa. They asked Naomi to join them, but she was too busy as always. That was going to change real soon. Mexico, Africa, here I come.

Africa. Dean. It had been six long years since she last spoke to him, but he was never far from her thoughts, especially when she was manless. He was the one who got away, the one she'd blown her chances with. Maybe they would have discovered they weren't meant for each other, but he had so many wonderful traits that were hard to find in a man, she couldn't help but wonder what might have been.

Still, she hated to think about that last encounter, even now. She had just broken up with Chuck when Debbie told her she'd run into Dean at the Giant supermarket on Queens Chapel Road, and she was so excited that she called his house the minute she got home.

"May I speak to Dean, please?"

"He stepped out," said a young voice. "Who's calling?"

"Naomi Jefferson."

"Hi. This is his sister. I'll tell him you called."

"When do you expect him back?"

"Any minute now. Is this about the wedding?"

Naomi's mouth went dry. "What wedding?"

"Oh, wait. He just came in."

Naomi numbed her mind while she held on. She didn't want to think about the prospect of Dean getting married until she knew it was a fact.

"Naomi?"

It was so good to hear his voice after all this time. She prayed some woman wasn't about to snatch him away from her forever. Dean living halfway around the world was bad enough. Dean married was unthinkable. There were bridges to Africa. Marriage would wash them away. "Hi, Dean. It's good to hear your voice."

"Good to hear yours too. I was going to call to give you the news."

Bridges . . .

"The only reason you didn't get an invitation is because this is kind of rushed."

Tumbling . . .

"We just got back from Dakar yesterday, and we go back right after the wedding."

Down, down, down. She had never hated the sound of the word "we" until now. "Uh-huh. When . . . when is it?"

"In two days. I'm in the import-export business, and I have to get back."

"Congratulations. Who's the lucky girl?"

"You remember Sonya?"

Of course. "I thought you broke up long ago."

"We did until she came to Dakar about a year ago—"

"Miss Jefferson?"

Naomi heard her name and realized that her mind had wandered to Timbuktu, or Dakar. She looked up from the copy of *Architectural Digest* in her lap and was surprised to see a man about her own age standing before her. She shook Dean from her head and stood up.

"Yes."

"I'm Marshall Underwood." He extended his hand.

"Pleased to meet you," she said, shaking his hand. He had such a formal air that it seemed the right thing to say.

"Come back to my office and we'll talk."

Naomi followed him down the hall. That earth-shattering conversation was the last time she'd heard from Dean—no more letters, no more phone calls when he came home to visit. For months after, she'd think how she'd blown all her chances with him forever, and found herself comparing every man she met to him. She had tried hard to kick that annoying habit, but it was futile. Even now, she noticed that the man leading her down the hallway had a brown complexion similar to Dean's, although he was not nearly as good-looking. He was very tall, well over six feet, and his attire, from the wing-tipped shoes to the dark gray suit and burgundy tie, was conservative yet tasteful. He wore old-fashioned wire-rimmed glasses. Naomi thought his looks would improve to where he could even be considered attractive if he wore a more stylish pair or got rid of them altogether.

When they reached his office, he folded his long body into a chair at a small conference table. "Have a seat," he said, and rested his lower arms on the table and linked his fingers together. Naomi had a feeling the formalities weren't just his office behavior. Dean was always so laid-back, so . . . Damn. She was doing it again. She bit her bottom lip and focused on the man in front of her.

"You're planning to build your own house?" he asked.

She nodded. "I'm mainly exploring the idea now."

"Have you picked out a location?"

She nodded. "Prince Georges County, maybe. Land is cheaper there than some other places in Maryland."

He nodded. "What size are you thinking of?"

"That depends on the cost. Nothing too big, since it's just me. But I would think at least twenty-five hundred square feet. Can you design something that small?"

He smiled for the first time, and his face seemed much less stern, even boyish. "I can design whatever you want. It depends on how much you plan to spend. What kind of work do you do?"

"I'm a manager at a technology research firm. Ever heard of SSI?"

He raised his eyebrows. "Sure have. They're one of the biggest around here."

"I'm up for the position of director of contracts and grants." That was not something she would normally have shared with someone she'd just met. What if she didn't get the promotion? But he made her feel comfortable.

"I'm impressed." He stood up. "Let me show you around."

He led her into a big bright room with two walls of windows. It held four large wooden tables with various design paraphernalia cluttered on top of them. Two black men stood at one of the tables, talking and looking at blueprints.

Marshall stopped at the table. "This is my partner, Lloyd Williams," he said, indicating one of the men. Naomi shook his hand. "And this is Michael Mckenzie. We're working on a restaurant he's opening in the city."

Naomi smiled again. It filled her with pride to see black people doing this kind of thing.

Marshall walked to a table in another corner and showed her some of their designs and scale models. As they talked, Naomi found herself becoming more and more impressed. She felt optimistic about going through with it, but she told him she needed time to think and promised to call him within a week.

As she drove to the SSI office and thought about some of the things Marshall had said, though, she became nervous about the whole thing. Design through construction would be a long involved process, six months at a minimum, he'd said. And much could go wrong along the way. But she loved the control it would bring her. She'd be able to pick out tile patterns, kitchen and bath appliances, and wall coverings. With control she now realized would come a lot of responsibility, though. When things went wrong, it would be up to her to set them right. And from what Marshall and others had told her about building your own house, things invariably went wrong. Marshall said to set aside more money than she thought she would need to spend. He also said he would guide her through the process and try to make things run as smoothly as possible.

So many problems, she thought, as she pulled into the underground parking lot at her office building. The house, the promotion, some woman in Chicago claiming to be the mother of Joshua's son—and no man to ease the burdens. The first thing she did when she reached her office was to ask her secretary if anyone had called from Mr. Gallows's office. Louise said no, and Naomi told herself to be patient. As she sat at her desk, with its piles of proposals to edit, she was thankful she was the kind of person who could put other things out of her mind when it was time to work.

By the end of the week, Naomi still hadn't heard anything about the promotion. Mr. Gallows's secretary had called to say she would hear from him by Friday or first thing Monday morning. Friday came and went with no news, and Naomi knew she'd have to suffer through the weekend in the dark. But she had to stay calm, she thought on Saturday morning, as she nibbled on a piece of toast at her kitchen table. Only two more days to go.

The phone rang and she picked up the receiver on the wall. "Hello?"

"Naomi, it's me," Mama said. "We got the pictures from Tisha, that woman in Chicago, this morning." At the mention of that name, all other thoughts flew from Naomi's mind.

"Do they look like Joshua?"

"Come see for yourself. What are you doing today?"

"The usual exciting stuff: washing clothes, grocery shopping." Worrying about the promotion. "Does it look like him?"

"Yes, very much. She also sent the birth certificate. It has Joshua's name as the father."

Naomi felt a sense of sadness wash over her. She knew that from this moment on their lives would never be the same. "I'll be there soon."

An hour later she sat on the sofa at her parents' house with the photo in her lap. She hadn't been able to take her eyes off it since she'd arrived ten minutes earlier. This handsome boy, whoever he was, was a browner miniature version of Joshua. He was younger-looking, of course, but there was no denying the resemblance. He looked exactly like Joshua had, at this age, and like her mother, whom Joshua had always favored. She fell back against the couch.

"Your father still wants to get a blood test," Mama said, sitting next to her. She took the photo from Naomi and looked at it for what Naomi was sure must have been the hundredth time.

"I don't blame him," Naomi said. "It's possible he just looks like Joshua and isn't his son."

"That's what I've been telling her," Daddy said. He stood up from the easy chair facing the couch and came over to look down at the photo.

"Then how do you explain the birth certificate?" Mama said.

"We don't know that it's real, for one thing," he said. "Maybe she knew Joshua at the time and just used his name."

Mama held the photo up toward him. "Can you look at this and tell me that's not your grandson?"

Daddy pushed the picture away. "I just want to be sure before we start sending this woman money."

"Did the detective come up with anything?" Naomi asked.

"I didn't hire him."

"Your father's too cheap to pay the man," Mama said. "We called Tisha this morning and asked her if she'd get a blood test if we pay for it."

"What did she say?"

"She said she would if we send her the money."

"That reminds me," Daddy said. "I need to mail a bill payment."

"I'll take it when I leave," Naomi said.

"No," he said. "I need to go out anyway, get some air."

Naomi nodded with understanding as her father slipped into his jacket. It was hard watching her parents go through this after what they'd been through with Joshua.

"Did you get the promotion?" Mama asked as Daddy closed the door behind him.

Naomi shook her head. "I won't know until Monday. It's driving me crazy waiting."

Mama smiled. "I'm sure it is, knowing you. You always want things done yesterday."

Naomi chuckled. "Where did I get that from?"

"I don't know. It probably has something to do with the times. Everything moves so fast these days."

Naomi looked at her mother closely. She and Daddy were still in good shape for their ages. But Naomi couldn't help but notice the gray hair and the slight bulges around the middle that weren't there a few years ago. "Ma, what are you going to do if it *is* Joshua's son?"

"What do you mean?"

"Are you going to try to get to know him?"

"I would hope so. If she'll allow it."

"You mean Tisha? I wouldn't send her any money if she doesn't."

"It would be hard not to. He's our grandson. This morning she told me Joseph has spent time in foster homes, although he's living with her now."

"Foster homes?" This was the first time Naomi had heard that.

"That's what she said."

"That's awful." Naomi felt a sense of rage that a son of Joshua's, her nephew, was growing up in foster homes. "Why can't she take better care of him?"

Mama shrugged her shoulders. "Who knows? We'll find out eventually. But he's family. Even if she's difficult to deal with, we still have to do what we can for him."

Any other time, the promotion would have pushed all other thoughts to the back of her mind. But as Naomi vacuumed the carpet in her living room that Saturday afternoon, her problems at SSI had been replaced by a boy halfway across the country named Joseph whom she'd never even seen. Her feelings zigzagged between fear and joy. He was her nephew, yet a stranger. She didn't know a thing about him but had known everything about his father—his courage, intelligence, ambition, sense of humor. She didn't dare hope this boy might be like Joshua, because he was bound to disappoint her. Yet she couldn't help but wonder about the possibilities.

She was just starting on the dining room carpet when the phone rang. She thought it might be her parents with more news, so she quickly shut off the vacuum and let the handle drop to the floor, then ran to the phone on the kitchen wall. "Hello?"

"Hello." It was a male voice she recognized but couldn't place. "I'd like to speak to Naomi Jefferson, please."

"This is she."

"Hi. It's Marshall Underwood."

For a moment the name didn't register, and Naomi frowned, trying to make it click.

"The architect. We met about a week ago."

"Oh, yes. Sorry about that, but something was on my mind when you called." This was certainly a surprise, she thought. Her brain went into high gear. It could be one of two things. Either he was wondering why she hadn't contacted him and was trying to drum up some business for his firm, or he was going to ask her out. She'd thought of contacting him a few times just for the sake of it, whether she planned to go through with it or not. He seemed as if he might be her type—successful, confident, well groomed. And she'd noticed he wasn't wearing a wedding band. But so much was crowding her mind now, with work and Joseph.

"Is this a bad time to talk?" he asked.

"Not at all. I'm glad you called."

"I've been thinking about your visit," he said. "It's not often that I meet a single woman planning to build her own house. It's exciting."

Naomi laughed. "It's not definite. I have a lot to think about before going through with something like this."

"That's why I'm calling. I have some brochures you might want to see. And if you're interested, I can show you one or two of the homes in the area that we designed."

Unfortunately, he sounded all business. Still, it wasn't a bad idea. Seeing one or two houses would be much better than looking at pictures and sketches. It would give her an indication of what these guys could do and what she would get for her money. And it would give her another chance to see him.

"That sounds like a good idea," she said. "Where exactly are the houses?"

"One is in Hyattsville, Maryland, and another in Fort Washington. A lot of nice new homes are going up there now."

"I've heard. But they're a bit on the expensive side, aren't they?"

He chuckled. "We can always design something within your budget. But the lot prices over there are quite reasonable compared to most of the metro area."

"It can't hurt to look."

"When is a good time for you?"

"Weekends are better, since I'm putting in a lot of hours at work these days."

"How about tomorrow then? After church."

"Tomorrow?" Naomi was perfectly free all day but hesitant to be so obvious about it. "Well, let me think. I guess I could manage a couple of hours tomorrow."

"How about one o'clock if I promise to have you back by four?"

"That should be fine."

"Good. I'll see you then."

" 'Bye. And thanks for calling."

Naomi smiled as she walked back toward the vacuum cleaner. She had a good feeling about this man. At any rate, an afternoon out would take her mind off all the other things going on in her life for a while.

One of the reasons she couldn't make up her mind about whether to go ahead with the house, she realized, was that it seemed like every time she turned around some new problem was shoved at her. Building a house now would be like throwing mud into a ditch she was trying to climb out of. Buying one already built would be so much simpler. Maybe if she got the new job, she would build the house. That way she'd be replacing one fulfilled challenge with a new one. If she didn't get the job—well, she hated even thinking about that prospect, but if it happened, she was going to have to start doing some serious thinking about leaving SSI, and she wouldn't want the added strain of building a house.

No need to think negatively now, though. She'd have plenty of time to do that if she got turned down. There was also time to deal with Joseph. She had her first date with a man in more weeks than she cared to think about—or at least kind of a date—and she was going to enjoy herself.

She turned off the vacuum and walked to the kitchen phone.

"Debbie? Hi, it's me. What are you doing this evening?"

"What do you have in mind?"

"Some shopping. Got a hot date tomorrow afternoon."

"A hot date on a Sunday afternoon? Now I've heard everything."

Naomi chuckled. "OK, so it's not exactly a date. That black architect I told you about just called. He's showing me some of his houses tomorrow."

"You're right, it doesn't sound like a date."

"It will be if I make it one."

"Excuse me. This guy must be something else."

"If I'm lucky, he'll turn out to be the one."

"Get out of here. You just met him."

"I know, but it feels right."

"You say that every time you meet someone new."

"This time is different. I hope. He's perfect husband material. Level-headed, successful." Single. Not living in Africa. "And I'm tired of being alone."

"Well, I hate to bother you about one small detail."

"What's that?"

"Love."

"Oh, *that*. That can come later."

"What a terrible thing to say."

"I mean, what is love, anyway? Drooling over a man who doesn't drool back? That's how it always turns out for me. Every time I get to drooling, I end up either disappointed in the man or disappointed in myself 'cause I can't hold on to him. I must be approaching it backward—looking for love, then hoping the person will fit into my lifestyle and be a good companion. Maybe I should look for the right kind of person, then fall in love."

"But what if you don't? You can't orchestrate this the way you do your job, Nay."

"I'm not. I'll take my time, see if it feels right. But I'm not going to expect starry nights in the beginning anymore. In fact, that's a red flag. I want the kind of love you build with time and respect and shared goals."

"This is crazy. You haven't even slept with him. What if you don't hit it off?"

"Then we'll see a sex counselor. The point is, that kind of thing can probably be fixed. But the basic personality has to be there."

"What if he doesn't agree to go to a counselor? Men can be funny about that."

"OK, so I'll make sure everything's going smoothly in bed first. But I'm definitely ready to take the plunge."

"That poor man," Debbie said. "You haven't even had your first date and already we're sending him to a sex counselor."

Naomi watched from her bedroom window as Marshall pulled up in a dark green Volvo and strolled along the sidewalk to her house. He was slimmer than she'd remembered him to be, but he was dressed in another nice dark suit and tie. In her mind, she put a few check marks in the plus column for stability, grooming, and income. Then she ran to the mirror over her dresser and checked her hair and makeup.

They could only drive past the house in Hyattsville. But Marshall knew the family living in the one in Fort Washington well and had made arrangements to walk her through. It was an English Tudor mini-mansion and much too grand for Naomi, with five bedrooms, four baths, a solarium, and a marble fireplace in the living room, but Naomi was impressed with many of the architectural details he pointed out. She put down a check mark for good taste.

After they left the house, he asked if she wanted to have dinner and she accepted without hesitation. In fact she'd planned to suggest it herself if he hadn't. As they talked and ate, Naomi thought he was turning out to be every bit as desirable as she'd imagined from their first meeting. He'd never been married, had no children, and no weird statements tumbled from his mouth. He was thoughtful and listened attentively to what she had to say. And he had no strange habits, unless you counted the twenty-dollar tip he left for a fifty-dollar meal. Either he was just generous to those less fortunate or trying to impress her. She added a check mark for generosity.

She invited him in when he brought her home, and they talked over wine and popcorn and watched the late-night news. Some men never seemed able to sit still or by now they'd be halfway on top of her, seeming to feel that they'd paid for dinner and now it was time for her to put out. Marshall seemed comfortable just sitting around relaxing and talking. She put several marks in the plus column.

At the door they talked some more, and since he didn't make a move to kiss her good night, she kissed him. Not so eagerly that he'd think it was a message to go further but passionately enough so he'd know she was ready to take this thing to the next level. He smiled when she pulled away, clearly surprised that she'd taken the initiative.

"I wasn't expecting that," he said.

"I got that feeling."

He chuckled. "You seemed like the kind who would want to take things more slowly."

"Not once I make up my mind about something."

"I see. Any more surprises for me tonight?"

Suddenly Naomi thought, Why wait? It was the one question she still had about him. Would they click in bed? She reached for his necktie and pulled his head down toward her.

An hour later she had her answer. He was more than adequate. He was not the most fiery lover around, but what he lacked in ardency he made up for with attentiveness and patience. Afterward they sat up in bed and talked, and she steered the conversation around, trying to learn his hopes and dreams, what he wanted out of life. He had it all figured out. A nice house in the suburbs, a waterfront retreat in Annapolis, two children, yearly vacations. Sounded good to her. And she was starting to like him too. What was there not to like?

He decided not to stay the night, and she agreed that he shouldn't. They both had to go to work early the following morning and were too practical to do anything foolish. They made plans to have dinner together at her house on Monday.

Twenty-four

Naomi smiled all the way to work Monday morning. A couple of drivers stared at her strangely, and she tried in vain to wipe the smile off her face by sucking in her lips. She hadn't felt this right about a man in ages, maybe never. Always before, she'd been hooked by passion. Well, passion was nice, but it didn't get you past the starry nights. It didn't get you through the rough moments once the sun came up and you climbed out of bed: the difficult bosses, family worries, bills piling up. For that you needed stability, dependability, reliability. These qualities and passion didn't often come ready-made in the same package. And when they did, the package wasn't available to her. Someone like Dean came along once in a lifetime, never for a lot of women.

By the time she reached her office her lips were under control. "Any word from Ed?" she asked Louise.

"No, but a Marshall Underwood called."

The smile was back again. Louise smiled too, when she saw Naomi's face brighten.

"Someone special, huh?"

Naomi crossed her fingers. "Let's hope so."

She closed the door to her office and dialed Marshall's work number.

"I can't stop thinking about you," he said.

"Same here."

"Should I bring my pajamas tonight?"

"You can bring several pairs if you like."

He laughed, and Naomi was still smiling when she hung up the phone. But by noon she still hadn't heard anything from upstairs, and the smiles had long since receded. She became especially worried when she ran into Patrick on the elevator as they both returned from lunch. He looked like someone who'd just won the million-dollar lottery.

Her phone was ringing as she walked into her office, and she ran to pick it up.

"Hello?"

"Naomi. I was just about to hang up."

It was Mama. When would they get around to calling her about the promotion? Even if it was bad news, she wanted to hear it. Anything would be better than not knowing. "Hi, Ma," she said, trying to keep the disappointment out of her voice.

"Have you heard anything?" Mama asked.

Naomi took a deep breath. "Not yet."

"Let me know when you do. I had a long talk on the phone with Tisha this morning."

"Is she going to get a blood test?"

"We didn't talk about that. I'm almost sure it's Joshua's son anyway."

"But you need to be absolutely sure before you get involved, Ma."

"That's why we're flying out there early next year. I'll know once I see him."

"Ma, this doesn't make sense. You should get the test done first. What does Daddy say about this?"

"Pretty much the same thing you do. And if he wants to get a stupid test he can. But it's not going to change anything."

Naomi could see her mother now, standing by the kitchen phone, one hand on her hip, determined to plow ahead. She sighed. "What did you talk to Tisha about?"

"Oh, just what Joseph has been doing all these years. It seems he's a very smart boy; she just can't handle him. I can understand that, in a way. It's hard raising a child alone, and her family doesn't seem to give her much support. Sounds to me like he just needs some guidance."

Naomi sensed something was coming. "Meaning what, Ma?"

"We'll have to see. But it may do him some good to come spend some time with us."

"Ma . . ."

"If we can work things out with her. Maybe next summer. Why not? She's shuffling him around to foster homes. That doesn't make sense when he's got family here. And I'd rather bring him here than just send her money and have no control over how he's raised."

Naomi shook her head. "I don't know if I like the idea of you two taking on a teenage boy at this stage of your lives."

"I admit it was not exactly what we had envisioned for our middle years."

"Then why are you rushing things? You're the one always telling me—" Naomi paused when the other line on her phone rang. "Just a minute, Ma. That's my other line." She put her mother on hold and pressed the button. "Hello?"

"Naomi." It was Louise. "Mr. Gallows's office just called. He wants to see you right away."

Naomi's heart skipped a beat. She closed her eyes. Too much was happening at once. She wanted to try to talk her mother out of moving so fast on this thing with Joseph but couldn't now. "Ma, I'll have to call you back. Ed Gallows wants to see me."

"Go ahead," Mama said. "And good luck."

"Promise me you won't do anything, like making plane reservations, until after we talk."

"I already made them for March."

"Oh, Ma. And you wonder where I get my rashness."

Mama laughed.

"Sit down, Naomi," Ed Gallows said, when she reached his office on the twenty-first floor. Naomi didn't like his tone. She didn't like the phony smile on his face, either. In the nine years she'd been there, she'd come to know her boss well enough to be able to read his expressions. For the head of a company that had grown to 150 employees, Edwin Gallows was still fairly accessible. Although reportedly well into his sixties, he had the energy of a man half his age. He met with his directors weekly and with the rest of the senior staff at least once a month. He held quarterly meetings with the entire staff, and at company gatherings he always made a point to stop and chat with each of his senior employees for a few minutes. He was the one who had given final approval to set up her unit. But this time she feared he was going to disappoint her. He had a smile reserved especially for bad news, and it was on his face now. She sat in the chair across from his big mahogany desk and crossed her legs, expecting the worst. She got it.

"I'm sorry, Naomi," he said. "You know how I like to get right to the point. We had two very capable employees vying for the same position, and it was an extremely difficult choice to make. But I've decided to go with Patrick Anderson."

Naomi sighed and sat back in her seat. "I see. May I ask why?"

"Of course. This is no reflection on you or your work. We've been pleased with what you've done for the division and for the company."

"Then why wasn't I chosen?"

"Patrick's been here a little longer."

"I thought promotions were based on merit."

"They are, generally. But when two people weigh in equally, we have to take other things into consideration."

This bull was insulting. She couldn't believe they would consider her work equal to Patrick's in any way, shape, or form. She put in longer hours, brought in more money, and had more influence with the other staff members. When someone had a question that didn't need the director's attention, they came to her, not Patrick. Ed couldn't just come out and say he didn't want a black woman in that position, so he zeroed in on the one area where Patrick had her beat—seniority—and ignored all the others. At that moment, Naomi wanted to get up and walk out for good. She wanted to scream and argue. But she knew it was no use to try to reason with him. From the look on Patrick's face earlier, they'd already given him the good news.

She stood up, planning to leave quietly, return to her office, and start looking for another job. But she couldn't go that way.

"Ed, I want you to know something," she said as he stood up. That special smile was still on his face but she intended to wipe it off. "To tell me I didn't get the job because my work is on a level with Patrick Anderson's and expect me to accept that is humiliating. And after all I've done for this company. I'm outraged."

The smile disappeared. Finally.

He squared his shoulders. "I'm sorry to hear you feel that way, especially since you'll be working under him now."

That was when it hit Naomi. Patrick Anderson would be her boss! She hadn't allowed herself to think of the possibility, assuming the company would act rationally and it would never come to this. But it had. She clenched her jaw.

"Is that going to be a problem?" he asked.

You're damned right it is. But she knew better than to express any more of the resentment boiling inside her. She'd already said more than she should have, considering she still had to work with these people. At least for a while. "I'll manage."

"Good," he said. "I'd hate for anything to disrupt the good work we've been getting out of the division."

That happened the minute you decided to promote Patrick Anderson, she thought with disgust.

Naomi headed straight for the software division on the seventeenth floor. She needed to unload all the stuff she couldn't say to Ed Gallows, and Carla was the only one at SSI she could tell. But Carla wasn't in her office.

"Where's Carla?" Naomi asked, approaching the division secretary.

"She had a meeting with the database management team."

Damn it, Naomi thought, looking at her watch. She had a meeting herself in fifteen minutes and she wanted to get some things off her chest before then. "When do you expect her back?"

"Any second now. Do you want me to ask her to call you?"

"Can I get a piece of paper so I can leave her a note?"

The secretary handed her a yellow pad, and Naomi leaned on her desk to write a brief note. Just as she pulled the page from the pad, Carla entered the suite. Naomi balled the note up in her hand and threw it in the trash. "Got a minute? I need to talk."

"Sure. Come on in."

They entered the office and Carla shut the door and walked around behind her desk, while Naomi paced up and down the floor.

"I just came from a meeting with Ed. I didn't get the job."

Carla dropped the folder in her hand on the desk and sat down. "You're kidding."

"I wish," Naomi said.

"They gave it to Patrick?"

Naomi nodded.

"Why?"

"Because he's been here longer."

"Oh, come on. That's what he told you?"

"Yes. But I don't believe it for a minute."

Carla blinked. "Did you point out that the company's policy is to promote based on performance?"

"You bet I did."

"What did he say?"

"Some bunk about our work being equal, so they had to consider seniority."

Carla crossed her legs. "I see."

Naomi leaned over and placed the palms of her hands on Carla's desk. "It's just like I told you. They aren't ready for someone like me in that position. They're afraid if some of those corporate hot-shots see me coming, they'll run a mile in the opposite direction."

"That's jumping to conclusions."

Naomi stood up. "How can you say that?"

"I admit it might look that way. But maybe they do see your work as equal. Patrick's job is important too."

Naomi folded her arms across her chest. "Carla, please."

"I have a hard time believing they'd turn you down just because you're black, especially with all this talk about promoting diversity."

"That's the problem," Naomi said, heading for the door. "It's just talk. I've had enough of it. I'm tired of fighting them."

"What are you going to do?"

"I'm going to start looking elsewhere, somewhere I'll be appreciated."

"You're appreciated here. They made you a manager. A lot of people would love to have your job."

"That's not the point. They're holding me back because of what I am."

"You don't know that, Naomi."

Naomi sighed and opened the door. If she was looking for empathy, she'd come to the wrong place. "*I* know it. Obviously, you don't. I don't know what it will take to convince you but it's not important." She turned and stepped out of the office.

"Naomi," Carla called after her. Naomi turned around. "I'm sorry you didn't get the job, for whatever reason."

Naomi nodded. "Thanks."

She walked down the hallway to the elevator. She should have known better than to expect Carla to understand. But it seemed so blatantly obvious to her that this was racism, and probably sexism as well. The scary part was that if Carla didn't see it, nobody else around here would either.

She stepped into the elevator and found herself among a sea of white faces. She recognized a couple of them and nodded. Funny how truly white they suddenly seemed. She'd worked among them for so long that she rarely thought about the differences. Oh, they were there, she knew. She always felt she had to work twice as hard as the next person and fight for promotions. But she'd convinced herself that one way or another she'd get what she deserved, and that ultimately the only limitations were her capabilities—not some arbitrary ones someone else set based on the color of her skin.

She got off the elevator at the nineteenth floor and walked toward her office.

"Naomi?"

She turned to see Louise, blond hair and blue eyes, staring at her. "Yes?"

"The meeting has started. They're looking for you."

To hell with their meeting, to hell with their precious company, to hell with them all. "I'm going to be late."

"Do you want me to call in there and tell them?"

"No." Let them wait. Leave them in the dark.

She went into her office and shut the door. When she got Marshall on the phone, she told him, "I may not be good company tonight. I didn't get the promotion."

"I'm sorry to hear that. What did they tell you?"

"Some crap about the other manager having seniority."

"White cat, right?"

"They all are, except me."

"Now you see why I started my own firm. It's a struggle, and I'd probably make more money working for a white firm. But at least I don't have to deal with all that on a daily basis."

"Tell me about it. I thought I'd left this stuff behind in college. I mean, it's 1983."

"You should take them to court if you're convinced it's racism."

She hadn't thought of that. She hadn't had much time to do anything except be angry. "I don't know. That would take so much time, and I've got enough to deal with as it is. I have to look for another job, for one thing."

"The one you have doesn't sound so bad. In your field, anywhere you go it'll probably be the same thing. There are limits to how far they'll let a black woman climb."

Naomi let out a deep breath of air. "You're probably right, but I have to try."

"I'm still coming over tonight," Marshall said. "You sound like you could use some cheering up."

Naomi hung up and thought about what he'd said. She didn't like the idea of suing. It could drag on for years and she might lose. And it would do nothing to move her career forward, just suck up valuable time and energy. But the idea of letting them get away with this was just as distasteful. Bringing a suit against them could pave the road a bit for the next black person who came along, not only here but at other consulting firms too.

She went to her file cabinet to look for her personnel files and anything else that might help document a case. She wasn't sure she'd go through with the idea, but she wanted the records just in case. She was in no mood for a meeting, anyway, and this helped her feel she was fighting back.

Twenty-five

Naomi's stomach was tied in knots as she waited at the gate with her parents for Joseph's plane to land at National Airport. Her mind was in a bad state, too. A part of her hoped this might be Joshua's way of reaching out to them, of keeping his spirit alive here on earth. Another part of her was much more suspicious of the boy and his mother and resented the intrusion. So much depended on the boy himself. If he brought joy into her parents' lives, fine. But all indications were that he was bringing a whole new set of problems with him. If he was having so much trouble in Chicago, why would he suddenly change here? What could they do to help him in one short summer?

Naomi could see from her parents' eager faces as they watched the planes come and go from the terminal that they were vulnerable. Even Daddy's attitude had changed from suspicious to eager since their visit to Chicago in March, and they had decided not to bother with a blood test. It was up to her to make sure some level-headedness prevailed in this mess.

"I hope Joshua's old room is big enough for him," Mama said, twisting the strap on the shoulder bag in her lap.

Naomi stared at her mother. She'd never heard her mother worry about whether that room was big enough for Joshua. "He'll be fine," Naomi said, reaching over to rub her mother's back. "From what you tell me about that apartment in Chicago, he shouldn't have any complaints."

311

"The place was a mess," Mama said. "They take their clothes off and throw them on the floor. And it looked like his mother hadn't mopped in ages."

"He was sleeping on a sofa bed in the living room," Daddy said. He was sitting on the other side of Naomi, on the edge of his seat.

"So you decided to put him in Joshua's room after all?" Naomi asked.

Mama nodded. "That seemed best." She patted Naomi's hand. "In case you ever want to come home."

Naomi sighed. "The way things are going at work, I just may have to do that."

"You'll find something else eventually," Daddy said.

"I'm not having much luck so far," Naomi said. "And I've been looking for six months. I could find something in a minute doing what I'm doing now. But I'm determined not to make a lateral move. I want to head a division."

"I thought you were doing that now," Daddy said.

"It's a unit within a division."

"Sounds pretty good to me," Daddy said.

"It's a good job. But I can do better, and I don't like the idea of someone else imposing limits on me."

"I still think you kids have got it made," Daddy said. "You can do things we never dreamed of."

"We're reaching new heights now, but don't fool yourself. Whites are still putting on the brakes."

"They've always done that," Mama said. "In our day it was just as much of a struggle to get good jobs as teachers and government workers and keep them."

Naomi twisted her lips. Sure it was rough back then, no denying that. She still didn't think it equaled working in a corporate environment. But she wasn't in the mood to debate with her parents about it now.

"Are you still thinking of suing SSI?" Daddy asked.

"I don't think so. I talked to a lawyer about it, and he thinks I may have a case, but the more I listened to him . . ." Naomi shook her head. "It started to feel like Atlanta Tech all over again. That's not my way."

"You're probably better off staying where you are or finding another job," Daddy said.

"I knew you would say that."

"Suing takes so much time," Mama said.

"I know. But I can sue and look for a better job at the same time."

"Will someone want to hire you, knowing you're suing the company you work for?" Daddy asked.

Naomi sighed. That was the dilemma she faced. "Suing will make that harder, maybe impossible. If I don't sue I can probably find something sooner or later, but I'd be letting SSI get away with murder."

"Well, the choice is yours."

"Some choice," Naomi said. "I keep thinking there's got to be a better way. Whites never have to deal with this kind of thing. They can just concentrate on getting ahead without having to worry about all this excess baggage."

"Oh, here comes the plane!" Mama said, jumping up as the announcement came over the loudspeaker.

Daddy looked at Naomi and smiled. "She's all excited."

"So are you," Naomi said, smiling. "You're convinced it's Joshua's son, aren't you?"

"When you see him, you'll know why. He not only looks like him in the face, he has Joshua's build, tall and lean."

She was starting to feel excited herself as she stood next to her parents. That could be Joshua's son on that plane. And in a moment he would be standing before them. What would he be like? Would he take to them? The anxiety was almost too much to bear as she stood on tiptoe trying to see above the waiting crowd as the passengers walked into the terminal.

And then she saw him. He was easy enough to spot, being the lone black teenage male in the crowd. But she would have known him anywhere, even in a throng of black men. He was wearing a Chicago Bears T-shirt and looked like a miniature Joshua.

He looked nervous and confused as her parents hugged and fussed over him. Suddenly Naomi's mind shifted to that afternoon so long ago when they'd fussed over Joshua in the same way just before he boarded his flight to Chicago. It was the same airport, and for all Naomi knew the same gate. In some eerie way, it felt as if Joshua were finally coming home to them. She swallowed hard. When her parents finally let go, she threw her arms around him. He felt stiff at first, but Naomi held on, and gradually he relaxed and let her squeeze. He probably thought they were all nuts, she thought, as she released him.

"Wow," was the first word from his mouth.

"I hope we didn't scare you," Naomi said.

He shrugged his shoulders and tried to smile. "It's OK."

"Let's go get the luggage," Daddy said, taking the sports bag Joseph was carrying.

As the four of them headed for the baggage claim area, Mama dropped behind and put her arm around Naomi's shoulder while Daddy walked alongside Joseph. "What do you think?" she whispered.

"The resemblance is uncanny, and with the setting and all . . ."

"I know. Now you see why we were so sure?"

Naomi nodded. But she also saw what a powerful hold this boy would have over them, and it frightened her. For although he looked like Joshua, he wasn't Joshua. He hadn't grown up around her parents, hadn't been exposed to their influence and values. And yet she knew her parents would settle for nothing less from him than they had expected of her and Joshua. Was Joseph up to the challenge?

Marshall took Naomi's hand as they left the downtown theater showing *Purple Rain*. Joseph walked along beside them.

"Thanks for taking us," Naomi said, squeezing Marshall's hand. He hadn't been all that eager to see the movie, but Naomi pestered him until he finally relented. It was the biggest hit of the year, she'd told him. And it was something they could do with Joseph. He had started hanging with some boys in a nearby neighborhood whom her parents didn't approve of, and they worried that he'd get into trouble if they didn't find more things for him to do. He had found a job working at Roy Rogers during the week and was always too tired to go out when he got home in the evening. He seemed to want to make up for it on weekends, though, by staying out in the streets at all hours.

"That Prince is a wild dude," Marshall said. "Too much for me."

"He's bad," Joseph said.

"I prefer Michael Jackson," Marshall said.

Joseph waved his hand. "Michael's all right. But Prince is the man."

"The two seem to be having a contest as to who can be the weirdest," Marshall said.

"Prince definitely wins that one," Naomi said. "But I enjoyed the movie. I want to get some purple boots."

"Don't wear them when you're out with me," Marshall said. Although he said it in jest, Naomi knew he was serious. Marshall could be very conservative about his women. It seemed she always ended up with men like that: Ralph, Chuck. She wondered if she was picking the old-fashioned ones out of the pot or if the pot was just filled with men like that.

"Want to get something to eat now?" she asked, as they approached Marshall's Volvo. "Maybe ride down to Chinatown?" It was after eleven, but Chinatown was always open.

"You can just take me back to Grandma's. I'm not big on Chinese."

"Then we can get something else," Naomi said. "How about pizza?" She was under orders from her parents to keep him out as late as possible, so he wouldn't have time to hook up with his friends after he got back home.

"Nah," Joseph said. "I'd prefer to head on back."

Naomi gave Marshall a beseeching look. They had to think of a way to keep him out longer.

"It's still early," Marshall said, unlocking the car door. "We'll get something to eat; then you can go home."

Joseph shook his head. "No, thanks, man. That's not for me."

"We're not giving you a choice here," Marshall said. "We're—"

"Look," Joseph said, pointing his finger at Marshall. "I don't need you or nobody else dictating to me about choices. I make my own choices."

"If you get in my car, you go where I go."

"Fine," Joseph said, throwing his hands in the air. "I'll walk." With that, he turned and pimped on down the street.

"Joseph," Naomi called. "Come back here. You don't even know where you are. How are you going to find your way back?"

"I'll figure it out," he said.

Naomi looked at Marshall in desperation. He rolled his eyes to the sky, then took off to catch up with Joseph.

"You need to just come on back here." Marshall reached out for Joseph's arm, but Joseph yanked it free.

"Get the fuck off me, man. You ain't my daddy."

Marshall backed away. "Fine. I don't give a damn what you do." He headed back toward the car, and Naomi ran after Joseph.

"Joseph, please come back."

He stopped and turned to face her, a defiant look on his face. "You going to take me back to the house?"

Naomi was torn between agreeing to what he wanted and slapping him. But hitting him would only make things worse, and who knew? He might hit her back. She wouldn't put it past him. And if she let him go, her parents would have a fit. "OK, if that's what you want. But if you talk to Marshall like that again, I'll put you out of the car myself."

He looked up the street, then back at her like he was trying to decide what to do. Finally, he headed toward the car. "Just keep him away from me," he said, tossing a spiteful look in Marshall's direction.

The three of them rode in silence all the way to her parents' house. Mama had said he could be difficult, but Naomi had no idea it was this bad. Mama had probably deliberately mini- mized the problem so as not to worry her. But now that she'd seen Joseph's temper, she was worried. He was almost as tall as Naomi and for a minute back there she'd thought he was going to strike Marshall. If Marshall, who was much bigger than her father, couldn't control him, what chance did her father have? She didn't want someone like this living with her parents for the rest of the summer.

When they got to the house, Joseph didn't even bother to go inside. He just got out of the car, walked up the block, and disappeared around a corner. Marshall waited in the car while she went to the door.

"Where's Joseph?" Daddy asked.

"He's gone up the street. Why didn't you tell me he was like this?"

He threw his hands in the air. "Your mother didn't want to worry you."

"Where is she?"

"Gone to bed. We thought he was taken care of for the night."

"Well, don't sit up waiting for him. I have the feeling he'll be out late."

"She's going to start worrying the minute she knows."

"I don't like this. You should send him back if he doesn't straighten out."

"She's not going to want to. You know that."

Naomi pursed her lips. "I can't stay now. Marshall is waiting for me in the car. But something is going to have to be done. That boy is dangerous."

"He's not that bad."

Naomi stared at her father.

"As long as you let him have his way," he said sheepishly. "He's not used to anybody telling him what to do."

She shook her head as she walked toward the car. What in the world had they gotten themselves into?

Naomi couldn't concentrate on her work, worrying about Joseph and her parents. It didn't take much to distract her these days, since she was so thoroughly disgusted with her job. She turned her chair away from the computer toward the window. She had gone back to her parents' house the day after the movie and tried to talk some sense into them. Joseph had stayed out until three in the morning, and he was back out again when she and Marshall arrived that Sunday evening for dinner. She wanted to put him on the next flight to Chicago, but her mother wouldn't hear of it. They had to do what they could during the little time they had him, Mama kept saying. Maybe they could make a difference. But Naomi believed it was hopeless after what she'd seen on Saturday night. She thought of trying to get him into a summer camp to get him away from her parents, but she knew he would never go.

Her thoughts were interrupted by a loud knock. She had started keeping her office door closed now, something she'd done before only when she met with someone or really had to concentrate on her work.

"Come in," she said, turning toward the door.

Carla burst in and slammed the door shut behind her.

"You won't believe what I just found out," she said breathlessly.

Naomi hardly cared. She had more important things on her mind than what was going on around SSI. If it had been anybody besides Carla, she would have said she was busy and to come back later.

Carla folded her arms across her chest and paced up and down the floor. "You know Norm Evans?"

Naomi wrinkled her brow trying to think. "Is he that systems engineer they just hired?"

"The one *I'm* training," Carla said, pointing to herself. "I just found out those bastards are paying him more than me."

"How do you know that?"

"Ever since what happened with you, I've become kind of paranoid. I was in Norm's office and saw his paycheck stub in the trash. When he left for a minute to get a file, I grabbed it. The sucker is making several thousand more than me, and he's only been here a few months. And I'm training *him*. It's out and out sexism."

"Maybe not," Naomi said. "Maybe it's because he's an engineer."

Carla glared at Naomi. "I don't care what he is. He's just out of college, and I've been here more than two years. I can analyze circles around that—" She stopped when she saw the look on Naomi's face. "Oh you smart-mouth. I probably deserved that, though."

"You had so much trouble believing they didn't promote me because I'm black, yet you don't seem to have a problem believing you make less money than this guy because you're a woman."

"All right, all right. You win. I thought there had to be more to it than racism 'cause it's so ugly to think of it being that way."

"What are you going to do?"

Carla sank into the seat opposite Naomi's desk. "I don't know. This makes me so mad. Confront them, I guess."

"Good luck. They'll probably just give you some crap about his background being more valuable or something."

Carla jumped back up and paced the floor. "This is ridiculous. I shouldn't have to put up with this."

"Hmm."

Carla stopped pacing and looked at Naomi standing by the window. "Are you planning on taking them to court? You haven't said anything about it for a while."

"No."

"Why not?"

Because she had an even better idea. She hadn't worked it out fully in her mind yet, but if she could carry it out, it would be the perfect solution. She'd be fighting back without jeopardizing her own career. The idea was so powerful, she hadn't told anyone at SSI, not even Carla. She didn't want to take the chance of its leaking out before she made her plans. But now that Carla was as spitting mad with SSI as she was, Naomi felt it would be safe to confide in her.

"I'm thinking of doing something else."

"What, shooting them all? If so, count me in."

Naomi laughed. "If I tell you, you have to keep it to yourself."

Carla zipped her lips with her fingers. "I won't say a word."

"I'm thinking of starting my own consulting firm. Nothing as big as this. I won't go into hardware engineering or anything like that. I'll just concentrate on software, at least in the beginning."

Carla's eyes grew bigger as she listened to Naomi. "I love it."

"I haven't made much progress planning it out. But I've already started to take in more freelance work at home. I spent some time last weekend in the library reading through *Commerce Business Daily* to get a better idea of the opportunities out there."

"I thought of doing something like that at one time, but I can't write to save myself."

"Writing proposals is no problem for me, of course. But if I want to go after the big money, at some point I'm going to need the help of someone with more of a technical background than I have."

"I'm your woman."

"It would mean working after hours. Because I doubt it'll be enough to leave SSI and support yourself, at least in the beginning."

"That's fine. I can use the extra dough. How soon do you think you'll start?"

"I'm going to make some calls this week to some of the people I do freelance consulting for. When I start competing for the bigger jobs, I'll let you know. Eventually, I hope to have enough work and money saved to quit and set up an office somewhere. But that's a long way off."

"When you reach that point, I want to be the first person you hire."

Naomi left work at three that day, claiming to have a doctor's appointment. The people in the office probably thought she had some terminal illness, with all the doctor's appointments she had these days. But Naomi didn't care. As long as she got her basic duties done, she dared them to fire her.

She went to the library, took notes, and made copies of several pages in *CBD*. She arrived home a couple of hours later and kicked off her heels. She was looking forward to reading everything more closely until Marshall stopped by at seven to take her out for dinner. She had just put on a Wynton Marsalis album when the phone rang. She turned down the volume, then went to the kitchen and picked up the receiver.

"Hello?"

"Naomi, he's gone. When I—"

"Wait a minute, Ma. Who's gone?"

"Joseph."

"What do you mean, gone?"

"When I came home from work he wasn't here. I looked in his room and it looked so deserted. Nothing on the chest, no clothes on the bed. He always has things lying around. So I looked in the closet, and all his things are gone. Just gone. Oh, God, I—"

"Ma, calm down."

"But what am I going to do? We're responsible for him."

"Did he leave a note?"

"I don't see one."

"Did you call Daddy?"

"He's on his way home from work. Said he would ride around the neighborhood and look for him first. Should I call the police?"

"Wait until Daddy gets back. He may be able to find him. In the meantime, try not to worry too much. I have a feeling Joseph knows how to take care of himself. And we'll find him."

"But he's only fifteen. Where could he possibly have gone?"

"I have no idea. Call me when Daddy gets there."

Naomi went back to the living room and slipped out of her suit jacket. Then she sat on the couch and picked up one of the photo-copied pages from *CBD*. But she couldn't read it knowing that Joseph was missing. She held the pages in her lap and chewed her thumbnail. Maybe she should go out and look for him herself. But where? Even though he'd been here a couple of months, she didn't know a thing about him—his habits or hobbies, what he did during the night when he was out, who his friends were. She was ashamed of herself for not spending more time with him, even if he did have problems. He was her brother's son.

The doorbell rang. Maybe it was Marshall arriving early. She sure needed someone to talk to. She jumped up in her stocking feet, ran to the door, and swung it open. There was Joseph, standing on the other side of the screen door, suitcase in hand, a uniformed cop behind him. He refused to look her in the eyes, just stared at his feet. Her first thought was that he'd committed a crime.

"Is this your nephew?" the cop asked.

"Yes. What happened? What did he do?"

Joseph rolled his eyes to the sky.

"He was hitchhiking out on Ninety-five. Thought he looked underage so I picked him up. He told me he was staying here with you. That true?"

Naomi looked at Joseph, who suddenly became interested in his feet again. "Yes," she said, opening the screen door. Joseph stepped in and walked to the living room. "Thanks, officer. Did he tell you where he was going?"

The officer smiled. "Chicago."

In the living room, Joseph was sitting on the couch flipping through her copied pages of *CBD*, his Nikes propped on her coffee table. "Get your feet down off that table."

He put his feet down and dropped the pages on the table. "Got any copies of *Hustler* lying around?"

Naomi ignored him and went to the kitchen to call home. "Ma, he's here. The police caught him hitchhiking on Ninety-five and brought him to my house."

"Thank God. Is he all right?"

"He seems to be fine."

"I'll send your father over for him when he gets here."

"Let him stay here tonight. I'll drop him off on my way to work in the morning. I want to spend some time with him."

"Good. Maybe you can get through to him."

"Don't get your hopes up."

Mama sighed. "At least we know he's safe. I'll call you tomorrow."

Naomi put the phone down and dialed Marshall's office. "Guess who's here with me."

"Who?" he asked, clearly having no idea.

"Joseph. He ran away from my parents' house. The police caught him hitchhiking on Ninety-five and brought him here."

"That boy is too much. Where the hell did he think he was going, home?"

"Exactly."

"Maybe they should have left him where they found him."

Naomi shut the door to the kitchen and lowered her voice. "Marshall, that's a terrible thing to say. Anything could have happened to him out there. Somebody could have grabbed him."

"I pity anyone who did."

Naomi chuckled. "I thought we'd all eat here and maybe rent a video instead of going out tonight."

"Uh-uh, count me out. I don't like being around him, and I think the feeling's mutual."

"Give him another chance, Marshall. He's just a kid."

"Thanks, but no thanks."

Naomi started to protest but then thought maybe it would be better if Marshall didn't come by. It would give her a chance to spend some time alone with Joseph. "Fine. I'll call you tomorrow."

"Wait a minute. You're going to stay in with him rather than go out with me?"

"I don't want to leave him here alone."

"Why don't you send him back to your parents? I don't like the idea of you being there alone with him, anyway."

"I haven't spent enough time with him since he got here."

Marshall let out a deep breath of air. "Maybe I'll have to come over there."

"I'll be fine. He doesn't scare me."

When Naomi went back into the living room, Joseph was

stretched out on the sofa with his eyes closed and one sneaker back on the coffee table. Naomi went over, lifted his foot, and dropped it on the floor. Joseph woke with a start and sat up.

"You like Michael Jackson at all?" she asked.

"Sure," he said, sleepy eyed.

She put *Thriller* on the stereo and went to the kitchen to see what she had for dinner. She was standing in front of the refrigerator with the door open when Joseph walked in. He pulled a chair out from the kitchen table, flipped it around, and sat on it backward.

"This your house and all?"

"I'm just renting. What do you want for dinner, chicken or steak?"

"Steak, by all means."

She removed a sirloin from the freezer and placed it in the microwave to defrost. "I'm thinking of building a house, though. Marshall is an architect. That's how we met."

"You two planning on getting married?"

Naomi laughed and sat down across from him. "We haven't known each other long enough to talk about that yet. Less than a year."

"Good, 'cause I don't think he's right for you."

"What makes you say that? You hardly know him."

"Trust me. You can do better."

"You just say that because he was firm with you and you aren't used to that."

"You got that right. You must have a pretty decent job, thinking about building your own house and all."

"I do OK."

"What do you do?"

"I'm a manager at a technology consulting firm."

His eyebrows shot up. "You mean you, like, write computer programs and all that?"

"Sort of."

"Not bad. A lot of money in that, right?"

"If you work hard at it. Do you use computers at school?"

"We got a couple, but they so old nobody uses them anymore. The school's always talking about getting more, but they never do."

"I've got a brand-new one. I can show you how to use it if you want."

His eyes lit up and he looked genuinely interested in something for the first time since he got off the plane.

"You got any games on it?"

"Some. A fighter-pilot one, but I haven't used it in a long time."

"Can you show me tonight?"

"I'll show you right after we eat."

"Cool," he said, smiling.

She got up to remove the steak from the microwave and put it in a pan. "You're in high school now, right?"

He shrugged.

"What happens after high school?"

"You mean after I graduate? Seeing as how college is out of the question, I haven't given it much thought."

"Why do you say college is out of the question?"

"Where am I going to get the money for college?"

"I see." Naomi felt silly for not picking up on that sooner. "Do you want to go?"

He twisted up his lips. "Never gave it much thought. Where's that computer?"

"Upstairs. Joseph, why did you run away from my parents' house?"

"I knew that was coming sooner or later. Look, I got nothing against them. But I'm just not used to being told what to do, all right? And your old man—he is one cheap dude. Can't get him to give me more than a few bucks a week."

Naomi couldn't help but chuckle at that. Daddy hadn't changed. "I thought you had a job at Roy Rogers."

He waved his hand. "I quit that the second week I was here. That's slave labor, man."

Naomi shook her head. Her mother hadn't told her that, either. "So you were going to hitchhike all the way back to Chicago. Do you have any idea how far that is?"

"Six hundred seventy-one miles."

"I guess that's supposed to impress me."

"You asked. I answered."

"I'm glad you at least went through the trouble to look up the distance, since you were planning to hitchhike all the way out there. But why did you tell the officer to bring you here?"

"I figured you'd be more understanding."

"Well, you figured wrong. You're welcome to stay here as long as you like, but not if you're going to run the streets all day and night. I'll probably give you more mouth about that than my parents did."

"Then I'm out of here first thing in the morning."

"I'll make a deal with you, though."

He narrowed his eyes at her. "I don't make deals."

"Can you at least listen first?"

"Shoot."

"Stay here through the summer. If at any time you want to go home, I'll put you on a plane myself."

"What's the catch?"

"What makes you so sure there is one?"

"Please. I wasn't born yesterday."

"OK, you've got to be in at a decent hour. But we can negotiate on the time."

"Uh-uh. No deal."

"I've got a pool and tennis courts. I'll give you passes, and you can use them during the day while I'm at work."

"You got a pool?"

"It's part of the town house complex. Olympic size, right out back. And don't forget about the computer upstairs. I'll have to use it most evenings, but it's all yours during the day."

Naomi could see he was giving this some serious thought so she decided to sweeten the pot. "What do you think would be a fair allowance?"

"Twenty bucks a week, minimum."

"I'll give you ten. But you have to be in by nine unless you let me know exactly where you're going."

Joseph jerked his head back. "Uh-uh. Forget it."

"No questions asked about where you're going if you're in by nine. Swimming pool and tennis courts during the day. Ten a week for allowance. Computer right in the room where you'll be staying. If you don't like it here, I'll pay your fare home. What have you got to lose?"

"Make it midnight and you got yourself a deal."

"Ten, and not a minute later."

He ran his tongue across his lips while he thought about it. Naomi didn't like the idea of letting a fifteen-year-old go out without having to tell her where he was going. But if she could get him in by ten at night, it would be a huge improvement. This was a boy who was obviously used to staying out all hours with no supervision. It was probably unrealistic to expect him to change overnight.

"OK," he said. "I'll give it a try. But if I don't like it, you send me back." He pointed his finger at her.

"Fine."

"Now where's the computer?"

Naomi laughed. "Upstairs. Come on. I'll set you up and you can practice while I fix dinner."

Things went fine with Joseph the first few days. While she was at work, he spent his mornings at the pool and afternoons on the computer. Naomi knew this because not a day went by that he didn't call her at work to help him unravel a problem he was having on it. The day before, she had had to come home during her lunch hour to show him how to set up the joystick.

More often than not, he was still on it when she got home from work, and she had to pull him away for dinner. He even wanted to take his meals at the computer, but she insisted they eat together. She looked forward to their conversations during dinner. Joseph knew almost nothing about his father, and what he did know had come from an unsympathetic mother.

"Tisha says he cared more about protesting than he did about her," Joseph said one day at dinner.

Naomi was having trouble getting used to Joseph calling his mother Tisha. She wondered what it must be like to grow up never calling anyone Mama or Daddy. "Why does she say that?"

"He was always doing this and that. She went along with him most of the time 'cause it was the only way she could be with him. The night of the car accident, she almost didn't go because she had just found out she was pregnant with me."

"Joshua was very much into the civil rights struggle. Lots of people were back then."

"Yeah, but he was obsessed by it. He went around doing crazy things."

"King had just been killed and a lot was going on. Your father had good intentions. A lot of the advantages you have now are because of people like my brother."

"Like what? I don't see no advantages."

"That's because you don't know what it was like before. Back in the fifties and sixties, black people couldn't sit at lunch counters in some restaurants and department stores. Some restaurants wouldn't let us in at all."

"What would they do? Have a guard stand around to keep them out?"

"They didn't need to do that. I remember one time it happened to us right outside D.C. The owner refused to seat us."

"And you just walked out and left?"

"What else could we have done?"

"You should have made him let you in. That's what I would have done."

Naomi smiled. "You sound like your father did then. But that wouldn't have done any good, because back then the law was on their side. We couldn't live in certain neighborhoods, and it was OK to deny us jobs just because of our race. They used all kinds of tricks to keep us from voting. And it was all legal."

"That's sick, man."

Naomi nodded. "That's what your father was protesting against."

"Then why doesn't Tisha see it that way?"

Good question, Naomi thought. "Some people just don't understand, that's all. They forget what it was like."

* * *

By the end of the week, Naomi's good luck with Joseph seemed to be running out. When she came home from work on Friday, he wasn't there and had left no note. His clothes were still around, and the computer was on, so she told herself not to worry just yet.

By 8:30 she had changed into Bermuda shorts and a T-shirt for a date with Marshall, but there was still no sign of Joseph. She and Marshall had planned to catch a 9:30 movie, so Naomi called him and suggested they go later.

"I want to be sure he's here before I go out."

"You expect him back by ten?"

"That was our agreement, and so far he's lived up to it."

"I'll come over around ten-thirty then. We can catch the last show, at eleven-thirty."

Her doorbell rang at 10:35, and for a second Naomi thought it was Joseph. Then she remembered he had a key and wouldn't ring the bell.

"He's still not back?" Marshall asked as he followed her into the living room.

"Do you see him?"

"Don't get on my case. I didn't keep him out."

Naomi sighed. "I know. But I'm starting to get worried. He should be back by now."

Marshall didn't say anything, just shook his head.

"What?" Naomi asked. "Go ahead and say what's on your mind."

"It's nothing you don't already know."

"You want to say 'I told you so.' But it's only a little after ten-thirty. He's probably on his way. He hasn't been late all week."

"Any idea where he goes?"

"Ma said he met some boys his age in her neighborhood and was hanging out with them. That's one reason I thought he'd be better off staying here."

"Obviously it doesn't take him long to make friends. Or maybe he went back over there."

"How would he get there? It's so far."

"All that money you're giving him for an allowance, he could have hailed a cab. That's probably why your parents didn't give him much."

"Ten dollars isn't much these days. And you can't expect to keep a fifteen-year-old boy who's used to unlimited freedom in chains."

"When they behave the way that one does, you do."

"That just makes them worse."

"Look, I don't want to sit here arguing with you. Are you planning to wait until he comes back? I have a feeling it'll be a long wait."

Naomi didn't know what to do. She hadn't been out with Marshall all week because she was trying to spend as much time as she could with Joseph. Things were going so well she'd thought it would be fine to spend an evening out with Marshall while Joseph stayed home. "Let's wait just a little longer."

Marshall sat back on the couch. "I just hope he gets here before the last show."

She sat beside him. "It would be nice if you'd show more interest in him."

"What's the point? The boy's nothing but trouble, and there's not a whole lot you can do in a couple of weeks. He'll just go back to Chicago and pick up where he left off."

"We still have to try. The more I'm around him, the more I feel that way. I don't like the things Tisha's been telling him about Joshua. He's growing up thinking his father was nothing but a troublemaker."

By eleven, Joseph still wasn't back. Marshall watched the news on TV while Naomi paced the floor. At midnight, Naomi jumped up from her seat on the couch next to Marshall and called her mother.

"I'm going to send him back to Chicago. I'm not putting up with this another minute."

"Send him back here."

"No. You shouldn't have to bother with it either. If he can't listen to us, he doesn't belong here."

"I'm not ready to send him back yet, Naomi."

"You wouldn't have put up with this kind of behavior from us, Ma. He's got to learn to show some respect."

"I wouldn't have sent you away, either. We have to be patient."

"I'm through with being patient. I—" She paused when she heard the front door open and shut. "I have to go. I think he just came in."

"Don't be too hard on him, Naomi."

"I can't believe I'm hearing this from you."

As soon as she hung up the phone, the sound of Joseph and Marshall arguing reached her ears. She rushed into the living room.

"Can't you show any respect?" Marshall was saying as she entered the room. "I don't know what you're used to at home, but—"

"Get off my back!" Joseph shouted. "I don't need this shit!"

"What you need is a good smack upside the head."

"You just try it, man."

"Don't tempt me."

"Stop it, both of you," Naomi said. "Where have you been, Joseph?"

"Out."

"Out where?"

"None of your damn business."

Marshall made a move toward Joseph. "Listen, you inconsiderate—"

Naomi reached out and stopped him. "I'll handle this." She turned to Joseph. "You remember our agreement?"

Joseph shrugged like it didn't mean a thing to him.

"I said I was going to send you back if this happened."

Joseph twisted his lips and turned his head away.

"That must be what you want me to do. It's after midnight."

"It's fine with me. 'Cause this is crazy. Who can deal with this? Can't even go out with my friends."

"Fine. I'll call and make reservations to Chicago in the morning."

"Fine with me."

"For a flight out tomorrow afternoon if I can get it."

"Fine," he said, and turned to go up the stairs.

Naomi watched him go in silence. She didn't really want him to leave. He'd done so well for a few days and this was the first time he'd broken their agreement. She would have gladly given him a second chance if he'd apologized or given any indication that he really wanted to stay. But he didn't. Her disappointment must have showed on her face as she watched him disappear up the stairs.

"Let him go on back, Naomi," Marshall said. "It's for the best."

She turned and looked at Marshall. He seemed to deeply resent the disruption Joseph brought into their lives. But then she couldn't really blame him. They had only been dating several months, and he had no reason to feel responsible for her nephew. Still, she wished he would try harder. It would do Joseph so much good to be around a strong male figure for a change.

"Best for who?" she asked. "Him or us?"

They walked through the metal detectors in silence. At the boarding gate, Naomi handed Joseph his ticket. He took it and turned toward the gate without so much as a glance her way. Naomi reached out and grabbed his arm. "Wait."

He stopped but wouldn't turn to face her. "I'm sorry this didn't work out and you have to leave this way," she said.

He shrugged his shoulders. "It's the story of my life. No big deal."

"What does that mean?"

"Nothing. Forget it."

"No, tell me."

"This isn't the first time I've had to pack up and leave. Won't be the last. I'm used to it by now."

Naomi clamped her mouth shut when she realized he was talking about his foster homes, and probably his mother's house. "I haven't given up. Maybe we can try again next summer."

"Yeah, sure," he said sarcastically.

"I mean it."

"Can I go now?"

She wanted to hug him but didn't think that wise. "Go on."

He walked off, handed his ticket to the agent, and disappeared through the gate without once looking back.

Twenty-six

The diamond was so big—at least two carats—it was hard to believe it was real. But knowing Marshall, it was very real. He liked the finest of everything.

She reached out for the ring eagerly, but Marshall pulled it back. "Wait. I think I should get an answer to my question first."

She smiled. His apartment balcony overlooking other buildings in Southwest D.C. wasn't the most exotic setting for a marriage proposal, but it would do. It was a beautiful fall night, cool and clear, and a ring like this made up for the backdrop. Besides, she'd decided months ago that she wanted to marry him.

"Yes."

He smiled and slipped the ring on her finger. Naomi realized with disappointment that it was a bit loose. This never happened in the movies. She held her hand out and admired it.

"I'll have to take it back and get them to size it," Marshall said, reaching for the ring.

Naomi pulled her hand away and switched the ring to her right finger. It fit perfectly. "I'll wear it on this hand until you do."

Marshall laughed and she kissed him. "It's gorgeous," she said.

He picked up the wineglasses from the balcony floor and handed her one. "A toast," he said. "To us."

Naomi raised her glass to his. "To us."

"When do you want to do it?" he asked.

"June is as good as anytime."

"June it is, then."

"Good," Naomi said. "That'll give us more than six months to plan."

"And build a house."

" 'Scuse me?"

He smiled broadly. "I thought we could build that dream house of yours together."

"Oh, Marshall. That's a nice idea, but I put that aside when I decided to start my own business. Sometimes dreams have to be postponed."

"I know. But together we could still do it."

"I don't know. I just got that project with Allied Research. It's going to take up a lot of my free time over the next few months. And I'm going to want to leave SSI soon."

"How soon?"

"A year if things go the way I plan."

"But by that time you'll have more income from the free-lance work, right?"

"Yes, but it won't be the same as having a steady income. For a while it'll be a lot less."

Marshall sat down on the glider and took a long sip from his wineglass. She sat beside him. "Having second thoughts?" she asked, only half teasing. "We can always put the wedding off until I'm earning more money in the business."

He smiled. "That won't be necessary."

She smiled back at him, relieved that he was beginning to understand.

"I think we can pull it off, as long as you have some income coming in."

She shook her head. Maybe he didn't understand after all. "It's not going to be available for building a house. I'm going to have to put most of it back into the business so I can open an office at some point." And into her own living expenses if they couldn't work things out, she thought.

"You're really serious about all this, about setting up your own office."

"That's what I've been saying all along."

"I knew you were serious about getting outside work, and I was really happy for you when things started picking up. But leaving your job and setting up an office—that's a big step."

"That's why I have to save. It doesn't take as much as many other businesses do but it does take some. The main expenses in the beginning will be office space, a small staff, and computer equipment."

"Why can't you just keep working from your house—or our house?"

She rolled her eyes to the ceiling. "You don't understand. I'm talking about starting a business, with an office, employees, the works, not just doing some work on the side. And when I start going after the big money, my clients will want to meet with me. I can't do that from my home."

"Then where will we live? This apartment is too small for both of us. And you live so far out of the city. I'd have to commute, and you know the kind of hours I put in."

"My house is not that far out. Certainly no farther than Fort Washington or anywhere else you might build. It'll be fine for us until I get on my feet."

"That won't take too long, I hope."

Naomi wondered what he would consider too long. Surely he realized it would be a few years before she had money to spend on something like building a house, if not longer. But she wouldn't go into that now. She didn't want to ruin this precious moment. She snuggled up to him. "We'll work it out."

Naomi sat hunched over the keyboard of her personal computer trying to find the darn bug in the program she was writing. Outside she could hear Christmas carolers at the house next door singing "Silent Night." When they knocked on her door a few minutes earlier, Naomi didn't even answer it. She was too busy. What a way to spend Christmas Eve, she thought, staring at the monitor. But this project was due the week after Christmas, and she couldn't possibly take a break. She had to work every day until then except Christmas.

She was about to call Carla for help when the phone rang. She picked up the receiver next to the computer without taking her eyes off the monitor. "Hello?"

"Naomi? It's Jennifer. How are you?"

"Oh, I'm hanging in there," Naomi said by rote. Her mind was still half on the software program. "Where are you?"

"Here for the holidays. If you're not busy, you should stop by."

As much as she'd like to see Jennifer, she couldn't possibly tonight. She'd put off her parents, Marshall, everybody to stay in and finish this job by the deadline.

"I can't. I've got some work I'm trying to finish up. But I'll make some time before you go back. Is your family with you?"

"Just my daughter. To make a long story short, Doug and I separated last month. He's involved with some white chick."

Naomi's eyes left the monitor for the first time since the phone rang. "What? When I talked to you last Christmas, everything seemed to be going so well."

"A lot can happen in a year."

"What went wrong?"

"Oh, everything. Doug likes the chicks, always has. I knew he was like that when I married him, but I was vain enough to think I could tame him. This isn't the first time he's had an affair."

"I had no idea." Naomi couldn't get over it. Not Jennifer, whose life was always picture-perfect.

"How could you? I didn't talk about it, hoping he would change and everything would be all right. But I'm tired of it."

Talk of good-looking men who cheat got Naomi to thinking of Ralph for the first time in ages. "Speaking of which, how's your brother doing?"

Jennifer chuckled. "He's fine. He's getting married this summer and moving to Florida. That's where Vicky, his fiancée, is from."

A chill ran through Naomi. She no longer had romantic feelings for Ralph, but he had a special place in her memories as her first real love. "Tell him I said congratulations. And Vicky too. Any woman who gets him to settle down deserves a pat on the back."

Jennifer laughed. "*If* he's settled down. Marching down the aisle doesn't guarantee a damn thing. I learned that the hard way."

"Oh, Jennifer, I'm so sorry things didn't work out for you."

"Don't be. I'm fine. I'm even thinking of moving back to the East Coast. I miss my family and friends."

"That would be great. But what about your job?"

"That's the only thing. I'm an executive vice president now."

"Go ahead! Last time we talked, you were director of personnel."

"I got the promotion about a year ago. I really got lucky with this company. They've been good to me."

"Don't think that way. They're lucky to have you."

"Thanks. But the problem is, if I move, I'd probably have to take something lower, maybe a director or manager or something. This firm is small, and when I put out feelers to other companies—"

"Sounds familiar," Naomi said, interrupting. "Go on."

"It's like, although I've proven myself to the people I work with, other firms assume I'm some kind of token and not really up to being a vice president for them."

"I know exactly what you mean. Something similar happened to me. Only in my case I couldn't even break beyond the manager barrier."

"I remember when I talked to you last year around this time you'd just found out that your boss was leaving and you were going to apply for the job."

"Right. I didn't get it. Went to some white guy."

"Figures. You should take them to court if you think it was discrimination."

"I decided I don't want something like that hanging over my

head for the next ten years. But I'm not going to let it get me down either. I'm moving on. Believe it or not, I'm trying to start my own business."

"Get out of here!"

Naomi laughed. "Seriously."

"What kind of business? Something to do with computers?"

"A technology consulting firm."

"Really? Heavy. How far along are you?"

"I was working on one of my projects when you called. I have another one lined up right after I finish this one. Everyone is computerizing, and they need people to design specialized software programs. I hope eventually to get enough work to be able to set up an office."

"That oughta show 'em. I'm so proud of you, Naomi. Have you left your job yet?"

"No. But I can't wait until the day comes."

"I'm rooting for you all the way."

"Thanks."

"So how's your love life?" Jennifer asked.

"Oh, I meant to tell you, I'm engaged."

"I don't believe this."

"Don't believe what, that I'm finally getting married?"

"No, not that. We've been talking half an hour and you're just getting around to telling me you're engaged."

Naomi chuckled. "It never seemed the appropriate time until now."

"You're unbelievable. When's the date?"

"We haven't set an exact date but sometime in June. I haven't even started planning it yet, I've been so busy with other things."

"More important things than your wedding?"

"It's not that. But you're right, I need to get started right after Christmas."

"What's he like?"

"His name is Marshall and he's kind of the serious type. He has his own architectural firm."

"You always liked the studious type. That's why I wondered what you saw in my brother."

"Girl, your brother is fine. And he's sort of studious. He was always studying, or at least I thought he was. It turned out that what he was studying was other women."

Jennifer giggled. "Then there was Merlon. I heard from a girl we went to high school with that he's doing very well now. Went to UCLA after he got out of the service."

"I heard about that too. I'm glad he straightened himself out. He's married with a couple of kids and lives around here somewhere. He's the one that got away, I guess, thanks to Ralph. Seems I always pick the wrong ones."

"At least you have it right now. You really seem to be getting your life together. I'm so jealous. Is Marshall good-looking?"

"He is to me. Not drop-dead cute, but he's got the kind of looks that grow on you."

"That's the best kind. You don't have to worry so much about other women coming in for the kill. Is he good in the sack?"

"You haven't changed a bit, have you?"

"Yes, I have. Before, that would have been the *first* thing I asked you about him."

"You're right about that. Listen, I've got a ton of work—"

"I know when I'm getting the brushoff. I didn't mean to talk so long."

"No, I'm glad you called. It was really good talking to you."

"Same here. Maybe we can get together before I go back."

"I'd like that. I'll call you right after Christmas."

The phone was ringing again. Damn it, she thought. She'd just finished talking to Jennifer not more than ten minutes ago. If this kept up, she'd never get her work done. Whoever it was, she was going to get rid of them in two minutes, tops. She was tempted to pick up and try to imitate a recorded message. *Hi, sorry I cannot come to the phone right now . . .* "Yeah?"

"Naomi?"

Her heart did a somersault. "Dean?"

He laughed, a soft deep sound that melted her heart.

"It's me. What do you know good?"

She closed her eyes and smiled into the phone. That was so like Dean. He never called when he came home to visit anymore— she had to assume that he *did* come to visit his family—and now he was acting like they'd seen each other only the day before. "Working, believe it or not."

"On Christmas Eve? Naomi, that's not good for you."

"It's a long story. Where are you?"

"At my mother's. Just got here yesterday."

"How's Sonya?"

"Wouldn't know. I haven't seen her recently. We were divorced last year."

Naomi was stunned. Dean divorced? "Uh . . . I'm sorry to hear that." She was. Really. She didn't know who wanted the divorce and didn't think it appropriate to ask. They weren't close like that anymore. But she'd heard divorce was always painful, even when you wanted it, and she hated to think of Dean being in pain. Despite all the years and all that had happened between them, he still held a special place in her heart. Always would.

"It was for the best. She really wasn't happy in Africa, and I wanted to stay."

"I assume you're just home for a visit?"

"I'll explain when I see you. Got any free time over the next few days?"

"I can always make time for you."

"How about now?"

Now? She looked at the work piled in front of her. "Now's fine."

"I'll be there in an hour."

Somehow, she'd have to find the extra time to finish her work, she thought, as she hung up the phone. She realized her hand was shaking a bit as she saved the software program and turned off the computer. The thought of seeing Dean again after all these years was making her jittery. She wondered if he'd changed, what he'd think of her. Then she remembered that her hair was a mess. She was planning to wash it in the morning before she went to her parents'. She jumped up, hopped into the shower, and bathed and shampooed in record time. Then she blew her hair dry and curled it with the electric iron. It was at these moments that she missed her Afro. But nobody wore them these days.

An hour later she was all dolled up in a short blue dress and blue flats. She didn't know why she was doing this. Dean was about the only man she knew who didn't seem to care about her looks. She smiled when she thought of the day he stopped by just before he first left for Africa. She had looked awful, just awful, and he barely seemed to notice.

She sprayed on some perfume, ran down to the kitchen, and opened the refrigerator. She remembered that Dean liked to drink beer, but since Marshall was a wine kind of guy she didn't keep it around much. She was relieved to see two cans sitting on the bottom shelf. But she didn't have much food. Maybe they could go out and get a bite.

The doorbell rang and she left the kitchen, pausing in front of her reflection in the china closet to make sure her hair was in place. Stop it, she thought, dropping her hand to her side. It was only Dean, not her fiancé.

She opened the door, and they stood on opposite sides of the threshold and smiled at each other. She could stand around looking into those eyes all night, she thought. He was dressed casually as usual, in a loose-fitting wool coat, jeans, and a shirt, but the man was so good-looking he could get away with wearing a paper bag. She reached out and pulled him in, and they hugged the way old friends do after a long absence.

"God, it's good to see you," he said, holding her. All of her problems seemed to fly out the door the minute she was in his arms: the job, the freelance work she had to finish, Joseph. She'd have to be sure to tell him about her newfound nephew, but not now. Dean was one of only three men who had ever made her feel she could overcome anything. One—her father— was of a different generation and didn't always understand, and the other was dead. She wanted to enjoy this moment. They were too few and far between.

"Thanks," she said when he released her. "I needed that."

"My pleasure," he said. "You smell nice. Would you like another hug?"

"Yes."

He seemed surprised but pleased that she accepted so quickly, and in no time she was back in his soothing grasp. Then they walked into the living room, arm in arm.

"Can I get you something?" she asked as she hung his coat in the closet. "I don't have much. I thought maybe we could go out."

"In a bit maybe. First I want to get reacquainted with you. It's been so long."

"Too long."

"Come sit with me." He sat on the couch and patted the space next to him. She sat down.

"So what have you been up to?" he asked.

She should tell him about Marshall, of course, and Joseph, and she would in time. But first she wanted to hear about him, about Africa, and what he was going to do with his life now that he was divorced. "You go first. Do you have any children?"

"No, no children." He smiled. "Sonya spent so much time back here, it was almost impossible."

"Hmm. Tell me about Africa. Last time we talked you were in Dakar."

"We moved to Banjul when we got married. They speak English, and I wanted to make the adjustment as easy on her as possible."

That was so like Dean, she thought, smiling. Always being considerate. "Where is Banjul?"

"In Gambia."

"That's near the place Alex Haley wrote about, isn't it?"

He nodded. "You're talking about Juffure. Anyway, after we separated, I moved back to Dakar. I'm helping this African friend set up and run an import-export business."

Naomi shook her head with awe. "You're hopping all over the place. Is it what you expected?"

"In some ways, yes. Others, no. It's a real heady experience being in a country where you're the majority. I think every black American should spend some time there, to feel that just once in their lives."

"I can't even imagine what it must be like. Are the people nice?"

"Very nice. They'll invite you into your homes and share what they have with you in a minute, even though it usually isn't much. Many of them are poor by our standards, but not starving, at least where I was, since they have natural resources. I spent many an evening down on the water in Dakar catching fish from the sea and grilling them on the beach with people who lived in nothing more than a hut. But they were happy enough."

"It sounds peaceful in a way."

"It is. But don't get the wrong idea. Poverty is poverty. Too many of them live on the streets begging. That can be infuriating when you see how well the whites live. Even those with moderate incomes have servants."

"That's disgusting."

"That's how I felt in the beginning. But then I realized I was looking at things through Western eyes. To us, making it over there would mean having a big house in the city with running water and servants. But the majority of the Africans live in the countryside. They don't have much, but they manage."

"I see what you mean. Still, in some ways it sounds so much like it is here, you know? Do any of the Africans live well according to Western standards?"

"Some of them do. Mohammad, the dude I'm working with now, has a nice house in Dakar with a swimming pool. I even met a few other blacks from the States, and they live pretty well too."

"What about the language? Is that a problem?"

"Not really. Even in the French-speaking countries, many of the most illiterate people you meet speak enough English to carry on a conversation. It put me to shame. They speak French, the official language, and then English, and one or more tribal languages."

"Amazing."

"Yes. Now tell me what you've been up to. Started any riots lately?"

She laughed out loud. "No, fortunately. Although I felt like doing that at work a few times. They passed me over for a promotion I really wanted. Gave the job to a white man."

Dean shook his head. "Whenever I come back to this country after a long absence, I go through a phase where I imagine that when I get off the plane I'll discover that racism and discrimination are gone."

"You have quite an imagination. Some things will never change. But I'm not going to mope about it. I'm taking freelance computer jobs, and one of these days I'm going to set up an office."

"Are you talking about starting your own business?"

"Exactly."

"I like to hear you talk like that. You don't know how proud that makes me."

"I just hope I can pull it off. There's so much to be done. I have an MBA but still I've just . . ."

He took her hand and she paused. "Naomi, don't even think for a minute that you can't do it. Think positively every second."

"You're right."

"And I want a phone call the day you open shop. Wherever I am, I'll come help you celebrate."

"Will I be calling you in the States or somewhere halfway around the world?"

He smiled and squeezed her hand. "Good question."

"I'm kidding. I've about given up on thinking you'll ever move back."

"Don't do that. I'm going to spend some time here, a few months, maybe even through the summer."

"And then what?"

"Depends. I was really comfortable there."

"Then why did you come back?"

He let her hand go. "Oh, different reasons. Some things I need to wrap up here."

"You've been away twelve years and still have things to wrap up here?"

He chuckled. "Pretty amazing, huh?"

Naomi sighed. "At least you'll be here for a while. It's good to have you back."

"It's good to *be* back, especially seeing you."

"Would you like a beer?"

"Don't mind if I do."

He followed her to the kitchen.

"How are your parents?" he asked.

"Fine." She took the two Miller Lights from the refrigerator, placed them on the countertop, and popped the tab on one of them. "And how are your mother and sisters?" she asked, turning to hand him the can. She hadn't realized he was standing inches behind her, and she had to jump back a little to keep from spilling the beer.

"They're all fine," he said, that deep voice of his sounding even deeper now. He took both cans and reached around her to place them down, then rested his hands on the countertop and looked down at her. The passion on his face made her tingle, so she looked away. But that didn't solve the matter of her arms, hanging limply at her sides. She tried folding them across her chest, but he was too close, breathing too hard, and somehow they landed on his chest. Oh, you naughty girl, she thought. This would be the time to tell him about Marshall and here she was with her hands and arms on another man's chest . . .

Her brain stopped working when he removed his hands from the countertop and wrapped his arms around her. He was so close, she could feel the muscles in his thighs, so she imagined he must surely be able to hear her racing heart. Now was definitely the time to mention Marshall.

She wiggled a bit trying to free herself—it was hard to think clearly with them all wrapped up like this—but he just moaned softly and backed her up against the countertop. She didn't breathe as he reached down and planted gentle kisses on the side of her neck, the front. Then he came after her lips, and she knew she had to put a stop to this. It had already gone too far.

"Uh, Dean."

"Shh." He kissed the corner of her mouth, and she thought her head would explode if she didn't get away from him.

"No," she said, trying to wiggle away. She was blocked from behind by the sink, so she stepped to the side. "You don't understand."

He dropped his arms and backed away. "What don't I understand? You seeing someone?"

She nodded and moved toward the kitchen table.

He threw his arms up in the air. "I should have known. You always are."

She always was? He'd obviously forgotten about Sonya, his ex-wife. "Not always."

"Is it serious?"

"Yes." She swallowed. "I'm engaged."

"What?"

She didn't say anything. She knew he'd heard her. He just needed time to let the news sink in.

"Why didn't you tell me before?" he finally said, clearly agitated.

"Before what? You just got here twenty minutes ago, and I only got engaged two months ago."

He looked up to the ceiling, then back at her. "You're not wearing a ring."

"It was too big. We're having it sized."

He exhaled and picked up a beer. When he turned back around, his lips were smiling but not his eyes. "Talk about timing. We can never seem to get it right."

She smiled thinly and rubbed her arms as he took two long drinks of beer. When he brought the can back down, it was empty, and he crushed it with his bare hands. "When's the date? You're not going to pull a fast one on me, are you?"

"You mean like you did? Not at all. It's in June, and I'd like you to come."

The smile fell from his lips. "Oh, no. Leave me out of it."

"Why won't you come?"

"I just can't."

"Even if you're still in the States?"

"I doubt if I will be."

"You just said you might stay through the summer. Why are you acting like this?"

"Why the hell do you think? I've been carrying a torch for you for years, that's why. I think I'm entitled to act any way I want."

He had some nerve. "You're the one who got married first."

"I know." He sighed. "It gets lonely in Africa, and you wouldn't come with me. I have to know, Naomi. Have you ever had any feelings at all for me? And I don't mean as a brother."

"What's in the past doesn't matter now."

"That's not what I asked you."

"Well, yes. But you've been away so long. And you're planning to go back. We can't just drop everything, like nothing that's happened these past twelve years counts. We've probably both changed anyway."

"You're right."

"Then you'll come to the wedding?"

He tossed the beer can into the trash. "I'll think about it." He didn't sound convincing.

"You're angry. I want us to still be friends."

He exhaled. "I'm not angry, just hurt. And I don't know about this friends business."

"I'm so sorry. I wish—"

"Hey, don't worry about me. I had no right to come in here acting like I own you. On the way over, I kept trying to decide whether to ask first if you were involved with anyone. But I decided to just go for it, since something or somebody always seems to be coming between us. It was stupid of me, and I apologize. You're engaged to be married. I respect that, but don't expect me to like it."

She put her hand to her forehead. The thought of losing him as a friend, just when she thought she'd finally gotten him back, was giving her a headache. He came up, cupped her chin in his hand, and tilted her head up. "Is this brother treating you right?"

"Oh, Dean."

"I mean it. Is he?"

"Yes."

"Good," he said, letting her go.

"So what do we do now?" she asked.

"Do? Nothing. I think we've had enough excitement for one night." He walked toward the living room. "I'll just get my coat and head on home."

"You're leaving?" she asked, following him. "You just got here. I thought we were going to get something to eat. We could—"

"I don't think so, Naomi. Not tonight."

She was tired of Dean leaving her, first for Africa, then marriage, now this. "I hope we can still be friends, Dean."

"Will you get off this friends kick? I just got the wind knocked out of me, baby. I need some time to regroup."

She backed down. "I understand."

After he left, she was too emotionally drained to do anything but sit on the couch and stare at the wall. What had just happened? Dean had expressed some pretty deep feelings for her, and she'd rejected him, that's what. She'd had a crush on this man for ages and now she was turning him away. Was she losing her mind? She shook her head. No. Times had changed; she and Dean had changed. She was building a foundation here in D.C.; he couldn't stay put. And being around him was too intoxicating. Marshall never left her feeling this way. He was stable and calm. He was safe. Even their arguments were sober.

She got up, went upstairs, and turned on the computer. Then she sat down in front of it and forced herself to work. She had already lost precious time. As soon as she got the day's quota done, she'd call Marshall.

"What's bothering you?" Mama asked as they filled the dishwasher. Daddy was in the living room talking with Marshall.

"What makes you think something's bothering me?" Naomi

asked as she scraped leftover turkey and cranberry sauce off a dinner plate.

"You've been so quiet all evening. Everything going OK with the freelance work you've taken on?"

"Couldn't be better."

"That's so exciting. We couldn't be more proud of you."

"I know. Thanks, Ma."

"Naomi, what is it? You seem distracted."

"I'm sorry. The truth is that I've had something on my mind."

"Something to do with the job?"

"No. With Dean."

"Is something wrong with him? You told me he was doing fine."

"He is, but something he said last night has my head spinning. It seems he . . . he"—Naomi wasn't even sure how to say it—"he's . . . liked me all these years."

"Liked you? That's nothing new. He's always been like a brother to you."

"That's not the kind of like I mean."

"You mean he's in love with you?"

Naomi flinched at her mother's words. "I guess you could say that."

"He told you that?"

"Sort of."

Mama did the strangest thing. She started cracking up.

"You think it's funny? It's not. I told him about my engagement, and he was pretty hurt."

Mama placed a wet hand on her hip and turned to face Naomi. "You little fool."

"Ma!"

"Sorry," Mama said, picking silverware up out of the sink. "It just slipped out."

"I thought you liked Marshall."

"Oh, Marshall will do just fine."

"But?"

"Dean is far more stimulating, and sexier."

"Ma, I can't believe I'm hearing you right. You're not supposed to talk like that."

"Maybe I *should* shut up. But you remember that day he stopped by to tell you he was moving to Africa?"

"Yes," Naomi said. "What was supposed to be two years turned into more like twelve."

"And you were so sad after he left?"

"Uh-huh."

"I told your father then I thought he had a thing for you. Your father couldn't see it. But I knew."

"He did say some things that day. But it was nothing like last night."

"What did you tell him? I hope you weren't mean about it."

"I'm never mean to Dean. But for the first time in my life, I was tongue-tied."

"So, is the wedding still on?"

"Why wouldn't it be? I mean, Dean is one of the most sensitive men I've ever met. When I'm with him, I don't feel he's sizing me up the way other men do. I love talking to him. He's always fascinating and understands what I'm feeling without me having to explain. He seems to get better-looking every time I see him."

"But?"

"He's been away for so long. We're two different people now. Am I supposed to throw all my plans out on a whim?"

"Do you feel all those things with Marshall?"

"All what things?"

"That he's sensitive, understanding, sexy."

"I didn't say anything about sexy. I said good-looking."

"I know. *I'm* saying it."

Naomi chuckled.

"Well, do you feel those things about Marshall?"

"Yes, in a different sort of way."

Mama frowned.

"I mean, Marshall is a good listener and he's patient, although he doesn't always understand right away."

"At least he listens."

Somehow that comment didn't seem right. It sounded as if

Mama was just trying to say something nice. "And I'm comfortable with him."

"That's good, too. Comfort's important in a marriage."

Twenty-seven

"You are so silly," Debbie said over the phone.

"I think I'm the one being level-headed. Everyone else is losing their minds. I showed Jennifer his picture when she was here last Christmas and she practically drooled."

"The man is electrifying, worldly. He's carried a torch for you for years. And what are you going to do? Go marry Mr. Boring."

Naomi had to admit that Debbie was right about Dean. But not about Marshall. "Marshall is not boring."

"OK. Mr. Comfortable, then."

"Comfort's important. I need comfort with all the other things going on around me in this crazy world. Dean never stays put. First Chicago, then New York, then Atlanta, then Africa, now back here. He's probably going off again any day now. Can you imagine being with someone like that?"

"Yes. Go for it."

"Get real, Debbie. I'm trying to start a business. I can't be with a man who wants to run around the world. And I think we should change the subject. You always manage to bring it up."

"Maybe he'd stop running around if he could have you."

"This is pointless. I've only talked to him once since Christmas Eve, to tell him about Joseph."

"When is he planning to go back to Africa?"

"He said maybe this summer."

"You'd better hurry and make up your mind. It's March."

"I've already made up my mind. Let's drop this. How's the budget section coming on the Walter Reed proposal?"

Debbie sighed. "Fine. I'll have it done within a week. But you should ask for more money."

"Not if I want to get the job."

"It sounds like a lot of work, Naomi. And you're working on what? Four other projects now?"

"Five."

"OK, five. You should budget in at least one analyst to help you on this one."

"Do you know how much analysts make?"

"Just part-time on the extra one."

"I don't know. I don't want to price myself out of the competition."

"Look, you've been doing this freelance stuff for years now. You've got experience, so you're worth more. And this new computer system at Walter Reed Hospital sounds like the big time. Don't sell yourself cheap."

"Maybe you're right. I know someone at work who might be willing to help without me having to bust the budget to use her. I just hate not paying anybody what they're worth."

"Ask her. We sisters have to help each other out."

"She's not black. She's white. But she's good people."

"Oh. Well, half-sisters then."

They talked about the wedding plans for a few minutes, and then Naomi hung up and made a dash for the bathroom and undressed. Marshall was picking her up for a concert at the Kennedy Center in thirty minutes, and she was nowhere near ready. She hated having to get up from the computer. It was where she spent most of her free time these days. When she wasn't working on one of her freelance projects she felt guilty, as if she were wasting valuable time. But Marshall was feeling neglected, and she couldn't work every single minute of the day.

She was so behind in planning the wedding that she hated to even think about it. It was three months away, and she hadn't done much except OK her mother's ideas. Thank goodness mothers did most of the work for weddings, or this one would never get off the ground. She still needed to finish her part of the invitation list and pick out dresses for herself, Debbie, Jennifer, Pamela, and Carla, who had all agreed to be bridesmaids.

She turned on the shower and stepped in. She smiled as she thought about her fiancé. One good thing about being with a guy who wasn't gorgeous was that she didn't always have to look just so. She'd had enough of living like that during her Chuck phase. She had never felt a need to impress Dean, either. But then maybe she'd taken him for granted. Her stomach flip-flopped every time she thought about him pressing her up against the kitchen countertop, moaning in her ear, kissing the corner of her mouth. God, why was he doing this to her? She had to focus on work, the wedding. She turned the cold water up full blast, but it didn't do a bit of good. Dean still had her pinned against the sink, was still moaning in her ear, still smothering her with kisses.

She shut off the shower and tried to shut off her brain. Here she was fantasizing about Dean when she was about to be married to another man. Not to mention that she and Dean were barely on speaking terms. He hadn't called once since Christmas Eve, not once, and when she finally got up the nerve to call him last week, he was as cold as the water streaming down her back a minute ago. The only time he showed even a little interest during that conversation was when she told him about Joseph.

"It's hard to believe he's Joshua's son," she said.

"Why do you say that?"

"He looks like Joshua, but he doesn't act anything like him."

"That's not surprising, given the circumstances."

"Did you know Tisha well?" she asked, trying to get the conversation warmed up.

"I was around her a few times with Joshua."

"What was she like?"

"OK."

"Was she pretty?"

"Yeah."

"Was she in school with you all?"

"No."

She stepped out of the shower and reached for a towel. She got about two more words out of him before they hung up. She had lost him as a friend, and that hurt more than anything. She missed him so much, more now than when he was in Africa.

She sniffed. Damn it. She had to stop this silliness. She threw the towel on the bathroom floor and pulled on her robe as she stomped off to the bedroom. This was exactly what she didn't want: all this blubbering, all this drooling. Whenever she got too emotionally involved with someone, she always ended up hurt. It would happen again with Dean. Oh, she could see it now. She'd call off the wedding, get involved with Dean, then he'd decide to run back off to his precious Africa. Well, no thanks, Mr. Electrifying. She was just getting control of her personal life, and she wasn't going to let anyone screw it up now.

She zipped her black strapless dress up in the back, removed her evening bag from a shelf at the top of the closet, and took it down to the dining room. She picked up her shoulder bag from the table and began transferring things to the evening bag. Everyone thought she was nuts, but they didn't understand.

The doorbell rang and she paused, closed her eyes, and took a deep breath. Marshall whistled when he saw the dress and kissed her lightly on the lips. She reached for his lapel, pulled him down toward her, and kissed him hard on the mouth.

"What was that for?" he asked, smiling.

"Just glad to see you."

"All ready to go?" he asked.

"In a minute. I just have to finish switching pocketbooks."

"Well, hurry," he said. "We don't want to be late."

"I'm coming, I'm coming," she said, as he followed her into the dining room.

"I met with a builder today," he said.

She threw her compact into the evening bag and rolled her eyes to the ceiling.

"Just to get an idea what it would cost," he said.

"Whatever he said, it's more than we can afford."

"Maybe not."

"How much?"

He shrugged. "Two, three hundred thousand."

She looked at him doubtfully.

"OK, maybe more like four, four-fifty."

"That's because you want sunrooms and decks and whirl-pools. We're not ready to do this yet."

"We would be if you kept working at SSI a while longer."

"I told you I'm not doing that. I'm planning to leave there by late summer."

"You think you'll have enough business by then?"

"Not if you build a half-million-dollar house."

"How much are you making freelancing?"

"I'm already bringing in half of what I make in salary at SSI. And I've cut way back on my spending. I haven't gone shopping since Christmas, and even then I bought only what I needed. And I'm still driving that beat-up old Honda. I'm miserable going into that office every day. I have to get out of there."

"I understand that. What I don't understand is why you can't wait until you're making more money at it. Then we won't have to put off our plans. That's the sensible thing to do. I mean, what if it doesn't work out the way you think?"

Our plans? This million-dollar house was his idea, not hers. "Will it kill you to wait to build a house? And I wish you had more confidence in me."

"It's not that. Starting a business is hard work."

"Don't you think I know that?"

"Look, we don't have time to argue about this now," he said. "Are you ready?"

"Maybe we should just stay here and talk this through, because it's got to be resolved before the wedding."

He picked up her evening bag and shoved it toward her. "Not now."

She sat through the concert but her mind wasn't on the music. String quartets weren't exactly her cup of tea, anyway. It was obvious that Marshall didn't understand how important starting her own business was to her. No matter how hard she tried, she couldn't get through to him. It was as if he thought she was playing a game: little black girl from nowhere who didn't know a thing about big business. Well, she'd show him just what a black woman was capable of. She'd show everybody.

She had set aside every penny she made from the freelance work and a big percentage of her income at SSI as well for several months. She'd put off buying a new car, although she was way overdue for one. And it was going to be like that for a while, maybe a long while. If Marshall wanted to marry her, he was going to have to be willing to sacrifice.

When they got back to her place that night and he reached for her, Naomi held a hand out to stop him. "We have to talk."

"Can't it wait until morning? I'm feeling amorous."

She laughed. "No, it can't."

"Fine," he said. He went to the couch and sat down. "What's on your mind?"

"I shouldn't have to tell you that," she said, standing in front of him.

"I look like a mind reader?"

"Marshall."

"OK, you're right. I know what it is."

"But do you understand?"

"I understand what you're saying. I just don't understand why you're so impatient about it."

"Do your doubts have anything to do with me being a woman?"

"I didn't say that. But naturally that's going to make it difficult to find clients in a technical field."

"So it *is* because I'm a woman."

"Naomi, you're twisting my words. All I'm saying is, Wait a few years until you're sure it will work out."

"I know I can do this. Why do you doubt me? *You* did it."

"That was different."

"How? You mean, because you were a man?"

"I had a partner, for one. And architecture is an old established business. This computer stuff is so new."

"It's the wave of the future."

"So you hope."

She took a deep breath. "When I was a little girl, I used to dream about someday owning my own business."

"I'm not saying give up your dream. Just be more cautious the way you go about it."

"I *am* being cautious, within reason. But I've got to be willing to take chances too. That's part of our problem. Too many of us are afraid to take chances. It's understandable, because we had to work our butts off to get to the point where we could get a decent nine-to-five. But our parents and the previous generations worked so hard and sacrificed so much to get us this far. I think in a way we owe it to them and to ourselves to move things up a notch."

"I'm already working on my own. That's another reason you should wait until your freelance work is more established."

She sighed. Hadn't he heard anything she said? "Your work is pretty secure, though, isn't it?"

"Nothing is ever a hundred percent. If interest rates sky-rocket I could be in trouble."

"There's always a 'what-if.' I can't let that stop me."

Naomi put the phone down and ran out of her office to the elevator. She'd just finished talking to the people at Walter Reed Hospital. She got the assignment, and the budget was big enough for her to pay two additional analysts. This was sensational, fantastic, spectacular! She pressed the button for Carla's floor, then stood in the back of the elevator as other people got on and off and tried not to laugh out loud. The elevator doors closed, and she realized she was the only one left on. She couldn't hold it in a minute longer. She pumped her fist in the air. "Go get 'em, girl!" she shouted at the top of her lungs. Little Miss Nobody from nowhere was gonna show them all a thing or two.

Carla had better be in her office, she thought, heading down the hallway. She rounded the corner, to find her on the phone. Carla waved her in. Naomi sat in the chair across from the desk, crossed her legs, and bobbed her foot up and down. She was staring at the carpet thinking about the call with Walter Reed when she heard Carla say something about "setting up an interview next week." Was that a job interview, Naomi wondered? Her eyes widened and she looked up. Carla winked.

"I've got an interview with Booz Allen next week," Carla said, hanging up the phone. "It's basically a lateral move in terms of position, but more money."

"They're so big you should have plenty of opportunities to move up."

Carla crossed her fingers. "That's what I hope. So what brings you in here? You look like you just discovered a pot of gold."

"I got the Walter Reed job."

"No kidding? When do we start?"

"Can you come over one night this week?"

"Name the day, I'll be there. I'm so excited about this!"

Naomi jumped up. "*You're* excited? Believe it or not, I got enough for two other analysts. I'm going to ask Wayne Yang. He did some work with me on another project way back. I'll call you after I talk to him to set up a time to meet." She walked to the door. "I have to run. I have a million things to do."

"Wait a minute. Slow down before you have a stroke, and congratulations."

Naomi laughed and dashed back to her office. So much was happening at once she felt dizzy. The consulting was booming. Then there was the wedding. It was only a month away now, and she still didn't have a dress. Mama called and fussed at her every day about going to look. At this point, she'd have to buy one right off the rack and hope it fit. But that was fine with Naomi. She didn't want one of those frilly, billowy white contraptions anyway. She'd just go to a shop on Connecticut or Wisconsin Avenue and pick out something elegant.

The phone rang as she grabbed her bag and briefcase. She was tempted to ignore it. Patrick was always calling and begging her to do something at the last minute. Since he'd taken over, the department was a mess. Word was going around that they were thinking of replacing him. Carla thought maybe they'd give Naomi a chance now, but Naomi was no longer interested. She picked up the phone, the word "no" already on her lips if it turned out to be Patrick.

"Naomi."

"Ma, I was just about to leave. Can I call you back when I get home?"

"No, I'm at work and I need to get back to my class. I just got off the phone with Tisha."

That was nothing new. Mama seemed to talk to Tisha about once or twice a month now. "And?"

"Joseph was arrested early this morning."

Naomi sank down into her chair. "Oh, no."

"He was caught riding around in a stolen car with some other boys."

"What did she want, money?"

"Yes. She's been calling around all last night and this morning trying to get bail money out there, but she couldn't. So she called me."

"And you're sending it."

"I called your father. He's going to take off work and wire it now."

Naomi let out a deep breath of air.

"What was I supposed to do?" Mama asked. "Let him stay in jail?"

"No, no. You did the right thing. I just . . . someone's got to get hold of that boy and straighten him out before it's too late."

"Tisha's talking about trying to get him into one of those boot camps."

"Oh, no."

"Maybe it's not a bad idea. She obviously can't handle him. She was so young when she had him and she didn't know a thing about being a mother. Even though she's trying now, it's too late because he doesn't respect her as a parent. He doesn't take her seriously."

"I still don't like the idea of sending him away again. He's sick of being shuffled around."

"He told you that?"

"Not in so many words. But it was obvious."

Naomi hung up and slumped back in her chair, her bag on her shoulder, her briefcase in her lap, and stared at the phone. It was painful thinking of Joshua's son in jail. She had a mind to call that Tisha and give her a good talking to. But she doubted if it would do much good. Talking to Joseph probably wouldn't make much difference either, but she could try. For a while when he stayed with her last summer, she thought they had connected. He really took to the computer and obviously had a good head on his shoulders. He just needed some direction. But how could she give it to him from hundreds of miles away?

"I want to get something I can wear again," Naomi said, pulling a skirt up over her hips and slipping her feet into heels at the same time. "I never saw any point in spending all that money for a dress I'll never wear again."

"Fine," Mama said. She was standing next to Naomi holding a blouse to match the skirt. "Just get something. Three weeks before the wedding and you don't even have your dress yet. Thank goodness I had the foresight to order the bridesmaids' dresses last month."

Debbie giggled from her seat on Naomi's bed.

"It's not funny," Naomi said, zipping the skirt up. "I've been so busy." Still, she couldn't believe it was only three weeks away—three weeks, and her whole life would change.

"You sure you want to go through with this?" Debbie asked.

What a silly question, Naomi thought. How could she change her mind now? The invitations had been mailed, dresses ordered, and her parents had spent loads of money on flowers and the reception hall.

"Of course I am. I . . . I want to be married. I'm dying to get married. I just don't have time for all this. I really shouldn't have let you talk me into going even now. I should be working."

"I've never seen a woman too busy to get ready for her wedding," Mama said, frowning. "And it's Saturday."

"Saturday doesn't mean a thing when you're trying to start a business," Naomi said, taking the blouse from her mother. "It's like any other day of the week. Sunday too. Oh, I forgot to set the printer to do the tables while I'm gone." She tossed the blouse on the bed, but Mama grabbed it and then Naomi's arm.

"Stop this. Whatever it is can wait until you get back."

"No, it can't." Naomi put her hand to her head. "Maybe we should do this another time. I have so much to do." Work, set up a meeting with Carla and Wayne. Get Dean out of her head.

"You don't have any more time," Mama said sternly, hands on her hips, "unless you want to get married in your jeans."

"I'm so pressed for time now I can't think straight." She pulled the blouse over her head. "I could just pick something out next week at Garfinckel's."

"It will still need to be altered. That takes at least—"

The phone rang. "Oh, darn," Naomi said.

Mama shook her head. "Don't talk long, Naomi. We've got to go."

Naomi picked up the phone while her mother buttoned the back of her blouse. "Hello?"

"Naomi, it's Dean."

"Dean?" Debbie got a big grin on her face. Mama narrowed her eyes.

"I wanted to ask you something," he said. "Got a minute?"

"Go ahead."

"Is your nephew going to be spending the summer with you?"

Naomi frowned. Joseph was out of jail, courtesy of her parents, but she hadn't found time yet to call him or his mother. She and her parents had talked about whether to have him back but hadn't made a decision. "We haven't made plans one way or the other. Why?"

"I'm going to be coaching a basketball team this summer, along with some other brothers. We'll practice and meet to play against each other. I thought if he was here he could participate."

That must mean he wasn't going back to Africa yet. "That's a good idea, but I don't know if Joseph will be here. If he is, I'll give you a call. That would be perfect for him."

"You do that. How have you been?"

"Pretty good. Very busy, though. And you?"

"Fine, just fine. Well, I'm not going to keep you."

"Dean."

"Yes?"

"Before you go, would you like to come by for dinner, maybe tomorrow evening? I'll cook and we can talk like we used to. It would be nice to see you again."

"Thanks, Naomi. But I've got plans for tomorrow."

"I see. Then how about another evening this week?"

"I don't think so. I've been real busy."

"Fine. Give me a call when you get some free time."

Let him go, she thought, as she hung up the phone. He's all wrong for you. She wasn't even sure how or why the invitation popped out of her mouth. He seemed to have a magnetic pull on her, tugging her one way when she wanted to go another.

When she turned around, Debbie was no longer smiling and Mama was busy fidgeting with something on the dresser. Naomi let out a deep breath of air.

"He's busy?" Mama asked.

Naomi nodded and went to the bottom of the closet for her shoes. The edges of her eyes stung, and she didn't want her mother or Debbie to see her face. It felt horrible being rejected by Dean. He never used to do that. Now he did it all the time.

"That one's lovely," Mama said as Naomi stood on the platform in front of the three-way mirror in Neiman Marcus in about the twentieth dress she'd tried on that day.

"I like the way it dips down in back," Debbie said.

It was a beautiful off-the-shoulder number in pale lavender. And it was something she'd be able to wear to formals in the future. But at $600, it was twice what she'd planned to spend. "Why does it cost so much?" Naomi asked no one in particular as she fingered the tag.

"It *is* expensive," Mama said, peering at the price tag for the third time.

"That's because it's a designer dress," the saleswoman said.

"Go ahead and get it," Debbie said. "It's gorgeous on you."

"Yes," Mama said. "We've already been to every shop on Connecticut Avenue and here at the Mazza Gallerie."

"Maybe I should go out to one of the malls in Maryland or downtown," Naomi said. "Before I spend this kind of money."

"I hear they have a lot of nice bridal shops in Baltimore," Debbie said.

"Don't tell her that," Mama said in a fake whisper.

"I don't want a typical wedding dress anyway," Naomi said. "I want something like this."

"Then get it," Mama said. "You don't have much more time."

"If I get a ready-made dress, I do. And I want to be sure before I spend six hundred dollars."

"Even a dress like this will need to be altered to fit perfectly," Mama said, tucking it in at the waist. She turned to the saleswoman. "Shouldn't this be taken in?"

"We'll take care of that for you."

"How long would it take?" Mama asked.

"About a week."

"Then you need to allow two," Mama said. "At least."

"That means I still have a little time," Naomi said. "Maybe I should hold off."

"Naomi, go ahead and get the dress," Debbie said. "You aren't going to find anything prettier. And it *is* your wedding."

"I know. But I need time to talk myself into spending this kind of money, especially since I'm saving for the business."

"I'll help you pay for it," Mama said.

"No. You're already paying for everything else, and we agreed I would take care of my dress. I just need a little more time. That settles it. I'll have a dress before the wedding. I promise."

"I certainly hope so," Mama said, not sounding convinced.

Naomi went into the dressing room and changed back into her street clothes. Then the three of them walked through Neiman Marcus toward the parking lot.

"Naomi, are you sure you want to go through with this?" Mama asked.

Naomi rolled her eyes to the sky. "Why do you keep asking me that?"

"Because you're taking so much time to do everything. It's like you're resisting."

Naomi shook her head. "I'm just busy."

"Are you sure that's it?" Mama asked.

"I know what you mean, Mrs. Jefferson," Debbie said. "When Naomi really wants something she charges full speed ahead."

Mama nodded in agreement.

"You're both wrong. I wouldn't go through with it if I didn't want to."

"Maybe you haven't taken the time to think it out," Debbie said.

"I admit I haven't had time to do much thinking, with work, the consulting, and worrying about Joseph." And Dean. Stop it, Naomi, she told herself. "I know what I'm doing. Marshall is good for me. Besides, you've already spent so much and the invitations just went out."

"Don't worry about that. I'd rather you back out now, if you're going to, than after the ceremony."

"I'm not backing out."

Naomi was in the bathroom washing her hands when the phone rang. "Debbie, will you get that?" she shouted as she shook her hands off and picked up a towel. When she walked into her bedroom, Debbie was holding the phone out for her.

"It's Joseph," Debbie said.

"In Chicago?"

"I guess that's where he is, since he's calling collect."

Naomi took the phone. "Hello?"

"Is this Naomi?"

"Yes, Joseph. Is something wrong?"

"Why you always got to think it's something wrong when you hear from me?"

"Sorry," Naomi said, biting her lip. She was glad he'd called, since it looked like she would never get around to calling him. "What is it?"

"Uh, can I ask you something?"

"You can ask me anything."

"Well, seeing as summer's coming up, I was wondering if you all planned to ask me to come stay out there."

Naomi nearly dropped the phone. "You want to come here? To D.C.?"

"I wouldn't mind."

"I thought you hated it here."

"I did. But I don't want to go to no boot camp. I'm tired of always going off to live with strangers."

"Your mother told you she was planning to send you away again?"

"She didn't say nothing. But I can tell she been thinking about it ever since I got in trouble."

"You mean about the car?"

"Yeah, but it wasn't my fault, see. I didn't know it was stolen."

"Is that the truth? Because I won't have you coming here if you can't be honest with us."

"It's true. I swear. I didn't know when I got in . . . but they did tell me later."

"Uh-huh. Does you mother know you're calling me?"

"She ain't even here."

"When will she be back?"

"Monday, probably."

Naomi's eyes narrowed. Monday? "Who's staying there with you?"

"Nobody."

"You mean you're in the house by yourself all weekend?"

"It's an apartment."

"Apartment then. Are you there alone?"

"It's no big deal. She does it all the time."

Naomi couldn't believe a mother would leave a sixteen-year-old kid home alone overnight, especially a troubled one. She didn't like this one bit. And there was something else she didn't like. Joseph's language seemed to slip when he was up there in Chicago. "I don't believe this. That's two whole days away."

"No kidding."

"Don't be funny. Where did she go?"

"Milwaukee."

Naomi shook her head. Joseph needed to get away from that

environment permanently, not just for the summer. But the last thing she needed was an unruly kid on her hands, especially now, with the wedding and all the consulting work she was doing. "I don't know, Joseph. If we let you come here, you'd have curfews."

"Don't I know it. But I'm older now, so I figured I should be able to stay out later."

"Whatever it is, you'd have to abide by it."

"Abide?"

"Obey it. Stick with it."

"No problem."

Naomi sighed. He was willing to promise anything to get away from there. "Let me think about it and call you back. In the meantime, you have to get permission from your mother."

"She don't care what I do long as I'm out of her hair."

"You still need her permission. And Joseph, do me a favor."

"Yeah?"

"Don't talk like that. You know better."

"Sorry, but, you know, that's my street rap."

"Then save it for the streets."

Naomi said goodbye and hung up. Then she dropped down on the bed. "That was the strangest call."

"Sounds like he wants to come back."

"Can you believe it? He's tired of being sent away. And I agree. He needs to be around family."

"That poor kid."

"I told him I had to think about it, but I don't see how I can say no."

"You mean he'd stay with you rather than your parents?"

"Since he called me, I guess that's what he wants. And I wouldn't want to put my parents through that again if he doesn't behave himself."

"But you'll be married by then. And I thought he didn't get along with Marshall."

"He doesn't."

"Then what are you going to do?"

Naomi fell back on the bed and looked up at the ceiling. "I

don't know. Maybe run away to the North Pole and bury myself under the snow."

"No, no, no," Marshall said, banging his fist on his marble dining room table. "A thousand times no. That boy is not living with us."

"It's only for the summer. He really needs this."

"No, Naomi. I don't see how you can even ask me, knowing we don't get along."

"You could be so good for him if you'd just try to work with him."

"I'm not wasting time on somebody else's ornery kid."

"He's not just any kid. He's my nephew, my brother's son."

"How can you spring this crap on me three weeks before the wedding?"

"Why do you have to be so narrow-minded?"

"I don't think it's too much to ask to want to spend the first few months of my marriage alone with my wife. If you'd just think about it, you'd see how ridiculous this idea of yours is. We don't need this in the beginning of our marriage. You want to start off on the wrong foot?"

Naomi sat back in the chair and folded her arms across her waist. "You're right."

"I'm glad you finally see it that way," he said, taking a sip from his wineglass.

"You're absolutely right that it's the wrong way to start a marriage. That's why we'll have to postpone it until after the summer."

"What?" He jumped up and followed her into the living room. "You're not serious?"

Naomi turned to face him. "Just until fall."

He flopped down on the couch. "I don't believe this."

"Marshall, try to understand. His call to me was a cry for help. I can't ignore it."

"But you can ignore me."

"I'm not ignoring you. I'm just putting the wedding off for a few months."

Marshall twisted his mouth and shook his head. Naomi sat down beside him.

"Come on. You're a grown man, and he's just a boy. Say you understand."

He stood and shoved his hands in his pockets. "That would be a lie. I don't understand this at all. The invitations have gone out, your mother's spent a fortune on deposits for caterers and the room at the Marriott. How can you do this now? Even though you still haven't gotten your dress." He tossed a pointed look her way. She smiled with embarrassment.

"I think my parents will understand. I'll have to give some of the money back to them."

"I hope they do, because I don't. For the life of me I don't understand. You never wanted to get married in the first place, did you?"

She looked away. "You're twisting things. All I'm asking is to postpone it for a few months."

"You didn't answer my question, did you? The answer is no. Either we get married June twenty-ninth or never."

"Why are you being so difficult?"

"It's not me. You're the one changing things with no regard for anyone but yourself. All for some kid who's just going to come here and take advantage of you."

"That does it," she said, getting back up on her feet. "It's off."

"Naomi—"

"No. You're right. He probably *will* come here and take advantage of me. But that doesn't mean I shouldn't try to help him. His father's dead, and he doesn't have much of a mother. But he does have us, and I can't ignore him. If you can't deal with that, I can't deal with you."

She grabbed her purse off his couch and marched to the door. It had a million locks on it, and she fumbled around, trying to get them all undone. She knew Marshall was standing right behind her, but she was too angry to ask for his help. Finally, she stepped back. "Open them," she said, without turning to face him.

He walked up beside her. "Are you sure this is the way you want it?" He sounded more irritated than anything else.

She looked at him sadly. "Yes."

He undid the locks.

Twenty-eight

Two weeks after breaking up with Marshall, Naomi was standing at gate 211 at National Airport, waiting for Joseph's plane to land. The flight was an hour late, and Naomi had spent the time going over and over the conversation with Marshall, just as she had done so many times during the past several days. That and the talk with her parents when she told them the wedding was off.

"Don't worry about the money," Daddy had said. "I'd much rather you do it now than later and end up in some messy divorce."

"I'm going to give you some of it back," Naomi said. "That's only fair."

"Keep it, Naomi," Daddy said. "Consider it our investment in your business."

"And you'll need money to keep Joseph," Mama said. "I'm sorry about you and Marshall, but I'm glad you invited Joseph back."

"Actually," Naomi said, "he invited himself. But I'm looking forward to having him."

"He really took to you," Mama said.

"I'm not so sure about that," Naomi said. "I think he sees me as the lesser of two evils."

"Nonsense," Daddy said. "The boy is smarter than we gave him credit for. He knows he's better off here with you."

"You're a perfect role model for him," Mama said. "And he needs that desperately."

"I hope I can live up to it," Naomi said.

"You don't have to live up to anything," Mama said. "Just go on doing what you've been doing. That's all the example he needs."

It was these moments when Naomi knew she was lucky to have such good parents. They were always so patient and understanding. They seemed to know just when to push and when to back off. She hoped that when she had children—if that day ever came—she'd do half as good a job.

She'd known the minute Marshall undid the locks on his door that she was relieved the wedding was off. Joseph had just been an excuse. Marshall was insensitive about two of the most important things in her life, her consulting business and her nephew. She couldn't marry a man like that. And she had to face it: she was thinking too much about Dean these days to marry Marshall or anyone else.

She hadn't yet called Dean to let him know Joseph was coming, partly because she wasn't sure of it until a couple of days ago but also because the thought of talking to Dean scared her now that she was a free woman again. He aroused emotions in her she wasn't sure she wanted to face yet—maybe never.

One thing she knew: the boy getting off that plane was going to have to straighten up. He was going to act right if she had to break every bone in his body. She was going to give him the game plan, and he was going to follow it.

As soon as she and Joseph walked through the door of her town house, she began to lay down the rules. Eleven P.M. curfew every night unless he told her exactly where he was, home every evening for dinner, chores on Saturday afternoon, room neat at all times, and basketball with Dean if she could arrange it.

"That's cool," he said about joining the basketball team. "But I got to think about some of that other stuff."

"Did I ask for your opinion? And another thing—none of that sloppy grammar around here. Makes my ears burn to hear you talk like that."

"No problem."

He went to his room to unpack, and she went to the kitchen and sat down near the phone. OK, so now it was time to call Dean and tell him Joseph was here, but what was she going to tell Dean about herself? Should she let him know the wedding was off, that she was available? Yes, her brain shouted. Her feelings for him scared the hell out of her, but they were too intense to ignore. No more fooling herself. Whatever might happen between the two of them, even if he made her fall in love with him and then ran off to Africa, the pain she would suffer couldn't be any worse than this.

She would call him and tell him that she'd been thinking about what he said and wanted to talk about it, then invite him over. She exhaled deeply. It was such a relief to finally give in to her feelings for this man. She put her hand on the receiver, took another deep breath, and dialed his apartment.

A woman answered, and Naomi's mouth went dry. "Uh, is Dean Davis there?"

"He's in the shower. Can I take a message?"

"Oh—uh, ask him to call—"

"Oh, wait," the woman said. "He's here."

"Hello?"

Naomi closed her eyes. Now what did she do? He probably had a towel wrapped around his waist and that woman snuggling up to him. It was amazing how one little female voice could change everything. "Um, I hope I'm not calling at a bad time."

"No, I just stepped out of the shower. What's up?"

Was it Sonya? Was she back in his life, planning to snatch him away again? "I was just calling to let you know that Joseph is here."

"Oh, good," he said. "Does he want to join the team?"

"Yes." Go ahead and tell him how you feel, she thought.

"Then send him over to Monroe Junior High tomorrow at one. We meet for practice every Saturday."

"OK." Don't let that voice stop you.

"Fine. I'll talk to you later."

"Um, Dean I wanted to ask you . . . "

She heard a muffled sound in the background and paused. "Hold on a second, Naomi."

Her mind slipped to visions of the woman opening the towel and sliding it slowly away from his moist body.

"Sorry about that," Dean said, a moment later. "What were you saying?"

If it was her, she'd probably tear that towel away . . .

"Naomi?"

She snapped out of it when she heard her name. "I'm sorry. I missed what you just said."

"I was asking what you were about to say before we were interrupted."

Someone giggled in the background.

"Oh. I . . . I was going to ask when the games are held."

"The first and second Sunday of every month at two. It would be good if you could come to one of the games. There's someone I'd like you to meet."

Fuck. He was going to introduce her to his woman. This was too much. Now she knew exactly how he felt when she asked him to come to her wedding. "Who is it?"

"A friend. The first game will be next month after we've gotten some practices in. I'll introduce you then."

At least he'd said friend and not fiancée. He wouldn't call a fiancée "friend," would he? "Fine." They said goodbye and she slammed the phone in the cradle. That had to be the worst conversation she'd ever had in her entire life. This was Ralph and Marlena all over again. No, not exactly. Dean wasn't hers, never had been, and now it looked like he never would be. He had simply gotten tired of waiting for her to come around, and she had no one to blame but her own stupid self. She sat at the kitchen table and stared at the phone until she realized it was getting dark. She hadn't heard a peep out of Joseph since he went up to his room. She turned on a light and climbed the stairs. His door was partly closed, so she knocked.

"Yeah," he said.

She stuck her head in. He was sitting at the computer with his back to the door. He had shoved all her business papers and books off to the side and set up the joystick. She opened her mouth to protest, but then closed it quietly. They were obviously going to have to come up with a system for sharing the computer but not tonight. It was so good to see him doing something constructive, and she would never be able to work now, anyway.

"Did you want something?" he asked, not taking his eyes off the monitor.

"No." She backed out and shut the door behind her and then went to her room and stretched out across the bed in the dark.

"You don't have to take me over there," Joseph said.

"It's your first time," Naomi said. "I want to be sure you find it. And I can introduce you to Dean." She didn't add that she was dying to see him herself. She'd known him for so long, maybe she could figure out for sure whether he was involved with someone else just by seeing him.

"I know where it is. It's just over the D.C. line. I can get the bus."

"Why get the bus when I'm willing to drive you?"

" 'Cause it's embarrassing having a grown-up take you places."

"Too bad. You'll have to be embarrassed today."

He sat on the couch and sulked while she squeezed into a pair of tight-fitting blue jeans and put on a little extra makeup. Then he stomped all the way out to the car. After they arrived and she parked, he jumped out and walked ahead of her. It had been years since she'd walked down these hallways. They seemed much smaller than she remembered them. She'd forgotten exactly where the gym was, but somehow Joseph knew exactly where to go. He'd obviously gotten around during the brief time he spent here last summer.

She stepped into the gymnasium, and there he was in the far corner talking to some boys about Joseph's age.

"I'm going into the locker room to use the john. You're not going to follow me there, are you?" Joseph asked, a big grin on his face.

She grabbed his sweatshirt and pulled him toward herself

playfully. "Before you go, I want to introduce you to Dean. He was your father's best friend in high school and college."

Joseph looked in Dean's direction, obviously curious. "So you told me."

Dean saw them headed in his direction and met them halfway. "So this is the man," he said, smiling at Joseph. He extended his hand, which seemed to surprise Joseph.

"I was just telling him you were Joshua's best friend," Naomi said, as the two of them shook hands.

Dean nodded. "You look a lot like him," he said to Joseph. "Only you're much more handsome."

Joseph smiled and folded his arms under his chest shyly.

"Go on, and I'll see you back home later," Naomi said.

Joseph made a beeline to the locker room.

"Damn," Dean said. "The resemblance is amazing."

"I know."

"I'm looking forward to getting to know him. How have things been since he got here?"

"Fine so far. But it's only been a day."

"I think he'll be OK."

"I hope so. You said you had someone you wanted me to meet."

"Yeah, I do. But he's not here today."

When Dean said "he," Naomi wanted to drop down on her knees and thank the Lord. But then she remembered the giggles on the phone. Who was that? "Maybe some other time, then."

"He's the other brother who was in the car up in Chicago. He's living here now and wants to meet you. He was a good friend of Joshua's too."

Fine, but who was the woman on the phone? "I see. I'd like to meet him too then."

He nodded. "I need to get back over to the boys and get this thing started. It was good seeing you."

"Um, it was good seeing you too."

He smiled and walked off, and Naomi found herself wishing it were possible to kick yourself. Why didn't she just come out and invite him over? Because she didn't want to hear him tell her no, that he'd found someone else or he was going back to his ex-wife. That's why. Boy, had she blown it, she thought, as she headed toward her car. When Dean wanted to get involved, she rejected him. Now she didn't know how to get him back.

Naomi was thankful she had planned to meet Carla and Wayne at her house at three that afternoon to work on the Walter Reed project together. Otherwise, she would have spent the rest of the afternoon staring at her monitor and fantasizing about Dean. She knew she had it bad when she realized she'd been looking at the thing for an hour and seeing not the words and figures up there but Dean making love to her in the shower, on a sandy beach, in the backseat of the old Firebird he had in college. She tried to shake the fantasies away, but it was pointless while she was alone.

When they finished work at seven, Naomi asked them to join her for dinner or a drink somewhere. But Carla had a date and Wayne an early-morning flight to visit family in Seattle.

Wayne Yang had been a godsend. He was referred by someone when she was looking for help on an earlier project. They set up a meeting at her house, but he obviously had no clue the woman he was about to meet was black until she opened the door to her town house. He was sure he had the wrong house, and for a minute Naomi thought she'd have to pull out her driver's license to prove she really was Naomi Jefferson.

His response didn't bother her, though. She had long since gotten used to getting weird reactions from people in the technology field the first time they met her. In fact she got a kick out of watching them as they went into shock and then quickly tried to cover it up. But like Wayne, they usually got used to the idea of working with a black woman once they realized she knew what she was doing. They'd better get used to it, Naomi thought. Because we're just going to keep coming, aiming higher and higher. She and Wayne had reached a point in their relationship where she could tease him about that first meeting. And as a Chinese-American, he had his own stories to tell.

After Carla and Wayne left, she called Debbie, and the two of them decided to meet at a Pizza Hut in Silver Spring at eight.

Thank goodness, Naomi thought, as she put down the receiver. She didn't care much where they ate; she had to get out of this house.

Joseph came in just before she left.

"How did it go?" she asked.

"Fine. Dean's all right. So's his woman. You ever meet her?"

Naomi swallowed hard. "No."

"Broad is hot."

"What does that mean?" She didn't tell him not to call the woman a broad, although she should have.

"You know, sexy."

Naomi rolled her eyes to the ceiling. So it was true. He *was* seeing someone else. "Is her name Sonya?" She held her breath while waiting for his answer.

"No, it's Marie."

She breathed a sigh of relief. At least it wasn't his ex-wife. She told Joseph she was meeting a girlfriend for dinner and asked if he wanted to join them.

"Nope. Got plans."

"Doing what?"

"I'll be hanging over at Dwight's."

"Fine. Just don't forget your curfew."

"Since I told you where I'll be, can I stay out later?"

"How much later?"

"Mm. Twelve? One?"

"Where does he live and how will you get there?"

"Over in Northeast. Not far from Monroe. I can get the bus."

"Give me his phone number and you can stay out until midnight."

"Go ahead and tell him how you feel," Debbie said, looping a string of cheese around her tongue.

"That's easier said than done," Naomi said, picking up another slice of pizza. "What if he tells me to get lost?"

"He won't do that."

"There's another woman in the picture now. His feelings have probably changed."

"Even if they have, from what you've told me about him, he

would let you down gently. He cares too much about you to be mean about it."

"It would still break my heart."

"He took a risk by telling you how he felt."

"And look what I did to him."

"I don't understand you, Naomi. You're so willing to take risks at work, why not in your love life?"

"I've developed a tough skin about work. You have to if you want to survive. But not when it comes to my personal feelings. I've been hurt so much."

"We all have, Naomi."

"I know. But I can't cope with it, especially when it comes to Dean."

When Naomi got back home around eleven, she curled up in bed with a book of short stories by black women writers and waited for Joseph. But she had so much trouble focusing, it took her an hour to get through one of the stories, even though it was only five pages long.

At least the consulting business was going well. At the rate the work was progressing, she'd be ready to set up an office very soon, maybe by the end of summer. It wouldn't be anything big or fancy to start, probably just one or two small rooms with space for a secretary.

She looked at the clock on her night table. It was 12:15, past Joseph's curfew but probably too early to start worrying. Still, she wished he would learn to get in on time. She smiled, thinking about all the nights her parents sat up waiting for her. Now she knew how they felt. Of course, she'd been nothing like Joseph. She would never have dreamed of staying out as late as he did or talking back to her parents.

She closed her eyes, and when she opened them again, it was 1:45. She jumped up and dashed to Joseph's room. The sofa bed hadn't even been pulled out. She looked in the closet on the off-chance that he'd come in quietly, packed his things, and left. She couldn't help but remember the night the police officer found him hitchhiking on the highway. She breathed a sigh of relief when she saw his things still hanging there. But where was he?

She went back to her room and dialed the number he left her. Someone picked up the phone on the first ring. "Hello?" said a groggy voice.

"Sorry to disturb you at this hour. But I'm looking for Joseph. This is his aunt."

"There's nobody here by that name."

"Is someone there by the name of Dwight?"

"Maybe, maybe not. Who is this?"

Naomi took a deep breath. "My name is Naomi Jefferson. My nephew gave me this number and said he would be there tonight with a friend named Dwight. He hasn't come in and I'm trying to find him."

"Oh. Well, Dwight lives here, but he's not home."

"Did they go out somewhere together?"

"I have no idea. Haven't seen Dwight since this afternoon."

"So Joseph hasn't been there?"

"No."

"Thank you." Naomi hung up. Damn. He'd lied to her. She went back to his room and looked around for any indication of where he might be—a phone book, a slip of paper with a name or number on it. She opened all the drawers to the dresser. First the top, then the middle. They were both filled with her own things. Then she opened the bottom drawer and saw Joseph's underwear and socks stuffed into a corner. She was about to shut the drawer when something familiar caught her eye. She moved a pair of his socks aside. It was a brown and white package of rolling paper. Memories of her days doing drugs with Jimmy tore at her mind. She picked up the package, and something shiny with a silver tip rolled across the drawer. A bullet.

She couldn't believe her eyes. She picked it up and placed it on top of the dresser, then tore through the rest of the things in the drawer, tossing them out one by one. If she found a gun in here, that was going to be the end of Joseph. She marched to the closet and looked around on the shelves. She found nothing else unusual, but one bullet was more than enough.

She went back to the dresser and stared at the bullet, still finding it hard to believe. Joseph was out in the streets, possibly high and carrying a gun. She had visions of him lying in a gutter somewhere with a bullet between his eyes. She wanted to get in her car and search for him around Monroe Junior High, but not alone at this hour. She dialed Marshall's number. She needed help and didn't know who else to turn to. She didn't want to worry her parents just yet and was afraid to call Dean. If that woman answered his phone in the middle of the night, it would be one more thing to fret about.

"Did I wake you?" she asked.

"No, I just got in about half an hour ago."

"I need to ask you to do me a favor."

"Now?"

"I wouldn't bother you if it wasn't important."

"What's the problem?"

She hated to tell him that Joseph was missing, since he'd warned her about him. But she was desperate. "Joseph is out and it's past his curfew. Can you come help me look for him? I have an idea where he might—"

"Naomi, it's two in the morning, and I just got in from a long trip. I'm tired."

She rushed through a summary of the day's activities. "And now I'm worried he could be hurt somewhere out there."

"Didn't I warn you about him?"

"Marshall, please. Just help me find him."

"Wait an hour before you drive all the way over to Monroe. If he's not back, call me and we'll go look for him."

She banged the phone down, grabbed her shoulder bag, and ran out of the house. The twenty-minute drive to Monroe took less than ten with the late-night streets empty and her foot pressed to the floor. She drove in front of the school and turned down a side street. At the opposite edge of the playground, she spotted a group of about six boys hanging around a picnic table under a streetlamp and was amazed to spot Joseph among them. She parked and walked across the grassy field. The playground brought back memories of her fist fight here with Henrietta. Now they fought with bullets.

Joseph saw her approaching and broke away from the

crowd. "What are you doing here?" he asked, clearly upset with her.

"Coming to get you. You were supposed to be home hours ago. And what is this?" She held the bullet out in her hand.

Joseph looked shocked but he quickly recovered and shrugged his shoulders.

"You may get away with this in Chicago, but not here. Let's go."

She took his arm but he yanked it away.

"I'm not ready to go yet." He shoved his hands into his pockets and walked back toward the boys.

"Joseph," she called after him.

He ignored her and kept walking.

"Joseph, come back here!" she said, but he ignored her. She was tempted to march right up to that picnic table, grab him, and drag him home. She didn't care if he was taller than she was. But she didn't know the other boys, and if they were out here at this hour they were probably bad news. What had she gotten herself into by agreeing to keep Joseph for the summer?

She got back in the car and flew up the street. Somehow she had to get the upper hand with this boy. He might be so far gone, it would be impossible to rein him in, but she wasn't ready to give up just yet. She had one more thing to try.

When she got home, she went straight to the phone and dialed Dean. The minute it rang, she panicked and thought about hanging up. What if that woman answered again? Don't be stupid, she told herself. Joseph was out there with drugs and a gun. Who cared about some silly woman? Dean picked it up on the third ring.

"Hello?" It was obvious he'd been sleeping.

"Dean, I'm sorry I woke you, but Joseph's over at Monroe and I can't get him to come home. He said earlier that he was going to a friend's near there, but when I called he wasn't there, and the woman who answered said she hadn't seen him, didn't even seem to know who he was. And then I found rolling paper and a bullet in his drawer. So I went—"

"Hold on a minute, Naomi."

She paused and realized she was out of breath. "Sorry, but I'm worried sick."

"I guess so. You found a bullet in his drawer?"

"Yes."

Dean whistled.

"He's over at Monroe, in back of the school with some boys."

"How do you know that?"

"I just got back from there. When I told him to get in the car, he refused to do it."

"You shouldn't have gone over in that area alone at this time of night. It's not like it used to be when you were there."

"I panicked when I saw the bullet."

"After basketball practice, he met some boys outside the gym. I didn't like the looks of them. I'll go over to Monroe and try to talk to him, if he's still there."

"I'll meet you."

"No. I don't want you out driving alone at this hour."

"There's no way I'm not going."

He let out a deep breath. "Don't get out of your car until I get there."

As soon as she pulled up near Monroe, she saw an old BMW parked on the street. She looked around and spotted Dean, dressed in a navy running suit and baseball cap, walking across the playground. The boys were still around, only now there were twice as many of them and they were shouting at each other. Naomi didn't like the looks of it at all. She got out of the car and scanned the crowd for Joseph.

As soon as her feet hit the playground, a shot rang out. Any other time, Naomi would have assumed it was a car backfiring, but not after what she'd found in Joseph's drawer. And not with the way Dean was running toward her.

"Get back in the car!" he shouted, waving and crouching as he ran. But she was still trying to spot Joseph. Dean reached her just as another shot rang out, and another. He grabbed her hand and pulled her to his car. Then he shoved her in through the driver's side and took off.

"My God," she said. "What's going on over there? Where's Joseph?"

"I didn't see him. Maybe he left."

"Oh, God. I hope so," she said, practically choking. "But what if he didn't? What if he's still there? What if—"

"We can't go back now, Naomi."

She blinked to keep from crying. "We have to find a phone and call the police."

"Did he get the bus out here?"

"I think so."

"Let's ride by a couple of the bus stops around here first."

Naomi fought to hold back the tears as Dean turned onto South Dakota Avenue and drove toward the nearest stop. They drove by slowly but the area was deserted. Naomi covered her face with her hand. She was going to start crying any minute. She felt the car swing around a corner and pick up speed. She glanced up. About a block away, a lone figure walked steadily up the street.

"Is that him?" Dean asked.

Naomi's heart bounced and she sat up. It looked like it could be. And as they got closer, she realized it was. She wanted to shout with joy. There he was, strolling along the sidewalk like he was headed for church on a Sunday afternoon. Dean sped up beside him, crossed over to the wrong side of the street, slammed on the brakes, and reached back and opened the rear door.

"Get in here!" Naomi shouted.

Joseph hesitated, obviously stunned, and then made a bee-line for the backseat. The three of them rode in silence until Dean pulled up behind her car. Naomi looked at him and suddenly realized why he was wearing the baseball cap. He hadn't bothered to comb his hair before leaving the house. She reached over and squeezed his hand. "Thanks."

"No problem."

She and Joseph both opened their doors.

"You ride back with me," Dean said, looking at Joseph through the rearview mirror. "I want to talk to you."

Joseph shut his door and slouched down in the seat.

"I'll follow you," he said to Naomi.

* * *

After they parked in front of her house, Naomi walked back to Dean's side of the car. Joseph got out, and Dean turned off the engine but remained seated. "Go on in the house," she said to Joseph. She knew her mind and heart were too full of conflicting thoughts and emotions to make sense tonight. She was confused, angry, relieved, tired, and disappointed all at once. It would be better to wait until tomorrow to talk to him.

Joseph shut the car door and stood on the sidewalk looking like he wanted to say something.

"What is it?" Naomi asked. It was all she could do to keep from snapping at him. She wasn't in the mood for one of his rude remarks.

"I just wanted to say I'm sorry for all the confusion I caused and all."

Naomi's mouth dropped open. She looked from Joseph down to Dean and back to Joseph. "We'll talk in the morning," she said, her tone softer.

Joseph turned to leave, paused, and turned back. "You going to send me back?"

Naomi looked at him. "That's exactly what I should do."

Joseph looked down and shuffled his feet on the sidewalk.

"But no," she said. "I'm going to make you stay here and learn to behave if it kills me." Out of the corner of her eye, Naomi saw a smile cross Dean's face.

"Go on up," Naomi said. Joseph turned and ran to the house.

"I'll call you in the morning to tell you what we talked about," Dean said. "But the long and short of it is that when things started heating up, he hightailed it out of there. The bus was taking so long, he started walking."

It made Naomi feel better to know Joseph had enough sense to leave when he sensed danger. But she was still pissed with him about so many other things. "What about the bullet?"

"He claims he borrowed the gun for a while and then returned it. I got on him about that." Dean lifted his cap and ran his hand over his hair, then put the cap back on. "I'll call you tomorrow," he said, turning the key in the ignition.

Naomi was exhausted but couldn't stand the thought of letting him go. "Why don't you come in for a while and tell me what you talked about?" She was too tired to worry that he would tell her no. But he didn't. He shut off the engine and walked with her to the house.

Twenty-nine

"He's a handful," Dean said as she shut the front door. "I'll tell you that." He stood in the middle of the living room floor, baseball cap on his head, hands in his pockets. Naomi thought he looked as if he wasn't sure what to do with himself, perhaps remembering the last time he was there. She wanted to reach out and comfort him, the way he had done for her so many times in the past. But she wasn't sure he'd be receptive after their last meeting, not to mention Miss Giggles.

She wasn't sure what to do with herself either, so she shoved her hands in her own jeans pockets and stood in front of him. It felt so awkward standing across from him like that in her own living room. "I know, but I can't give up trying to straighten him out. When I look at him, I see all the pain and suffering of the past but I also see hope, if I can just get him on the right path."

"I admire you for that."

"Do you?"

He nodded. "A lot of people would have had him on the next plane out."

"That's what I did last summer, and now I regret it." That wasn't all she regretted. One of these days, she was going to learn to do the right thing the first time around, but thank God for second chances. She might regret what she was about to do. If Dean rejected her again, it would tear her to pieces. But she couldn't stand here one more minute looking at him, not knowing how he felt.

"And going out there tonight to get him." Dean chuckled and shook his head. "That took . . ." He paused in midsentence, as her nervous fingers reached up for his cap, and gave her a funny look as she tossed it onto the couch. She took a deep breath and swallowed hard. She had to move fast or she would chicken out. She quickly tucked one arm around his waist, then the other. He removed his hands from his pockets but didn't seem to know what to do with them, so he let them drop to his sides. Uh-oh, she thought. This was where he was supposed to take her in his arms and kiss her passionately. Instead he was just standing there. So what did she do now? She tilted her head up and looked into his eyes, hoping he would take the hint. But he didn't. He stiffened, grabbed her arms, and pushed her back.

She thought she would collapse in misery. She covered her face with her hands.

"What exactly are you up to, Naomi?" he asked.

Making a fool of myself, she thought. She let out all the air she'd been holding in since she removed his cap. "Something I wish I'd done a long time ago," she said, shoving her hands into her back pockets. "It's the woman who answered your phone yesterday, isn't it? You're involved with her?"

He didn't answer, so she looked at him. His smile told her what she didn't want to know. She glanced away.

"Aren't you supposed to be engaged?" he asked.

"We broke up."

"Well, I'm sorry to hear that. But you don't expect me to just drop everything going on in *my* life, do you?"

She shrugged. No. Well, yes. She could hope, couldn't she? "Are you in love with her?"

"You can't play with my feelings," he said, ignoring the question. "Jerking me around like this."

"I know. I'm sorry. I—"

"One minute cold, the next hot."

OK, OK. She got the point.

"I'm leaving now." Out of the corner of her eye, she saw

him walk to the door, and a pang of despair ripped through her heart. Don't do this to me.

"I'll call you sometime," he said, bitterness still in his voice.

She heard the door close quietly behind him and she squeezed her eyes shut to stop the tears. When would she learn that this kind of love wasn't meant for her? This was the pain she had wanted to avoid. This was—

She was still standing when a knock came at the door. Her heart jumped. He was back. He'd changed his mind. She whirled around and . . . saw his cap on the couch. Her shoulders slumped with disappointment. He'd come back for that, not her.

She opened the door. "It's on the sofa," she said and stepped to the side. He looked at her, then the couch. He strode across the floor, picked up the cap, and turned back toward the door to find her blocking his path.

"Dean, whoever she is, she's all wrong for you." Her voice was cracking, but she didn't care.

He raised his eyebrows. "Now how would you know that?"

"Because . . . *I'm* right for you."

"You don't say."

"She doesn't have the history with you that I do. That counts for something." She paused. "Doesn't it?"

"Uh-huh."

She looked down at her feet. This wasn't going well at all. "I . . . I guess she's very pretty—"

"Not nearly as pretty as you."

"Huh?" She looked up and saw the smile in his eyes and almost choked with relief. "Well, there you go," she said, and smiled herself.

He chuckled. "To tell you the truth, this is not what I came back for." He tossed the cap back on the couch. "*This* is what I came back for." He stepped toward her, but she was in his arms before he could cross the room. He lifted her head and kissed her, first gently and then more passionately, and all the years of searching slipped away. She didn't need the doctor or the house on the Gold Coast or the boutique to feel like a whole woman. *This* was what she needed.

He let her lips go and kissed her forehead, her eyes, her nose. Then he held her tightly, and she buried her face in his chest. The fit was just right.

She led him across the living room to the stairs. It seemed to take an eternity to climb them, so she clenched his hand and ran up, pulling him along behind. They laughed as they reached the top, and the minute she shut the door to her bedroom, he grabbed her around the waist and filled her mouth with his tongue. His kiss was long, urgent, and it felt as if she'd never *really* been kissed before until this moment.

His hands traveled down her back to her buttocks and pressed, and she rubbed against him, thinking she would explode from craving him. He moaned—a low, deep sound that sent quivers up her spine. She grasped the bottom of his sweatshirt and pulled. He let out a deep breath of air, put his hands on her shoulders, and gently pushed her back. She thought she would swoon.

He took her head in his hands and kissed her nose. "I want to take this slowly, love," he said, his deep voice a whisper, his breath coming hot and heavy.

Slowly? Slowly? She tried to slow her own panting while contemplating that idea. It took her about an eighteenth of a second to make up her mind. She had dreamed about this moment in her sleep and fantasized about it when she was awake. And now he wanted to go slow? Not on your life, sweetie. "We'll go slowly next time," she said, grabbing his sweatshirt.

He chuckled as she pulled it over his head. Then he yanked hers off and backed her to the bed. They fell on top, and she wasn't sure what happened next or how. Maybe he took her clothes off or she did herself, maybe he undressed himself or she did it for him. It happened so quickly. But she knew exactly what was happening as he slid inside her and rocked until she thought she would burst. He was filling every desire, every dream, every fantasy she'd ever had and some she'd never known about. And every time she thought she'd reached the mountaintop, he took her to new heights.

An hour later, after they'd both had time to catch their

breaths, they were back at it again. Only this time, they took it slowly.

Dean tried to get out of the house the next morning before Joseph got up. But Naomi didn't want him to leave—not now, not ever. So she kept thinking of ways to hold him there, like leading him to the bathroom for a long, hot shower. When he came down fully dressed, baseball cap on his head, she was in the kitchen wearing a big old T-shirt making breakfast. She held up the coffeepot and fanned the aroma in his direction.

They sat at the table and he removed his cap. Maybe with some sixteen-year-olds she would have wanted Dean out of there, but Joseph was no innocent. Besides, the two of them got along well, and Naomi wanted Dean there to help her talk to Joseph.

"Uh-oh," Joseph said, when he came down and saw them sitting at the table.

Naomi told him to take a seat so they could talk.

"I'm in for it big time, huh?"

"Not really," Naomi said, getting up to fix him a plate. "But we do have some things to get straight." She and Dean had agreed it would be nearly impossible to enforce any kind of punishment on Joseph, so they would try to use firmness and reason.

"I already know those dudes I was with are bad news," he said, pulling out a chair.

"Dean told me you left when things started getting rough over there."

"Man, those dudes are crazy. All of 'em got guns."

"Why did you bring one in this house?"

"Just curious, I guess. They would have thought I was a punk if I acted scared of it."

"What do you care what a bunch of thugs think?" Dean said. "Guns are nothing to play with."

"What if it had gone off?" Naomi said. "Someone could get badly hurt or worse. Not to mention that it's illegal."

"I know," Joseph said. "I wasn't thinking."

"Don't ever do that again," she said. "I was worried sick about you."

He didn't say anything, just stared at his food.

"Did you hear me?" Naomi said, her voice rising despite her efforts to keep her temper in check.

"I thought you was telling, not asking," Joseph said. "But OK, I got it."

"Good. I didn't mean to yell. But it was so hard on us when Joshua died. I can't stand the thought of someday seeing you lying somewhere with a bullet in the back of your head."

"Me neither," Joseph said. He actually looked frightened at the possibility, so Naomi thought she'd made her point.

"Joseph," Dean said, "How much do you know about your father?"

"Some."

"Not much at all," Naomi said.

"In some ways you remind me of him," Dean said.

"That's what Aunt Naomi and all of them tell me. 'Cept I know I don't act nothing like him."

"I wouldn't go that far," Dean said. "You've got a good head on your shoulders. You may not always use it the best way, but it's there."

"That's the difference, Joseph," Naomi said. She pointed to her forehead. "Your father had no more up here than you do, neither does anybody else. But he made the most of what he had. He knew from an early age that he wanted to make a difference in this world, and he set out to do it."

"Yeah, and look what it got him. Killed before he was twenty-one. What's the point in even trying to get anywhere?"

Naomi and Dean exchanged looks. Is that what he thought? That everything was pointless because his father died trying to reach his goals? Was that why he didn't try to make something of himself?

Naomi stood and walked around the table to Joseph. She took the fork from his hand and made him stand up, then she put her arms around him and hugged him tightly. "I thought the same thing right after Joshua died. I was mad at the world, and I thought, Why bother? It seemed pointless. We have to work twice as hard for everything, only to have obstacles thrown in our faces again and again. It's always been like that and maybe always will be." She held him at arm's length. "But you know what I finally learned? So what if we have to work twice as hard? It makes us twice as good."

"We'll always have disappointments and setbacks," Dean said. "But we can never give up trying. We take two steps forward, one step back, but slowly we're making progress."

Joseph sat back down in his chair and leaned back. "What progress? I don't see no progress. If anything, things are harder for us now."

"No, they aren't, and I don't even want to hear you say that," Naomi said, shaking the fork in his face. "You think life is harder for us now than it was during slavery? Or when we were lynched in the South for just looking at a white person the wrong way? Or when we couldn't vote or live in certain neighborhoods? Those things didn't stop your grandparents from getting ahead then, so I don't want to hear any talk about things being too hard now."

She paused to catch her breath. "You know this business I'm setting up with computers and all? Your grandparents could never have dreamed of doing something like that. It was hard enough for them just to get decent jobs, but they did it anyway. You can't see the progress because you haven't been around long enough. But before you leave here this summer, I guarantee you'll see it. Now sit down and eat."

"I'm already sitting down, Aunt Naomi. I'd be eating, too, if you'd hand me my fork."

Naomi laughed.

Thirty

In August, Naomi walked away from the SSI offices for good. It had reached the point where she had to take off too much time to keep up with her consulting work: meeting with contractors at their offices, writing proposals, looking for new work. The day someone from Bell Atlantic phoned and said he wanted to come by to discuss the work she was doing for them, she knew it was time to start hunting for office space away from home. She couldn't take them up to the room where the computer was, since Joseph stayed in that room now. So she went up and got what she needed and met with them in the dining room.

After the meeting, Naomi called Debbie, who by now knew more about the financial side of things than she did. And Debbie refused to take a dime from Naomi for keeping the books, telling Naomi to save it until she could afford to pay her what she was worth.

"You've got more than enough set aside now to move to an office," Debbie said.

"Are you sure?" It was what she'd dreamed of, but now that everything had fallen into place she was afraid to take the plunge.

"It'll have to be small, but yeah. And get cheap furniture. At least you already have a computer. I've heard of people doing it with less."

Joseph came into the house with a towel wrapped around his

swimming trunks and a copy of *Invisible Man* in his hand, and ran up the stairs, taking them two at a time. Naomi smiled. When she asked him if he'd read it, as well as a few other books by black authors, he explained that he was assigned to read it in school last year but had only skimmed through enough to write the required paper. She gave him a copy and told him to really read it this time. When he'd finished, they would discuss it.

"I'm going to leave that computer here for Joseph and get another one."

"But he's going back to Chicago in September."

"I'm hoping he'll stay longer."

"Seriously?"

"If I can get him and his mother to agree. He's doing so much better. He still stays out later some nights than I think any boy his age should, but I'm finally getting through to him. Dean comes over almost every evening after he gets off from work and takes him to the park to shoot basketball. I'd hate to have to send him back to that environment in Chicago now."

"Does that mean Dean's not going back to Africa?"

"I wish. But it's a temporary job. He's supposed to leave next month too."

"You sound so calm about it."

"It's making me crazy, but what can I do?"

"Did you ask Dean to stay?"

"Not yet."

"What are you waiting for?"

"He still talks about Africa so fondly. I think he misses it. I should have grabbed him years ago, 'cause the man's got wanderlust in his soul now."

"You mean live here?" Joseph said. He sat up and placed *Invisible Man* on the sofa bed.

"If you want and your mother agrees," Naomi said, putting freshly laundered underwear in his drawer.

"What about school?"

"We'll have to enroll you here in Maryland."

"But how long are you talking about?"

"As long as you want to stay."

"You mean like, forever?"

"Well, I imagine you'll want to go to college or get married and move out one day. But yeah, if that's what you want."

He stretched out on the sofa bed and stared at the ceiling. Naomi busied herself straightening out the top of his dresser, trying to think what she would say if he turned down the offer. Should she just let it go or try to—

"OK."

She blinked and turned to face him. "You mean, just like that? I don't have to promise you a new car or anything?"

He bolted upright. "That's not a bad idea."

"Forget I said it."

He chuckled. "I'd rather you used the money for the business anyway."

Naomi watched as he got up from the bed and sat in front of the computer. That was probably the nicest thing Joseph had ever said to her. She had planned to do some work now, but what the heck. She wanted to call Dean and her parents with the news that Joseph had agreed to stay. "We'll call your mother tonight," she said, walking toward the door.

"You better let me do that," he said. "I know how to handle her."

"Fine." She stepped into the hallway and shut the door partway. Then she opened it back up, walked up behind him, took his head into her hands, and bent over to kiss his cheek. He practically fell out of the chair trying to get away, but she still managed to land a nice juicy one.

"What the heck are you doing?"

"If you're going to stay here, you'll have to get used to them."

"Man."

She laughed and closed the door behind her.

By the end of August, she still hadn't asked Dean to stay. They saw each other almost every day, but she kept putting it off. She knew what was holding her back. She was so happy now, and hearing him say no would change that. As long as she didn't ask and he didn't turn her down, there was a glimmer of hope.

But she'd feel worse if he left and she'd never asked him to stay. So on the very last Friday of the month, she arranged for Joseph to spend the night with her parents and invited Dean over for a nice cozy dinner with candlelight and wine. After the meal, she put an Al Jarreau album on the stereo, while Dean took their wineglasses to the couch. She sat next to him, and he put his arm around her.

"There's something I've been meaning to ask you," she said.

"Go ahead. You can say anything to me."

"I know, but this is hard 'cause I suspect you'll say no. And if you do, I'll understand. Or I'll try to."

He frowned. "I can't imagine telling you no."

She smiled. "I hope you don't."

He put his wineglass down and picked up her hand and squeezed it.

God, she was going to miss this man if he left. "Would you consider staying here instead of going back to Africa?"

"Is that what you want?"

"Yes, very much."

"Well, I've already made arrangements to go back in two weeks. I promised to help Mohammad set up his business, and he's expecting me."

She slipped her hand out of his and stood up quickly with her back toward him. She'd known he would probably do this and tried to prepare herself. Still, it hurt so much to really hear him say it, her eyes stung with the pain.

"But I'm not planning to stay long. Probably only six months or a year at most."

He'd said something like that when he left the first time. She wished she had listened to him then, when he told her how he felt about her. She wished she had listened to her heart, telling her how much this man meant to her. Funny how you can run around looking for something that's right under your nose all along. "I understand. I love you and don't want you to go. But I understand."

"I'd ask you to come with me, but I know the consulting business is too important to you. And Joseph."

"You're right," she said, fighting the lump in her throat.

He walked up behind her and wrapped his arms around her. She closed her eyes and rested her head against his shoulder.

"Will you wear this until I get back?"

She looked down. He was holding a ruby ring in front of her.

"It's not a diamond," he said, as if apologizing. "I don't believe in them, with all that's going on in South Africa. But it means the same thing. I love you and want you to marry me. Will you?"

Naomi thought it was the most beautiful thing she ever saw. She nodded and then turned around in his arms and clung to him. She didn't say anything just yet. She was crying too hard to speak.

Epilogue

She hadn't been all dolled up like this in ages. The silk gown—a Gianfranco Ferre original, mind you—had cost a royal fortune, not to mention the Chloe slingbacks and the Chanel handbag. But what the heck. It was a big celebration, the Oscars of the black business world. And she was one of the stars. They were paying tribute to her, African American businesswoman extraordinaire, right up there along with John Johnson, the night's featured guest. She deserved to splurge.

The limo driver pulled up in front of the Plaza Hotel and rushed around to open the door. Naomi stepped out and wrapped her fingers around Dean's tuxedoed arm. This was definitely her kind of night. A chandeliered ballroom full of illustrious people—all black, bold, and beautiful—laying out big bucks for charity while coming together to praise and support each other and, yes, check each other out. Many of the people in this room started with almost nothing, yet today they were sitting on top of the world, commanding business empires in publishing, television, entertainment, technology, and finance. Along with four or five others, she was giving a speech after they dined on seared salmon, roasted leg of lamb, and a bunch of other goodies. It should be a fascinating evening.

She stopped to chat with a few familiar faces. As soon as they reached table number four, Naomi kissed everyone and ordered Dom Pérignon all around. As powerful as many of the surrounding faces were, the people at this table were the most important in her life: family, friends, coworkers. They helped her become what she was today, and Naomi hated to even imagine where she'd be without them. Goodness knows she'd slipped dangerously close to the gutter often enough.

That was why tonight was so special. She intended to enjoy every moment of it. Some folks would accuse her of going overboard—of showing off—with the limo, designer rags, and hundred-dollar bottles of champagne. But she couldn't care less. She'd worked her butt off to get where she was and deserved every glorious bit of it. Nobody ever accused whites of those things when they pulled out all the stops. Sometimes, we could be so hard on each other, as if the outside world didn't beat on us enough. But that was all right. That was how some of us got to be so tough.

"And now the founder and president of Dynamic Data, the largest black-owned information technology service firm in the country and one of the top ten such firms overall!"

Naomi walked up to the podium, adjusted the microphone, and waited for the applause to die down.

"People are always telling me I'm lucky. 'Girl, you are so lucky.' 'Luck just seems to follow you around.' 'How come you always have such good luck, Naomi?' I tell them, Yeah, I've been lucky. But do you really know what luck is? One percent good timing and ninety-nine percent preparation. I was fortunate to come into this world at the beginning of a technology boom and after important civil rights laws had been passed. But I was only able to take advantage of that timing because of all the preparation that went on before me.

"That preparation started the day my ancestor stepped off a ship, hands and feet bound in chains, and made up his or her mind to survive no matter what lay ahead. It continued with each successive generation despite beatings, mutilation, rape, lynchings, segregation, dogs, hoses, and assassinations. They learned to read and write, even when it was illegal, they managed to feed and clothe their families, even when there were too few jobs, and they encouraged their children to hope and dream for a better future, no matter how bad things looked.

"With all that behind me, how could I miss?

"That's why I get miffed when I hear us talk about how it's harder to make it today. I was once guilty of thinking that way myself. I can remember looking at my parents as a young woman and thinking 'teacher,' so what? 'Government worker,' big deal. That's nothing compared to going up against a bunch of whites in the corporate world to become a manager or director. What was so easy to forget was that this teacher was a woman who went to school in a one-room shack with barely enough books to go around, whose mother got down on her hands and knees to scrub the kitchen floors of rich white folks to earn a living. And that this was a man whose father shot pool, not bullets, to get enough money to put shoes on the feet of his seven children. With preparation like that behind me, how dare I miss? How dare we give up when the going gets rough?

"Our children are our most valuable asset. If they don't do a little better than we do, there's no progress. It's that simple. Other ethnic groups know this. We once knew it too, but for some reason we've forgotten. Remember the woman scrubbing the kitchen floor to make a better future for her daughter? She knew it. She was a single mother for years, but that didn't stop her. Why doesn't the unwed teenage mother living in the run-down tenement housing with *her* mother know it? Why doesn't she do something about it? Why don't the fathers help? Do the rest of us even care?

"Oh, we all pay lip service to it. But how many of those of us who are more fortunate reach out with a hand to pull in that young nephew or niece or cousin swimming against the tide, before he sinks? Each and every one of us in this room knows someone like that. They are all around us. Despite our fur coats and designer gowns and the fancy cars we rode up in, few of us are more than a generation or two away from poverty.

"I want to introduce you to a young man I'm very proud of. Stand up, Joseph."

Joseph stood and smiled, looking fine in his new tuxedo.

"This is my nephew, the son of my beloved brother, who's no longer with us. When Joseph was a teenager, he was a handful. But we worked with him and now he's twenty-five and tremendously successful. He's a graduate of MIT and is employed at Price Waterhouse. One of these days, I'm going to snatch him away and lure him to my firm."

A few laughs drifted through the crowd.

"Thank you, Joseph. I have some other people at that table to thank tonight, all employees of mine. Most of us go way back. I want each of you to stand when I introduce you.

"First, there's Deborah Young, vice president of finance, Jennifer Jones, executive vice president, and Carla Reed, vice president of operations. And Walter Johnson and Wayne Yang, two of the most brilliant technology analysts you'll find. But don't get any ideas. I'm paying them all far too much for you to even think about stealing them from me."

The audience laughed.

"Next, I want to introduce you to my husband. Stand up, will you, honey?"

Dean stood, and that chocolate face looked as magnificent as it did the day they got married.

"He doesn't work for me. I'm just pointing him out so that all the women here know he's taken."

The audience roared.

"Finally, I want to introduce the two people most responsible for me being where I am today. Mama, Daddy, will you stand up for a minute?"

Her mother and father stood, and the audience applauded.

"They steered me in the right direction, when it seemed I was getting off track, and stood on the sidelines and cheered the loudest whenever I made a hit. But most important, they set good examples.

"With folks like that, how could I miss?"

Acknowledgments

For this one, I've got several gutsy women out there to thank. I'm grateful to two in particular who found the time to talk to me about some of their experiences as they blast their way up the mountaintop. First, my cousin Joanne Reneé Harrell, just promoted to vice president, Nebraska, U.S. West Communications. She's leaving the rest of us in the dust on her way to the summit. I'm always bragging about her and now I get to do it in print. And Rose McElrath Slade founded a *real* technology research firm, Strategic Resources, Inc. This is not the life story of either of them, but it's women like them who inspire me. I have to thank Karen Singleton and Nate Whitaker (a gutsy guy), two of my oldest and dearest friends, for making my breaks from writing so pleasant as we travel around the world. I also want to thank my editor, Peternelle van Arsdale, who is encouraging, patient, and fun to work with. And what would I do without Wanda Newman, my interpreter, who is always available, even at the last minute? And last but certainly not least is the woman with whom this all started. If asked to describe the perfect agent, I'd need only two words: Victoria Sanders.

If you enjoyed *Big Girls Don't Cry*,
you won't want to miss . . .

SISTERS & LOVERS
by
Connie Briscoe

Beverly, Charmaine, and Evelyn are three sisters living in the
same Maryland town outside Washington, D.C., each wishing her life were just a little different. Beverly is twenty-nine
and single. She's a successful magazine editor who would
love to be in love. The problem is, no man can meet her
high standards. Charmaine longs to finish her degree, but
meanwhile she has to juggle a thankless job, a beautiful
child, and an irresponsible husband she doesn't quite have
the nerve to leave. Evelyn seems to have it made. She has a
successful psychology practice and her husband is a partner in a prestigious law firm. But there's trouble in paradise,
and Evelyn refuses to face the facts.

Warm and bittersweet, believable and real,
SISTERS & LOVERS is a novel of family and love,
heartache and hope, and above all the
triumphs of sisterhood.

SWEET SUMMER
Growing Up With and Without My Dad

by Bebe Moore Campbell

Written with the narrative force of fiction and the lyrical motion of poetry, **SWEET SUMMER** is Bebe Moore Campbell's elegy to her extraordinary father, a bittersweet evocation of a divided childhood with its family secrets, surprising discoveries, loneliness, and love.

"Fearlessly unveils the pain of loss and the ecstasy of love. I am grateful for Bebe Moore Campbell and for such a **SWEET SUMMER.**"

—Maya Angelou

Published by One World/Fawcett Books.
Available in bookstores everywhere.

YOUR BLUES AIN'T LIKE MINE
by Bebe Moore Campbell

A *NEW YORK TIMES* NOTABLE BOOK

WINNER OF THE NAACP IMAGE AWARD
FOR BEST LITERARY WORK OF FICTION

A black man...a white woman...a single
sentence spoken in a Mississippi roadhouse
leads to the tragedy that will transform and
haunt these people's lives forever.

"**YOUR BLUES AIN'T LIKE MINE** is rich,
lush fiction set in rural Mississippi beginning in
the mid-'50s. It is also a haunting reality flowing
through Anywhere, USA, in the '90s....There's
love, rage, and hatred, winning and losing,
honor, abuse; in other words, humanity....
Campbell now deserves recognition as the best
of storytellers. Her writing sings."
—*The Indianapolis News*

"Absorbing...compelling...highly satisfying."
—*San Francisco Chronicle*